To Mike

Every Little Thing She Does

Andrew Muir

All the best
Andy
Jan 2012

Published by YouWriteOn.com, 2011

First Edition

A CIP catalogue record for this title is available from the British
Library.

This book is dedicated to the memory of Allan Weston

For my dad, my family, my friends and especially as ever, for Karen.

Darkness makes me fumble
for a key to a door that's wide open
Darkness, The Police

Andrew Muir is married and lives in Steyning, West Sussex.

When Andrew was a teenager, he was a big fan of The Police, and yes, on occasions alcohol tends to play havoc with his stomach.

However, despite these similarities, Andrew is keen to stress yet again that he and Tim James are certainly *not* one and the same person....

Andrew's previous book featuring Tim and co., *Does Everyone Stare The Way I Do?*, was published by YouWriteOn.com in 2009 and is available online.

Cover design by Andrew & Duncan Muir.

For more information, go to www.andrewmuirwriter.com

Part One

September 1980 - March 1981

1- Shadows In The Rain

Sting was singing to me again. He seemed to have a song for every occasion.

It was late in the afternoon and it was growing dark. Raindrops dripped down the back of my shirt collar as I stared through the window of Brighton's HMV store.

I hummed along with the song my hero was singing in my head. But I didn't have any answers for him. I gave up. After all, just how *did* you explain shadows in the rain?

My mind wandered back to the conversation that I'd had with Jacko, over the phone, the night before.

'Honestly, Tim James, you're such a gutless, spineless chicken!' my mate had told me.

I'd just been forced to confess that I still hadn't worked up the courage to speak to her, so I didn't argue.

Nevertheless, Jacko wasn't finished.

'You have absolutely no balls, do you? You are a cowardly eunuch of the highest order.'

A bit harsh. Especially coming from Jacko.

Why was I taking relationship advice from Jacko anyway? We're talking about someone who had only ever had one relationship with a member of the opposite sex in his entire life - if you didn't count the ongoing one his right hand had with the underwear section of his Mum's Littlewoods catalogue - and that was when he was thirteen. And that had barely lasted a fortnight.

'I'm just biding my time,' I'd protested.

'You can say that again mate!' he spluttered, 'what is it now? Three weeks since you first saw her?'

'Nearer four actually,' I muttered shamefully.

I'd first seen the beautiful red-headed girl in HMV when I'd gone to spend the cash that Dad had given me for passing my O-levels.

She'd been serving someone who had been buying Zenyatta Mondatta, the new Police LP. She had this lovely giggle and a smile that lit up the whole shop.

The girl and the customer got talking about The Police; the band I just happened to worship. The beautiful shop-assistant told the bloke

7

her name was Roxanne, which was also the name of one of the Police's biggest hits.

I mean, what were the chances of that? It had to be fate didn't it? Surely, we were meant to be together, weren't we?

As a theory that was all very well; the only problem was, that despite practically setting up home in HMV ever since that day, I couldn't actually bring myself to talk to her, no matter how hard I tried.

'Mind you,' Jacko said, 'four weeks is nothing by your standards is it? How long did you have a stiffy on for Alison Fisher without actually telling her? Four *years* wasn't it? I suppose you've got a fair way to go before you break that record.'

'Yeah, well, things were slightly different with Alison weren't they?'

'How do you figure that then?'

'Well, it's the *little* details I suppose. You know, like the *minor* fact that she was going out with my *best mate* all through that time?'

'Well, she wasn't going out with Humph when you first fancied her was she?'

'Maybe not,' I grunted, grudgingly.

'Well, that's why you need to do something now and not leave it until some other punter makes a move on her.'

'And how do I know she's free in the first place? A girl that gorgeous; it seems unlikely'

'Well you will never know unless you ask, will you?'

'I'm getting there, OK?'

'Eunuch.'

It had only taken twenty minutes of standing there in the rain for me to finally admit to myself that Jacko was right. A third of one hour of utter procrastination; stood there with my nose pressed up against the glass.

This was no way for a Sixth Former to behave. I'd been in the lower sixth for four whole days and here I was, still acting like I was twelve.

'He's right, you're a eunuch.'

Try as I might to goad it into action, my reflection didn't seem bothered.

8

The rain was getting heavier and the wind was getting up. The concrete canopy of Churchill Square shopping centre gave little shelter from the weather at the best of times, but in the driving wind, it was useless. I pulled my duffel coat around me as the sky grew darker. The figures inside the shop grew vague and shadowy.

So, how do you explain - Shadows In The Rain?

Someone switched the shop lights on. The shadows came into focus. It didn't brighten my mood.

It was the fourth time this week that I'd stood there like that.

Each time, I'd followed the same post-school routine. Got on the number 14 bus, all pysched up. Convinced myself today was the day. Told myself that *nothing* would stop me; that I was going to do it.

The resolve, as always, had stayed with me all the way into Brighton town centre; but as soon as we were halfway up North Street, I'd started to waiver. And by the time we pulled in at Churchill Square, I'd been so nervous that I'd been tempted to stay on the bus; by now having not just second, but third and fourth thoughts.

As on previous days, I'd been forced off of the bus by the sheer irresistible tide of foreign students heading for the shopping centre. All of them blonde, all of them carrying their EF bags; all dying to spend their holiday money. I'd followed them, dragging my sorry arse all the way to the doors of HMV, by which time, as usual I'd well and truly mislaid my bottle.

Each day I'd stood there, hesitating for ages, before deciding that I'd only been kidding myself all along and feeling utterly miserable, I'd turn around, walk back to Western Road and catch the bus home again.

So far, today had been no different, except that, as if to make things worse, and in an effort to make me feel even more pathetic than ever, the weather had decided to be bloody awful. Frankly, someone up there was taking the piss. There was a bright flash of lightning, followed almost straight away by an enormous clap of thunder. The storm was sitting right over Western Road. I was getting soaked. My nose was running and I had a sudden fit of sneezing - serve me right if I caught my death of cold. I didn't feel much like talking to Roxanne at all now. The rain clouds had stolen my thunder.

As the driving rain blew in gusts against the glass, two large raindrops ran down the window, right in line with my face.

9

'OK,' I told myself, 'if the raindrop on the right reaches the bottom of the window first, I will go back in and talk to her. If it loses out to the one on the left, I'll head back to the bus-stop and call it a day.'

My entire future happiness hinged on the outcome of a random two-way race between drops of rain-water.

The lightning lit up the window display, advertising Barbara Streisand's new album. They'd changed the display earlier in the week. The *Zenyatta Mondatta* posters from last weekend had given way to conky Barbara and the beardy one from the Bee Gees. From the sublime to the ridiculous. The hairy couple were all loved up, both dressed in white; teeth on full beam. There's something about Barbara though. She may have stupid hair and a nose that sticks out of her face like a pillion passenger, but she's got nice eyes; *really* blue.

My two rain drops headed towards the top of Barbara's poodle-permed head. Then the drip on the left took a detour around a greasy smear on the glass. It veered off at right angles. It had no chance of winning.

Next, the wind caught the one on the right, causing it to pool and send a side-shoot spreading across the window. Now they were on a collision course. At this rate, there would be a messy pile-up. The race would be declared null and void. What did that mean? Twist, stick or bust?

The wind had really got up now, driving the rain against my back. At least the foul weather gave me an excuse to keep sheltering under the concrete canopy without looking like a complete stalker. The shop's life-size cardboard Jack Russell cocked its ear to the sound of His Masters Voice over in the corner. It looked just like my Dog Chalky, except this one had more patches. He seemed to be peering past the huge gramophone and watching me knowingly. *'You're going to bottle it again aren't you?'*

Crap. I'd taken my eyes off the raindrops - they'd disappeared – there was just an ever-spreading puddle forming under Barry Gibb's beard (was it Barry or was it Maurice? - I never knew which was which - and frankly, I couldn't care less either).

Stalling for time again, I checked my watch. They were only open for another half hour.

'Come on Tim, it's now or never.'

10

Returning the Jack Russell's meaningful glare, I wiped my nose on the sleeve of my coat, counted to ten and worked up sufficient courage to walk through the door, scanning the shop-floor as I went.

Maybe she wouldn't be here? Maybe it was her day off?

Then I clocked her, over by the David Bowie "Scary Monsters" display. She was talking to a colleague; a spotty kid with a Terry Hall flat-top. He's the lead singer from The Specials. (Terry Hall that is; not this spotty berk). The hair-style looks cool on Terry Hall. This bloke looked a complete git with his lop-sided grin and all those zits on his forehead.

Roxanne was giving him the benefit of *that* smile – those dimples, the cute crinkles around the eyes. I felt dizzy. I thought I might be physically and violently sick any minute.

"You can do this, you can do this."

I wanted to walk straight back out. But it was Thursday. This was getting silly. Then again, there was always Friday.

My master-plan, as far as it had got, was to buy a single – it was all I could afford – and if I timed things right, get Roxanne to serve me.

I'd decided on "Stand Down Margaret / Best Friend" by The Beat (it was a double A side, so in my mind, good value for money). I don't really know much about politics but all the cool bands seem to be dead against the prime-minister, Margaret Thatcher. I don't like her much either. She uses far too much hairspray and she's got a horribly creepy voice. I didn't know whether they were really sufficient grounds to want her to "stand down" but who cared? I loved the song anyway.

I'd carefully rehearsed my opening gambit.

'Any idea when the new Blondie single is out?'

Of course I already knew the answer; Simon Mayo had been playing it on the radio. It was out in a couple of weeks. I wasn't a huge fan, unlike Jacko, who worships Debbie Harry. But I reckoned Roxanne would like Blondie; Roxanne had red hair with dyed black bits at the back – a sort of red version of Debbie's hair. Not that Debbie was naturally blonde – any idiot could tell that. I wonder what colour her hair was naturally? Maybe she was originally a red-head? It was possible - after all, she might have changed her hair colour just to tie in with the band name - after all, "Gingerie" wouldn't be such a catchy name for a group would it?

Biding my time, I practised my question, whilst strategically positioning myself by the bins marked "autumn sale", next to three scandinavian students, all looking uncannily like Olivia Newton John.

Pretending to be interested in the sale, my hands flipped robotically through the tatty old singles, whilst all the time, I trained my eyes on Roxy (Christ I'm sad, I haven't even spoken to her yet and I'm giving her a pet name); waiting for my moment. I had to time it right.

Suddenly, she was looking straight at me. Had she sussed me? I stared down at the single in my hand.

Oh God. Boney M!

Roxy was looking straight at me and I was holding a Boney M single.

Oh shit.

I stuffed it back into the pile and risked another glance. Now, Roxy was serving a customer; some long-haired, leather jacketed greaser.

'Right', I decided, 'this is it.'

I headed over to the chart-singles rack and found "Stand Down Margaret". As quickly as my trembling legs would carry me, I took up position behind the greasy looking bloke; fumbling in my trousers for my last pound note.

The greaser was buying loads of Motorhead stuff – an LP, a poster, and a badge – this guy was seriously into warty heavy-rockers.

Roxanne smiled as he pulled a mouldy old fiver from his dirty jeans – I reckoned she was trying not to laugh. Bloody Motorhead; what a din.

'Yes sir, can I help you?' I heard a boyish voice say.

It was the spotty Terry Hall-alike. He'd taken up position on the next till. Bugger. I glanced at Roxy, she was giving Lemmy his change. I pretended I hadn't heard him.

'Sir?' Spotty tried again. I ignored him, casually focusing on the carpet.

'Thank you, sir,' Roxy smiled, her transaction completed.

Great, get in there Tim! I took a step forward.

Grease-head started to walk away. Then he turned back.

'Excuse me,' he said, slightly red in the face, 'Do you know when the new Judas Priest single is out?'

'I'll just see if I can find out for you,' Roxy said and turned away, heading through a swing-door into the back office.

When was the new Judas Priest single out? What sort of an obvious chat-up line was that?

'Can I serve you sir?' Spotty said in a loud voice.

Oh knickers.

Outside it was as dark as midnight. I felt miserable, I was sneezing again and my head felt like I'd been hit by a bus. I pocketed my change, tucked my new Beat single under my arm and shuffled along under the canopy.

It was still peeing down. I took one pathetic glance back.

Spotty was shutting the doors behind me. I strained my eyes as the shop lights dimmed. I couldn't make out Roxanne or anything else in the shop now.

Not even shadows in the rain.

2 - (Still) Can't Stand Losing You

Denton School and Denton Sixth form college were, effectively, one and the same place. They were housed in the very same buildings, on exactly the same site. Inside, the classrooms, which may have had a lick of new paint during the summer holidays, still smelt the same as ever - a fragrant cocktail of disinfectant and B.O.- and were still furnished with the same old rickety desks and chairs as they'd always been.

Outside, the playing fields were unchanged; if perhaps a little greener than they'd been six weeks before. The same trees, the same bike-sheds, the same tennis courts. Ninety-five percent of the kids who made up my new sixth form colleagues had been there in the fifth year. Even the teachers were the same. Denton Sixth Form College (or DSFCL6, as the sign above the lower sixth common room announced it was now to be known) and Denton High School were in all ways obvious to the naked eye, identical; yet, to me, they felt like entirely different places. "DSFCL6" put me in mind of some new life-form from Star Trek; and it might just as well have been an entirely new planet, without my old mates.

On the first day back, in early September, I'd looked at my watch as I walked up the access road, kids all swarming towards the entrance gates, like bees returning to a hive.

Eight forty-five a.m. Right about now, my best friend Chris Humphreys, would be being picked up in his works van by one of his new workmates. Too weird. I'd still half expected to see Humph on the back seat of the eight-twenty bus. Instead, his seat had been taken over by a couple of those cocky fourth years - or fifth years, as they were now.

There was no sign of Humph's gorgeous girlfriend, Alison Fisher, either. For a moment I wondered if she had changed her mind about staying on and gone off to get some glamourous job as a model or an air hostess - then I remembered she was still in Florida with her family. She wouldn't be back for another week.

Later, getting off the bus, I'd forlornly hoped that by some miracle, I'd see Martin "Jacko" Jackson waiting for me by the gate, his Adidas bag thrown over his shoulder.

He wasn't there either.

There was no Declan Kelly, parking his old bike around the back of the science lab, and no Ray O'Brien, spitting out his gum and sticking it in his hankie outside class 44.

There was no mouthy Sam Jessop, telling anyone who'd listen, that she'd snogged Steve Andrew's face off at the weekend, and no Dan Chester, moaning about the weather or asking me if he could copy my homework.

I'd felt very alone that first day. Adrift in a strange new world. Beam me up Scotty.

A week in, and things felt just as alien.

'Good Morning Tim,' said Miss Morris, my personal tutor and History teacher, as I shuffled into room 74 on the second Monday morning of term.

'Morning Miss. Morris...er Candice,' I replied, taking my seat next to Gary Hurst.

There were a couple of stifled sniggers.

This calling teachers (sorry, "tutors"), by their first-name business was going to take some getting used to. To be fair, "Candice" Morris had always been one of the more friendly teachers - and calling her by her christian name didn't seem as peculiar as it did with some of the older teachers. But she didn't seem at all like a *Candice*.

Candice sounded like a film-star, like Candice Bergen. My Dad liked her. She was a real sex-kitten type according to Dad. Miss Morris, with her horn-rimmed glasses, grey hair and frumpy clothes, was definitely no sex-kitten. Not with her legendarily thick ankles.

'Today, we're going to be looking at The Dissolution of The Monasteries. Page 154 of your text books,' Candice announced, as she scribbled the word "Dissolution" on the blackboard.

I tried not to fixate on her ankles. She was wearing thick grey ankle socks.

More Mavis than Candice.

Calling "tutors" by their first names didn't seem right.

And it wasn't the only change at 'DSFCL6'.

We didn't have to wear uniform anymore - we could wear smart-casual now; which apparently meant "anything, except denims or bermuda shorts". Not much chance of bermuda shorts this term; it was bloody freezing.

15

The whole situation was bizarre - in July, we all had to wear school colours and stand up when a teacher entered the room and now, six weeks later, we were all wearing cords and sweat-shirts and acting like the tutors were our new best mates. Apparently, in the eyes of the educational system, we'd gone from children to adults over a six week period.

I was still looking for page 154 when the door opened.

'Oh, sorry I'm late Candice, my Dad's car got a flat tyre!'

Alison Fisher bounded into the room, cradling her text books to her chest. She looked flushed, like she'd been hurrying. She took a seat next to her best friend, Sara Potts and hung her purple velvet jacket over the back of her chair. The two girls hugged each other.

'Alison!' said Candice, 'so good to see you back. Did you have a good holiday?'.

'Yes, thanks Miss, er Candice,' Alison said, 'it was great.'

'Where was it, America somewhere wasn't it?'

'That's right, Florida!' Alison beamed.

'Oh, did you do Disney?' asked Sara.

'Oh yeah, it was fantastic!' said Alison, smiling as she looked around the room, noticing the rest of the group for the first time. She gave me a little wave.

As usual, Alison Fisher looked like a million dollars. She'd always been the best looking girl in the year. Now, with a fantastic tan and her sun-bleached hair, she looked even more incredible than ever. I told myself not to gawp and then, as ever, gawped anyway.

Alison was tall and slim. She had lovely long legs which were normally on full display in one of a series of very short mini-skirts, bit today, she was wrapped up against the cold in her full hippy-chick outfit; purple jacket, matching scarf, fluffy pink polo necked jumper and long flowing ankle-length black skirt, complete with tassels.

'Well, we'll catch up after the lesson and you can tell me all about it OK?' Candice said, 'Ok, what do we know about the Monasteries before the reign of Henry the eighth?'

Gary Hurst, who was a right swat, was as always, the first to offer his expertise. I didn't really take-in what he was saying. I was still studying Alison.

I hadn't seen Alison much since the start of the holidays when she'd had her cousin Collette from Solihull staying at her place. Collette and I had exchanged saliva and phone numbers and for a

16

couple of weeks, I'd convinced myself I was madly in love with her. Then Collette went back home. I pined for ages - well, a week or two, and then, when she sent me her photo, showing off her newly cut hair, I realised I hadn't really fancied her that much at all.

What suddenly dawned on me as I sat there watching Alison chewing the end of her biro, was that these were the first summer holidays since 1976 that I hadn't spent the whole six weeks counting down the days to when I'd be back at school, so that I could see her again.

This was a good thing; Humph and I had already had one major falling-out over her. Besides, now I'd met, well...seen... Roxanne. Things were going to be different now.

How did Alison shape-up next to Roxanne? Well, Alison was undeniably still gorgeous but the irony was that now that I had got to know her as a friend, I reckoned that she wasn't really my type. For a start, she didn't seem to get my sense of humour at all - and don't get me started on her musical taste - Abba, Kool and The Gang, Earth Wind and Fire. Oh please. We simply weren't compatible at all. More to the point though, who was I kidding? How could someone like me ever compete with the most popular, best looking guy in the whole year? No, they were made for each other were Alison and Humph. I'd moved on I reminded myself. Roxanne was the one for me now. And all I had to do was work up the courage to speak to her.

Minor detail.

'So, how are you doing Timbo?' Alison asked, sitting down next to me and pecking me on the cheek.

I ignored the familiar thumping under my rib cage as her knee brushed against my leg. I was sitting on one of the old leather sofas in the common room, trying to make sense of The Canterbury Tales and listening to "Zenyatta Mondatta" on the crackly old school record player. The common room was pretty deserted; apart from the two of us, there was only a group of lads, playing cards in the far corner. I put down my Chaucer and tried to appear relaxed

'I suppose this was you?' she said, swaying her head gently to the music.

'Of course!' I said,

'Oh dear, I really started something there didn't I?' she laughed.

'Uh?'

17

'Well, if I hadn't bought you that single for your birthday, maybe you'd be into something else by now? I dunno - maybe Chic or...AC/DC?'

'Pah! Unlikely,' I smirked.

Alison had given me "Can't Stand Losing You" on blue vinyl for my birthday a couple of years back. It was the first Police record I owned. Come to think of it, it was the first record I'd owned.

'Ah well, it could have been worse eh? They're pretty cool aren't they? Is this the new album?'

'Yeah, this one's great; it's called "Driven To Tears".'

'I know the feeling,' she muttered with feeling, 'and how's Chris been behaving himself whilst I've been away?' she said, folding her arms moodily across her pink, fluffy chest. She was trying to sound like she was only casually interested but I could tell she really wanted to know.

'To be honest, I've only seen him once or twice, but I'm happy to report that he was on his best behaviour.'

That wasn't strictly true; the last time I'd seen him, he'd got extremely pissed. Jacko, Humph and I had visited a back-street pub, near Brighton station, on a Friday night - which had been all Humph's idea. But I didn't know how much if anything he'd told Alison about it - after all, it probably wouldn't sound too good for Humph that the first time he'd ever suggested visiting a pub was the very week she'd gone to Florida.

'Still, I bet he's looking forward to seeing you!' I said, trying to lighten the mood.

'Has he missed me then?' she asked, playing with her scarf.

'Of course!' I said.

I couldn't actually remember him mentioning her in the entire time she was away but I was sure he must have missed her. Who wouldn't?

'Huh!' she said, crossing her long legs, 'that wasn't how it seemed yesterday.'

'Oh so, you've already seen him then?'

'For all of an hour or so, yes. That was all of his precious Sunday evening time he could spare me apparently. He was off to play snooker with his new work mates,' she said sulkily.

'Pete and Doddsy? Yeah, he seems to be spending a lot of his time with them. Bonding I suppose?'

18

'He's always with them!' she said, 'I don't know why I bothered rushing around there as soon as I got home. I was really jet-lagged but I wanted to see him. He didn't even bother opening his present.'

'Did you get him something good?'

She looked embarrassed. 'It was a bit of an impulse. It was just a bit of a joke really,' her mouth was twitching, her lips curling at the edges, like she was trying not to laugh.

'What?' I asked

'A Mickey Mouse wrist-watch.'

'A what?' I said. I let out a snort of laughter before I could stop myself. Thankfully, she was laughing too.

'Do you think he'll wear it?'

'Oh yeah, all the time,' I said.

We both laughed.

'So,' she said, when the moment had passed, 'how are you finding the lower sixth?'

I shrugged, 'not that great actually...' I started to say.

A bell rang. Alison looked at her watch.

'Crikey is that the time? I'd better be off. I've got Commerce,' she grabbed her large straw bag from the floor and started to dash off. 'Doing anything for lunch tomorrow?' she asked, looking over her shoulder.

'Might pop to the Ritz,' I said sarcastically.

'Good, I'll meet you in the canteen - I'll show you my holiday snaps - I'm picking them up from the chemist this afternoon.'

'Cool,' I said.

Oh bugger.

Alison's holiday snaps, from hot and sunny Florida.

Beach shots.

Alison in a bikini.

God help me.

'So, this is us at Disney again - that's Ade with Elliott.'

I must have looked stumped.

'You know, Pete's Dragon?' Alison explained.

And indeed, there was Adrian, Alison's kid brother, pictured with a man in a seven foot-tall Dragon costume. Adrian, who was fifteen, looked really cheesed off. When you're fifteen, seven-foot dragons don't seem as cool as they do when you're say, six.

I took a munch out of my ham and tomato roll, doing my best not to get butter smears on her newly developed prints.

Alison was eating a jacket potato; we'd managed to find a corner table in the canteen. Hardly any of the sixth formers used the canteen - most of them ate in the common room. We were surrounded by noisy, younger kids but effectively, I had Alison Fisher all to myself for lunch.

'And this one's me with Baloo from Jungle Book.'

As in most of the shots of the Fisher family, who had been snapped with assorted Disney characters, the Disney employee in the bear costume had his arm around Alison. I couldn't help noticing though that Baloo had moved in for a particularly intimate bear-hug, both arms around Alison, one around the waist of her skimpy white shorts and the other suspiciously positioned somewhat higher up on her pale blue capped-sleeved t-shirt.

Yep, there were no two ways about it, Alison Fisher was being well and truly 'pawed' by Baloo the Bear. Now I knew what he'd meant by looking for his bear-necessities. Crafty bear.

There were numerous Disney themed photos; assorted Fisher combinations with other cartoon characters; parades of amazingly decorated floats; brilliant firework displays and loads of the Fisher family enjoying scarily impressive, huge looking roller-coasters. Then there were several pictures of what Alison told me were the Florida Everglades and something called a manatee, that looked like a cross between a seal and a hippo. Then we moved on to the beach photos.

'Ooh, I'm not showing you that one,' Alison said, putting a photo back in the Boots envelope, 'oh, or that one, that's far too embarrassing. Bloody Adrian, I could kill him sometimes.'

I guessed she was being coy about her bikini shots. I was relieved but at the same time disappointed. I mean clearly I would have liked to have seen them; in fact I would have been quite happy to take them away, studying them at my leisure - but it would have been mortifying, looking at them with Alison there. I'd once spent the day at Brighton beach with her and her family a couple of summers ago, when Humph was in Spain. Alison had worn a lime-green bikini. That bikini had caused me some pretty sleepless nights.

'And this one's of the four of us at Florida Keys,' she said, passing me the next snap.

Sure enough, there they were on a fantastic looking sandy beach; Mr. Fisher, looking sunburnt in speedos which were years too young for him; Mrs. Fisher, looking shapely and tanned in a white one-piece and Adrian in his Liverpool football shorts. But, if I'm being honest, I hardly noticed any of them; I was too busy trying to prevent my eyes from popping out onto my cheeks. Alison, looking every inch like a Greek Goddess, had apparently gone to the beach wearing nothing but three small triangles of black material that sewn together wouldn't have made a decent sized face-flannel.

Oh my God, I realised, if she was happy for me to see that one, what the hell wasn't she wearing in the ones she'd vetoed?

'Blimey,' I said, aware of Alison's eyes burning into the side of my face, 'look at the colour of that sea! I've never seen water so clear.'

'I know, the scenery around that coast was stunning.'

You can say that again. I couldn't drag my eyes away.

Five minutes later, I'd seen approximately eighteen photos of Alison in various bikinis.

It had been torture; wonderful, hideous, torture.

Finally, Alison placed them back in the top of her straw holdall and the wonderful agony was over.

'So, you were telling me about your first week in sixth form then,' said Alison, her rosebud mouth sucking some 7-Up through a straw.

'Yeah, it's alright, I suppose.'

'You miss your mates, don't you?' Bloody hell, she was good.

'Well, sort of.' I didn't want to sound like a complete prat.

'Well, that's not surprising, I miss Sam.'

I shivered.

The mention of Sam Jessop's name always had that effect on me. I'd supposedly gone out with her for five months but I'd never really liked her that much. I'd only pretended to fancy her because she was Alison's best mate. Not that Sam was any better, she fancied Humph. I suppose from that point of view, we'd deserved each other. Alison might miss her. I can't say I did.

'Yeah, but you've still got Sara,' I said, 'I've lost Humph and Jacko - and practically all the other lads from our class.'

At the mere mention of Humph's name, Alison's sulky face reappeared.

'Now who's got a gob on?' I said, giving her playful shove.

She half-smiled.

21

'Things still not too good between you?' I guessed.

'What do you think of his new mates?' she suddenly asked.

'Pete and Doddsy?' I wasn't sure what to say. Did she like them?

'Yeah, tweedle-dum and tweedle-dummer,' she said.

That would be a "no" then, I guessed.

'They're OK, I suppose, making allowances.'

'Making allowances for what?'

'For the fact that they're complete morons?'

That put the smile back on her face.

'What does Humph see in them?' she asked, 'he's got no time for me at all.'

'I'm sure it's just a novelty thing,' I said, 'you know, he's just started a new job. He has to work with these new mates. He's just getting to know them, that's all. Things will be back to normal once he's settled in.'

'I hope so Tim.'

So did I, but I wasn't convinced.

'So, talking of new mates. That's what we need to find you, eh?'

'Oh yeah? Like who?' I huffed.

'Well there's....Gary Hurst for a start.'

'Gary Hurst? Be serious Alison! Gary Hurst?'

'Well, he's a useful mate to have. He's very clever.'

'And very boring. Do you know his favourite band? The Shadows! The ruddy Shadows!'

'Ok, not Gary then? How about William Gregory?'

I shook my head. 'Dr.Hook.'

'Martin Yates?'

'The Commodores.'

'Ok, how about Luke Watson?'

'Mmm nice. Village People.'

'Oh right, so you determine people's worthiness solely by their taste in music do you?'

'No, not at all, but ....'

'So what about Trevor Tiler?'

I pulled a face.

'What?' she said, exasperated.

'He supports Palace,' I said, smiling.

She grinned. Shook her head. She gazed out of the window. A group of lads from our year strolled by. One of them, Dave Booth, was kicking an empty Coke can along the path.

'How about David Booth and his crowd?' she said, waving at Dave. He waved back, blew her a kiss. His mates waved too.

'Love themselves,' I said. Dave Booth and his mates had been in a different class to me and mine. We never mixed with them. Poseurs.

'Well, maybe David does a little,' she smiled. I watched as they walked around the corner, heading for the door to the canteen.

'A little? He's president of his own fan club!'

The door opened right on cue. Dave Booth and his mates strolled in, laughing and joking as ever. Showing off.

'He's so cute,' Alison muttered, looking over at them

'Dave Booth? You're joking?' I said, glancing around at the three boys as they headed for the service hatch,

'No, not David. Karl Bloom.'

'Really? Karl Bloom? Why?' I looked over at one of the lads who was, as always, with Dave Booth. Karl was blonde and skinny; loppy looking.

'Ooh, there's definitely something about Karl,' she said, a dead sexy smile on her face. Bloody hell, I bet she'd never smiled like that when my name had been mentioned.

'Really?'

'Yeah, all the girls think so.'

I just shrugged. I'd never understand women.

'Kevin's a nice lad too,' she said, pointing out the third lad in the threesome.

Kevin Clarke was a quiet, red-headed boy who always seemed to be hanging back slightly from the others. He was one of those kids, was Kevin; still wore the uniform, even though it was no longer strictly necessary,

'Don't know him,' I said dismissively; still trying to work out the Karl Bloom thing.

'He's funny is Kevin, a really good laugh'

'Really? He always seems dead quiet.'

'You don't know him that's all. Strikes me you don't know many of the boys who've stayed on. I can see we're going to have to widen your circle of mates!'

'Well, maybe.' I said. I wasn't convinced about that either.

23

'And in the meantime, I'll just have to be your best friend. Ok?' She smiled, put her arm around my shoulder and kissed me on the cheek.

I shivered.

'Right, I don't know about you, but I've got some catching up to do. See you on the bus home?' she got up, putting on her purple jacket and throwing her holdall over her shoulder on in one move and then before I had a chance to answer her, she was off, leaving only a trail of perfume and some vivid pictures in my head of a beach at Florida Keys.

I took a last sip of my Coke and got up to go. That's when I saw it.

On the canteen floor by the chair where Alison had been sitting. A black photo envelope. I bent to pick it up and looked around for her but she'd already gone.

Turning the envelope over in my hand, the flap fell open. There was Adrian with Elliott the Dragon looking up at me. I glanced around. The canteen had emptied out; only a few last kids, finishing up their lunches. No-one paying me any attention. No one had see me pick up the photos. Oh well, I would give them back to her on the bus tonight. I started to slip them inside my Adidas bag.

Then, in my head, I heard Alison's voice saying *"Ooh, I'm not showing you that one."*

"... or that one, that's far too embarrassing."

I was never good at ignoring temptation. I'm not proud of the fact but there it is.

I sat back down and making sure no-one was watching, slipped the pile onto the table and quickly rifled through, until I came to the two photos she wouldn't show me.

Oh blimey. There was one with Alison sunbathing on a beach towel, reading a novel. Adrian must have crept up on her. In the next one, she was just starting to stand up; she looked angry; still clutching her book in one hand, grabbing the towel in the other, her mouth wide open, as if she was shouting at someone; presumably her brother, who had obviously caught her unawares.

And in both cases, the stunningly attractive Alison Fisher was completely topless.

Oh. My. God.

Of course I should have ran after her - after all, she could't have got that far in those couple of minutes.

'Here Alison', I should have said, breathlessly catching up with her, 'you left your holiday snaps behind.'

That's what I *should* have done. What I *should* have said. But I didn't of course.

I thought about it. But then I hesitated; firstly I had to have another look; to make sure I'd seen what my disbelieving eyes couldn't quite believe they'd seen. And once I'd done that there was no going back, no running after her and giving them to her, face-to-face. She'd have *known*.

She'd have been able to tell, as clear as light is day, from just looking at my guilty face. She'd know I'd looked at them; that I'd gawped over the very photos she'd expressly chosen not to show me - because she was too embarrassed. And if she asked me and I lied, she'd have seen right through me. And she'd probably never speak to me again.

So, I sat there, the wad of revealing photos in my grubby mitts, wondering what I should do.

I could hand them in at lost property.

Or to one of the dinner ladies, there in the canteen

But then what if they told Alison it was me who'd handed them in?

Maybe I could give them back via a third party - say via Gary Hurst or Sara Potts? No, they'd just tell her it was me who found them and I'd still not be able to look her in the face.

I could always check her locker - put them in there after school. But what were the odds that she'd have left it open? She never left her locker open. Nope, that wouldn't work either.

So, I'm not proud of myself but I admit it. I panicked. Instead of taking any of the more sensible options open to me, I left them there, in the canteen, on her seat, for someone else to find. Someone else could have the dilemma. Besides, as soon as she realised, it would be the first place she'd look. Yeah, it would be fine. And she'd never have to know.

I'd only been home half an hour when she rang. She was in a flap.

'Please say you found them!'

'Sorry Alison, the last thing I remember was you putting them in your bag.'

25

'Did I definitely?'

'Yeah, I watched you. You put them on top of your books.'

'That's what I told my Mum. She's so upset. I can't believe I've been so stupid!'

'Don't worry. You must have dropped them somewhere, that's all.'

'But where? Mum called the bus company. There's no sign of them.' She sounded like she might burst into tears.

I was such a terrible friend.

'You wait and see. Someone will have found them and handed them in by tomorrow.'

'Oh God,' she groaned.

'What?'

'I just hope it's a girl. Or someone kind; someone discrete!'

'Why?' I said, trying my best to sound confused.

'Nothing. It's just a bit embarrassing, that's all. I hope they don't fall into the wrong hands.'

'Aren't you being a little....I don't know...melodramatic?'

'If you'd seen them, you'd understand,' she muttered.

'But I did see them. I mean, er, you showed them to me.'

'Not all of them Tim!' she said impatiently, like she was waiting for a very large penny to drop.

I gave it what I thought was sufficient time for even a dense idiot like me to get the picture and then I said, 'oh, I see.'

'That's just it. I'd rather you didn't!' she said.

Having assured her repeatedly not to worry and having promised to help her search for them in the morning, a distraught Alison finally hung up.

I felt really awful. And what was worse was that, even though I knew how upset she'd been, I still couldn't shake off the image that was burning a hole in the back of my smutty little retinas. The secret image that I tried, unsuccessfully, to blank out, as I ate my tea and as I watched TV that evening.

It was no good. It was clear to me that I wasn't destined to get much sleep that night. I knew I'd be tossing and turning.

3 - Canary In A Coalmine

Tim James and 'DSFCL6' was not a marriage made in heaven.

During those early weeks of term, I felt completely out of place. I was like a square peg in a round hole. A rabbit caught in headlights. Or, as Sting would have it - a Canary in a Coalmine.

The Police's song "Canary in a Coalmine" was my favourite from Zenyatta Mondatta. I thought about the words a lot; trying to get my head around just what it was Sting was actually trying to say. I asked Dad. He listened to the song, pulling a face as usual, making comments about Sting's "girly' voice.

'What do you reckon he means though?' I said, doing my best to ignore him.

'Miners used to use canaries in the pits. They could detect gases like carbon monoxide. They'd start flapping their wings if they caught a sniff of it. That way the miners would know it was dangerous and get out of there pretty sharpish. Cruel though really - keeping a beautiful little bird like that down a dark hole. They didn't deserve that. They didn't belong down there.'

At that early point in my sixth form life, that was exactly how I felt about staying on at sixth form and taking my A-levels. I didn't belong.

DSFCL6 was a drag; even though the ever-lovely Alison had been doing her best to jolly me along. During most of those early term lunchtimes, I joined her and Sara Potts in the school canteen; sitting there patiently, listening to their bizarre conversations. It didn't take me long to realise that Joe Jackson had been spot on when he sang "It's Different For Girls". Nevertheless, I did my level best to play the honorary girl-friend. I smiled along, and chipped in with the odd rude comment, when they argued who was better looking out of Bodie and Doyle from The Professionals. I stifled my yawns as they debated, at some length, as to which brand of hairspray Toyah had used to such devastating effect in her latest video. I even listened in to a fascinating conversation about the respective merits of Lil-lets and Tampax; a subject on which I wasn't exactly qualified to offer much of an opinion, so I just sat there feeling distinctly uncomfortable. Still, I knew they were only trying to help me feel more at home at DSFCL6 and I was grateful that they were making such an effort. The two girls had really taken me under their respective wings. They were being really supportive with the studying too - making me revise with them in the common room when I'd sooner have been listening to old records and feeling really sorry for myself. But it wasn't the same. Unlike the fifth year, most of the people who had stayed on were here to do some serious learning. There was less larking about, fewer jokes, fewer opportunities to act the fool. I felt unsettled. During those first few days of the new term, I'd almost made up my mind to leave about half a dozen times. Did I really want to go to University; to study to be a journalist? I was far from sure. I'd under-estimated how much I'd miss my old mates. If it hadn't have been for Alison and Sara, I would have spent those entire weeks, doing very little work and moping around Denton's lonely corridors. As it was, even with their encouragement, I still couldn't help wondering if I'd done the right thing; wondering if the journalism idea was just a stupid pipe-dream and if so, what the hell I was going to do with the rest of my life. Even if I got my A-levels - a big "if", if my shoddy performance to date was anything to go by - would I really have what it took to work in Fleet Street? Or even on a local rag?

Jacko, Humph and I had discussed my plans as we'd sat in the pub one Friday; three nervous, under-age drinkers, pretending to be grown-ups and in the words of the XTC song, "Making Plans for Nigel" - or in this case, *for Tim*. They both knew that I'd long dreamed of being a music journalist, working for Sounds or the NME.

'But they talk bollocks!' Jacko pointed out, as he'd done many times before. 'I can read a review of the new Talking Heads album half a dozen times and be none the wiser what the reviewer thought about it - they just use big words for the sake of it.'

'Yeah, maybe,' I knew what he meant - but then "review" was a big word where Jacko was concerned.

'Go straight to the end of the review and see how many stars they give it out of five. Just go by that; ignore all the poncey crap they come out with,' he said, displaying his usual level of intellectual wit and wisdom.

So, if I didn't want to be the chief-writer for the NME, what did I want to do? And more importantly, how would I afford to go out and enjoy myself for the next five years? And there, perhaps, was the real crux of my problem; did I want to get an education or did I want to go out with my mates, get drunk, meet girls in night clubs and buy loads

28

of LPs? I asked myself that all the time and I wasn't entirely sure that I liked the answer I kept coming up with.

My old mates were working; earning money they didn't know how to spend. All I had was a couple of quid a week from my paper-round and a pound pocket-money from Dad - and that didn't seem to stretch very far since my mates had introduced me to lager and the delights of the Pedestrian Arms on a Friday Night. I had to make my money stretch. I watched on enviously as Humph and Jacko spent and spent – but there were no daily additions to the record collection for me; no new skinny legged jeans and black Fred Perry t-shirts; no seventeen games of pac-man or Space Invaders down the pub. I was skint, I missed my mates and I was beginning to think that staying on was the worst decision of my life. And what's more, who was I kidding? I was never going to work up the courage to speak to Roxanne in a month of Sundays. In short, I was the canary and Sixth Form was the proverbial coal mine.

But that was before the day that Dave Booth came to my rescue.

'Anyone sitting here?'

I looked up from the pages of my magazine. Dave Booth was dripping wet, carrying a Cornish pasty and a bottle of Coke. Raindrops ran down from his fringe, dripping from his nose onto the table.

'Raining is it?'

It was a stupid question.

Dave gave me a look, 'There's no flies on you, are there Sherlock?' he laughed.

'Where've you been then?' I asked.

'It's that bloody Bo Derek!' he said, shaking drops from his wet blazer and sitting himself down in the vacant chair.

'Sorry?'

'Bo Derek. She keeps pestering me; phones all the time. Bloody nuisance. I told her - "Bo, get real - it's raining, we can't go doing it in the long grass again in this weather." But you know what these women are like; won't take no for an answer.'

'Must be tough,' I laughed, wondering if he was on something.

Bo Derek was a seriously sexy Hollywood actress. She'd been in "10" with Dudley Moore. Dave would have more chance with Bo Peep.

29

'Still, my own fault I suppose. Once these women get a slice of Dave Booth, they want the whole package.'

'Really?' I smirked

'Yeah, and besides it was either that or spending another boring lunch hour going over the shops for a pasty and coming back here to revise Economics!' he winked and delving into his bag, retrieved an enormous and slightly soggy looking Economics text book.

'Do you have Mrs. Holloway?' I asked.

Mrs. Holloway was the school's Economics teacher. She was really lovely. All the boys fancied Mrs. Holloway.

'*Have* her? She should be so lucky! Like Bo would ever share me with Sabrina!'

'Sabrina? Is that her name?'

'Yeah. Suits her doesn't it? She's tasty isn't she? I mean, I would, wouldn't you?'

A stupid grin broke out on my face, which I just knew was flushing at the thought of the sexy Sabrina. It was pretty embarrassing; Dave talking about a teacher like that.

'I bet she's the only reason you're doing Economics isn't she?' I laughed.

'Of course, why else? And if Bo ever gets tired of me, which, let 's face it, is pretty unlikely, the fair Sabrina might just be in with a shout.'

Dave Booth was clearly quite mad, but I was relieved just to have someone to talk to

Before he'd come in, rambling on about his soggy, fantasy-rendezvous with beautiful Bo, I'd been sitting, bored out of my tiny mind, in the school library, thumbing through an old Smash Hits that I'd rescued from the common room bin. I'd tucked it inside my History text book, just in case Candice Morris or any of the other teachers came snooping around. I was only in the library because it was warm and dry; it wasn't that I was swatting; and I suppose if I'm being honest, the other reason for being there, was that I was avoiding Alison.

The three of us; Alison, Sara Potts, and I, had searched high and low for Alison's bloody photos that morning. I'd never seen Alison so upset. They weren't in the canteen; which was obviously the first place I'd suggested looking.

'Well, that was the last place you saw them; they're bound to be there,' I'd said, more in hope than anything. I'd had an ominous feeling they wouldn't be there. I'd been right.

They weren't in any of the classrooms she'd used the previous afternoon; they weren't lying on the path anywhere and they weren't on the bench at the bus-stop as Sara had predicted. I assured Alison they would turn up and I was now hoping and praying I was right. By late morning she had enlisted the help of practically every female member of the lower sixth to help with the search. I felt more terrible as the morning went on; especially after she'd thanked me and told me what a great friend I was, for spending all my free time helping her look for them. Finally, at lunch time, Sara had calmed her down enough to persuade her to go back to the canteen and have something to eat. I declined the invitation to join them and skulked off to the library to hide; to take refuge from the storms which were gathering both outside and inside the common room.

Smash Hits wasn't exactly a challenging read. It consisted mainly of the lyrics to current chart hits, printed on glossy, colour photos of the artists responsible. Ian Dury grinned at me from the front cover. I looked out of the rain spattered window and wondered what reasons he had to be so bloody cheerful - one, two, three? I couldn't even think of one.

'Anything good in there this month?' Dave said, looking over my shoulder.

'Not a lot....' I said, feeling a bit stupid that he'd rumbled the old text book ruse so easily, 'it's an old one, from a few weeks back.'

I showed him the cover and then flipped the pages, coming to rest on a colour photo of Grace Jones, accompanying the words to her latest hit.

'Grace Jones is weird, isn't she?' Dave said, studying the photo, 'not sure I'd want to wake up to find that face on my pillow first thing in the morning eh?'

'Yeah, dead weird,' I agreed.

Grace Jones was a tall, scary, butch looking black woman, who'd had a couple of singles in the charts recently. In the photo, she wore a dress with massive out-sized shoulder pads. Her hair was cut in this amazingly severe flat-top and her skin was shiny, like she'd been polished with Mr. Sheen. Seriously weird.

Dave tucked into his pasty.

I tried to think of something to say - but I didn't know a lot about him really; other than the fact that Alison had assured me he didn't love himself as much everyone thought. Judging by his comments, she was either very wrong or he had a very strange sense of humour. Dave and his mates had been nodding acquaintances of mine right through senior school - but they were in a different class; a different house - always on the opposing teams. Dave was big mates with Karl Bloom and Kevin Clarke. They were really cliquey and they'd all stayed on to take A-levels together.

'What do you think of them?' I asked, making conversation. I pointed to the centre-spread photo; Dexy's Midnight Runners. They were all dressed in black coats and matching bobble hats.

'Brilliant! Geno - what a great song that is eh?'

'Yeah, it's great isn't it?' I said, relieved I'd found some common ground between us.

'Ugly buggers though. That lead singer's got a face for radio if ever I've seen one,' Dave said through a mouthful of minced meat and pastry.

I smiled. He was right. Kevin Rowland wasn't exactly a looker. The next page had a photo of Paul Weller from The Jam.

'Your mate Jackson would like that, wouldn't he? I've seen him in his Ben Sherman shirts and his Harrington jacket; reckons he's a right Mod, doesn't he?' Dave smiled.

'Yeah,' I agreed, 'wouldn't be so bad if he had a scooter and not that Raleigh Chopper!'

'He doesn't still ride that thing does he? What a prat!'

I laughed along, but I didn't really like him calling my friend a prat.

'He's OK really,' I said.

'No, don't get me wrong!' Dave said, 'He's great is Martin - a good laugh, I used to go to junior school with him, you know?'

'Oh yeah, I'd forgotten that - was he a prat then too?'

We both fell about. He was alright was Dave Booth. He asked me what Jacko was up to now. He was amazed when I told him.

'A bank? Martin Jackson working in a bank?'

'Yeah, bit of a turn-up eh?'

'I should say, I had him down as a barrow-boy on the open-market - or maybe a bookie, or an antique dealer? Well, I never! Martin Jackson - a banker?'

'With a capital W.'

Dave liked that one; he almost choked on his pasty.

'If you had money, would you seriously trust Martin Jackson with it?' Dave laughed.

OK, you've made your point Dave; it was a good one though, to be fair. Jacko wasn't the most responsible bloke I'd ever met; not by a long chalk. Mind you, he'd only got the job because his Dad's mate was the branch manager.

'What about that other lairy mate of yours, Chris Humphreys? What's he up to these days?'

'He's an electrician - well, an apprentice anyway.' I wasn't too sure about the abuse he was handing out to my mates - but we were on a roll now, having a bit of a laugh. I let it pass.

'Is he still seeing the gorgeous Alison Fisher?'

I nodded.

'God, she loves herself though, doesn't she?'

I bristled but said nothing.

'Mind you,' he continued, laughing, 'she's got pretty good taste eh? I mean she is bloody horny, isn't she?'

I just smiled. 'She's not exactly hideous,' I conceded.

'So, Chris Humphreys, a sparky eh? Following his Dad then?'

Then Dave said something that surprised me, 'well, good for him. Good to have a trade. Very sensible. My old man's always telling me I should get a trade. Trouble is, I'm crap with my hands. The world's least practical bloke, that's me.'

'Huh, you can't be as bad as me,' I said, 'I can't even wire a plug!'

'Me neither! Or change a light bulb!'

Brilliant. I'd found someone else as useless as me.

We chatted for ages, talking about all our old class mates and what they were up to. Dave told me about Stuart Fletcher, who was working in a butchers shop and Mark Brooks, who had joined the Army. I told him about Dan Chester and Ray O'Brien. Dan was in heating and ventilating - whatever that was, and Ray was training to be a Carpenter - or a 'Chippy' as Humph called them. Then there was Declan Kelly; Dec was working in insurance, which sounded dead boring. Even Tony Di Marco, the thickest kid on the planet, had got a job; even if it was only as 'Head Waiter' in his dad's pizza place.

Having exhausted that topic, I went back to Smash Hits and Dave finished stuffing his face with Cornish pasty.

'What do you fancy doing after school?' he asked a few minutes later.

'Oh, thanks but I'm probably going into town, to have a look around HMV,' I said.

Dave laughed, spluttering flakes of pastry into his Coke, 'After you leave sixth-form, I meant, you prat! Are you going on to Uni?'

'Oh, right!' I laughed, 'No idea really, you?'

'Me neither,' he shrugged, 'still, at least two years yet before we have to think about it eh? And if we go to Uni, at least another five before we have to think about a job! Ah well, we don't want to rush into things do we? Fancy a bit?' he offered me the last bite of his snack.

'No thanks mate.'

Mate?

So, it seemed I'd made a new friend; a bloke with about as much clue as to what he was doing there as I had. And I'd always thought Dave Booth was the sort of bloke who knew exactly where he was going. He'd always seemed so cocky. Suddenly, I felt a whole lot better about my own aimless life.

'Oi, Boothie, what you up to?' said Karl Bloom, as he and Kevin Clarke came bounding into the library.

Karl stuck a damp looking satchel down on the table next to Dave. It was covered with assorted pin-badges - Man United, Joy Division. This was the bloke that Alison said all the girls fancied. I couldn't see it myself; he still looked tall and loppy to me. Actually, with his blonde hair and gangly limbs, he reminded me a bit of Stewart Copeland, the drummer in The Police.

'Hope you're not actually revising!' he teased Dave, ignoring me completely. 'Come on, it's stopped raining, we're going to have a kick-around on the tennis court. Fancy it?'

'Yeah, OK,' said Dave, lobbing his empty Coke-can into the nearest bin. He picked up his bag and made to follow his mates.

'Hey Tim; fancy a kick-around?' he said, turning back to me.

'Er no, you're alright thanks Dave,' I said, feeling a bit self conscious.

'Oh come on, it's as boring as hell in here. What do you think lads? Two on two eh?'

'Yeah, good idea!' smiled Karl Bloom, 'come on Tim, you can't be any worse than Clarkey; he plays like he's got webbed feet!'

34

I hesitated but Dave made up my mind for me. He picked up my bag and started heading off. 'Come on mate, we've only got half an hour - get a move on!'

That evening, I sat on my bed listening to records as usual; nursing a badly grazed knee. Mum had gone mental about the dirty patches on my trousers. Bloody Dave Booth was a really dirty player. But all in all, things were looking up. The day had certainly finished better than it had started. I'd bumped into Alison on the bus home. She'd been smiling as I sat down behind her and Sara.

'Look what I've got!' she said, holding up the packet of photos.

She looked as relieved as I felt.

'Great. Where were they?' I asked.

'The school office had them. Someone had posted them through the letter box.'

'Oh really, did they know who?'

'No. No-one saw anyone. They reckoned it must have been after the office had closed.'

'Oh right.'

'Still,' she said, smiling, 'goes to show that there's some pretty nice people about doesn't it? Almost restores your faith in your fellow man!' she laughed.

'I suppose,' I said. Then I suddenly had a horrible thought. 'Were they, you know, *all* present and correct?' I asked, crossing my fingers in my lap.

'Seem to be, yeah.'

Ah well, all's well that ends well eh? No harm done.

I turned the volume up on my music centre and sang along to "Canary in a Coalmine". Maybe sixth form was going to be OK for this particular canary after all. I'd give it a few weeks more anyway. Who knew what DSFCL6 had in store for me?

Dave and his mates had invited me around Kevin's place that Saturday for a Scrabble marathon and maybe a game or two of Subbuteo. I thought it all sounded a bit childish but I decided I'd probably go; after all, I didn't have anything better to do. And I might get to meet Bo Derek.

4 - De Do Do Do, De Da Da Da

The last few months of 1980 and the times, they were-a-changing.

School had become sixth form college and I had made some new mates. Wispy hair had suddenly appeared on my upper lip, my spots grew bigger and angrier. I'd started going to pubs. Or at least one pub; the Pedestrian Arms, near Brighton station. Oh, and I'd started drinking lager. But I wasn't that sure if really liked the taste yet.

'Cheers mate!' Jacko raised his pint of Carlsberg.

'Cheers, happy birthday Jacko.'

Martin Jackson. Seventeen and never been kissed; well, almost never; if you ignored Fay Carpenter in the third year. She'd dumped him when he'd tried to experiment with the French form of kissing. Lord knows why; after all, he hadn't even mastered the English version.

'Blimey, I've just had a thought!' Jacko was rubbing his bum-fluff covered chin. I think he was trying to look intellectual. He didn't. He just looked like a spotty teenage prat, rubbing a bum-fluff beard.

'Come on them, let's hear this massive pearl of wisdom,' I said, anticipating some joke at my expense - as per usual.

'No seriously Timbo, do you realise, we'll be able vote this time next year?'

'True.'

Crikey, I hadn't thought of that.

'So, given that....'

Here we go, I thought.

'Isn't it about time your balls dropped?'

'Ho, bloody ho,' I muttered, supping my lager. I still had a half pint to get through.

Lager? I just wasn't sure what the fuss was about, but at least it wasn't making me gag as much as it had that first time, a few weeks back, when Humph had turned up at my door with a surprise.

'Hi, mate, what are you doing here?' It was a Friday evening, in early September. I'd just finished my tea and had been heading upstairs to listen to some records, when there had been a ring on the bell.

'Christopher's here for you!' Mum had shouted as I climbed the stairs.

Humph stood in the hallway. He was wearing new clobber; black Levi's, a button-down shirt and red Dr. Martens. His hair was all spiked up with gel; he looked dead cool. No wonder Alison had fallen for him. The git.

'You look smart Chris. Have you got a date with Alison?' my Mum asked.

'No, Mrs. James, she's on holiday with her folks. I was just wondering if Tim wanted to play out?'

Mum laughed. 'Are sure you want this scruffy bugger tagging along?' Mum chuckled.

'Yeah, thanks a bunch Mum.'

'So where are you boys off to?'

'Oh, not sure, really,' Humph said, 'Jacko's sorting something, maybe a film or ten-pin bowling.'

'Oh, well, that's nice. Have you got enough cash Tim?'

I never had enough cash.

'Yeah, I'll manage,' I said.

Mum lingered in the hall. What did she want, an encore?

'Well, I'll see you later then Mum OK?' I said, dropping a subtle hint that the pleasure of her company might not be required any longer.

'Oh, OK, well you lads have fun - but don't be too late!'

I pulled on my trainers and grabbed my coat.

'What's going on then?' I said as I closed the front-door behind me.

'We're off for a pint. Thought you might fancy it?' Humph said nonchalantly, like it was something we did every week.

'What, in like...a pub?'

'No, down the all-night chemist. Yes, of course, in a pub, Brainiac!'

Instinctively, I rummaged in my pockets - a pound note and some odd coppers.

'I've only got a quid...and... sixteen pence,' I said, counting the change in my hand.

'Don't worry, I'm sure me and Jacko can club together to buy you a bottle of Cresta.'

'Very funny,' I gave Humph a two fingered salute.

'It's Frothy man!' he said, returning the gesture.

Frankly, I'd have happily have had a Cresta too. But I'd succumbed to peer pressure of course.

That first taste of lager had made me want to retch, and even all these weeks later, I wasn't exactly loving it. All the other lads knocked their pints back like seasoned drinkers. There was nothing for it; I'd have to bluff again. Holding my breath as much as I could, I tipped the glass and knocked it back in one; after all, I didn't want to be seen as a wimp. I'd have given anything for a mouthful of Orange Squash.

As I soon discovered, lager didn't like me much either. It seemed to have a very nasty effect on my stomach.

I belched loudly.

'Windy Miller!' said Jacko, laughing.

My stomach grumbled like a wind-turbine.

'Joking aside though Tim,' said Jacko, swilling the last dregs of the amber liquid around the bottom of his glass, 'doesn't it feel weird, still being at school at our age?'

'Shhh!' I hissed.

By now, we were just about on first name terms with Fred, the barman at the Peds. Thankfully, he was busy washing glasses and he didn't look up. To my relief, nor did any of the other punters. This under-age drinking lark scared me shitless.

'What?' Jacko said.

'Keep your bloody voice down will you?' I said in a stage whisper, 'do you have to talk about me being....at *school*?' I grimaced, anxiously looking around the bar.

I was terrified we'd be rumbled; even though I knew I was letting my imagination run away with me, I had these horrible visions of us all being nicked and ending up in a cell for the night. I could just picture my Dad collecting me from the police station in his car; he'd go mental.

Fred the barman seemed OK - but he always gave us a knowing smile when we ordered the beers - I figured he knew perfectly well we weren't old enough. It was only a back-street pub; I suppose there wasn't too much chance of a raid up here. But even if Fred was prepared to turn a blind eye, he still had his licence to consider. So far, he'd never asked us for IDs but Jacko talking loudly about my time at "school" wasn't going to help our cause if Fred did decide to get awkward one of these evenings.

Despite Jacko and his enormous gob, I was relieved to see that no-one had batted an eyelid. Not that the Peds was exactly a hive of activity; there was an old bloke in a tatty trilby, studying the Evening Argus, and two hard looking labourers in orange and black donkey jackets, supping guinness and smoking fags. With me, Jacko, Humph and his two mates, that made eight. Eight punters - the total clientele of The Pedestrian Arms on a Friday night. Jacko's 17th birthday celebration. We knew how to live it up.

We'd been coming to the Peds every Friday night since that first time, several weeks now. For the first couple of Fridays, it had been just me, Jacko and Humph; it had been a laugh. But then Humph had started bringing his new workmates with him. I wasn't at all sure about Pete and Doddsy but I was trying hard to give them the benefit of the doubt for Humph's sake. I'd preferred it when it had been just the three of us.

'I need a slash,' Jacko announced. He jumped down from the bar stool and reached into the change pocket of his Levis. 'Why don't you feed the jukebox? Here's fifty pence. Go mad - it's my birthday after all!' Jacko tossed the coin at me, as he turned and made for the Gents.

The pub was a bit of a dive really. But the beer was cheap, there was a pool table, a games machine and a one arm bandit. Furthermore, they did great meat pies and best of all, we got served, with no questions asked. The best thing about the Peds for me though, was the fantastic jukebox. I loved that thing. I wanted one just like it for my room at home. But I knew I'd never squeeze it in between my bed and the wardrobe.

Seven choices for fifty pence. A bargain. It was so cool; the way the singles lined up side by side; the way you could watch the bar move over, pick up your chosen record, and move it into position on the turntable. I loved the crackles it made when the needle landed on the grooves. Heaven. I peered down through the glass cover. It was still there. The one piece of white vinyl in a sea of back. "Can't Stand Losing You" by The Police. The first 45 I'd ever owned. My copy was on blue vinyl. White was pretty rare as far as I knew - maybe only available for the jukebox market? My plan was to get really pally with Fred - maybe then, if they ever decided to take it off, he might let me have the precious white vinyl copy.

39

A6. I punched in the digits. The bar moved along the black line and picked out the white disc. It flipped into place with a flash of the tell-tale A&M label. The needle landed and the opening bars kicked in. Sting started singing.

"Called you so many times today...."

'Oh bloody hell Timbo, not again!' shouted Humph. He was playing Pac-Man with his work-mates Pete and Doddsy, at the other end of the bar. They all groaned. With perfect timing, the old boy in the trilby started folding his paper and got up to go. The two builders moved to the bar, giving me a dirty look. Fred gave me a rueful smile as he cleaned a pint glass, holding it up to the light to check for smears. Bloody hell - did no-one in this God-forsaken dump have any musical taste?

Jacko came back from the loo just in time to see the door closing behind Mr. Trilby.

'Good old Sting. You can always rely on him to empty the place out!' he laughed, ' have you heard their new one?' he said, sitting back on his stool, '"Diddums da da" or something like that?'

'Piss off Jacko,' I said, slurping the dregs of my second Carlsberg.

I wasn't taking the bait. The song in question was called "De Do Do De, De Da Da Da". It was the second single from "Zenyatta Mondatta". It wasn't as great as the first, "Don't Stand So Close To Me", but it was still pretty good - better than most of the crap Jacko liked at any rate.

'It's something like that anyway. Kiddy speak it is. My nephew George, you know Nick's kid- he's three now- he loves it - sings along with all the words.'

'Yeah, right - all the words? I expect he gets a bit tongue-tied around "poets, priests and politicians" then?' I said smugly.

Jacko ignored me. 'Do Do Do, Da Da Da,' he sang in a babyish voice, 'their best yet eh? You Police-ettes will buy anything won't you? I bet if Sting recorded himself farting into a jar, you'd have to have it wouldn't you? I can see it now. Jimmy Saville; Top of the Pops - "Okay, guys and gals, here's The Police with their latest number one smash, Fart in A Bottle."'

'Very funny.' Farting was no joking matter as far as I was concerned; the lager was playing havoc with my guts; hot air was escaping from both ends at once - I felt a bit like a punctured li-lo. I was likely to burst any minute.

'Do do do, da da da,' Jacko repeated in his baby voice.

'Piss off Jacko,' I repeated, a little too loudly.

This time, Fred did raise his head. He gave me a look. I smiled at him apologetically.

I looked around the bar. Jesus. What a way to celebrate your birthday. The Peds was hardly likely to rival Coasters, The Sea House, Smugglers, or any of the other bars in the town centre. Humph's older mates thought we were mental, drinking in a "dump" like this. I could see their point, but I wasn't ready to brave the town-centre pubs yet. Despite my feeble attempts at growing a moustache and Jacko's pathetic beard, I knew we still looked nothing like eighteen.

A couple came through the door and approached the bar. Fred moved across to serve them. The girl looked vaguely familiar; bleach-blonde hair; pretty, in a tarty sort of a way. Short skirt - more like a tea-cloth - and far too much make-up. She was with a tall, dark-skinned bloke, in a flash suit.

'So, how *is* school anyway?' said Jacko.

'Shhh!'

'Sorry,' he whispered, 'so how *is* kindergarten?'

'Sixth form college, Jacko, it's sixth form college - it's totally different from school,' I said.

'True. There are differences I suppose.'

'Exactly.'

'Yeah, all the cool people have gone and you're left with the nerds. That's what's different. Same bloody teachers - same boring lessons.'

'They're not all nerds!' I protested.

There were a few though, to be fair.

'And for your information Martin, we do different subjects now,'

'Like what?'

'Well, like....er.. Commerce and.... Economics!'

'Wow, Economics and Commerce eh? Oh, no! Why didn't I stay on?' Jacko said sarcastically.

'I would have thought they were the sort of subjects that would come in useful working in a bank actually'

'Not if you're filing record cards all bloody day they're not!'

'Well, sixth form isn't all that bad you know, maybe you should have stayed on? You might have been trusted with something a bit more arduous that filing if you had some A levels.'

'What? And end up skint *and* miserable like you?'

41

'I'll be earning in a couple of years,' I said, trying to sound convinced. It was what my Dad was always telling me.

'S'pose so. But you'll owe me a lot of bloody beers by then! You might as well hand over your first pay packet.'

'Well, I'm not sorry I stayed on. It'll be worth it.'

Was I trying to convince Jacko or myself?

There was a commotion from the Pac-man machine. Humph was still struggling to get past level one. Pete and Doddsy were jeering and laughing.

'They're putting a lot of money into that machine,' I said, 'they've got more money than sense, these apprentice electricians.

'That's not saying much is it? They could be completely skint and they'd still have more money than sense!'

'Wan - kerrr!' shouted Pete and Doddsy in unison.

The machine beeped and played that familiar little tune. Another life lost. Another ten pence on its way down the drain. Another five minutes of life that Humph would never get back.

'Toss-errr!' his new mates shouted.

Pete and Doddsy had a limited vocabulary.

Fred was giving them a dead dirty look now. I looked down at the bar and said a silent prayer. It didn't work; they were still there when I looked up. Worse still, they were walking over.

'Knob-head here just can't get past level one!' announced Doddsy, ruffling Humph's hair playfully.

'So, who's round? Pete asked, 'the school-kid's turn is it?' he said, looking at me.

'Shh!'

Pete knew I didn't have any money - he was just winding me up.

'Yeah right, Fred really believes you're eighteen, in your Police T-shirt and your school uniform trousers!' laughed Doddsy.

As usual, he punched me playfully on the arm. As usual, it was bloody painful. I wan't going to rub it though, I'd learned already with these two; never show a sign of weakness. If it had been Jacko winding me up, I'd have told him to piss off - but it wasn't; it was John Dodds, and like his mate, Pete Mackay, he was nineteen and bloody hard with it. I said nothing.

Fred was still serving the new couple; he hadn't heard. The girl had a high pitched giggle. She laughed at something her boyfriend had said and we all looked around.

Pete pulled a face and Doddsy smiled, 'She'd do eh?' he said, just a little too loudly.

'No chance mate,' said Pete, 'looks like she prefers Camel Jockeys.'

The dark-skinned man looked over, obviously hearing the remark. He glared at Pete for a moment and then looked away, before his tarty looking girlfriend led him away to the safety of a table in the corner.

Doddsy snorted and I saw Pete wink at him. They were trouble those two.

The silence that followed wasn't the only thing that was uncomfortable. My stomach began to complain noisily about the lager. I felt really warm; I took off my leather jacket, revealing my Regatta de Blanc T-shirt in all it's glory

Pete smirked, 'Talking of The Police, have you heard that new one?' Pete laughed.

'Yeah, how does it go? Da Di Dum-Da Di Dum or something isn't it?' Doddsy said.

Jacko was grinning from ear to ear. 'Told you mate!' he said, looking pretty pleased with himself.

'Piss off Jacko,' I muttered. My stomach groaned. 'Popping to the loo,' I said, sliding off my stool, just as Pete strolled past on his way to the fag machine.

'God, have you dropped your guts Jacko?' I heard Pete say, as I was walking to the loo.

I didn't look back.

I really wasn't sure about this lager business.

For once, it wasn't raining as we walked home. It was a cold, cloudless night; I fastened the zip on my jacket. I wished I'd worn a jumper like Mum had told me to.

Humph and his mates had headed into town; Pete and Doddsy were confident that they would get Humph into Sherry's. To be fair, Humph, who was six feet-plus in his bare feet, did look older than seventeen. If any of us could get in there it was Humph. Jacko said he wasn't fussed about clubbing.

'They play crap music,' he explained.

'How the hell do you know? You've never been there in your life!'

'I've been there loads of times!'

'Like when?'

43

'With...Wilf and the blokes from the bank.'

He was such a liar.

'Besides, it's a disco isn't it? They play disco music don't they?'

'I suppose.'

Disco music was crap. Those Americans in Chicago had it about right. They had burned a huge pile of disco records in a park. I'd have happily lit the match. Anyway, according to Doddsy, it cost a couple of quid to get into Sherry's. I couldn't have afforded it even if I'd been brave enough to try it.

Jacko and I were sucking on extra-strong mints. Neither of us had told our folks we were pubbing on a Friday night; they thought we were either bowling or at the flicks. I'd lost count of the number of films I'd supposedly been to see. I'd already had to make up the plots to loads of movies; Airplane, The Blues Brothers' all sorts. For example, I'd since found out that apparently, The Elephant Man didn't even *have* a trunk. Still, hopefully by the time it came on the TV, Mum and Dad would've forgotten all about my made-up version.

'So, I keep meaning to ask you,' Jacko slurred, as he used the kerb as a balance-beam, his arms stretched out wide. He teetered, then slipped into the gutter, 'have you been into HMV this week?'

'No, not this week.'

It was only a *white* lie. I'd only been in there three times.

'So, you still haven't spoken to the ravishing Roxanne then?'

'Not exactly,'

'What do you mean, not exactly?'

'Well, I did ask her if they sold head-cleaners for my cassette player.'

'And?'

'They don't. She suggested WH Smith's.'

'And?'

'Smith's do them but they were too expensive.'

'So, you didn't ask her anything else then?'

'I didn't need anything else.'

'What you need my little yellow friend, is a kick up the arse! How much longer are you going to wait?'

'I've sort of gone off her a bit.'

That lie was a bit darker.

'Oh, yeah, right! God, you're something else you, aren't you?'

'Oh and you're such a big man when it comes to the ladies aren't you?' I said, 'you're not exactly copping off with Hazel O'Connor are you?'

'I've got more chance of copping off with bloody *Des* O'Connor than you have of ever pulling a bird, the way you're going.'

'Yeah, you probably have, you're such a shirt-lifter!' I laughed.

Jacko leant over and flicked me really hard on the ear. 'And that's for being a lippy smart-arse.'

'Ow! Bloody 'ell Jacko! That ruddy hurts!'

'It'll be more than your ear hurting if you don't get in that shop soon. I'll tell you what, I'll take you up there tomorrow and we can sort you out good and proper!'

'No thanks, I'm probably going to the Albion with my dad.'

That was a really black one.

'Ah, well, I'll go up there on my own then, put in a good word for you.'

'Yeah right, you're all mouth,' I said. I was right of course, he was. The trouble was he had a bloody big mouth. You never knew what was going to come out of it. Ah well, he was sloshed; he'd have forgotten all about it by tomorrow.

I woke up in the middle of the night with a headache and a burning need for the loo. Afterwards, I couldn't get back to sleep. I kept thinking about Jacko's threatened visit to HMV. He wouldn't really go up there would he? Nah, he was bluffing. He didn't have the balls. Still, I thought, maybe I should just head up there first thing, before he does anything that I'll regret. Yeah, I told myself, feeling brave in the wee small hours, head up there, bite the bullet and strike up a conversation with her. What was the worst that could happen? She could only say 'no' after all. Or laugh out loud?

'Come on mate, you can do this,' the three pints of lager told me, 'easy peasy, lemon squeezey!'

I got up, turned on the bedside light and grabbed my pen and note book from my school bag. I began to scribble down ideas for things I could say to her when I got up there. I crossed out the first effort and started again. The second attempt was even more feeble than the first. The third idea was just pathetic.

45

Face it Tim, I told myself after I scrapped the the fifth or sixth ridiculous chat up line; you're completely clueless when it comes to talking to girls.

Fifteen minutes later I had a page full of scrawled through rubbish. I admitted defeat and gave up. Before I switched off the light, I wrote one last note, in large letters, at the bottom of the page.

DE DO DO DO, DE DA DA DA,

THAT'S ALL I WANT TO SAY TO YOU.

5 - It's Alright For You

'It's alright for you. You were drinking pissy-weak Carlsberg. That Stella Artois is lethal!'

'Serves you right,' I chuckled.

'Your sympathy is greatly appreciated,' Jacko said, holding his head in his hands.

Something about Jacko's face reminded me of the Bakewell Tart that Sara Potts was tucking into. His face was white and pasty, his eyes red and glazed, like glace cherries,

'God I feel rough. I didn't wake up until mid-day. Grandstand was already on the box when I got downstairs.'

'Why do you boys think it's so big drinking so much? You look awful,' said Sara, talking with her mouth full and giving us all a lovely view of the mashed-up contents of her podgy little gob.

I thought Jacko was about to throw up. I'd still had a bit of a headache myself when Mum had come into my room and pulled open the curtains, at the ungodly hour of eleven o'clock. However the walk up to Churchill Square had done me good and I was feeling much better as I drank a second cup of tea.

I'd been pretty worried when Jacko had called me to say we were all meeting up at Acres The Bakers. I thought he was about to make good on his threat to take me up to HMV.

'So, are you still thinking of going to the Albion with your old man?' he'd asked on the phone.

Oh blimey, I thought he might have forgotten about that. Perhaps he hadn't been as sloshed as I thought he was last night.

'Er no, I was getting confused. They're away today. It's next week I'm going.' I was such a liar.

'Good, Humph needs bailing out! I'll be round in a minute.'

What was all that about, I'd wondered? But at least he hadn't mentioned bloody HMV.

Half an hour later, when he'd got to my place, Jacko had explained that Humph had called him from a phone box; Humph had arranged to meet Alison up town to do some Christmas shopping and she'd brought Sara with her. They were trying on loads of clothes and dragging him from shop to shop. He'd said he was bored stiff. He'd pleaded with Jacko to go up and rescue him. For some reason, Jacko had decided this involved me going along for the ride too.

Another half hour later, we were sitting in a corner table in Acres.

'My legs are killing me!' Humph said, rubbing his calf-muscles.

I was desperately trying not to laugh. He'd been moaning ever since we got there.

'It's alright for you! You haven't been frogmarched around every women's clothes shop in town!' Humph groaned.

'Don't exaggerate Christopher!' Alison said, playfully pulling a face and sticking her tongue out at him.

'When you said Christmas shopping,' Humph told Alison, 'I thought you meant for presents and stuff. Not trying on bloody frocks.'

'I did mean presents but then Sara said she'd got a new dress for the Christmas party. So I had to ask Mum for a loan. I mean I've got absolutely nothing to wear.'

'Nothing to wear? You've got a branch of Miss Selfridges in your bloody wardrobe?'

'I have *not!*' Alison laughed, 'anyway, I can't wear the same dress as I did last year, can I?'

Why not, I wondered? The same pair of trousers had lasted me for two years. I'd worn them pretty much every day at school during that time. The knees were a bit shiny but I reckoned they had at least another six months in them.

'You didn't need to try on every flipping' dress in Brighton!' Humph said. He was laughing now but you could tell he was pretty hacked off.

Sara and I were laughing too. Jacko looked like death.

'I wouldn't mind,' said Humph,'but do you know what she did?'

I shook my head.

'After we've traipsed around every sodding clothes shop in Sussex, she goes back to the very first shop we went to, at five-past-frozen-to-death this morning, Miss Selfridges of course, and buys the very first dress she tried on.'

'Yeah, but she might have found something she liked better!' said Sara, standing up for her mate.

'Exactly, you can't just rush in and buy the first thing you see can you?'

'Yes!' said Humph, 'Yes, you bloody well can!'

'If you want to look like a bunch of tramps like you three!' laughed Sara.

A tramp? I had on my best sleeveless jumper, my one and only button-down shirt and my smart black jeans. These were my best clothes.

'So, about this party?' Jacko suddenly piped up, coming back from the dead, 'will *all* the girls from school be going?'

'All the girls from *sixth form* will be there, yes Martin,' said Alison.

'Sorry, I stand corrected Miss Fisher. Will the girls from the Denton sixth form finishing school for ladies be gracing the soiree with their attendance?' Jacko sneered.

Humph and I snorted.

'Any young lady in particular that you're interested in, is there Martin?' Sara chuckled, a stray piece of cherry falling from her mouth onto the plate.

Jacko pulled a face. 'Don't choke on that will you?' he said.

Sara stuck out a sugary tongue. She was vile.

'Well, for your information Martin, yes I suspect Fay Carpenter will be going; as it's obvious that's what you were really asking,' said Alison.

Humph, Sara and I all sniggered.

Jacko's face went from ghostly white to crimson in sub-speed-of-light time. 'Never crossed my mind,' he said; his face now as red as a baboon's bum, 'I was just curious that's all.'

'Yeah right!' said Humph.

We all laughed. Jacko had gone out with Fay for about three weeks back in the third year. She'd dumped him for Dan Chester. Jacko had never got over it. Jacko had about as much luck as me with girls. Precisely nil.

'I don't know what you're laughing about Timbo. Don't think I've forgotten about your little girlfriend in HMV. We're heading there after aren't we? You can ask her to the party eh?'

Now it was my turn to do a Captain Scarlet.

'Oh, so what's this about a "little girlfriend" then?' asked Alison teasingly, as she sipped on her coffee.

Brilliant; it was one thing my mates taking the mickey, but it was quite another thing for Alison to join in.

'Nothing,' I said, 'just ignore them.'

49

'Just a girl he's had the hots about for weeks,' said Jacko.

'Don't tell me - he hasn't worked up the bottle to speak to her?' Humph laughed, 'as per bloody usual!'

There was a chorus of "aah's" from the girls.

'He only fancies her because her name's Roxanne!' said Jacko.

'Really? Like The Police song then?' said Sara, who had a degree in stating the obvious.

'I bet she looks just like bloody Sting too!' Humph laughed.

'Lovely biceps. Green jump-suit.' said Jacko

'Well, he does sing like a girl!' Humph smiled.

Humph and Jacko were really enjoying themselves now.

'Well, I think it's sweet,' said Sara, 'don't you Alison? You're so sweet Tim,' said Sara.

'Ooh, you're so sweet Timmy, so sweeeeeet!' said Humph in a little-girl voice.

'Bugger off!' I said.

'Yeah, leave him alone Chris!' said Alison, 'don't be so mean. I expect he's just working up to speaking to her, aren't you Tim?'

Was she taking the mickey too? I could never tell with Alison.

'Yeah, in 2010 at this rate, I should think,' Humph said.

'Well, I need the loo,' said Jacko getting up from the table, 'and then I think we should all wander over to the shop and see the lovely Roxanne for ourselves.

Oh, Knickers.

'It's alright for you!' I said to Humph, as he dragged me by the arm through the crowded shopping-centre, 'you got to know Alison at school. At least you didn't need to go up and talk to a total stranger in the middle of a packed record shop on a Saturday afternoon.'

Jacko and the girls were marching on ahead, making a bee-line for HMV.

'Stop whingeing you old woman!' Humph said with typical sympathy, 'lets get this over and done with. Think positive. You could have a date with a sexy girl this evening.'

The flying pigs zoomed overhead as we approached HMV.

'So, point her out then, which one is she?' said Humph as we walked through the door.

HMV was absolutely full with early Christmas shoppers. I'd hoped and preyed, as they'd dragged me across Churchill Square, that this would be Roxanne's day off; but the moment we walked through the glass doors, I'd spotted her on the far-side of the shop, next to the Film-Score section, showing albums to two women - a mother and daughter by the looks of it. I immediately looked away and pretended to be scanning the whole shop floor for her. There were dozens of customers and loads more staff than there normally were. Saturday girls and boys; taken on for the pre-Christmas rush. There must have been at least ten girls altogether.

'Oh dear, I don't think she's here,' I said weakly.

'Crap!' said Humph,' come on, which one is she then?'

'I bet it's that little dark-haired one with all the Punky make-up,' said Jacko, pointing to a girl serving at the counter. A queue of around eight or nine customers were waiting to be served by her.

'No, I've never even seen her before,' I said, quite honestly.

'OK,' said Sara, 'is it that blonde girl?'

'Yeah, I bet it is,' said Humph, 'the one with the enormous...'
Alison elbowed him in the ribs and glared at him.

'...earrings! I was going to say earrings! Enormous earrings!'

I had seen the blonde girl before. She was standing at the customer service desk and she did have large earrings; *and* an enormous chest.

'No, that's not her either,' I said, 'not my type.'

'Oh right. The busty blonde isn't your type? In that case, it must be the chunky one with the braces on her teeth is it?' said Humph, pointing to a large girl who was stacking singles from a cardboard box.

'Do me a favour!' I said.

'Oi, don't be so rude and nasty!' Sara squealed, thumping me on the arm.

'And what happened to "Timmy, you're so sweet" then?' Humph sniggered.

My friends continued to point out a other girls in HMV T-shirts, most of whom I had never seen before. We were running out of candidates and Humph and Jacko were scanning the shop for more. I glanced over to where I'd seen Roxanne; there was no sign of her, although the women she'd been serving were still in the same section. Then Roxanne's head appeared; she had obviously been reaching down for something under the record racks. She was now showing the women an LP. Even from across the shop, I recognised the famous cover of Jeff Wayne's 'War Of The Worlds"; the huge Alien Tripod firing down on a ship.

'I suppose she could be upstairs?' I said quickly to the others and started heading over to the stairs.

'What about that girl over there?' I heard Sara Potts say as I hurried away. I didn't look back. It may not have been Roxanne she was referring to but I wasn't taking the chance. I had my head down as I started taking the stairs two at a time, desperate to get my friends away, both from Roxanne and from inevitable embarrassment. Humph, with his long legs was matching me stride-for stride. I glanced around to make sure Jacko and the girls were following.

'Hello Tim!' I heard a familiar voice say. I almost collided with Karl Bloom, who was coming down the stairs, clutching an HMV carrier bag.

'Alright Karl?' asked Humph.

'Blimey, Karl!' I said, relieved for a second to see another friendly face.

'What are you lot all doing up here then?' Karl grinned, 'Hi Alison, Sara, Jacko,' he said.

Oh bugger, here we go I thought. One word from Jacko or Humph and my little infatuation would be all round The Sixth Form. Mind you, now that Alison and Sara knew, I supposed I was on a hiding-to-nothing on that score anyway.

Before the others could speak, I chipped in with a question of my own, to Karl, 'so what's in the bag mate?'

We were all stopped on the stairs. We had to make way for customers going up and down. Karl, Humph and Alison had their back pressed to the wall; Jacko, Sara and I stood by the hand-rail on the shop side, as people jostled by. It as hardly an ideal location for a conversation.

'Oh, Christmas present for my kid-sister, Madness tape,' he said, holding up the carrier bag.

'Well, at least she's got good taste!' said Jacko, across the heads of people rushing by, 'not like Tim and his Police obsession!'

'Piss off Jacko.'

'So, what *are* you guys after then?' asked Karl again. An obese woman wobbled past, panting as she climbed the steps. I had to practically hang over the side of the railing to let her pass. I could see the top of Roxanne's head; she was still talking to the War of The Worlds fans.

'Not, what, who!' I heard Humph say.

52

'Eh?' said Karl.

'We're trying to save Timbo here,' Jacko said, now crossing the stairs to stand between Humph and Karl.

'Save Tim from what?'

'From life-long virginity!' Jacko snorted.

I stuck two fingers up, almost taking a passing kid's eye out.

'Tim's got the hots for one of the girls here,' Alison explained. Was it my imagination or was she pouting? Sara was fussing with her hair and trying, unsuccessfully, to catch Karl's eye.

'No? Really? I hope it's not my sister!'

'What, your sister works here?' giggled Sara.

Shit, I didn't know that.

'Yeah, she's downstairs on the tills!' Karl laughed. Oh bugger, it couldn't be could it?

'Which one's your sister?' Alison asked

'What's her name?' Jacko said, looking at me. I could feel the colour draining from my face.

'Poppy!' said Karl.

Thank you God.

'Blonde, tallish...'

'Big...' Jacko started to say.

'...ear rings?' I said, butting in.

'Don't know about the earrings but she's got massive boobs!' laughed Karl.

'Blimey, that's your sister?' Jacko spluttered, 'she's alright isn't she? Can you introduce us?'

'She'd have you for dinner mate!' Karl laughed.

'Sounds good to me,' Jacko said.

'So, does Poppy know a girl called Roxanne?' asked Alison, before I could divert the question.

'Roxanne? Yeah, I know her, she's been round our place a few times; they're really good mates,' said Karl.

My stomach was doing somersaults.

'Blimey, Tim, you're a dark horse. Why didn't you mention this before? I can get Poppy to introduce you. Mind you, she's a bit out of your league mate!'

I really didn't like the way this was going. How could I dig myself out of this one? Maybe if I fell down the stairs and broke my leg...?

'Great, we're going to fix the two of them up. He's been coming up here for weeks, trying to pluck up the courage to speak to her!' laughed Jacko, 'he's such a tit!'

'Not exactly weeks...,' I weakly started to protest.

'So, bit of a looker is she this Roxanne?' asked Humph, laughing.

'Not that you're interested of course!' said Alison, thumping his arm.

'Only for Tim's sake,' Humph said.

'Well if you'd call a red-headed version of Goldie Hawn a looker, yes I guess she is!' joked Karl.

'Goldie Hawn? She was dead sexy - especially in that film with Peter Sellers!' said Jacko.

A red-headed version of Goldie Hawn? Roxanne? Nah, I couldn't see that - she was more like Felicity Kendal...

'So, do you know if she's here today?' Humph asked.

'Er...' Karl said thoughtfully. His eye caught mine. I tried to shake my head without actually shaking my head. I couldn't breathe. Please don't say 'yes', please, please.

Karl gave me a little smile. 'Er, no, I haven't seen her,' he said, 'now I come to think of it, I think Poppy mentioned it was her day off today.'

'Oh, no! Bummer,' Jacko said.

'Well, maybe I can put a word in for you with Poppy?' Karl smirked.

'Maybe,' I muttered.

'Oh well, I'd better be off. I'll see you on Monday mate. Nice seeing you guys!' Karl said breezily. He started off downstairs. I saw him turn his head as he reached the bottom of the stairs. He winked.

I finally exhaled. I just about managed to prevent myself from collapsing in a heap on the stairs.

'Oh well, we might as well bugger off too,' said Humph.

By some miracle, I managed to get them all out of the shop, without anyone spotting the attractive red-headed Goldie Hawn / Felicity Kendal hybrid, who was now serving at the next till to Poppy Bloom. I breathed another huge sigh of relief.

'Don't think you've got away with it that easily, pipsqueak!' Humph said, as we walked back through Churchill Square.

'Too right, there's always next week,' Jacko warned.

Oh, Knickers.

My saviour, Karl Bloom, phoned me later that evening.

'Cheers mate, I owe you one,' I said.

'Thats OK, I could tell you were a bit hot and bothered. I'd have been dying of embarrassment myself in that position.'

'Tell me about it.'

'Mind you, you should let me have word with Poppy. What have you got to lose? Apart from your virginity like Jacko said!' he laughed.

'Huh, it's alright for you,' I said, 'some of us don't have women flocking all over us whenever we walk into a room!'

'What? I wish!'

'What about all those fifth years who follow you about?'

'What fifth years?'

'You must have noticed!'

'The only thing I've noticed is the one girl that I actually like, doesn't seem to know I exist, so we're not that different are we Timbo?'

'Really?'

What was he on about? He could have his choice of most of the girls in school.

'Don't ask. Maybe I'll tell you about it one of these days. So, do you want me to have word with Poppy or not then?'

No I bloody did not.

'Let me think about it, OK?' I said.

'OK, but don't leave it too long, I happen to know she has other admirers!'

'Really? Who?'

'Well, a certain mutual friend of ours for one. Someone who think's he's God's gift?'

'No? You're joking?'

'Yep, Mr. Booth is a fan of the lovely Roxanne too. Met her at my place back in the Summer holidays. He went on about her for weeks after.'

'But has he done anything about it?' I said, trying to sound like I wasn't bothered.

'Not yet, but you know what's he's like!'

I did. Only too well. Bugger. Well, there were plenty more fish in the sea.

55

I walked Chalky around the block that Sunday evening.

It was bitterly cold. I had two jumpers on under my coat and I'd dug out my gloves. It was going to snow I reckoned. Chalky took ages; stopping at every lamp-post, sniffing at them and cocking his leg up. I don't know why he bothered, no dog alive had that much wee. He was marking his territory with nothing but air. Finally, I forced him through the gate and up the path. There was a girl standing outside my door, ringing on my doorbell. As I came up behind her, she turned around and smiled.

'Hello!' she said.

I recognised her instantly; it was the tarty looking girl I'd seen that night in the Peds. I thought at the time that she'd looked familiar. I hadn't placed her in the pub; now it was all falling into place.

'Hi, it's Stacey isn't it?' I said.

Stacey Groves worked with my sister, Cheryl. I'd met her once when I'd gone with Dad to pick Cheryl up from the Salon. It had been raining. Dad gave Stacey a lift to Brighton station. I hoped she didn't remember me from the Peds. For a start, I hadn't told Mum and Dad - or Cheryl - that I was pubbing, and for another, Pete and Doddsy had been trying to pick a fight with her dark-skinned boyfriend.

'Yeah, that's right!' she said, in a high pitched squeal.

Stacey Groves was certainly pretty, but she wore far too much make-up. She had long pink finger-nails and she smelt of shampoo and bubble-gum. Even though it was freezing, she had bare legs under a thin coat, and she wore high-heeled sandals.

Cheryl opened the door. She was obviously expecting her.

'All right darlin'?' Stacey screeched.

'Hi Babe!' Cheryl screamed.

Cheryl was dressed like a right tart too - I mean to say; fingerless gloves and a stringy top in this weather?

The two girls hugged each other like they hadn't seen each other for years, even though they worked together six days a week! Stacey took off her coat in the hall, as I let Chalky off his lead. He jumped up at her. Stacey was wearing possibly the shortest skirt I'd ever seen; even shorter than any of Alison's. Stacey's legs were really brown. Where had she got such a good tan in the middle of winter? I mean she only lives fifteen miles up the road, in Burgess Hill, which is not exactly renowned for it's exotic weather.

56

'Quick, come upstairs,' shrieked Cheryl, 'I've got Spandau Ballet's album!'

'Triffic!' said Stacey, 'ah, look at this little dog of yours Cheryl, he's triffic! What's his name again? Oh I remember,' she said, crouching down to tickle Chalky's ears, 'Hello Timmy! What a cute little doggie you are! Yes, you are! You're a cute little doggy-woggy aren't you Timmy?'

Timmy? Bloody Timmy? Who does she think I am then? Bloody Chalky?

'The dog's called Chalky! Timmy's my little brother you complete Muppet!' Cheryl said. She was laughing so much, her eye-liner was running.

'Oh, I'm so sorry Timmy!' said Stacey, slapping my arm, 'ah, he doesn't mind though ,do you Timmy? No - he's triffic is your brother - and cute with it!' Stacey winked at me.

'Oh stop it, you'll be making him big-headed!' said Cheryl, winking at me. I could feel myself blushing.

They started climbing the stairs, giggling and slapping each other - like two complete Muppets. I watched them go.

Stacey Groves' legs were quite sexy.

And she'd said I was cute.

Looking at myself in the mirror the following morning, I remembered what Stacey Groves had said.

Was I really cute? Was I? Well, I suppose if I could ever get rid of the spots. Yeah, I was alright. Just as good looking as bloody Dave Booth anyway.

6 - Friends

The audience went wild as I climbed up to the podium.

'Thank you all so very much, I love you all,' I blew my adoring audience a kiss.

They responded with wild applause; the screams of hundreds of teenage girls rang in my ears.

My peers looked on approvingly. Sting, Stewart & Andy of The Police; Paul, Bruce & Rick of The Jam; Elvis Costello, Feargal from The Undertones and those two blokes from Orchestral Manouevres In The Dark - they were all there; the assembled masses of British pop royalty. Our compere, Noel Edmonds, standing to one side of the stage, clapped and smiled; Pamela Ewing from Dallas stood beside Noel, her dark mane of hair shimmering in the stage-lights. She looked ravishing in a revealing, black, back-less evening dress. They'd called on her, as one my most famous celebrity fans, to present me with my award. She gave me that knowing smile from across the stage. It was no good though I told myself, what we'd had together had been fun whilst it lasted, but she was far too old for me; she'd just have to find another toy-boy to amuse her between series. I'd just have to let her down gently.

"Best Newcomer" in the NME awards for 1980; it was, if I say so myself, richly deserved of course. All those hit singles; the album that had stayed at number one all through the summer. Everyone had agreed; there'd been no real competition. Debbie (Harry) and Kate (Bush) gazed up at me from the front-row of the packed auditorium. They'd both already propositioned me backstage of course. I'd have to make a decision soon I supposed. It was a tough choice. Debbie was old enough to be my mother - and could therefore clearly teach me a thing or two - then again, Kate was more my age and she had lovely lips. Not so much of a dilemma actually - after all, I'd had Kate on my bedroom wall ever since Wuthering Heights. Never mind Debs, maybe next year eh?

'There's so many people I'd like to thank,' I continued, waving my gold statuette in one hand, 'Dave Booth, Martin Jackson, My Dad, & most of all....John Lennon. Without you wonderful people, I wouldn't be standing *here* tonight.'

Here was in fact my bedroom, where I stood in front of my mirror, in my pyjamas, using a hairbrush as a microphone. My gold statuette was actually a can of Old Spice deodorant. Blimey, that was a huge spot on my chin. That really needed squeezing. I threw the brush back on the dressing table, turned the light off and jumped into bed. The sheets were bloody freezing. Roll on summer. Ah well, no NME award for Tim James this year, but Dave, Jacko, Dad and the recently departed Mr. Lennon were all very much in my good books and deserved my grateful appreciation anyway. It was thanks to them that I was looking forward to seeing my second Police gig, in a couple of weeks time, just before Christmas.

It was Dave Booth who'd planted the idea in my head. If it wasn't for the invite from my new mate, I wouldn't have seriously thought about travelling all the way up to Tooting in London to see them; without Jacko, I wouldn't have been able to afford the price of a ticket; without Dad's support, Mum would have kicked up a song and dance about me going (even though it was nearly two months past my seventeenth birthday!); and finally, without John Lennon, my parents would probably never have understood how badly I wanted to go.

I'd been knocking around with Dave Booth and his mates for a few weeks by then. I'd got to know them much better; I understood the dynamics of the group. There was Dave himself; he was a really good laugh but was pretty full-on, fancied himself as a comedian and came across as a bit of a big-head at times. By contrast, Karl Bloom was like Dave's straight man and in a lot of ways, was his complete opposite. Karl wasn't very confident, even though he had all sorts of talents. He was probably the fastest runner at Denton and he was good at practically every sport going; and then there were the hidden talents. According to the others, Karl was a good singer and he played guitar in a band. How cool was that? Last but by no means least, there was Kevin Clarke. "Clarkey" was an odd fish. Easily the brainiest of the bunch, he had passed twelve O-levels or something ridiculous. Despite this, or maybe because of it, he was the butt of a lot of Dave and Karl's jokes. But he was very funny in a dry sort of way. I hadn't been sure about Clarkey at first, but he was growing on me. But it was Dave who was the ring-leader, the ideas man. Where Dave lead, Karl and Clarkey followed; and pretty soon, I was following too.

One lunchtime, Dave suggested we bunk off for the afternoon and head into town to see "Bananas", an old Woody Allen film, at the Duke of Yorks - a well known fleapit cinema on the main London Road. Dave was really into Woody Allen - he quoted his jokes all the time. None of us knew much about Woody - Dave called us philistines and said he'd have to "educate us". We were sitting in the back row, sharing a huge bag of Maltesers, waiting for the film to start, when Dave leant over Karl and prodded me.

'Here Tim, I've been meaning to say….'

Here we go, I thought. I had been waiting for one of them to bring up the subject of Roxanne ever since we'd bumped into Karl that day. I was sure he would have told the others by now. I braced myself.

'You're really into The Police aren't you?'

'Yeah,' I said, waiting for some kind of punchline. I was used to taking abuse from non-believers. The Sting backlash was well and truly in flow now that The Police were so successful.

'Cool, well, we're all going up to see them in Tooting at Christmas, aren't we lads?' Dave said.

'Really?' Instantly, I felt massively jealous.

'Apparently, they are playing in a huge circus tent or some-such,' Clarkey explained.

'I know,' I said, 'I read about it in the Record Mirror.'

The paper had reported that the band were returning from a world tour to play a one-off Christmas gig for their UK fans. They were playing in this huge tent on Tooting Bec Common - wherever that was. It would be the only chance to see them in England for ages.

'Are you going?' asked Karl.

No I bloody wasn't. I was stunned. I had no idea any of my new mates were Police fans.

'Doubt it,' I said, not explaining why I doubted it. I wasn't ready to admit to my cool new mates that my Mum and Dad would never let me go.

'The tickets are going on sale the weekend after next - up in London - we're going to take sleeping bags and queue over night, Dave explained, 'you should come with us!'

'Wow, really?'

'Yeah, come along Tim; it'll be ace!' said Clarkey, to whom everything seemed to be "ace" - especially Grand Prix drivers - and David Bowie, who was apparently "double ace".

'Yeah, of course you should come,' said Dave, lowering his voice as the Pearl and Dean advertising tune started up.

'In fact, why don't you bring some mates? You know, Martin Jackson or Chris Humphreys? Maybe even Alison?' Dave said, very quietly, still leaning across Karl. The boys exchanged looks and smirked. I sensed Dave had a hidden agenda.

'Are they still together? Only I'd heard a few rumours,' he said casually.

'As far as I know, they're great, yeah.'

Alison had confided in me that they were far from great but I wasn't telling Dave that. Was there any girl on the planet he didn't fancy his chances with?

'Well, perhaps they'll both come, or if not, you know...Alison's welcome to join us either way,' Dave said.

Karl sniggered.

'Nice try Dave,' Clarkey said.

'Shh!' we heard from two rows in front.

'We're going up by train - the more the merrier,' Dave whispered.

'Ok, I'll ask them,' I said excitedly. I was getting a bit carried away with my new found friends. I doubted Humph, Alison or Jacko would be interested and I would still have to tackle my parents - still, surely if there was a whole bunch of us, they would be alright about it? What about the money though? I was skint. Maybe I could talk nicely to Jacko - yeah, that would be fine - Jacko would be good for a quid or two.

'How much are the tickets?' I asked Karl. There were more shush noises from in front.

'A fiver if you get them in advance.'

A fiver? Bloody hell. I was going to have to do Jacko some *big* favours.

'OK, count me in.'

I went to Jacko's house on the Saturday morning. We often went out on our bikes on Saturday - cycling up to town for a coffee in Acres The Bakers, or sometimes up to the Dyke, or to the Beach if the weather was half-decent. It was raining - as it seemed to have been for weeks, so I didn't take the bike. I took my dog Chalky instead. Jacko loved the dog. I needed him in a good mood.

'Pop up the park shall we?' I suggested, standing on his doorstep, as he put on his black Harrington jacket. I noticed him sneak something into pocket. Fags. Jacko had taken up smoking since working at the bank. He'd been hanging around with a bloke he called "Wiffy Wilf" who worked in the bank's post-room. Wiffy Wilf apparently rolled his own. Jacko seemed to think that was the height of cool. I hadn't met him yet but he didn't sound too savoury and he seemed to be having a bad influence on Jacko. Not only was there the fags but he'd started listening to hippy music like Led Zeppelin and Pink Floyd. According to Jacko, Wilf had an 'amazing' record collection - everything from The Beatles and Bob Dylan to obscure sounding groups like Magazine and Fischer Z. Jacko was always borrowing Wilf's LPs and copying them on to tapes. Jacko had always been into Punk at school - Punk and nothing else - now he dressed like a mod and listened to all sorts of old hippy crap. He was having an identity crisis I reckoned. It was dead confusing.

'You should broaden your horizons,' he was always telling me.

I was hoping this new musical open-mindedness, might have extended to The Police, who he'd always sneered at. I was sure he liked them really - he just didn't want to admit to liking anyone that I liked so much. According to Jacko, who was a self-proclaimed music-guru, The Police had "sold out" on punk and "gone all Top of the Pops". Jacko worshipped The Clash because they'd always refused to go on TOTP. Jacko could be a right pretentious berk sometimes. But he had something I needed – cash.

I hadn't been sure how to approach the subject of a loan. I decided to jump straight in.

'So,' I said, as we walked up the hill towards the park, 'The Police are doing this big gig on 21st December. Up in Tooting. That's London apparently.'

'Yeah? Parents getting you and Cheryl tickets for Christmas are they?'

Mum and Dad had got me a ticket to see The Police at the Brighton Dome for my last birthday - on the condition that I went with my older sister. Jacko still thought it was hilarious that I'd had to be chaperoned. Usually, I would tell him to piss off but for obvious reasons, I laughed along.

'Good one mate,' I said cheerily, 'do you fancy it then?'

'Fancy what?'

'The gig.'

'Are you serious?'

'Yeah, a whole bunch of us are going.'

'What, Dave Booth and his cronies?'

'Yeah, me, Dave, Clarkey and Bloomer.'

'Clarkey and Bloomer? Do you mean Kevin Clarke and Karl Bloom? Since when have they been "Clarkey and Bloomer"?'

'They're alright are Clark....Kevin and Karl.'

'Bunch of stuck-up tossers. They were all in Miss Megson's class - the old dragon. 5 Beta. Thought they were the bees knees, that bunch.'

All the classes at Denton were named after letters of the Greek alphabet. We were in Delta. Alpha and Beta were the top classes - or so they reckoned - they didn't mix with us in Delta, except when we were united in defending ourselves against Steven Andrews and his thugs, who were in Kappa. Kappa were bullies – they picked on everyone; especially the poor sods in Omicron. But then *everyone* picked on them.

'They're OK,' I argued, 'Dave Booth says you're a good laugh actually.'

'Really?'

'Really. And he thinks Humph is cool.'

OK, the word he'd actually used to describe Humph was 'lairy" but it was practically the same thing.

'Yeah, well' Jacko said after a minute, 'I suppose Dave's OK. We were mates a few years back - but I'm not so sure about "Clarkey and Bloomer",' he sneered, making speech marks with his fingers.

I opened my mouth to say something clever but thought better of it. After all, I hadn't even got to the subject of the fiver loan yet.

'So, what do you think?'

'Not really my cup of tea. They're just a bunch of Punk sell-outs.'

Here we go.

'...and Sting's girly voice brings my ears out in a rash.'

I grimaced but said nothing, forcing a false chuckle. By now we'd reached the park and Jacko sat on a bench whilst I threw a ball for Chalky.

'Jacko?' I said, not turning to face him, as he lit up a fag.

'Yes mate?'

'I hate to ask like but....'

'How much?'

'A fiver.'

'What a rip-off,' Jacko said, shaking his head and pulling a note from his jacket.

'Cheers mate!' I said, now grinning from ear to ear. I offered to pay it back. I suggested fifty pence a week. I reckoned I could just about manage that.

'Think of it as a Christmas present - it will save me a shopping trip.' Jacko smiled.

'Really? Oh, thanks Jacko - that's brilliant!'   Jacko was a good mate really - underneath it all. I held out my hand for him to shake it. He just stared at my hand and smirked.

'Don't start getting all Starsky and Hutch on me, you bender - you're not my type!'

With part one of my grand master-plan completed, I pondered how to tackle part two; my Mum and Dad.

'So, have your old dears sanctioned this little trip then?' asked Jacko.

'Of course; no problem.'

Jacko just smirked. Like my Dad says, "never kid a kidder."

I'd worked it all out.

If Albion did the business, a good time to ask him would be when Dad got back from the football. Dad was a huge Albion fan. He went to all the home games. They were at home to Sunderland that Saturday and I reckoned they had a good chance of winning - so Dad should be in a good mood. Then, he could talk Mum round.

I watched the results come up on the vidi-printer on ITV.

Brighton 2 - Sunderland 1.

Great.

'Good match then Dad?' I asked, even before he'd got his blue and white scarf off.

'Not bad. You missed a cracker by Andy Ritchie.' Dad beamed, 'you should've come along.'

'You don't want me tagging along Dad,' I said, feeling guilty as usual. I used to go with him to the Goldstone when I was a kid. I still went with him occasionally, but I wasn't into it as much as Dad would have liked me to be.

'Or more to the point son, you don't want me cramping your style. There are some nice bits of stuff going to the Goldstone these days. You should get along there with those mates of yours.'

I hated it when Dad talked about "bits of stuff" and things like that. It was so naff. He still thought it was the seventies. Still, he was clearly in a good mood. It couldn't be going better if I'd planned it.

'Would you mind if I went up to London with the lads Dad?' I said dead casually.

'What, like to an away match or something?'

'Yeah, well maybe...or to a gig or something.'

'Yeah, I suppose you're old enough, if a few of you were going.'

'Brilliant. Thanks Dad!' I blurted out.

'What? Hang on a minute,' Dad said creasing his eyebrows, 'what have I just walked into?'

I explained the situation.

'Jacko's lent me the money. There's a load of us going.'

Dad nodded along. 'OK, as long as there are a whole bunch of you and you'll make sure you get the last train home - even if it means missing an encore, OK? And ....'

'Yeah, sure, thanks Dad.'

'And Tim...*if*, and only *if,* your mother agrees.'

Bugger.

'Up in London?' said Humph on the phone.

'Yeah, there's a few of us going. It will be a laugh.' I said.

'On a Sunday night? I dunno mate; I've got to be up early for work the next day.'

'I thought you guys would be really into the idea,' I said, meaning him and Alison - maybe even Sara Potts too.

'Well, yeah, I could ask Pete and Doddsy; I don't think they're really into The Police though.'

Pete and Doddsy? Crap. 'No, I was thinking more of the girls, you know - Alison and Sara maybe?'

'Ali?' Humph sounded surprised, 'Nah, I doubt it, she's not really into music,'

'She liked Grease.'

'Exactly - she's not into music.'

We both laughed. He had a point.

'Well, you could ask her at school - you'll probably see her before I do. But I'll think about it and let you know.' Humph didn't sound keen.

'Fair enough, but you'll need to decide soon - the tickets go on sale on Sunday.'

'Well, if I don't get back to you, just leave me out. Thanks for asking though mate.'

Humph never did get back to me. Still, at least it meant I wouldn't have to put up with bloody Pete and Doddsy.

'But Mum! Dad said it would be OK.'

'That's not *exactly* what I said is it son?' said Dad, waving a fork at me, as he walked past. I was leaning on the kitchen work-top, arms crossed. I knew Mum wouldn't be keen.

'I'm not so sure love, you hear of all sorts of things going on up in the city - you've never been that far with your mates before.'

'I'm not twelve anymore Mum, I'm seventeen!'

'Only just.'

'Seventeen and two months!'

Like two months made all the difference.

'I'm not stupid you know - I'll be careful.'

'Come on love,' said Dad, 'he's got a point. He's big enough and ugly enough to look after himself.

'Thanks Dad!' I said, smiling.

Mum didn't look convinced. She was cooking dinner; Dad was laying the table - coming in and out of the kitchen.

'I just don't like the idea of you being in London on a dark December evening with all those crowds. You get pick-pockets and everything up there.'

'Mum, I'll be careful, Ok?' I said, sliding my arm around her shoulder.

'When are these tickets on sale?'

'Next Sunday morning - Ten O'Clock, Shaftesbury Avenue - Dave reckons it's quite near Oxford Street.'

I had no idea where anything was in London. Oxford Street *was* London as far as I knew. I'd been up there a couple of times with Mum and Dad when I was a kid. I couldn't believe how busy it was - there were millions and millions of people. My Mum had loved the shops -

she'd bought me an Action Man for my eleventh birthday. I'd wanted one for years.

'You'd need to get up there early. I wouldn't be surprised if there's a queue. I've heard they're quite popular - for some reason,' Mum smirked. I reckoned she was coming around to the idea.

'Yeah, we will,' I didn't want to add that we wanted to queue up over night. If I could get her to agree in principle, I would tackle that problem next.

'OK, let me...'

'Brilliant! Thanks Mum - I'll be careful!' I leant over and kissed her on the cheek.

'I was about to say, *when* you've finished creeping, let me think about it!'

'OK Mum.'

The deal was as good as done. We all sat down to watch Not The Nine O'Clock News and laughed like drains. I was dead excited. Mum and Dad were in a really good mood too.

That night, John Lennon from The Beatles was shot. And as it turned out, that sealed the deal.

It was Wednesday morning when I heard the news. Mum woke me for school as usual and told me what had happened.

'Come on love, you'll be late,' she said, pulling open my curtains, 'your breakfast is on the table,' she said as she left the room - only to pop her head around the door seconds later, 'oh, - it's really sad but someone's shot John Lennon.'

'So, is he badly injured?' I said, coming through the kitchen door, pulling my jumper on over my head. As I brushed my hair out of my eyes, I looked at my Dad. He seemed to be in a daze.

'He's dead love. It's so tragic,' explained Mum.

Dead? Blimey. Dad didn't speak. He looked all done in. He got up and headed for the hall.

'See you later Dad,' I said.

There was no reply.

'He's in shock,' whispered Mum.

She went out in the hall. I heard them whispering.

'See you son,' my Dad called back from the hall. He sounded gutted.

The front door closed behind him and Mum came back in to the kitchen - her eyes had all welled up - it was like that time our old dog Patches had died.

'Is Dad really upset Mum?'

'Of course son, we both are. John Lennon was one of our heroes. Your Dad loved him. Imagine if your beloved Sting died - how would you feel?

'But I thought Elvis was his favourite?'

'Yes, but he loves the Beatles too, you know that.'

'Not as much as Elvis though - or the Stones. He loves Mick Jagger much more than Paul McCartney or John Lennon.'

'Yes, but we don't all just worship the one pop star you know- we all have lots of favourites don't we? One day you'll realise there's more to music than The Police!' She sounded annoyed.

'I don't just like The Police, I like other stuff - there's The Undertones, there's Elvis Costello, The Jam, Squeeze, The Beat....'

'OK, well imagine how you'd feel if the singer from Squeeze died for example.'

'Glenn Tilbrook or Chris Difford?

Mum just looked at me.

How would I feel if someone shot Glenn Tilbrook or Chris Difford? Well, sure I'd be annoyed; Squeeze were really good – but Glenn Tilbrook wasn't Sting, just like Lennon wasn't Elvis. I didn't understand the fuss.

That night, TV was full of Lennon's murder. It was all over the news. And there were special documentaries all about his music. It was amazing how many Beatles songs I knew - far more than I realised. Actually, I had to admit; the Beatles were pretty good.

The news showed Paul McCartney being interviewed. They asked him how he felt. He said it was "a drag".

'I'm really sorry about John, Dad,' I said, as I watched the footage of The Beatles playing at Shea Stadium - which was somewhere in America I think.

'That was their last ever live performance you know. I never did get to see Lennon live.' said Dad.

Mum and Dad exchanged a look. I saw Mum wink.

'So Tim, when you get to see your heroes up in London at Christmas, make sure you enjoy it - and remember every minute of it.' said Mum. She smiled at Dad.

'Ok Mum, I will.'

I loved John Lennon.

7 - Contact

It finally happened during a free-period.

I thought I'd got away with it but I'd started my chicken counting far too early. I'd been expecting something ever since Karl had announced that I had a rival for Roxanne's affections; one David Booth.

Free periods were boring. If you weren't part of the card-schools, or didn't want to read in the library, you were kind of left to your own devices. I suppose we were meant to be studying but my heart just wasn't in it. Luckily, I wasn't the only one. Dave, Karl and Clarkey felt the same. We were all sitting in the common room, reading music magazines, eating Wagon-Wheels, and playing records on the old record player. I wondered what Jacko was up to in the bank; what Humph was doing in his little white van. It had to be better than this. What was I doing with my life?

I'd brought in "Zenyatta Mondatta" to play. I thought it would get us in the mood for the gig at Tooting, which was fast approaching.

'God, this one's rubbish!' said Karl Bloom, looking up from his Melody Maker, as "De Do Do Do De Da Da" came on.

'I think it's great,' I said flatly.

'It is a bit...basic though isn't it?' said Kev, 'Sting must have taken all of five minutes thinking up those lyrics!' he laughed.

The others nodded and grunted their agreement.

'Have any of you idiots actually bothered listening to the words?' I said.

I was fed up with people knocking the song. It seemed to be getting a pasting, not just from my mates, but from the music press and the media. It was misunderstood. I knew the feeling.

My new found friends exchanged glances. I knew I was letting them wind me up far too easily but I'd had enough.

'It's about how difficult it is when you....you know,....can't ..sort of ...well, you know what I mean...can't find the right words....when you're, you know, what's that word?...'

'What do you mean?' said Dave Booth, 'sort of....you know....er....er .. when you can't find the ....er right....er words....like when you're a bit......er thick...'

70

The others started to snigger.

'....inarticulate!' I said. 'He's talking about when you talk to a girl or something - how you get all tongue-tied!'

'Oh, right, so it's not just a pile of shite then?' said Karl.

They all guffawed.

I gave up.

'Anyway, speak for yourself,' said Dave, who was watching a girls netball match from his vantage point at the window, over-looking the courts, 'personally I have no problem speaking to the fairer sex. My pillow talk is legendary. Bo Derek said I was a ten and as for Jessica Lang....well, let's just say I've had no complaints!' Dave laughed.

The others jeered.

'Yeah right Dave, you're a proper little Warren Beatty!' I smirked.

'Thank you Timothy. I've had my moments, if I say so myself.'

'So, how come I've never witnessed any of them?' I asked, putting down the sleeve to Zenyatta Momdatta, which I'd been studying for the zillionth time.

'What?' said Dave.

'How come I've never seen any of these "moments" of yours.'

'You haven't known me long enough. I've just been taking a bit of a breather from women. It's pretty exhausting being a sex-symbol you know. Normally, I'm having to fight them off with a big stick, I can tell you. I refer you to my learned friends who will vouch for my legendary success with the ladies...' Dave turned away from oggling fifth year girls in short skirts and gestured theatrically towards Karl and Clarkey.

They looked at each other and shrugged.

'Well, now you come to mention it....I can't remember any of your moments either,' laughed Clarkey, 'can you Karl?'

'I'm struggling to recall....'

'So, other than the imaginary lunch-times with film-stars, exactly when did you last cop-off with a real flesh and blood female then Dave?' I said, warming to the theme, now that I'd received some much needed, if unexpected support.

'Oh ye of little faith!' Dave said, picking up the LP sleeve and sitting down next to me on the red plastic sofa, 'a gentleman doesn't kiss and tell!'

71

'Well, you're not a gentleman,' Clarkey laughed, 'so come on, who exactly are you 'kissing" at the moment then?' Clarkey crossed his arms and waited.

'Like I said, I'm between engagements at present, Dave said dismissively, leaning over to the formica topped coffee table and stuffing his face with a Wagon-wheel, 'but I do have my eyes on that lovely red-head from HMV.'

Yeah, I suppose I'd asked for that.

I looked at Karl. Had he said something to Dave about our meeting in HMV? Karl looked a bit sheepish. I had my answer. Then I came out with it. The moment I said it, I regretted it.

'So, why don't you do something about it then?'

'Well, I don't want to cramp your style. After all, maybe you saw her first!' Dave winked at the others.

Clarkey laughed. At least Karl had the decency to look a bit embarrassed.

'You haven't got the balls!' I said.

'Do I hear a challenge in your voice Mr. James?' said Dave, giving it his full-on cocky smile, 'are you prepared to put your money where your mouth is?'

'Huh,' I grunted, already beginning to back-track. Why had I allowed myself to be wound up so easily? Had I misjudged Dave Booth? Was he all mouth and trousers? What if I was wrong?'

'Right Timbo, I bet you a quid I can get her to come to the sixth form Christmas do with me.'

No, you're alright,' I said, beginning to regret the whole conversation.

'Chicken,' Dave muttered.

Now the others were jeering me.

'Right, you're on!' I said, all too hastily. I held out my hand and we shook on it.

What had I started?

For the rest of that week, I made a point of avoiding Dave and the others after school. It was difficult. Twice I had to deliberately miss the bus.

'We'll all go up to town one day after school and pop into HMV shall we Tim? I'm keen to win that fiver!' Dave had said, as we'd sat in the common room one morning.

72

'We said a quid!' I said.

'Oh yeah, a quid - well, I'm still keen to prove my talents!' he grinned.

There was no way I was giving him the chance to win that quid. I couldn't afford it for a start; but that was the least of my worries. I had a feeling I was being set up for something. Going up to HMV with them was bound to end badly; at best plain embarrassing, and at worst, in the highly unlikely event that Dave won his bet and Roxanne actually agreed to go to the party with him, excruciating. It was a no-win situation as far as I could see.

I caught the later bus home again. I was surprised to see Alison on there too. She explained that she'd been helping her Drama teacher to set up the lighting for the school Christmas play. When she asked me why I was late, I explained.

'So, Dave Booth fancies this Roxanne too?'

'Yeah.'

'And you've had a bet with him that he won't ask her to the Christmas party?'

'I know; stupid. Don't rub it in.'

'Do you think he'll do it?'

'What do you think?'

'I think he's all talk. I told you.'

'Really?' I felt relieved.

'Yeah, take it from me, he's not half as confident as he makes out. Don't you remember how nervous he was before the O level exams?'

'Really?'

'Yeah, Chris said he'd seen him throwing up in the Gents. He looked as white as a sheet.'

'Yeah, I remember Humph saying something about that. But that's different. He's dead cocky with the girls.'

'Rubbish!' Alison smirked.

'Isn't he?'

'If I tell you something,' she said looking around her, as if she was about to spill highly sensitive Government secrets, 'promise you won't tell anyone - especially Christopher?'

'Ok, what?' I said, puzzled.

'Dave Booth asked me out once, back in the third year.'

'Yeah, exactly my point. He's dead cocky. He must have known you were going out with Humph.'

73

'Yeah, but that's just it. He didn't actually ask me himself - he sent poor Kevin Clarke over with a note in Physics. Didn't even give me the note himself. He looked dead embarrassed.'

'What, Dave?'

'No, poor Kevin! He went dead red - and that's not a good look with ginger hair and freckles, I can tell you!'

'Poor Clarkey,' I said.

I could imagine. Kevin Clarke blushed bright red at the slightest provocation. I though I was bad with the cherries, until I met Clarkey. He lit up like the Human Torch in the Fantastic Four.

'Ah, he's a nice lad is Kevin,' said Alison.

'Yeah, he is, isn't he?' I smiled.

'So, what did you do, when you got the note?'

'Well, I just sent a note back with poor Kevin. I wrote, "thanks but no thanks". And I reckon that's what this Roxanne would tell him too, if she's got any taste.'

'D'you think so?' I asked, breaking into a smile.

'Yeah of course.'

'Thanks Ali,' I said.

'Mind you, if Karl Bloom had sent me a note, it might have been different!' she laughed.

Brilliant. What if I'd have sent her a note?

'What is it with Karl?' I said, 'there's this group of fifth form girls. They follow him everywhere. They're always there, five yards behind him, at lunch times, break-times and after school, giggling and showing-off every time Karl so much as looks in their direction. Dave and Clarkey think it's hilarious.'

'Well, at least the girls have good taste! said Alison. She had a dreamy expression on her face as she looked out of the window.

Bloody Karl. What did he have that I hadn't got?

There was a brief silence as the bus pulled up at the stop before ours.

'So, what are you going to do then?' Alison asked as the bus pulled away.

'About what?'

'About Roxanne silly! I think you should get in there before Dave does.'

'Maybe.'

'No "maybes" Tim, just do it! And whatever you do, don't ask poor Kevin Clarke to deliver a note to her for you. It's so naff!'

Mum had the hump when I got home; she'd had to keep my sausages and chips warm in the oven.

'You could have phoned!' she barked.

'Sorry Mum, I was doing revision in the library.'

'That's the third time this week. I hope they aren't working you too hard,' she said, handing me the plate. 'Careful, it's hot.'

I felt bad about lying to Mum, but at least I wasn't getting into trouble or doing drugs or anything.

'And I'll be late again tomorrow. I've got that try out for the football team.'

For once I wasn't lying about my reason for being late home. I *was* actually having a trial for the "DSFCL6" team. I hadn't represented the school at football before; at least not for Denton; I'd played for the juniors at Mellor Park - but Mellor was a small school. The team had been rubbish. Denton always had a good team - but then most of the good players like Humph, Rob Jennings and Grant Doyle had all left at the end of the fifth year and that meant the also-rans like me, and Clarkey would get a look in.

Going to the trial, like most things, was Dave's idea. Along with Karl, he was one of the few proper footballers left in our year; he'd persuaded us to try out for a couple of the half dozen places that our sports master, Mr. Beattie, still needed to fill. Dave said he remembered me being pretty good in matches during P.E and that I should go along. Par for the course, I was a sucker for flattery, so I deluded myself, that I stood a fair chance of creeping into the side. Now that I was sitting there in the pungently smelling changing rooms, doubt crept back in with a vengeance.

There was a hubbub of excitement as I walked into the changing room. Most of the other lads were gathered in one corner, all standing around looking down at someone who was sitting on the changing benches, underneath the clothes hooks over in the corner. At first I couldn't tell who was the focus of such interest but as I searched for a spare hook, I heard Dave's tell-tale dirty laugh, chortling from the middle of the scrum. Karl and Clarkey were amongst the crowd standing with their backs to me.

75

'Unbelievable eh?' I heard Dave saying.

One of the boys wolf-whistled. There was some jeering.

'Bloody hell, how the hell did you get hold of that?' a voice said.

'Crikey, can you get me a copy?' asked another.

I was curious but I was too nervous to pay the commotion too much attention. I sat down on the bench and opened my Adidas kit bag. My stomach was churning. I always got like this before playing a match. Never mind a poxy school trial, you'd think it was the ruddy European Cup Final the state my guts were in.

'Alright guys?' I said to the cluster of backs facing Dave.

Hearing my vice, Clarkey jumped and almost tripped over the lad next to him as he turned around.

'Oh, hi Tim!'

'Blimey you're jumpy mate. And I thought I was nervous!' I laughed.

A couple of the other lads turned around.

'Tim!' said Karl. He looked startled too. The other boys went quiet, started moving back to their seats.

'Hi mate!' said Dave from across the room. He was slipping something into his bag.

'Oh yeah, what are you up to now?'

'Oh nothing,' he said, looking even more sheepish than usual, 'just some fags for after the match. You know?'

'Fags? Bloody hell Dave, you don't want old Beattie to catch you with them in here. He'll go bloody mental!' I said.

'Absolutely!' said Clarkey.

'Totally!' agreed Karl.

'No problem mate,' said Dave, holding up his bag, 'they're safely tucked up in the old jock-strap. No-one in their right mind will go looking in there.'

Everybody laughed.

'Yeuck!' I said.

As I pulled up my Brighton-blue socks, I surveyed the competition. In addition to Dave and Karl, there was Frank Little, the school goalie and Jez King, affectionately known as "Kong" to his mates. He was huge. Even compared to Frank, who was a big lad - you had to be to keep goal - Jez was massive. He had muscles in places I didn't have places. His thighs were like two small trees. He played in defence. He *was* the defence. Then, there were a couple of other lads who could

76

also actually play - the rest of the two teams were to be made up by me, Clarkey and about a dozen other plebs who weren't good enough to get anywhere near the first team in the past. As old Beattie had put it; "desperate times called for desperate measures". Charming.

Still at least the trial had the advantage of being after school; so there was no way of Dave and co. dragging me up to town before the shops shut.

'Where have you been hiding the past few afternoons then Timbo? We were planning to go and see that little red-head in HMV, weren't we guys?' said Dave, as he pulled on his boots.

'Hiding? Huh - no, I was looking out for you - you must have dashed off pretty quickly,' I lied.

Dave exchanged glances with the the others; they didn't look convinced.

'Well, we'll meet up tomorrow shall we? Let's say 3.45 sharp, at the bus-stop yeah?'

'Cool,' I said.

Oh knickers.

The trial started badly.

'The fifth form are wearing the bibs for cross-country,' announced Mr. Beattie. Then he uttered the words that all of us skinny kids dreaded. 'So, it will have to be shirts v skins.'

It was bloody freezing. No-one wanted to play in skins. Skins wasn't my best look. People like Kong loved playing in skins. He didn't need a second invitation to get his shirt off. If he had been green, he'd be a dead ringer for The Incredible Hulk. Humph had been another one who loved playing in skins in his day. Humph looked like Sting - Sting was always taking off his shirt - but then again, so would I, if I looked like Sting. The local punk band The Piranhas had a great song called "I Don't Want My Body" in which their singer described his ribs as "looking like a toast rack". That was me. "Little Weed" Jacko used to call me, after the character from Bill and Ben The Flowerpot Men.

'Frank's team will be in shirts; David's in skins.'

No prizes for guessing. Yep, I was in Dave's team.

We kicked off and more or less straight away, Kong whacked the ball straight at my chest. It stung like hell, leaving a red ball-sized mark smack between my nipples. Running around with my lily-white skin, I looked like a mobile version of the Japanese flag.

'Ok Tim?' asked Mr. Beattie, as he hurtled past me, whistle in hand.

'Fine, thanks Sir,' I said, biting my lip and resisting the temptation to cry like a baby.

Dave was good; almost as good as Humph used to be; but not quite. Karl wasn't bad either - what he lacked in ball-skills he made up for in speed. With his long legs, he moved like a greyhound. His fan-club of fifth form girls had turned up and cheered every time he touched the ball. Karl looked good without his shirt on. Even though he was tall and thin, he had a proper chest; one with hairs on and everything. I looked like The Milky Bar Kid doing a strip-tease. The real surprise though was Kevin; he was like a tiger in the tackle; twice he up-ended Kong in full flow and Kong was twice his size.

'Nice tackle Kevin' said Mr Beattie approvingly. Karl's fan-club giggled; I reckon they were having similar thoughts about Karl.

Half time came. We were losing three - one.

'Did you see my goal' Dave boasted, as we came off, 'I took it down on my chest; one touch to steady myself and whack,' he kicked the air, 'first time with my left foot, curled right into the corner. Frank Little never stood a chance!' he said, raising his arms aloft in triumph.

It was only a school kick-around - you'd think he was playing at Wembley in the bloody cup final the way he went on.

Playing out on the wing, I'd touched the ball about three times in the entire first half - once when it whacked me on the chest and the other two times when Dave made a point of passing to me and I instantly lost it to the opposing full-back Graham Everett, who was quick and dirty in equal measures. As we sucked on our orange segments, I only had a red chest and bruised shin to show for my efforts. I should have brought some shin pads.

Karl was off talking to the gaggle of fifth year girls who followed him everywhere. I watched him laughing and joking with them. I know Alison keeps saying he's really fanciable and everything but I don't really see it myself. There again, I can never really tell when a bloke is good-looking from a girl's point of view. I mean I can see what Alison sees in Humph - he's tall and good at sports and he's got great hair like Sting. But what does Lady Diana Spencer see in that Prince Charles? I mean she's really pretty; he's far older than her and he dresses like a right old fuddy-duddy. And look at those ears! Like my Dad always says, if there was a strong wind, he'd take off. Women were a complete mystery to me.

'So,' I said to Dave and Clarkey as we sat on the grass, chewing our orange segments, 'I've been meaning to ask, what exactly is it with Karl and those fifth years? Is he going out with one of them?'

They laughed.

'It's complicated,' said Clarkey, his face glowing like the Olympic flame, 'one of them, that Glenda Craven, has got his name written all over her exercise books apparently. It's hilarious.'

I smirked. Why did all these girls love him? I just couldn't see it.

'Unfortunately for Karl, he fancies one of the others, Juliette Bradshaw,' said Dave, orange juice running over his chin.

Juliette Bradshaw? She must be the girl that Karl had talked about on the phone that time; the one who apparently doesn't know he exists.

The three fifth form girls were loud and giggly. Two of them were quite pretty. There was a tall, attractive, sporty looking dark haired girl; sort of a taller version of that Scottish singer Sheena Easton. Karl seemed to ignore her most of the time; he was mainly chatting to the shorter fair haired one, who seemed to do most of the talking - Karl and her seemed to be getting on pretty well - I was guessing that was Juliette. She seemed a bit too chatty but she was easily the best looking of the three. I could see why he fancied her. She had a lovely smile and a great little figure. The third girl was plain looking; podgy, with a spotty complexion. If Karl's luck was anything like mine; that was Glenda. She looked like a Glenda. There was a girl on Crossroads called Glenda - she looked like her.

'Who's the other one?' I asked.

'Oh, that's just Heidi. She's in the fourth year. She plays in the school orchestra with Juliette and Glenda.'

I studied the dark haired girl, who stood slightly apart from the others. She was tall for a fourth year.

'So, I think we should change things around a bit for the second half,' Mr. Beattie said, interrupting our conversation.

Great, does that I mean I can put my shirt on, I wondered?
It didn't.

'I want you all to change positions - defenders play up front, attackers play in midfield, midfielders become strikers. Mr.Bloom...'

79

he shouted across the field, '...if you can drag yourself away from the ladies...?'

Both teams jeered Karl. The girls giggled. Karl came trotting over, looking bashful.

'Ok, let's get cracking' Mr Beattie shouted, 'it's turning a bit nippy!

Turning a bit nippy? I couldn't feel my nose and my fingers were blue.

The changes meant I was playing up-front with Clarkey. He was the only boy on the pitch who looked more red than I did. He looked like someone had peeled his skin off. He was red raw.

I spent the first ten minutes or so, running backwards and forwards, chasing the opposing team, who were clearly much better than us. Pretty soon, I was knackered. But then it happened - the most memorable moment of my football career thus far; I would never forget it.

I was running back towards our own half, just behind Stuart Tucker, who was meant to be marking me. Suddenly, Dave got the ball and whacked it up the pitch. It was sailing over my head and I turned and started running after it. The ball landed in a puddle and stopped dead about ten feet in front of me.

'Offside! Sir, he's offside,' I heard Stuart yelling.

I half expected Mr. Beattie to blow his whistle. There were no linesmen though and Mr. Beattie had been back in the other penalty area when Dave thumped the ball up field.

'Play on!' I heard him shout.

I didn't look back. I could hear Stuart Tucker bearing down on me from behind. He was quite a hefty lad was Stuart; he was wheezing as he tried to catch up. I wasn't in Karl's league when it came to sprinting, but if I say so myself, I'm pretty quick. Tucker would never catch me in a million years. So, all I had to do was keep going and beat Frank Little in the opposing goal.

I knocked the ball forward and looked up in time to see Frank come hurtling out of the penalty area. Should I shoot or take it closer?

'Go on Tim, shoot!' I heard Clarkey shout.

I touched the ball again. Too firmly; it was running away from me. Frank was bearing down on me; he was going to get there first; oh crap, I was going to waste my big chance.

The ball stuck in the mud again. Frank shaped to kick it as I was about a foot away. I saw him smile as he whacked it as hard as he could. He slipped as I turned my back; the ball thumped against me - bloody hell, that hurt. I turned back - the ball was ballooning over Frank's head and towards the open goal. I kept running as I followed the ball. It sailed goalwards. Frank was lying flat on his back in the mud, looking back at me, over his shoulder. The ball landed with a splash at my feet, three feet from the goal-line. I was already lifting my arm in celebration as I carefully side-footed it over the line.

Afterwards, when I recounted the story to friends and family, I told how the ball hit the back of the net with a satisfying thwack. It didn't - it sort of trickled over the line almost apologetically. I turned, thrusting my clenched fist in the air. I heard David Coleman commentating in my head "And it's there! A great goal by Tim James!"

The roar (from the three fifth year girls and an old man walking his poodle) was deafening. My team-mates mobbed me. I was a hero. If only we weren't losing 7-2.

'What a goal eh Dave?' I said as we trotted back to the halfway line.

'Yeah, bit flukey mate - but yeah, well done,' he said begrudgingly.

My moment of triumph didn't last long. Sensing I was onto a good thing with Stuart Tucker's lack of speed and the absence of linesmen, I took up position next to him and waited for my next opportunity. Sure enough, a few minutes later, another high ball came sailing our way. desperate to atone himself, Stuart launched himself at the ball, which came down with a thud and skimmed clear off the top of his head, straight into my path. It was deja vu - clear through on goal again, with only Frank Little to beat. I skated away. I heard footsteps and heavy breathing behind me but I wasn't concerned - Tucker moved like a tranquilised hippo, wallowing in the mud.

This time I would let fly; hit it from distance; catch Frank unawares. A real Liam Brady special. I caught up with the ball and shaped myself as Frank came off his line. That's when the train hit me from behind. Next thing I knew, I was face down in the mud with my ears ringing.

'Ref! Penalty!' I heard the boys shouting, followed by a piercing whistle from Mr. Beattie. I shook my head and peered across the pitch - a dozen feet were converging on me; I couldn't stop my head from swimming. A meaty hand grabbed me by the arm and started to haul me up.

'Oops, sorry mate!' said the voice; although the tone was far from apologetic.

Kong's blurred face came slowly into focus. Dave and Clarkey hauled me up on my shaky pins. Mr. Beattie was asking me to count how many fingers he was holding up. Four fingers gradually became two as the boys led me over to the side of the pitch.

'Get some of that water will you girls?' said Mr. Beattie, pointing to his trainers's bucket. Sheena Easton grabbed the bucket and handed it over to the pretty little fair-haired girl; the one Karl had been chatting to. She put her hand in and pulled out a sponge, which she splashed all over my head. I gasped; the water was freezing. The girls laughed.

'OK,Tim? I think you'd better sit the last few minutes out don't you?' said Mr. Beattie.

The small fair-haired girl smiled and giggled as I tried to sit up.

'Yeah, perhaps I should,' I said.

'Right' said Mr. Beattie, 'It's a penalty kick for the skins and you Mr. King will be taking an early shower!' he said to Kong; whilst pointing in the direction of the changing rooms.

'Aw, sir!' protested Kong.

'No arguments Mr. King or you will be suspended from the next two school matches!'

'Right, I'll take the penalty!' said Karl, grabbing the ball and smiling at the girls. The podgy one yelled her encouragement. The small girl was still leaning over me. She had a really pretty smile.

'Are you alright now?' she said.

'Yes, thanks,' I said, glad that my face was already bright red from my exertions. It covered my blushes.

She started walking back to her friends, ready to watch the penalty.

'Great goal by the way!' she called back giving me a thumbs up.

Karl had definitely scored. Both from the penalty spot and also from what I could see, with that pretty little girl. I could tell by the way she hugged him and kissed him on the cheek as he left the pitch at the end of the match. We'd lost 7-3. The podgy girl leant in to congratulate him too but Karl pulled away. She looked crestfallen; poor girl.

Karl walked back across the playing fields and into school with the girls. I walked gingerly, supported by Kevin and Dave.

'Sure you're OK?' asked Mr. Beattie.

'Just winded I think.'

'Well, I hope you're fit for next week, we've got a match,' he grinned.

Bloody Hell. I'd made the team. How had that happened?

Back in the changing rooms, I sat wearily but happily on a bench whilst the others ran around in the showers, flicking each other with damp towels. Fortunately no-one targeted me; I think they still felt sorry for me. Even Kong shook my hand, apologised for half-killing me and said 'well played'.

'Yeah, well played Tim. Sounds like you're in then!' said Karl.

'Thanks Karl. You too eh?' I said, winking.

'Uh?'

'With Juliette Bradshaw I mean! She's pretty isn't she?'

'Do you think? I'm not so sure. I think she's playing hard to get.'

'Oh come off it mate, she was all over you at the end, hugging and kissing you.'

'What?'

'Juliette, she was kissing you at the end. I saw you!'

'Oh, no, you twerp,' he laughed, 'that's my little sister Heidi; she's in the fourth year. You must have seen her before? Juliette is the tall one; looks like Linda Carter.'

'Oh!' I said.

What a pillock I was. Mind you, Linda Carter? Not from where I'd been sitting. Juliette was definitely more Sheena Easton than Wonder Woman.

'So, you think my kid sister's pretty then?' Karl smirked, pulling on his trousers.

'Well, I didn't say that exactly...'

'Hey lads, guess what.....' started to shout Karl across the room.

Me and my big mouth. Would I never learn?

The glow of scoring a goal and getting selected for the team stayed with me for the rest of the week. I felt six inches taller as I walked around the corridors; I imagined that the younger kids were prodding each other as I strolled past.

'That's Tim James, he's the Paul Mariner of the Sixth Form.'

I felt on top of the world. I wasn't even too phased when I bumped into Heidi Bloom and her mates; they all giggled as I walked past. Had Karl told her what I'd said? Well what if he had? I expect she'd be proud to have the star of the Sixth Form team making admiring comments about her. She certainly seemed to be smiling whenever I saw her. Or was it laughing? Anyway, she was only fifteen - I suppose if she developed a crush on me that would be understandable. I just had to remind myself that Karl Bloom's little sister was definitely out of bounds.

Somehow, I missed my rendezvous with the others at the bus-stop, after school the next day - possibly, because I walked right around the other side of the building to avoid them, before doubling back to catch the next bus.

So, the whole week passed without me having to face the potential agony of going to HMV with Dave Booth and the lads. I still had to face the potential threat of Jacko, Humph and the others dragging me up there again at the weekend. That was easily remedied too though. Rising ridiculously early that Saturday morning, I decided it was safer to get out before they rang. Anyway, I had a genuine reason to visit HMV, so I decided to go up there alone. The early bird catches the worm.

Christmas was only two weeks away. Cheryl wanted the Adam and The Ants album. Mum had given me the money to get it. She always did that - every year. The Ants were quite cool, so if Roxanne was to serve me, it would do my street cred no harm at all.

As anticipated, HMV was already bustling. I found the album and had a bit of a look around - looking at records I'd like to buy but couldn't afford. Maybe I should consider that Saturday job at Fine fare that Cheryl was always droning on about? I couldn't be a paper boy forever. Or maybe I could get a job here; work with Roxanne....

There were four or five people serving behind the counter; I couldn't see Roxanne. There was a queue at each of the tills, so I stood at the back of the nearest one. It took a few minutes and I was happily daydreaming and singing along to The Pretenders "Brass in Pocket" before I realised that I was at the till and the girl was taking the LP from my hands. She was blonde and when she leant over to get a plastic bag from beneath the counter, her loose top fell open and I got a right eyeful. She had a cleavage like the Devil's Dyke. It was Poppy Bloom, Karl's older sister. She had a name badge on. I would have tried to read it - but it was positioned far too close to her boobs. I didn't want to be accused of being a complete pervert.

'Three ninety nine please sir,' she said.

I fumbled around in my pocket for the right money. Then the shop phone range.

'Excuse me a moment sir,' she said, marching away to answer it.

A door behind the counter opened as Poppy Bloom passed it, 'oh Roxy,' I heard her say, 'be an angel will you and finish serving this young man.'

Roxanne appeared from nowhere. My heart started playing a samba; it was as much as I could do to stand still; fighting the urge to turn and run. She was looking a bit flushed; her face was almost the colour of her red hair. She must have caught my questioning look.

'Stock taking!' she said by way of explanation, 'some of those boxes are dead heavy!'

I couldn't speak. I managed a small smile.

'Ah, Adam and the Ants. He's so good looking isn't he?'

Was he?

'Sorry, I don't suppose you'd think so! What am I thinking? Such a busy morning. I expect Debbie Harry's more your type eh?' she said laughing and shoving my album into a bag.

I smiled and nodded.

She didn't notice, she was busy with the till. She was pushing the buttons but nothing was happening.

'It's been playing up all morning this till, I am sorry sir. Geoff! It's doing it again.'

A smart looking young black man in a suit came over from the other end of the counter and started fiddling with the till. I noticed his name badge. *"Geoff. Assistant Manager"*

'Sorry about this.' Roxanne said.

"Roxanne. Senior Customer Advisor" her badge said.

'No problem,' I squeaked. They were the first actual words I'd ever spoken to her. I was a smooth-talking bugger and no mistake.

Geoff prodded at the keys.

'So, are you up to anything cool this weekend?' Roxanne asked. I thought for a moment she was talking to the Assistant Manager. Then I realised she was was still looking at me.

'Er, yeah, I'm going to my scho....er sixth form college party,' I said. My mouth was dry and my voice sounded ridiculously croaky.

'Oh really? I'm going to a sixth form party too. Which college are you at?'

Bugger. I had a sinking feeling.

'Denton,' I said, my voice finally returning to near normal.

'Yes, I think that's the one.....Poppy, here a minute!'

Oh no, had Dave Booth been down here already?

Poppy Bloom looked up from the phone. 'OK sir, AC/DC, yes, we'll put that aside for you,' she put her hand over the receiver, 'what?' she mouthed to Roxanne.

'Which sixth form is it that your brother goes to?'

'Denton,' she said, putting the phone down. Poppy's boobs wobbled across the room. She followed a few feet behind.

'There! See, we're going to the party too. We'll see you there then!' said Roxanne.

Poppy looked less than excited at the prospect.

'Know my brother then do you?' she asked.

I tried not to stare at her chest, which was difficult.

"Poppy Bloom. Senior Customer Advisor".

I looked more closely at her face. For some reason I hadn't noticed before but she was an obvious cross between Heidi and Karl, except with a chest like a small battleship.

'Karl Bloom, do you know him?'

'Yeah, I know Karl,' I said.

'Cool,' said Roxane.

'Cool,' I smiled, 'so Karl invited you to the party then?'

'Yeah, that's right, 'said Roxanne, 'should be a laugh!'

'Karl invited you?'

'Yeah, why?' Roxanne smiled, looking puzzled.

'Oh, nothing. It should be a cool party.'

Karl had invited her? Not Dave then.

I had a sneaking suspicion that I might get a different version of events from the crafty Mr. Booth.

8- Voices.....

Sting sang to me as I got dressed for the party.

The song was called 'Voices Inside My Head'. As usual, he was spot on. These days, there were always little voices inside my head, telling me one thing and then another.

"Roxanne's coming to the party, this could be the night."

"Don't kid yourself, you've got no chance,"

"You never know, stranger things have happened."

I wished they'd just shut up.

'Timothy, don't forget Martin's waiting for you down here!' Mum shouted up the stairs, 'shall I send him up?'

'Won't be a minute, nearly ready!' I shouted back.

I took off my button-down shirt and put on my Regatta De Blanc T-shirt. What if Roxanne didn't like The Police though? Maybe the plain white t-shirt and the sleeveless blue pullover? Too dull? Oh, bloody hell, just choose will you?

'Blimey mate, what took you so long?' asked Jacko, perched on the end of my bed, rifling through my record collection.

'Didn't know what to wear,' I said.

'Such a girl!' he smirked.

'Piss off Jacko,' I said, doing an Anthea Redfearn twirl, 'so what do you think?' I'd opted for my Jam "Tube Station" capped-sleeved T-shirt with black jeans.

Jacko looked me up and down; shook his head, as if in disbelief. 'Good choice of T-shirt,' he finally conceded.

Jacko loved The Jam.

He picked up the dusty box of Andrex from the bedside cabinet, 'Are you sure that's what you were doing up here?' he sneered.

'I've had a cold.'

'Yeah, right, that's what they all say mate. Just be careful you don't yank it right off one of these nights OK? I know it seems unlikely right now, but one of these days you might just need it.

'Ho bloody ho,' I said, pulling on my black Dr. Marten shoes.

'Blimey though mate, seriously you do want to be careful,' he said, a small pile of LP's on his lap.

'What?'

'Well, some of these records aren't even by The Police!' he said, holding up The Buzzcocks's "Love Bites" in one hand and Dexy's "Searching For The Young Soul Rebels" in the other.

'Yeah, very funny Jacko. Excuse me while I stitch my sides back together. You're killing me.'

He was right though. I was becoming a tart. A tart with a fickle heart. I seemed to fall in love with someone new every other week these days. My first love wasn't over but it had challengers.

Those heady days of 1978. Annie Nightingale had introduced me to The Police. Just a few bars of Can't Stand Losing You and I was instantly smitten. I was a Police fan and I was convinced in those early days of carefree love that they would remain my favourites forever. It would have been unfaithful to admit I considered myself a fan of anyone else. I liked other bands, of course I did, but I wasn't a Boomtown Rats fan and I wasn't a Gary Numan fan - I was a Police fan. Now, suddenly it was 1980; nearly 1981, and I wasn't so sure anymore. I'd fallen in love several times over the last twelve months; one minute I was swooning over The Jam, down in their tube station at midnight, then I was seduced by Dexy's and "Geno". I was madly in love with Dexy's for several weeks. Then I heard "Mirror In The Bathroom" and my head was turned by The Beat. Ever Fallen In Love With Someone You Shouldn't Have Fallen In Love With? Oh yes, I loved The Buzzcocks too! Now, posters of all these bands, plus others, like Squeeze, The Specials, OMD and Joe Jackson were vying for space on my over-crowded bedroom walls, together with older favourites like Blondie, Siouxsie and The Banshees, The Undertones, Kate Bush and of course, The Police.

Yet more musical confusion and excitement had come along with the discovery of the sixth form common room record player. Dave Booth brought in his Dad's "Beach Boys Greatest Hits" LP and we played it on the knackered old Ferguson. It only played at 33rpm, so you couldn't play singles properly. Although someone from a previous year had left an old copy of "Maggie May" hanging around and Rod Stewart sounded dead funny slowed down. Even funnier than normal.

Since we couldn't really afford albums ourselves, most of the lads raided the collections of their dads or older brothers. The boys always seemed to have first say over what was played, I noticed. Sharon Chapman had tried to play Barry Manilow a couple of weeks back. It hadn't gone down well with some of the lads. I wonder how Sharon's Mum reacted to that huge scratch when she got Barry home?

On reflection, and with the benefit of my all of my seventeen years of experience, I had to admit that contrary to my earlier belief, not *all* old music was crap.

I discovered that I really liked The Beach Boys, The Kinks, The Who, David Bowie and T.Rex. I even quite liked the Stones and The Beatles but I would never admit that to Dad - he was always going on about how much better music was in 'his day' and how everyone in the charts was "ripping off" his old favourites. I still didn't think that was true of course, but I had come to realise that for example, The Jam owed a certain debt of gratitude to The Who, and that Squeeze's Difford and Tilbrook weren't necessarily the first great songwriting duo in musical history, as I had supposed them to be. All of a sudden I'd become a right musical old scrubber.

Now, it seemed I was in danger of becoming the same when it came to girls. Like my love for The Police, I had been obsessed with Alison Fisher practically right through school - the fact that she clearly had no interest in me and was going out with my best friend hadn't deterred me in the slightest. Like The Police, back then, there were no other charms that could sway me from my true love. Since I had turned sixteen, my hormones had run riot and I seemed to fall in love with any girl that smiled at me - which didn't happen that often, or not as often as the admiring glances that Karl Bloom seemed to attract for example. Thank God; I think I would have needed air-traffic control in my trousers if I'd been Karl.

Was I in really in love with Roxanne now? I mean I didn't even know her. My obsession with her was like hearing one single by a band and deciding they were the best thing since sliced bread. What if I didn't like the follow-up? Maybe Roxanne was like Collette, Alison's cousin, my summer holiday fling. She'd turned out to be just a passing fancy; an infatuation like Dexy's and Geno. Only time would tell if Roxanne was my true Sting or just a Plastic Bertrand; a one-hit wonder with no staying power.

Now there was Stacey Groves, my sister's friend from the Salon. Although she was tarty and loud, she was undoubtedly sexy. Whenever I saw Stacey, I got a peculiar tingling in my stomach, which somehow seemed a bit...sordid; a bit like I felt when I listened to T. Rex, or Roxy Music - I knew they were really too old and glamourous

89

for me, but just as I was strangely drawn to Glam Rock, I seemed incapable of resisting Stacey's charms. And what about Heidi Bloom? Far, far too young and innocent for me - she was the schoolgirl equivalent of Spandau Ballet and their weird songs and even weirder kilts. To Cut A Long Story Short, I couldn't get either of them out of my head, no matter how much I told myself it would be better for me if I did. And just like posters on my wall, I stored up mental snapshots of other girls I'd seen and admired. My mental gallery included the vast majority of the girls in the Upper Sixth, at least half a dozen in the fifth year, Sabrina Holloway, the school's Economics teacher, the girl who worked weekends in the local chippie, Sarah-Jane Smith from Doctor Who and the woman in the Shake 'n Vac advert on telly. A complete and utter tart - that was me.

We were each allowed to take one guest to the party, which was to be held in the main school gym. Jacko was my guest, Humph was going with Alison; the whole crowd was going to be there.

Despite the strict rules laid down by the headmaster about the availability of alcohol, it was also likely that it was going to turn into one almighty piss-up. The two teachers left in charge, Mr. Knight ("Justin") and Miss O'Connor ("Sue", a.k.a "Des" for obvious reasons), were both soft touches. Everyone knew they'd be turning a blind eye to any cans or bottles being smuggled in under large winter coats. The word was that random searches would be conducted on the door, by upper-sixth Prefects. That was a laugh; we all knew what they were like. They liked to let their hair down more than we did.

As Jacko and I approached the school gate, small knots of kids were already gathering outside, some of them openly wielding cans of Carlsberg and Hofmeister. Whilst most of the boys were dressed like me and Jacko - chords or jeans, t-shirts and trainers - the girls had taken the opportunity to dress up in little black party frocks or spangly tops with skin-tight trousers and high-heeled shoes. With their faces made up, some of them were instantly transformed - suddenly you couldn't take your eyes off of girls who you wouldn't have given a second glance to in their dowdy school gear. We entered through Reception. The large arched windows had been stencilled with Christmas decorations in fake white snow; a santa, a snowman, a robin and an angel. There was a huge Christmas tree, with home made decorations and paper chains draped all over the room. At the other end, we could see coloured lights flashing through the Gym door;

flashing perfectly in time with the butterflies in the pit of my stomach. I glanced around. No sign of Roxanne. Maybe she wouldn't come? God, I was such a chicken.

One of the first people we bumped into, as we were hanging our coats, was Fay Carpenter, Jacko's all-too-brief snogging partner back in the third year, with her best friend Shelly Tranter, a mousy looking girl with a turned-up nose and an overbite, which Jacko rather cruelly referred to as her "flick-knife" teeth.

Fay looked amazing. I watched Jacko's Adams-apple do a triple-salco.

Wow! There had always been something vaguely attractive about Fay beneath her pink horn-rimmed glasses and starched white blouses, but I'd always dismissed her as brainy Fay. She was probably the cleverest girl in our year. But I could never quite see what Jacko had seen in her.

Tonight was different.

Now I understood.

In her strappy, low-cut top, and high-heels, she was a dead-ringer for one of the Nolan sisters. The good looking one at that. Her purple satin trousers appeared to have been sprayed on.

'She looks......different, doesn't she?' I whispered as she teetered towards us, leaning on Shelly for support.

Jacko didn't reply. That would have meant using his tongue, which at that moment had vacated his mouth.

'Hello Tim!' Fay said, smiling warmly. Then she turned towards Jacko, her smile faded and raising one eyebrow like Mr. Spock, she addressed him with cool detachment.

'Oh, hi Martin.'

That's all she said.

Jacko's face resembled a puppy that had just been offered a particularly juicy bone.

Fay and Shelly exchanged knowing glances, giggled and headed towards the door.

'Is she still seeing Dan Chester?' asked Jacko, his eyes on stalks which appeared to extend to within mere inches of Fay's purple satin backside.

'No idea mate, you'll just have to ask her won't you?'

'Uh?' he muttered, still mesmerised.

Fay turned and smiled back at us, as she went through the door.

'Unless you're too much of a eunuch of course?' I added, smiling to myself.

The prefects had done a great job of decorating the Gym. Over to one side, there were trestle tables with plates of grub covered in tin-foil and cling-film. Another table had been set up for the officially sanctioned selection of drinks - i.e. lemonade, Coke and various other soft drinks. Jacko and I had each brought four cans of Cider - the so called bouncers hadn't even looked in our plastic bags, even though the name *"Unwins the off-licence"* was emblazoned across them in giant letters.

As usual, Colin Doyle was the DJ. Colin was an ex-Denton pupil, who always did these parties. He'd set up his equipment at the far end, under the Southampton wall bars. There were two huge amps and twin record-decks, with coils of coloured lights draped over the front. As we entered, he was playing "Rock Lobster" by The B-52's. No-one was dancing yet, but a few of the girls were standing around the edge of the cleared dance floor area, shuffling their feet; waiting for the first brave one to head out under the flashing lights.

Fay and Shelly had sat themselves at a table on the far side of the room. It took Jacko's built in radar all of five seconds to spot them. He caught me looking at him, looking at Fay, and looked away, trying to act dead casual.

I sniggered.

'What?' he said.

'Nothing,' I said, doing my best to keep a straight face., 'oh look, there's Clarkey.'

Clarkey was sitting alone in one of the corner chairs on the opposite side of the Gym. He'd Brylcreemed his red hair into a slicked back, teddy-boy D.A.

I waved over; he raised a can of Hofmeister in salute

'I didn't know Kevin Clarke had joined The Stray Cats,' said Jacko. The Stray Cats were a rockabilly band with tattoos and very large quiffs.

'Clarkey got up and started to wander over. I hoped Jacko wouldn't give him any more stick about his hair.

'Hi Clarkey, you remember Jacko don't you?'

'Hi Kevin,' said Jacko coolly.

'Martin,' Clarkey nodded in acknowledgment.

92

There was an embarrassing pause.

'Looks cool eh?' I said, gesturing around the Gym.

People were arriving all the time now. Frank Little, the school goalie, walked in with a girl that I didn't recognise. Frank was dressed in a button down shirt with a skinny leather tie and drainpipe trousers, topped off with a really cool denim jacket covered in sew-on badges. He looked the biz - and so did his girlfriend - she was dressed in a similar trousers and skinny-tie combo, with a purple blazer - but it wasn't really her clothes we all noticed. She was beautiful - coffee coloured skin and a mass of brown frizzy hair with incredible doe-eyes.

'Who's that with Frank?' Clarkey asked.

'No idea,' said Jacko, 'but I wouldn't mind finding out.'

A hundred male heads turned as she walked across the room. They sat down at table near Colin's decks. Then Jacko grabbed my arm.

'Look, who's here!' he shouted in my ear, trying to compete with The B-52's, as he gestured over to the door.

Alison spotted us too. To my surprise she was with Sara and not Humph. The two girls waved and started to head over. Predictably, Alison looked fantastic in a her little black party dress. She seemed to be attracting even more admiring glances than usual, as she glided across the gum towards us. I noticed boys nudging other and winking; mouths gaping. I'd been aware of the "Alison effect" for years. The older she got, the more marked the effect became. She looked more grown up these days, what with that red streak running through her long blonde hair and the black make up around her eyes a-la Chrissie Hynde. She was passing a group of lads, who all followed her every step, eyes on stalks.

'Hi Alison, nice dress!' I heard one of the boys say as she passed by.

'Going away on holiday again soon?' said another, for no apparent reason.

The group of boys sniggered.

'How's your tan?' a voice shouted.

Weird.

'What was all that about?' Sara was asking as they joined us.

'No idea. Ignore them. I do,' Alison said, turning to face me and Jacko and critically looking us up and down.

'Glad you two made an effort to dress up!' she said.

93

'Hi Alison, you look....' I was lost for words. But as ever Jacko was on hand.

'Good enough to eat?' he muttered.

'...amazing,' I said.

'Why thank you young sir!'

'And don't tell me, I look amazing too?' said Sara, posing in her flouncy pink satin party dress. It did nothing for her. If anything it made her hips and bum look even bigger than ever.

'Large enough to eat,' muttered Jacko, flashing her a smile.

I moved in to kiss her plump cheek, deliberately elbowing Jacko in the mid-riff as I did so.

'Of course you do Sara!' I said gallantly. 'So Ali, where's Humph tonight?'

'Meeting me here later. He's been working. Doing a "private job" he said. Cash in hand apparently.'

'Sounds dodgy!' Jacko observed.

'Well if it's with those two clowns Pete and Doddsy, I wouldn't be at all surprised,' Sara agreed.

Alison looked fed up. She changed the subject.

'So, is this picture of loveliness your big date for the evening Timothy?' laughed Alison, poking Jacko in the ribs.

'He looks better in subdued lighting,' I said.

Alison laughed. 'I doubt it. Still, the night is young eh? she smiled, 'the young prince might still find his Cinderella at the ball tonight.'

'Yeah right.'

I'd be lucky to pull one of the ugly sisters.

- - -

By nine o'clock, I was really nervous. There was still no sign of Roxanne, or of Dave and Karl. I had just visited the loo for the fourteenth time. I wandered back out into the corridor, still adjusting my flies. With my head down, I practically walked into her.

'Sorry!' we both said at once.

The girl looked down to my hands.

'Sorry!' I said again, 'button flies,' I explained. Idiot.

'Oh,' the girl said.

'Too much information eh? Sorry.'

'So, how are you?'

'Ok, thanks,' I said.

'You don't remember me do you?' she said.

94

She was small and dark and undeniably pretty. She looked like Dana. Her hair was done up in a bun on the back of her head and her big blue eyes were heavily made up. She was wearing a shiny blue blouse and a short dark skirt. She looked familiar but I couldn't place her. I must have looked pretty blankly at her.

'Heidi? Heidi Bloom? Karl's sister?' she said, blushing slightly and laughing, 'I spoke to you at the football match.'

'Heidi? Blimey, sorry, it's your hair...you've gone dark!'

She touched her hair self-consciously and blushed more noticeably.

'More like my natural colour really - I only make it lighter with lemon juice and stuff. Does it suit me? I'm not sure if I've made a hideous mistake!'

'Er, no it looks fine.'

It did. She was really very pretty. I'd always fancied Dana. All kinds of everything reminded me of her.

'Have you seen Karl?'

'Not yet.' I said, still trying to get over Heidi's transformation, 'are you coming to the party?' I asked - a fairly dumb question in hindsight. Heidi looked a little sheepish.

'Hopefully. Karl said he would get us in.'

'Us?'

'Yeah, I'm with Juliette,' she pointed in the direction of the foyer, where her friend was sitting on a stool.

'Ah!' I said - Juliette's presence explained why Karl had promised to get his little sister into the party.

'Did you bring a guest?' Heidi asked.

'Yeah, afraid so,' I said; suddenly wishing that I hadn't.

'Oh right, you've got a date then?'

Did she sound disappointed? Probably. After all, she'd just realised she couldn't use me as a free ticket to the party.

'No, just a mate,' I said.

Heidi smiled. 'Oh, right.'

'Heidi! There you are!' Karl appeared, dragging Clarkey by one arm and a nerdy lad called Simon Fletcher by the other, 'is Juliette with you? I've found you two chaperones! I can get you into the party.'

'Why can't you and Dave take them in?' I asked.

'We've already got guests,' Karl said, shrugging.

'Who?...' I started to ask but Karl was too busy flirting with Juliette.

'Juliette, this is Kev. He'll get you in. Simon can get Heidi in. Kevin, Simon, Congratulations, you've pulled! This is Heidi and Juliette.'

Heidi sniggered.

Juliette blushed.

Simon looked like he might faint.

Clarkey took Heidi's hand, 'follow me young lady!' he said, cheerfully.

'Hang on a minute. Weren't you bringing your brother?' I asked Clarkey.

'He's sick. Chicken Pox,' Kevin shrugged.

'Grant's got the pox?' said Karl, pushing Kevin away from him, 'bloody hell Kev, I haven't had that!'

'I have!' I said cheerfully, heading back to the gym.

I saw Dave as soon as I walked back through the door. He looked insufferably smug as he came bounding over.

'Hi mate, there you are! I've been looking all over for you. Have I got news for you?'

'Yeah?' instinctively, I knew what he was about to say. He didn't disappoint.

'You owe me a quid!' he said, a broad grin on his face and the palm of his hand stretched out in front of him.

'Oh really? I said, acting casual, feigning surprise, 'how do you work that out then?'

'Follow me, I'll show you,' he said, grabbing my arm.

'Tim, this is Roxanne,' Dave smirked as he winked at me.

Roxanne was standing near the dance floor. Dave handed her a plastic cup of what looked like Coke. Unlike the other girls, Roxanne was dressed in jeans and pumps, with a smart blazer over a black and white hooped t-shirt. She looked dead causal, although she had clearly taken time over her brushed-back red hair. I thought it looked a bit like Bowie's in his "Ashes To Ashes" video. Clarkey would be dead jealous.

'Hi Roxanne, you and Poppy made it OK then?' I said as breezily as I could, even though my stomach was doing little cartwheels.

Dave looked utterly confused. Good, teach the cocky sod right.

'Oh, hi there, how are you? Poppy's just powdering her nose. So, what did you think of the Ants?'

Dave's face was a picture.

'Not heard it yet - it's a present for my sister.'

'Ah, that's dead sweet of you. I wish my brother was that thoughtful.'

Dave's mouth was gaping.

'By the way, love the t-shirt!' Roxanne told me, touching my sleeve, 'The Jam are so cool aren't they? Bruce Foxton's gorgeous isn't he? Oh God,there I go again, I don't suppose he's your type either is he?'

'Not really....'

'Hang on a minute,' Dave was saying, 'do you two....?'

'So, you were right the other day; looks like it's going to be a cool party,' Roxanne said.

I was beginning to enjoy myself; relishing the bewilderment on Dave's face.

'Yeah, I'm really glad Karl invited me along,' Roxanne said, 'my feet are killing me though. I've been standing up in that shop all day. Fancy a sit down?'

'Yeah good thinking....' said Dave.

'Oh, er David was it?' Roxanne said, draining her drink in one and holding the empty cup out to Dave, 'you wouldn't be a star and get me another would you? I'm parched.'

Dave looked from me to Roxanne and back again to me.

I grinned what I hoped was my smuggest grin, before leaning over to whisper in Dave's ear.

'So what was that about *me* owing *you* a quid?'

Dave just looked at me; his mouth hanging open.

'Never mind mate,' I said, 'you've still got Bo Derek.'

He hesitated for a moment, looked at Roxanne's empty cup; then he turned and skulked off back to the drinks-table.

Roxanne took my arm and led me across to a free table. Blimey, I couldn't believe my luck. Maybe Alison had been right all along. Well, hello Cinders!

Roxanne pulled out a chair, took off her blazer and draped it over the back. She had silver bangles on both arms, right up to her elbows. She was so cool.

'Sorry about that!' she said, placing her hand briefly on mine as I pulled up the chair next to hers. 'That friend of yours is a bit full on isn't he? He was all over me like a rash. I was feeling pretty claustrophobic. Thanks for rescuing me.'

'No problem. He's alright though when you get to know him,' I said.

What was I saying?

'Too full of himself for my liking,' she said, tossing back her red hair. It glinted as it caught the light, 'besides,' she added, I don't go for younger men.'

Bugger.

'Not *usually* anyway,' she smiled.

And what exactly did she mean by that?

'....and so, anyway, have you seen Adam & The Ants live? They are totally mega!'

The next five minutes seemed to last forever.

Roxanne knew absolutely shed-loads about music; she was really funny and seemed really interested in my opinions. She even laughed at some of my feeble jokes. I was starting to relax. The music was really loud, so she had to lean in really close as she talked to me. I could feel her hot breath on my cheek. She smelt like rose petals.

It was only when we were interrupted by the the others that I actually remembered we were at a party. Karl and his two sisters pulled up chairs beside us. Juliette was hovering. There were no other chairs. Karl retrieved one from a nearby table and engineered it so that he was sitting right next to Juliette. Clarkey looked uncomfortable. He stood up behind Heidi. Simon Fletcher had disappeared. I guessed Karl had made sure he was given the elbow as soon as he'd got Juliette into the party.

'So, are you looking forward to tomorrow night then Tim?' asked Karl.

'What?' I said, still intoxicated by Roxanne and her warm scent.

'Queueing up for tickets! You know, for The Police! London and all that!'

Shit, I'd forgotten we were going to queue up overnight. I hadn't even mentioned that to my parents; I'd been too distracted by everything - the football trial, the party and of course, Roxanne.

'Er, yeah,' I said.

'You guys are going to see The Police? Brilliant!' said Roxanne, 'Did you hear that Poppy, they're going up to London to see The Police.'

'That's so unfair!' Heidi was telling Juliette, 'Mum and Dad will let Karl go but not me!'

'Shame. It'll be double ace!' Clarkey said; putting his hand on Heidi's shoulder.

She shrugged him off and pulled a sulky face.

'Er, Karl, I was going to ask,' I said, 'do we all have to go and queue or can we get more than one ticket each?'

'Why, are you bottling out about the queueing over night idea then?'

'No, it's just...'

'Don't be such a girl. It'll be cool!' said Karl.

'It does sound like a bit of an adventure - sleeping bags, a bottle of wine, take the radio up, that kind of thing!' said Roxanne, 'come on Pops, why don't we go with them? I've heard The Police are great live. What do you say?'

'Yeah, they *are* great live Poppy,' I said.

Poppy pulled a face. She was spilling out of a very low-cut red dress.

'Have you seen them before?' asked Roxanne.

'Yeah, last year, at The Dome.'

'Brilliant! And were they as good as everyone says?'

Roxanne looked dead impressed.

'Better,' I said.

'Oh, come on Pops, let's go for it!'

Poppy said she'd think about it.

Dave finally came back with some drinks and plonked one down on the table.

'Think about what?' Dave asked Poppy.

She didn't reply. Dave might have got an answer from talking to her face instead of her chest.

'We're coming to queue up for tickets for The Police with you guys!' said Roxanne.

'Really?' said Dave.

'I only said I'd think about it!' said Poppy.

I wasn't sure if I liked Karl's big sister. She was a bit sulky. She'd probably be really pretty if she tried smiling occasionally. She sort of looked like a cross between Karl and Heidi. She had Karl's nose and Heidi's eyes. She was a big girl was Poppy; and not just her chest. She was what my Mum would call big-boned. Not fat exactly, but not what you'd call slim either. I remembered Karl saying his Mum was half-German. Poppy looked a bit like one of those East German shot-putters from the Olympic Games. They'd won loads of medals in the Summer. Dad reckons they're all on steroids.

'Yeah, go on, it will be a laugh Poppy!' I heard myself say.

'Maybe,' Poppy said. She still looked stony faced but I sensed she was cracking under the pressure.

'Go on Poppy!' said Heidi, 'if you go, Mum might let me and Juliette go too.'

I looked at Karl. It was like someone had just turned a light on. He was beaming.

'Would you fancy it then Juliette?' he asked.

'Yeah, if everyone else is going. Would you be able to get us tickets though? I don't think my Dad would let me queue overnight.'

'Come on Pops,' Karl said, suddenly really enthusiastic, 'Heidi's right. Mum and Dad will let her and Juliette go, if you go too.'

'Yeah, go on Poppy!' said Heidi again.

'How about it Pops. I really fancy it,' Roxanne added.

'OK, OK! Stop ganging up on me!' Poppy said, 'I'll come along, OK?' At last she was smiling.

I was right, she was quite attractive; even if she was on steroids.

'So Dave, do we all have to queue up?' asked Karl.

Huh, when I'd asked that, he'd called me a girl.

'I think we can get two tickets each,' Dave said.

'There, you can get them for us Karl!' said Heidi. 'Poppy, if you talk nicely to Mum about me and Juliette...'

'We'll see,' Poppy said, giving her little sister an affectionate pat on the arm.

'Yeah!' said Karl enthusiastically, 'And Tim, if Dave, Clarkey and I go up with Poppy and Roxanne, you don't need to come and queue either!'

'Er, no, that's alright - I can come too,' I said, 'I'm actually looking forward to it.'

9 - ...Inside My Head

The party was going brilliantly

Colin the DJ played some epic music; "Cars" by Gary Numan, "Fade to Grey" by Visage, "Going Undergound" by The Jam. That got all the boys dancing. Then, Dave, clearly trying to get me away from Roxanne, dragged me up to dance to "Rat Race" by The Specials. I say "dance" - more like "shuffle" - I felt really self - conscious. My feet wouldn't move properly.

All the girls were up and dancing. Deborah Castle put her handbag down on the floor. All the girls followed suit. Soon there was a small heap of PVC, around which the girls held hands and danced in a little circle.

Five minutes later, Colin dimmed the lights and started playing a slowie. It was Fern Kinney singing "Together We Are Beautiful". Roxanne and Poppy were sitting next to me. My heart started pounding. My mouth was dry.

"*Ask her, ask her,*" a voice in my head said.

"*Bugger off,*" replied another.

"*Chicken!*" the original voice taunted.

Right! I was going to ask her.

'Fancy a dance Roxanne?' Dave said, beating me to it.

Roxanne exchanged glances with Poppy, who was smirking like mad.

'Sorry, but I've already promised this dance.........to your friend Tim,' Roxanne said.

Lucky Bugger, I thought.

Hang on a minute, did she say "Tim"?

Roxanne smiled, taking me by the elbow.

Pinch me, I must be dreaming.

She dragged me onto the floor and put her arms around my shoulders. I was conscious of several sets of eyes watching us. I tried to ignore them by staring at the floor. I wasn't sure what to do with my hands. Static electricity seemed to be shooting up my arms as I put my hands on Roxanne's hips. A fire was breaking out in my jeans.

'He's definitely a bit pushy your mate isn't he?' Roxanne whispered.

Then she grabbed my wrists and placed my arms around her waist. Her perfume filled my nostrils and with her body pressed against me, my legs turned to jelly. I couldn't dance for toffee. We just sort of went around in little circles; a couple of times I stood on her toes. She didn't seem to mind. It was brilliant. Fern Kinney. She knew a thing or two. Together we were indeed Beautiful. I was praying it was the twelve inch version, but it seemed to be over all too quickly. Next up was Johnny Logan doing "What's Another Year" from the Eurovision Song Contest. A truly awful song. Normally I wouldn't be seen dead dancing to that. I went to move away, thinking that my 'turn' was over. I saw Dave waiting by the chairs. Roxanne pulled me back.

'Dance with me again. He'll get tired of waiting soon,' she said.

So, we danced for another blissful four minutes or so. I knew I'd never be able to hear Johnny Logan again without thinking of this moment. The song truly did stink for England but I didn't want it to ever end. When it did, something magic happened. For the briefest but most perfect moment, Roxanne kissed me full on the lips. It was such a brief kiss that for days after, I wondered if I'd imagined it.

'I need to sit down now Tim,' she said, 'my feet are really killing me.'

'Sorry about that,' I said, 'two left feet!'

She laughed. 'You need a bit of practice that's all.'

Michael Jackson was next; "She's Out of My Life". And as quickly as that, she was.

We walked back to the table, sat down and started talking to the others. I stood there, trying to be calm; my arms were trembling; I could still smell her scent on my T-Shirt. The room seemed to be spinning. What should I do now?

Dave was saying something to me but I didn't hear a word. I was staring at Roxanne. Had I just imagined the whole thing? And then, as I stood there like an idiot, staring at this beautiful girl, I saw Heidi Bloom stroll up to her and whisper in her ear.

Roxanne laughed and nodded.

I couldn't hear what they were saying over Michael Jackson - who like me apparently didn't know whether to laugh or cry.

Heidi came over and grabbed my hand, pulling me back onto the dance floor. I looked over at Roxanne but she was laughing at something Karl had said.

'Don't worry, lover-boy, she says it's OK!' Heidi said.

'What?'

'I asked Roxanne if she minded me dancing with her boyfriend. She said it was OK.'

'You asked what? Her what?'

Heidi giggled, wrapping her arms around my back; she couldn't reach my shoulders. Under normal circumstances I would never have danced with a fourth former in front of all my mates. It was asking for trouble; but at that moment, I didn't care at all. After all, if Roxanne didn't mind, why should I?

I must've danced with Heidi for the next three songs. It was all a bit of a blur. She was laughing and commenting on the songs. I wasn't concentrating on what she was saying though, especially when I noticed her brother dancing with Roxanne to Donna Summer.

"Oooh, I feel love, I feel love, I feel love" Donna sang.

I knew how she felt.

I was glad when Colin started playing "Y.M.C.A" and I could make my excuses and make a run for it. I noticed Karl, Poppy and Roxanne were doing the Village People dance, making the signs of the letters with their arms. So uncool.

Kevin Clarke sat down on the chair next to me; I think he was talking about the Grand Prix or something totally uninteresting. I wasn't really listening to what he was saying. I was too busy trying to catch Roxanne's eye as she sang along to Village People; laughing and joking with Poppy and Karl. She seemed to have forgotten I existed. Had that kiss meant nothing?

Then Dave came rushing over.

'Crikey Tim, you're mate ain't half getting some stick out there!' he laughed, gesturing towards the corridor.

'Uh? Who? Jacko?' I said.

In all the excitement, I'd completely forgotten about Jacko. I hadn't seen him since the others had arrived.

'No,' said Dave, picking up his can of Heineken, 'The other one. Chris Humphreys!'

'Humph? Who's giving him grief?'

'Alison. She's going mental!'

A small crowd had gathered in the corridor, watching the drama unfold.

Humph leant against the wall; looking annoyingly cool in a smart jacket and trousers; it was as near to a suit as I'd ever seen him wearing. Alison was standing in the middle of the corridor, staring daggers at him. Her arms were crossed across her chest. There were big smudges of black mascara around her cheeks, which reminded me of Chi-Chi The Panda. She'd been crying.

'So,' she was shouting, 'what's it to be? Staying here with me or going to Sherry's with your mates? Think very carefully before you answer Christopher!'

Humph rolled his eyes.

'Don't roll your eyes at me Christopher Humphreys!'

A couple of people giggled; someone gasped.

I inched my way through the gathering audience and stopped, standing a few feet from the action.

'I told you, I promised to meet Pete and Doddsy. It's Pete's birthday next week...'

'Next week? You just said it was today! Make your mind up!'

'He's away next week - so this is the only chance....'

'Yeah, that's right! It's your only chance - to stay going out with me!'

There were more stifled giggles.

'Look, piss off will you, you lot!?' Alison suddenly shouted, turning to face the crowd. A sob caught in her throat.

I had to intervene.

'Come on guys,' I said to the crowd,' give them a break will you; lets leave them to it eh?'

I started gently pushing people up the corridor, including Sara Potts, who looked like she'd been crying too. She helped me usher people back int the gym. I could still hear Alison and Humph.

'You're always doing this to me lately,' Alison said, 'it's not fair. It's my Christmas Party and you just want to go pissing it up with your bloody mates!'

Humph looked over in my direction; looking for support. I didn't want to take sides. Besides, frankly, I agreed with Alison; ever since he'd started to work for a living, he wasn't the same old Humph. It was like we'd already lost him and Alison was only just realising.

I shrugged my shoulders. What did he want me to say?

'Ruddy Hell Alison - it's only a kids party!' he said.

Really bad move; lighting the touch-paper without retiring.

'And what does that make me then? Just a kid I suppose? I'm only two bloody months younger than you, don't forget. Oh, but you're so bloody grown up now that you've got a proper job! That's it isn't it? You think your too adult to go out with a ...school-girl! You're ashamed of me aren't you?'

'Don't be so ridiculous. It's just...'

'It's just what Christopher?'

'It's just...well..this party's so.... boring. Everyone's talking about what happened today in Chemistry or which bloody book they're reading in English. It means nothing to me!'

'*I* mean nothing to you then, is that it?'

'I didn't say that Ali!'

'Don't *Ali* me! Go on, piss off and play with your grown up friends. I'm getting back to the kid's party. See you never Christopher!'

And with that, Alison stormed off past me; with a waft of perfume and the sound of stilettos clomping on the wooden floor.

I turned to Humph.

He shrugged, turning to walk away.

'Not staying then?'

'Better not eh?'

'Well, have a good evening then.'

'Yeah, you too.'

Back at the party, our table was unoccupied. It was nearly ten o'clock. The party was scheduled to finish at eleven. Things were hotting up. Colin was playing "Geno". The dance floor was crowded.

Legless by now, Karl and Dave were were pogoing around the dance-floor like maniacs. Poppy and Roxanne were dancing too, ignoring the boys even when they bumped into them for the third time. Heidi and Juliette had their arms around each others shoulders and were doing that weird kicking dance that the singer with The Skids does. Karl put his arm around Juliette's other shoulder - you couldn't blame him for trying - and soon a load of other kids had joined in and there was a whole chain of people kicking and singing along. Heidi spotted me and grabbed me, dragging me into the melee and before I knew it, I had one arm around Heidi's shoulder and I too was doing the punk can-can. Dave Booth linked arms with me. I saw Roxanne heading back to the table but I was surrounded on all sides; there was no escaping.

At about half ten, Colin Doyle announced it was time to slow things down again as we were coming to the end of "our allotted time together." A lot of couples started smooching; some of them looked like they were propping each other up, they looked so tired. Roxanne was still talking to Poppy. Karl finally asked Juliette to dance and by the time Dr. Hook got to the Chorus of "When You're in Love With A Beautiful Woman", Juliette had twice pushed his hand off her bottom.

'When you're in love with a beautiful woman, it's hard!' said Dave nudging me, as we watched Karl's attempts to get Juliette to kiss him.

'I can see that!' I said.

We laughed.

'Where's Jacko?' said Dave. Blimey, yeah, where *was* Jacko?

My sweaty T-shirt clung to my back in the chill night air. At least it wasn't raining. Hunting for Jacko, I bumped into Alison and Sara Potts. They were sitting on the steps between the gym and the canteen.

'He's just not worth it Ali,' I heard Sara saying.

She had her arm around Alison, who had her head down between her knees.

Alison was still crying. I stood behind them, wondering how to get past without disturbing them, when two drunk lads fell up the stairs, swigging from cans of Carlsberg. One of them almost tripped over the girls.

'Oh, Hi Alison!' he said. It was Graham Everett, who I knew from the football trials. He nudged his mate, William Gregory.

'Look Wills, it's Alison. I almost didn't recognise her!'

'Looks different with clothes on!' William Gregory replied, leering suggestively.

What? I was beginning to get a very uneasy feeling. There'd been a few very odd comments aimed at Alison tonight.

'Piss off you morons!' said Sara, sticking up for her friend.

Alison hadn't looked up.

Graham and William stumbled off towards the gym, sniggering and swaying as they went.

'What were they on about?' I heard Alison mumble, through her hair, which was hanging over her knees.

'No idea. Like you said, morons!' Sara said.

'What was that about looking different with clothes on?' Alison asked, tilting a wet cheek towards her friend.

'Juvenile boys and their fantasies, that's all,' Sara said.

I wasn't so sure. I kept remembering those photos. I was putting two and two together and I really didn't like it when it added up to four.

Navigating my way around them was impossible. They were smack bang in the middle of the stairway.

Sara spotted me as I tried to creep past.

'Alright Tim?' she asked.

'Hi,' I said.

Alison still didn't look up.

I smiled at Sara. 'Is she OK?' I mouthed.

Sara shrugged.

'Hey Alison,' I said, putting my hand on her bare shoulder.

She was freezing.

'I'm...really sorry about Humph.'

'Why?' Alison said, suddenly jerking her head up, shrugging my hand away. 'It's not your fault he's a selfish bastard!' Alison snapped.

'Well, no but sorry anyway,' I shrugged helplessly and spoke softly to Sara, 'have you seen Jacko?'

Sara pointed to the canteen block at the bottom of the stairs.

'Last seen investigating the contents of Fay Carpenter's blouse,' she whispered.

'OK, right, thanks,' I sniggered.

'They're all the bloody same - just after one thing,' muttered Alison. She didn't look up.

I shrugged again at Sara.

She jerked her thumb down the stairs. 'Go on, he might need rescuing from Fay. The quiet ones are the worst.'

'OK, cheers, see you both later.'

Jacko and Fay were snogging each others faces off, leaning against the drinks machine in the canteen lobby. They were totally oblivious to me. I was within a couple of feet of them and could hear them slurping and groaning. I thought about interrupting but I didn't think Jacko would be too pleased.

Well, at least *he'd* had a good night.

I left them to it. No doubt, Jacko would be giving me a blow-by-blow account next time I saw him. Besides I had more pressing matters to attend to.

I'd had a few too many. I felt stupidly careless.

'Right Tim, get up there and be a man!' I told myself.

I would go back up there, ask Roxanne to dance and finish what I'd started; or at least what Roxanne had started. But as I walked through the door to reception, I was ambushed by Alison.

'Oh, Tim!' she sobbed, appearing from behind the door and throwing her arms around me. 'I'm really sorry I was horrible earlier!' she spluttered through her tears. My nose was assaulted by a cocktail of perfume, fags and Pernod. Her arms were were covered in goose-pimples.

'Er, that's OK,' I said.

'I didn't lean on your shed,' she seemed to be saying as she buried her head in my shoulder.

'My shed?'

'What?'

'What was that about my shed. What shed?'

Alison pulled her head back. She looked at me as if I was mental. 'I said "I didn't mean what I said", you idiot!' she laughed, wiping a tear away from her cheek. Her hands were black, covered with mascara. I glanced down. There was a huge black smudge all over the top of my clean white t-shirt. Bruce Foxton's head had disappeared.

'I know all blokes are not the same really,' she said, putting one black hand on my cheek, 'I just wish there were more boys like you.'

'Er..no..well...er....'

Her lips were on mine before I could say "thank you very much." Her mouth was cold and damp and tasted like burnt liquorice. I'd never been very fond of liquorice - I'd once been very ill after eating half a hundred-weight of Bassetts' Allsorts at my Namps' place in Wales.

Instinctively, I pushed her away. She looked puzzled; offended. She pulled my head back and started kissing me again. Despite the unpleasant taste of liquorice, this time I started to respond; I was only human after all. But even as I probed her mouth with my tongue, I felt awful. This was wrong. I was no idiot - as soon as she sobered up, Alison would regret this - and so would I. So, I pushed her away again.

'Stop! Alison, stop it ,OK?'

We were standing below one of the big arched windows - the one with the angel stencil - the artist wasn't great - it's wings looked as if they were dropping off. A fallen angel.

'But, I thought you liked me?' she said, moving in for another assault. 'You *do* like me don't you Tim?' she said in a very sleazy drunken drool; a poor impersonation of some cheap-hooker from an American cop show.

'Of course I like you...' I had a sudden vision of her topless on a Florida beach. I gulped. Was I mad? I was pushing her off!

'Well,' she pulled my head back for a third round, 'I'm single now, so what's stopping you?'

Then I heard someone clearing their throat behind me, followed by muffled laughter. Startled, I pushed Alison aside. We had an audience; consisting of Roxanne, Poppy and half a dozen Upper-Sixth formers.

'Blimey Tim. Girls just throw themselves at you!' said Poppy, 'what's your secret?'

The upper-sixth formers all laughed.

Only Roxanne said nothing.

'Come on then guys, let's be off, shall we?' Poppy said, turning to the others.

'Where are you off to?' I said.

'Sherry's,' said one of the lads.

'We were coming to find you to invite you along,' Poppy sniggered, 'but it looks like you're busy.'

'But...I could..,' actually I wasn't sure *what* I could do, but as it happened I never got the chance to finish my sentence anyway.

'He'd never get in dressed like that anyway,' said Paige Nelson, an upper-sixth former with Dallas shoulder pads and a Sue Ellen attitude. She looked down her long nose at me as they all walked past.

'That'll stain,' Roxanne said, pointing to my smudged t-shirt. Alison was still lolling against my shoulder.

'See you tomorrow then?' I said to Roxanne's retreating back.

She didn't turn around.

I took a couple of steps after her, 'see you tomorrow?' I tried again, 'you know, to queue for tickets?'

She didn't turn around. The door swung shut behind her and she was gone.

'Bloody hell Alison...' I said. But Alison was gone too. Back to the party I guessed.

'Great night's work Tim,' I said to myself.

As Clarkey and I walked out into the cold night air, fifteen minutes later, I heard a voice behind us.

'Hey, do you need a lift?' It was Heidi Bloom. Her cheeks were really pink, her eyes twinkling.

Juliette came up beside her, closely followed by Karl, who was wearing a face like a slapped arse. I guessed I wasn't the only one whose night hadn't turned out as planned.

'That would be great,' Clarkey said.

'Oh, right,' Heidi replied, suddenly noticing Clarkey, 'well I suppose we might be able to squeeze you both in. How about you Tim?'.

'Well, I suppose...'

'Great. My Mum's picking us all up. She'll be here in a second. I'm sure she'd drop you off en-route,' Heidi said.

'It's a bit out of the way,' I started to say.

'Thanks!' said Clarkey.

'Good idea,' said Karl. 'It'll be a tight fit though, one of you girls will have to sit on a lap,' Karl smiled at Juliette - she blushed.

Mrs Bloom arrived a couple of minutes later. She pulled up and wound down her window. 'Did you have good time love?' she asked Juliette, 'sit up front and tell me all about it.'

Karl's face dropped.

And that's how I came to travel home with Heidi Bloom perched on my lap.

'Behave yourself with that nice young man Heidi!' joked Mrs Bloom, looking in her rear-view mirror.

'Mummm! Shut up will you?' Heidi giggled, pulling a face. I felt her dig her fingers into my thigh. I gulped, smiling back at Heidi's Mum.

Heidi and Juliette gave Mrs Bloom a full account of their evening - laughing and giggling - Heidi fidgeting and shifting on my lap. I really liked Heidi Bloom. I mean, *really* liked her. But she was far too young. 'She's only fifteen, she's only fifteen', I kept saying to myself. Still, she was far less complicated than Roxanne or Alison.

Karl sulked all the way home and Clarkey fell asleep, his head nodding against the window.

Heidi left her hand on my leg the whole way home.

'Here we are then, Derwent Close!' said Mrs Bloom, 'That'll be three pounds please,' she said, holding out her hand.

110

I hesitated, wondering how much money I had on me.

'She's pulling your leg,' smiled Heidi, pushing open the back door and clambering out - not before giving my thigh one last squeeze.

'Goodnight young man.' I heard Mrs Bloom say, as I climbed out.

'See you Tim!' said a chorus of voices.

'Bye Tim, see you at school,' giggled Heidi, standing on tip-toe and kissing me on the cheek.

Someone wolf-whistled.

'Put him down Heidi!' Karl said.

The boys laughed.

'Heidi, get in the car - now!' said Mrs Bloom, 'and leave that poor boy alone!'

'Mummm!' Heidi said, climbing back into the car, 'shut up will you?'

I was glad to get to my bed. I'd drunk too much and my legs ached from dancing and from being cramped up in the back of the Bloom's Cortina. I didn't have the energy to undress, and my head was buzzing. The voices inside my head were having a field day.

"Roxanne kissed you, that must mean something,"

"But then she saw you with Alison, you blew it"

"And what about Alison - you missed a chance there boy. You Muppett!"

"Nah, she doesn't really like me, she was just feeling sorry for herself,"

"And what about Heidi Bloom?"

"Too young, much too young."

"Rubbish, she's only two years younger and it was nice having her sat on your lap wasn't it?"

'Oh shut up will you? Shut up!!' I said out loud.

The voices didn't shut up for ages though and it was the early hours before I finally fell asleep.

10 - Visions Of The Night

Thud Thud Thud.

I woke with a start. My head was throbbing and my mouth was as dry as a lizard's armpit. I was lying on the bed, still wearing my party clothes. They say a fox can't smell it's own den; well I could certainly smell mine. Lager, cigarette smoke and old perfume, which could have been either Roxanne's, Alison's or Heidi's but was most likely a bouquet of all three. What a tart I was.

Thud Thud Thud.

That noise again, it wasn't just inside my head.

'Timothy! Phone! Can you hear me?' Mum shouted from the landing, as she pounded on my door.

'OK. OK,' I groaned, glancing at the clock. Eleven o'clock. Bloody hell - how had that happened?

'Tim?' said the female voice on the end of the phone.

I was barely awake; I wiped sleep from my eyes and cradled my aching head in my free hand.

'Yeah?'

'Tim. Hi, it's me, Alison,'

Bloody hell - why was Alison ringing me at the crack of dawn?

'Hi, Alison..'

'Tim, I'm really sorry about last night. I was really out of it.' Her voice was croaky, 'I'm sorry if I...you know....showed myself up.'

'That's OK...I understood...'

'I'm such a mess. I don't know what to do about Humph. It feels like I'm losing him..,' she barely got the last word out before she started to sob again.

'I'm sure you'll get back together,' I said.

'Do you think so?' she sniffed into the receiver.

'Of course. Don't you always?' the last word was barely out of my mouth before I was regretting it.

'What do you mean *always?'*

'Well, I mean, it's not the first time....'

'We've never split up before!'

Only a million times.

'Well, no, but you've had.....disagreements, haven't you?'

112

'And who's fault is that?"

'I wasn't blaming you...or Humph..' Bloody hell, how had I got myself into this? I felt lousy as it was; this was the last thing I needed.

'Look Alison, why don't you just call him?'

'I'm not calling him....he should call me!' she sobbed, 'he's the one who needs to apologise.'

This was going nowhere fast and I was desperate for the loo.

'Look Alison, I'm really sorry but I've got to go...I'm meant to be taking the dog out - he's going bananas here,' I improvised.

'Are you going over the park? Can we meet up for a chat?'

Bugger.

'Yeah, of course, why not?'

Alison talked at me for over an hour.

'Humph this, Humph that.'

She kept apologising for throwing herself at me and thanking me for not taking advantage. Actually, I was quite proud of myself for that too.

The park was empty. It was a cold, windy day. We were sat on a bench, whilst Chalky ran around on the grass. I kept having to get up to throw his ball for him - each time, Alison carried on talking about her and Humph; by the half hour point, I was barely listening.

'Look, do you want me to talk to him?' I said at one point. I was instantly shot down in flames.

'Don't you dare! I don't want him to know that I'm bothered!'

'But isn't that kind of the point?'

'Of course not. If he cares about me, he'll call and apologise.'

'He may be on the phone right now; perhaps you should head off....'

I was feeling like death warmed up; I had hardly had time to wash and my chin was covered in little zits. I didn't want to appear uncharitable but frankly, sitting there, on a bench, in the freezing cold, listening to her prattle on and on, was just about the last place I wanted to be at that precise moment.

'Good, I'll make him wait - let him sweat it out for once!' she said, with a grin.

Even though she'd apparently had a sleepless night, and despite wearing no make up, she was so irritatingly pretty. She patted me on the hand and said thanks yet again "for being such a good friend" and then she kissed me on the cheek. I felt really guilty for wanting to go home.

After a while, we started walking back in the direction of the gate.

'Can I ask you something?' Alison said.

'Yes, I really do think you and Humph will get....' I started to say.

'No, not that; something else.'

'Sure, what?' I said, grabbing the dog by the collar, so I could put his leash back on.

'I know I was pretty out of it last night, but did you hear some of the boys making odd comments to me?'

'How do you mean, odd? What lads?' I said, slightly uneasily; sensing what might be coming.

'Weird stuff. That Graham Everett and Wills whats-his-face for example.'

'Gregory?'

'Yeah that's him. When I was sitting on the stairs with Sara. They said something about me "looking different with my clothes on."'

'Are you sure?'

'Yeah, Sara heard them too.'

Yeah, so did I.

'Really? That *is* weird.'

'Yeah it is. And all evening, other boys kept asking me if I'd had a good holiday and talking about my tan and stuff.'

'Well, what's so odd about that?'

'I got back three months ago!'

'So? Your tan did last pretty well.'

'Yeah, but I've been thinking....'

So had I.

'...about my holiday photos. You know, when they got lost?'

Yeah, I'd been thinking exactly the same thing.

'You don't suppose it was one of those lads that found them, do you?'

'Nah!'

'Well, how else do you explain it?'

'I dunno', maybe they just saw you in your swimming cozzie, in the school pool or somewhere.'

'I haven't used the school pool all year. It's scummy!'

She wasn't wrong.

'God,' she said, 'I'm really worried now. It fits doesn't it?'

114

'No, you're just being over-sensitive.' I said.

'Do you think?'

'Yeah, of course. I'm sure there's a perfectly reasonable explanation.

And I was sure there was. I just had a horrible feeling it might well be the one she'd just mentioned.

'Ok, thanks Tim, you're a star,' she said.

We'd reached the gate.

'I don't suppose...' she said, 'no, that's a bad idea.'

'What is?'

'Oh hell, why not?' she said. 'Do you fancy coming around to watch a video tonight. Mum and Dad are going to the Theatre. I could really do with some company.'

Oh God. Was Alison Fisher actually coming on to me? My heart was jumping like a pneumatic drill under my rib-cage.

'Er, I'm really sorry Alison, I can't.....'

'Oh, sorry, right, I don't blame you,' she said, looking miserable, 'after what happened last night...'

'No really, I can't Alison - I'm going up to London with Dave Booth and the others,' I said, realising that I still hadn't broken that particular piece of news to Mum and Dad yet.

'Really? What for?' she said excitedly.

I told her the whole story of our plans to queue up for Police tickets.

'Cool!' she said, 'when are they on?'

And that's how Alison ended up coming with us to London.

Mum and Dad had amazed me - when I'd casually mentioned queueing overnight, Dad didn't seem at all bothered. Even Mum was pretty easy-going. She barely batted an eyelid.

'So, there are a whole bunch of you going?'

'Yes Mum, I said,'

'And you'll all be staying together?'

'Yes Mum.'

'And you'll take your father's sleeping bag?'

'And you'll wrap up warm and take the flask of hot soup and some food'

'And you won't get drunk and do anything silly?'

'And you'll be back by Sunday afternoon for dinner?'

115

By Mum's standards, that was her barely batting an eyelid.

'Clarkey's not coming,' announced Karl as we waited by the ticket office at Brighton station. 'The little ginger sod's gone and got chicken pox. If he's given it to me I'll bloody kill him,' he added sympathetically.

'Bummer. Poor Clarkey,' I said. 'I've got some news for you too....'

'Yeah?'

And before I could speak, right on cue, Alison walked onto the concourse, accompanied by Dave Booth.

'Look who I bumped into on the bus!' said Dave cheerfully, 'Alison's coming with us, isn't that great?' he gushed, putting his arm around Alison's shoulder. She beamed one of her mega smiles - like a five hundred watt bulb. Well at least Dave was happy with the idea. He and Alison went off to get their train tickets.

'You dark horse!' Karl whispered to me, 'Good on you. Bloody hell - Alison Fisher eh?'

'Shhhh! It's not like that!'

'Yeah right, pull the other one! Get in there my son! Mind you, you'd better keep an eye on Dave though; he's fancied her for years.'

Well, knock me down with a feather, who would have guessed?

'So, does that mean you've given up on Roxanne?'

'I think I might have blown it there,' I said, 'I'll be pretty surprised if she turns up.'

'Ah well, Alison Fisher's pretty good compensation!'

'Karl, it isn't like that. She's not into me!'

'Are you sure? The way I heard it, she was pretty into you last night!'

We waited what seemed like an age. Then, as I'd just about given up on them, Poppy and Roxanne came jogging up the steps from Trafalgar Street. There were about two minutes to spare, before out train to Victoria was leaving.

'Sorry everyone,' panted Poppy, panting. Her chest wobbled up and down like fun-size space-hoppers. 'Roxanne's Mum's fault - bloody old banger's useless.'

'That's no way to talk about my mother!' laughed Roxanne. She seemed happy; relaxed. Then she noticed Alison. 'Oh how nice Tim, you've brought your friend from the party.'

'Hi, I'm Alison,' Alison said, holding out her hand, ignoring the edge in Roxanne's tone.

'Hello, I'm Roxanne.'

'Oh really, Tim's...er...friend from HMV? Excellent, I'm so glad to meet you after all this time.'

Roxanne looked puzzled. 'After all what time?'

' ...and this is Poppy...' I said, quickly changing the subject, 'Karl's sister.'

'Oh hi!' said Alison 'yeah, I can see the resemblance.'

Roxanne looked at me and then at Alison, 'so, did you enjoy yourselves last night?'

Karl sniggered.

Alison blushed.

'I was a bit drunk,' said Alison, 'I'd just split up with my boyfriend.'

'Alison's going out with my friend Humph,' I was keen to point out.

'That's *was*, Tim - was!' Alison said.

The journey up was frustrating. I didn't get to speak to Roxanne at all. I wanted to set the record straight about Alison; to gauge whether I was still in with a shout. The Victoria train was jam-packed with day-trippers, making their way back from Brighton. We were just in time to hear the guard blow his whistle. When we clambered on, there was only one double seat left. Roxanne was first on. She grabbed the seat and Poppy sat with her. Dave grabbed a seat across the aisle from them and Alison sat opposite Dave. Karl and I had to stand until Haywards Heath and when we did eventually get to sit down, we were sitting with our backs to the others. I could hear Dave flirting with Alison. I only caught snippets of their conversation.

'Odd comments? What sort of odd comments?' I heard Dave say at one point.

I craned my neck trying to hear but Alison was whispering.

'Why is that so odd? You did go on holiday...' I heard Dave say. '....really, was it that long ago?......really, what an odd thing to say........well, Sara's right, they probably were just fantasising. Take it as a compliment.'

After a while Dave went quiet; all I could hear was Alison talking...and talking....and talking... about her and Humph. Served him right. Still, if Roxanne was listening, she'd surely know there was nothing going on between me and Alison?

The tube was no better than the train; we were crammed in like sardines. We had to change at Green Park and crowd onto another train to Piccadilly Circus - fortunately it was only one stop and soon we were all walking up Shaftesbury Avenue.

London was amazing. It was enormous; there were hundreds, no thousands, of people milling about, heading for the restaurants and theatres.

'Crikey, look at that queue!' said Karl, 'I'm glad I'm not going to that show!'

'Er, I hate to say this mate,' said Dave, 'but I think that's our queue. People don't queue for a theatre on a Saturday night with sleeping bags and ghetto blasters.'

He was right. It wasn't even eight o'clock and there was already an enormous queue of people camped out on the pavement. The ticket office didn't open until ten the next morning. People had pillows, sleeping bags, garden chairs and in some cases, even foldaway tables and picnic baskets. I heard at least three different Police songs playing simultaneously from various cassette players. The queue snaked out of sight, around a far distant corner.

'Bloody hell!' said Karl, 'I didn't realise they'd be this popular!'

'Could be something to do with the number one hits and platinum selling albums?' I suggested sarcastically.

We searched for the end of the queue, walking around the first corner, a second and a third, eventually heading back on ourselves, down a street which ran parallel to Shaftesbury Avenue. I felt suddenly panicky.

'Do you think we'll all get tickets?' I asked.

I was doing the maths. Five thousand tickets for sale, limited to two per person - that mean there only had to be two and half thousand people and we'd miss out.

'Why didn't we come earlier?' I said.

'Relax Tim, there's more than enough to go around,' Alison said.

118

'How do you know though, have you counted all the people in the queue?'

'Yeah Alison - why don't you just do that?' laughed Dave, showing off as usual, 'let's go and do a headcount eh?'

'Well, we're certainly going to have enough time!' Roxanne said, putting her bags down on the pavement, 'come on everyone, we might as well settle in for the night.'

'Hey,' whispered Karl, 'fancy spending the night with Roxanne eh?'

'Yeah, not quite what I had in mind.'

The pavement was cold and uncomfortable. After less than an hour or so, my back and legs were already killing me. We were sitting in twos; Roxanne and Poppy up front, me and Karl behind and Dave and Alison behind us. Someone near us was playing The Police hit "The Bed's Too Big Without You" on their ghetto-blaster. I would have killed for a bed at that moment. Karl and I took it in turns to lean against the wall. He and Dave had bought carrier bags full of lager and crisps. They really took the piss when I got out Mum's flask of hot soup and my bag of sandwiches.

'Blimey Tim, you're so molly-coddled!' said Dave.

'Such a Mummy's Boy!' added Karl.

Mind you, I noticed both of them were keen enough for a sip of soup when I offered it around.

Although we were all chatting away and having a bit of a laugh, I couldn't really get to talk to Roxanne properly. I was still puzzling over that kiss at the party. Had it meant anything or was Roxanne, like Alison, just a bit drunk? Soon, however, I had more pressing matters on my mind.

'Bugger, I really need the loo,' I said.

It was half past nine.

'Yeah me too,' said Roxanne.

Everyone said they wanted to go too.

'Where are we going to find a loo around here?' Poppy groaned.

'Well, we can't all go,' said Dave, 'we'll lose our places in the queue.'

'Come on Tim,' said Roxanne, 'let's see if we can find somewhere. You'll keep the pavement warm for us won't you guys?'

119

Roxanne and I walked the length of Shaftesbury Avenue, past theatre-goers and endless lines of Police fans. There was a real buzz in the air. We made small talk as we went but I was still no clearer as to whether I had any real chance with this sexy, older girl or whether she was just humouring me.

We'd almost completed the block; there were no obvious loos or signs for public toilets anywhere.

'Well I don't know about you Tim but I'm going to wet myself if we don't find one in a minute!'

'Yeah, me too,' I agreed. I felt numb with cold and the pressure on my bladder was unbearable.

'Come on,' she said pointing to a busy, and expensive, looking Italian restaurant, 'let's have a pizza. We don't need to tell the others. We can use their loos and warm up at the same time.'

'Er, I'd love to Roxanne, but the thing is, I'm skint,' I said, feeling incredibly inadequate.

'Well, I got paid yesterday, so it's my treat!'

We had to wait to be seated, which seemed to take ages. Roxanne smiled at the Italian waiter and asked if she could use the loo. The young Italian - far too good looking for my liking - gave her a personal escort to the WC's, flirting and joking with her as he walked. Flash Italian git.

Eventually, we were shown to a seat in a corner and I made my excuses and finally went off to relieve myself. When I returned to the table, the smarmy waiter was hovering.

'...And garlic bread for two to start,' I heard Roxanne say.

'Grazie - and will there be anything else for the Signorina?'

'We'll just check the menu,' Roxane smiled.

'Of course!' The waiter flashed his perfect white teeth, before disappearing into the kitchen.

'Pretty boy,' I muttered, opening a cellophane-wrapped bread-stick and hungrily devouring a mouthful.

'You're not jealous are you Tim?' Roxanne smiled.

'A starter?' I said, trying to ignore the comment but more than slightly aware of my burning cheeks, 'but shouldn't we be getting back soon?'

'Why? They're not going anywhere in a hurry are they? Anyone would think you didn't want to spend time with me.'

'No, not at all....'

'Or is just the lovely Alison you want to get back to. Don't trust her with David - is that it?'

'You're not jealous are you Roxanne?' I said, suddenly feeling braver.

'Touche good sir!' she laughed, 'no, you've no cause for concern there, Dave's a nice enough lad but he's not my type *at all*! He's far too sure of himself that one!'

'Ha ha!' I smiled, 'that's not what I meant. There really is nothing going on between Alison and me.'

'That's not how it looked last night.'

'Alison was just drunk.'

'You didn't seem to be exactly fighting her off!'

'But I did!'

'Took you a while though eh?'

What could I say? There was an embarrassing pause. The waiter strolled past with a tray of drinks in his hands. He smiled at Roxanne. She smiled back.

'So, if Dave isn't your type, who is?' I said, 'that flash Italian git with the Bee Gees teeth?'

'Well, that's for me to know and for you to find out!' she smiled.

The garlic bread arrived with a wink from lover-boy and two large glasses of lager.

'Do all Italians love themselves that much?' I said, the garlic running down my chin.

Roxanne laughed out loud, 'Relax, he's not my type OK?'

I smiled. Things were going well.

'So tell me about yourself Mr Tim...Hey, I don't even know your surname!'

So, I told Roxanne all there was to know of interest about the one and only Tim James. It took all of two minutes.

'So, you fancy some sort of journalism? Well good for you! Most people your age don't know what the hell they want to do!'

"Your age?" What was she, my Mum or something? Still, I didn't want to rock the boat, so I let it pass - almost.

'And what about you? You know, what with the benefit of your advanced years - what do you want to do?'

'Cheeky!' she said, laughing and flicking a large piece of bread-stick in my general direction. Then she told me about herself.

Roxanne Delaney was eighteen and three quarters (not nineteen yet, which for some reason I was insanely happy about - after all she wasn't even two full years older than me!). She was from Surrey (very posh!) and she had two brothers. She explained that she was taking a year off. She was intending to go to University in September.

'So, your on your crack year then?'

'Crack year?' she guffawed, 'I think you mean gap year!'

'That's it Gap year!'

Had I really just called it a "crack year"? What a total dingbat.

'Yeah, Sussex is one of the Uni's I'm going to apply to....'

Brilliant.

'Either that or Bristol, or Leeds, or maybe even Edinburgh.'

Knickers.

'So, did you come down to Brighton to suss it out then?'

'Not exactly.'

'How do you mean?'

She looked embarrassed.

'Well, if you must know, I was kind of...escaping.'

'Escaping what?

'Not so much a "what",' she said, 'more a "who"'. Her smile had disappeared

'Oh...'

'A fifteen stone, six feet three, rugby playing, two-timing, prattish bastard of a "who" called Robert actually.' Her mouth smiled, her eyes didn't.

'Oops, sorry.'

'Well, it's worked out OK. I'm sharing a pad with my friend Jackie, who's never there - she's engaged to a copper from Haywards Heath - and I like working at HMV. Brighton's a brilliant place and I've made shed-loads of good mates like Poppy....and..,' she smiled, 'it turns out I don't need him anyway. Cheers!' she raised her glass.

The pizzas arrived a few minutes later. We wolfed them down without saying too much more. Roxanne had gone all quiet on me. It had been going so well. I had to go and ask, didn't I?

It was when we were walking back to the others in the queue that she suddenly asked me an odd question.

'So, these big plans to go to Uni and become a journalist; where does the lovely Alison figure?'

'Uh?'

'Relationships often don't survive that sort of separation you know.'

Relationship? What relationship?

'Er, I told you. I think you've got the wrong end of the stick Roxanne, there is no relationship. Like she said, Alison goes out with, or at least was, going out with my best friend!'

'*Was* Tim, *was.*' Roxanne smiled knowingly, 'I think she has moved on. I think she's got you firmly in her sights!' she giggled.

'Rubbish!'

'So, let me get this straight; she's all over you like a rash at the party; she's never particularly been into The Police before, yet she drops everything and travels all the way up here with you, and yet she's not interested in you?'

'Huh, I wish....' I spluttered, 'that is....I mean...she's never been...'

'That's OK, I wouldn't blame you if you *did* wish, she's an absolute stunner isn't she?'

'Well, yeah she's OK.....'

'OK? She's a beautiful girl. And she's got her eyes on you my little friend!' Roxanne teased.

'I really don't think so.'

We rounded the corner and saw Dave and Alison up ahead in the queue. Dave was clearly laying on the charm; Alison was laughing like mad and tossing her blonde hair over her shoulders. The way things were going, Dave would be passing Kevin Clarke another note to deliver before long.

'See,' I said, 'she's more interested in Dave than me!' I said.

'We'll see,' said Roxanne, still smirking.

'Listen, I'm telling you; Alison Fisher is not interested in me!'

Roxanne just smiled. We walked towards the end of the queue.

'We know what you've been up to!' shouted Dave, as we walked along, causing the whole queue, including several wannabe-Sting-lookalikes, to turn around and gawp at us.

I ignored him.

'Where are the Blooms?'

'Gone to find the loo, like you did an hour ago!' said Alison. She sounded angry.

Roxanne looked at me and raised her eyebrows.

She was wrong. Alison was not interested in me.

123

By midnight, the temperature had dropped. It was so cold.

'If I had tits, I'd be freezing them off!' said Dave, as he shuffled his feet.

'If you had tits, I'd be warming my hands up on them!' Karl said.

'Karl Bloom!' said Poppy, 'I shall be having a word with mother when we get home. You're disgusting!'

The girls all laughed though.

Dave was hardly dressed appropriately in his jeans, sweatshirt and denim jacket. Karl was no better in his jeans, thin jumper and leather bomber jacket. Neither of them had brought sleeping bags along. Surprise surprise.

The girls were already in their sleeping bags and I expected some abuse from the boys as I unrolled mine. Instead, Dave asked if he could get in with me.

'Sod off you bender!' I laughed.

'Aw, go on Tim, it's brass monkeys out here!' said Dave.

'Aw go on Tim, I'm so cold, let me cuddle up to you....I promise I won't get a stiffy,' said Karl, mocking Dave.

Dave gave him a two fingered salute. Then, he turned to Alison - I knew what was coming.

'Alison..,' Dave started to say.

'No way!' she said.

'Bloody hell, I could freeze to death out here!'

There was little chance of getting any sleep; people were talking excitedly; the music of The Police drifted along the frosty pavements. By about two o'clock, it was seriously cold and things were starting to quieten down a little, although new people kept joining the ever-lengthening queue. Clubbers were making their way home, some of them curious, as they stumbled past.

'What you lot queueing for?' was a common question; the reply provoked various comments and abuse.

Poppy was the only one sleeping; we could hear snoring coming from her bag. Dave was still complaining about the cold, shivering and chattering his teeth for effect. Even Karl was starting to stamp up and down; rubbing his arms and legs.

'Jesus I'm so coooooooold!' said Dave, 'come on Tim, can't I borrow your bag for half an hour, just to warm up?'

'Oh bloody hell David, I'm trying to sleep here!' said Alison. She undid her zip and started to pull her bag down over her legs. 'Here, come on, if it's the only thing that will shut you up, you can have my bag!'

Dave looked gobsmacked. He looked from me, to Karl and then to Alison and then broke into a huge smile.

'Great,' he said, 'I won't fidget too much!' he said.

'Fidget all you like, I'm not getting in with you!' said Alison. She leant down and started to undo the zip on my bag, 'Right Tim, budge up, I'm getting in with you!'

'Uh?'

'Come on, if I've got to share with one of you, you're the only one I trust, move over!' and with that, Alison Fisher, the girl of my teenage dreams, climbed into my sleeping bag.

'Woooo-ooooo!' yelped Karl, 'Behave yourself in there you two!'

Dave stood half-in Alison's sleeping bag, half out. He looked stunned.

Karl's hollering had woken his sister. I could just make out Roxanne's face in the pale lamplight. They both looked at me, then looked at each other and smiled. One of them snorted, before they both laid their heads back down and closed their eyes. I stared at the back of Roxanne's head, wondering what she was thinking. Alison pushed herself down in the bag, slipping her arms around my waist, her warm stomach resting against my back. Two small mounds pressed against my shoulder blades. A picture of her lying topless on a beach came into my head. Ruddy hell.

'Thanks Tim, at least that should shut Boothie up for ten minutes,' she whispered. She rested her head on the back of my neck, her warm breath blowing down the back of my shirt. I laid there absolutely rigid - and not in a good way.

I didn't get much sleep. That bag wasn't designed for two. Alison didn't seem to mind though. She hardly moved at all. I think she fell asleep pretty quickly and after a while, I became less aware of the contours of her body pressing against me. I didn't know whether to laugh or cry. Part of me - and not just the predictable part - was loving every minute of this. Another part of me cursed. Why now? Once again, Alison had demonstrated lousy timing. What was she playing at? It did feel good though - feeling her pressed up against me. I prayed I wouldn't show signs of enjoying it too much though. I was terrified of moving - there was no way I was going to turn and face Alison, put it that way. I could hear Sting singing "Bring On The

Night" on a cassette player a few yards away. 'No mate,' I thought. Bring on the morning.

There was an enormous sense of anticipation as people started stirring from their bags. Fortunately, thanks to my determination to face away from Alison all night, the anticipation was the only thing that had become enormous. All I had to thank for my efforts were a very dead left arm and a frosty reception from Roxanne.

'Sleep OK?' I said to her, when she finally turned around and opened her eyes, to find me staring at her from a matter of inches away.

'Not bad, better than you I should think?'

At last, Alison started to stir too and I felt her turn around, so that her bum was pressed against mine.

'Morning Alison!' I heard Dave say brightly, 'I hope that pervert didn't try anything on last night!'

'So what if he did?' she said.

'I didn't!'

'No, you were the perfect gentleman!' said Alison.

'More's the pity eh Ali?' said Poppy.

The girls all giggled. Roxanne gave me a funny look.

'He's such a bender!' I heard Dave say to Karl.

I turned over, trying to ignore the fact that Alison's bottom was now dangerously close to my crotch.

'Look at these two, Tim,' Alison said, sniggering.

I raised my head. Karl and Dave were both now in Alison's bag.

'So when are you two announcing your engagement?' I said.

'He was a good shag actually!' said Karl.

'Yeah, but my arse ain't half sore this morning!' laughed Dave.

'Oh, gross!' I heard Poppy say.

'Euuucch! Not in my sleeping bag!' Alison added.

'Such benders!' I said.

As ten o'clock approached, the excitement mounted. I was tired but buzzy; I'd be seeing The Police in just seven days time. Everyone was checking their watches; except the girls of course who were too busy re-applying their make-up. There was a loud cheer signifying the ticket office was open and soon we were picking up our stuff and shuffling

126

forward. It seemed to take ages for us to get to the front; well over an hour.

'Look at that queue. It goes on forever!' I said.

'There can't be enough tickets to go around,' Dave speculated.

'Not if everyone gets two each,' I said, trying to convince myself, as much as him.

'The touts will have a field day!' Karl said, yawning and stamping his feet.

'Hey, we should get two each; we can sell the spare ones on the night – we'll make a killing!' Dave beamed.

'Er, excuse me, but where are we meant to get the extra money to buy them in the first place?' asked Karl, echoing my own thoughts.

'Yeah. Fivers don't exactly grow on trees Dave!' I said.

'Well, I've got a tenner - I'm getting two!' Dave said.

'You do that,' I said, 'I owe Jacko as it is, I'm going to be paying him back for weeks.'

'But that's just it – if you get a spare ticket, you can sell it on the night – you'll probably get twenty quid for it!'

'Really? You think?'

'Yeah, there's always buyers on the night – how do you think the touts earn their money?'

'I'll lend you a fiver,' said Alison, 'it's the least I can do after you letting me share your sleeping bag!'

'Blimey!' laughed Dave, 'She's paying him to sleep with her now!'

'Oh, you're so funny!' said Alison.

'Yep – my mouth – the home of comedy!' said Dave proudly.

'Funny,' said Alison, 'I thought that was your pants.'

And so it was, that I found myself with two tickets to see The Police and indebted to both Jacko and Alison to the tune of five pounds each. Dave Booth had better be sodding right about touting, otherwise I would be skint until Easter.

We were completely knackered by the time we boarded the train home from Victoria.

Alison instantly fell asleep with her head on my shoulder, to the sound of much tittering from Poppy and various rude gestures from the boys. Only Roxanne said nothing. She leant her head on the window and by the time we were at Clapham Junction, she was asleep. We all followed suit by East Croydon and it was only at Brighton that I came

to, with a sore shoulder and muscle cramps. But we had the tickets. I
was on my way to see The Police.

That evening, I went straight to bed after watching The Muppets
and eating my sunday tea of cheese on toast. Maybe it was the cheese
that did it but that night I had a weird dream. I was sharing a very
crowded sleeping bag with Alison, Roxanne, Heidi Bloom, Stacey
Groves, Daisy Duke from the Dukes of Hazzard and all three singers
in the Three Degrees.

I woke up feeling incredibly stiff.

11 - Bring On The Night

Outlandos D'Amour. Regatta De Blanc. Zenyatta Mandatta.

The week of the gig, I played them all to death. I couldn't wait for the weekend. Bring on the night.

It was just as well it was the last week of term, I couldn't concentrate on my studies. In the common room, the gig was our only topic of conversation; thankfully, replacing the previous week's gossip about who'd got off with who at the Christmas party. The only downer was that Clarkey was still poorly with the pox. It didn't look like he would make it. And then on the Thursday, things started to go really tits-up. Karl wasn't in school. Dave Booth phoned me that evening.

'It's official, Karl's got Chicken pox.'

'Oh no, that's terrible.'

'You haven't heard the worst – both his sisters have got the symptoms too – it looks like we might have a Bloom-free gig.'

'Oh no!'

'Yeah, I know, that means we'll have to flog their tickets too!'

Bloody hell.

I felt really sorry for The Blooms. They spent the end of the week in quarantine at their family home. None of us were allowed to visit. Dave spoke with Karl on the phone. Karl said he was going to murder Kevin Clarke.

'But what about Roxanne?' I asked Dave.

'What about her?'

'Well, will she still come, now that Poppy's sick?'

'Blimey, I hadn't even thought of that,' said Dave.

I had. It had been the first thing I'd thought of.

I made a special trip up to HMV. There were only four shopping days until the big day, so the town was was packed with frantic people, searching for last minute Christmas gifts. As far as I was concerned, the big day was Sunday and I wanted to make sure Roxanne was still coming. I needn't have worried.

She spotted me, as soon as I walked through the door; like she'd been looking out for me. Noddy Holder and his supersonic tonsils were announcing to the whole of Sussex that it was Christmas.

'Tim. I'm so glad you came in.'

Music to my ears in HMV.

'I was going to get your number from Poppy. Have you heard? The whole family's bed ridden with chicken pox?'

'Yeah, it's a real shame,' I said, 'you are still coming though eh?'

'Yes of course!' she beamed, 'I wouldn't miss it for the world. Is it just, you, me, David and Alison?'

'And Juliette, you know Heidi's friend?'

'Oh of course, will she still come along? Without Heidi I mean?'

'Yeah, so Dave says,' I said.

'I bet Karl's hacked off; missing his big chance with her?' she said.

'Utterly!' I laughed.

'So, just the five of us.'

Roxanne seemed distracted for a moment. Then she snapped her fingers in the air, 'actually, that's OK. I've got an idea.'

'You didn't tell me she had a car,' Dave told me, as we walked from his front door to the old Mini.

'I didn't even know she could drive!' I said, 'besides it's not strictly hers, it's her brother's,' I explained as we reached the car. Alison and Juliette were already in the back.

'Hi Roxanne, this is kind of you - and your brother,' said Dave.

'Well Patrick doesn't mind. He's touring around Europe by train with his girlfriend – until their money runs out, kind of thing. So I'm sort of looking after it. It's a bit of an old banger, but it will get the five of us up there. Much better than relying on the train, don't you think?'

Blimey, I was sort of seeing a girl, who sort of had a car. How cool was I?

So it was that we travelled to Tooting Bec common in a very old (D reg – 1966) green Mini, owned by Patrick Delaney, and driven by Roxanne, who had apparently had a full driving licence for all of two months and who was driving the car for precisely the third time. She crunched the long gear stick every time she changed gears. She drove too fast and far too close to the car in front for my liking. But I didn't care, it was nearly Christmas, it was the school holidays and we were driving up to see The Police, with their music blaring out from the car's cassette player. Life didn't get much better than that. It felt so...adult.

As usual, Dave wasted no time in flirting with Alison.

He tried it on with Juliette too, but she was understandably quiet, which wasn't that surprising, given she'd probably said no more than five words to any of us before. We'd picked her up at the Old Steine, where her parents had dropped her off. They seemed really nice. I was amazed she'd still come along without Heidi. That took some guts. She was very shy and obviously felt awkward without her more confident little friend along for the drive.

'So, are you looking forward to the gig Juliette?' I said from the front passenger seat, trying to spark up a conversation, as we travelled up the A23 past the pylons and out of Brighton.

'Yes thanks,' she said politely, still peering out of the window.

'And what's your favourite Police song?'

'I like all of them really,' she said, giggling coyly as she realised she was the centre of attention in the car.

'Me too!' said Roxanne. who turned her head to face Juliette, as she spoke.

She was driving. Call me old fashioned but I would rather she was facing forward.

'Sting's gorgeous isn't he?' I heard Alison say.

Juliette giggled. 'Uh-huh, he's alright.'

'I quite fancy Stewart Copeland myself,' said Roxanne, turning her head again.

We veered slightly to the right. A lorry blasted it's horn.

'Oops, sorry!' said Roxanne, 'maybe I should keep my eyes on the road?'

'Maybe best,' I gulped.

'People say I look a bit like Stewart Copeland!' Dave piped up from the back.

I glanced in the rear view mirror. I saw Alison and Juliette exchange looks – both of them burst out laughing.

'What?' protested Dave, 'they do, honestly!'

'You should stop hanging around St. Dunstans Dave,' I said. All the girls laughed. St. Dunstans was the local home for the blind.

'I'm glad I don't look like him anyway, you'd probably fancy me if I did!'

I didn't turn around. I merely stuck two fingers up. Dave leant over and tweaked my ear really hard.

Yep, we were such adults.

I was useless at map-reading. Once, on the way to my Namps house in Pembroke in Wales, I was given the job of navigator. We ended up practically in Birmingham. So when Roxanne asked me to give her directions, I knew we were in trouble. But I didn't want to appear totally useless, which of course, I was.

'According to my Dad,' Roxanne had said as we started out that afternoon, 'it's straight up the A23, you can't miss it.'

We could if I had anything to do with it.

Half an hour from Brighton, things were getting a bit tetchy.

'I'm not used to map reading - my Mum always does it, whenever we go anywhere!' I explained as we looked for an exit off of the London ring road.

'Now he tells us!' I heard Dave mutter.

'But why did you say turn left if you weren't sure?' Roxanne said. She looked really annoyed.

'Well I thought we wanted the ring road...'

'No, I said straight up the A23!' she snapped.

Blimey, we sounded just like my Mum and Dad. We were having our first map-reading argument.

Roxanne leant over to the passenger seat look at the map in my lap. The car veered slightly to the right. Juggernauts boomed by on each side. The mini rattled.

'I think you might want to stay in the left hand lane,' Alison suggested, with just a hint of sarcasm.

The cat and the pigeons had just been well and truly introduced.

'Why? Do you know the fucking way all of a fucking sudden?' Roxanne blurted.

I'd never heard Roxanne swear before. Something told me she was a bit anxious. I could tell. I seemed to have a sixth sense for these things.

'No, but if you're looking for a sodding exit, they'll be on the fucking left hand side of the road!' said Alison.

Things were definitely getting a bit fractious.

Roxanne glared at Alison in the rear-view mirror, before veering back over to the left. There was a screech from behind as a white Ford Transit driver suddenly had to steer out to the middle lane to avoid us. The driver blasted his horn and glared as he passed us.

'Bloody hell Roxanne! Take it easy will you?' said Dave.

'Would you like to take the fucking wheel smart-arse?'

132

Roxanne was getting even more anxious by the minute. I could tell. I definitely had a sense for these things.

'God, why didn't we take the train?' muttered Alison.

'Yes, why didn't *you* take the bloody train?' Roxanne spat.

'At least we might have got there in one piece AND on time!' shouted Alison.

'Don't blame me if we're late!' Roxanne retorted, 'I wasn't the one who directed us on to wrong side of the ring road!'

Roxanne was a funny purple colour. Definitely signs of anxiety. I could tell. I have a sixth....

'Look, there's a turn off coming up!' shouted Alison, right in my ear.

'Yes,...thank...you....Alison...I HAD SPOTTED THAT!' Roxanne hissed, turning around.

The car slalomed into the middle of the carriage-way, before she turned back and yanked on the steering wheel. There was a loud screech and the smell of burning rubber as we took a dramatic forty-five degree turn onto a slip road.

I swallowed hard.

'Oh Jesus, oh sweet Jesus,' I heard Dave muttering.

'I never knew you were religious Dave!' I joked, trying to lighten the mood.

No-one laughed. No-one spoke. No-one dared breathe. I stared fixedly out of the window and zipped my lip.

An hour later, after several terse exchanges between Alison, who had taken charge of the map, and Roxanne, who drove in near silence, we all breathed a huge sigh of relief when we saw a signpost for Tooting. I was tempted to point out that Roxanne's Dad's directions had not been *strictly* correct and that it wasn't really just "straight up the A23". However, judging by Roxanne's stony face and the fact that she hadn't spoken a word to me since the ring road incident, my handy sixth sense suggested to my mouth that perhaps I shouldn't mention it.

'So, where do we park?' asked Dave as we drove slowly in a queue of traffic up Tooting Bec High St.

There were crowds upon crowds of pedestrians, all heading in the same direction.

'Good question,' said Alison.

Roxanne still wasn't speaking.

I saw a policeman talking on his radio.

'Hey pull up Roxy, I'll ask this copper where we can ditch the car,' I said breezily.

Roxanne said nothing but pulled up at the kerb.

Fifteen minutes later, we were gratefully climbing out of the Mini and parking in what looked like someone's front garden.

'Three quid to park here?' said Dave, 'what a rip off!'

We had a whip round and rustled together the money to pay the dodgy looking bloke at the gate. Then we set off on foot, following the masses along the road. There was a real buzz in the air; everybody was obviously looking forward to the gig. And there were loads of touts about – we had been offered tickets three times even before we had gone a hundred yards. The touts were a shifty looking bunch; blokes with dodgy footballer's perms and gold dripping off them like Jimmy Saville.

'Tickets for tonight's gig, I'll buy or sell,' one said as we passed.

'How much are you buying for?' asked Dave, stopping in his tracks.

'Face value,' the tout announced.

'Are you serious?' said Dave, sounding every bit like John McEnroe arguing with an umpire.

'Any tickets? Buy or sell?' the tout said, ignoring Dave and walking on.

'So much for your profiteering then David!' laughed Roxanne.

It was the first thing she had said since the M25.

In my relief, I laughed a little too loudly and a little too obviously.

'Don't forget you've got to sell as well Tim!' she said, a smug smile playing on her lips.

She was right. I couldn't help feeling I would be crap at this touting business - and there were loads of coppers around too, which made me feel really nervous. Wasn't touting illegal?

'We'll never sell them - there's hundreds of touts here!' I said.

'Oh, give it to me! said Roxanne, grabbing my spare ticket from my hand,'watch and learn!' she said.

Roxanne took her coat off and handed it to me. She was wearing a tiny mini denim skirt over black tights and pink leg warmers. Her red silky blouse-top fit her so tightly, it looked like she was trying to escape from it. Dave and I exchanged glances.

'Spare ticket for The Police gig. Who wants to buy a ticket?' she said, sashaying up the street. She hadn't walked five yards when two shifty looking blokes in Arthur Daley camel-hair-coats strolled up. One of them said something, at which point Roxanne laughed, throwing her red hair back over her shoulder. The whole thing took seconds. The taller bloke shook hands with Roxanne. Then he bent his head to kiss her hand, before both Arthurs walked off.

'There! Doubled your money!' Roxanne smiled. She handed me a ten pound note.

'Wow that was amazing Roxanne!' said Juliette.

'Impressive,' Alison added.

'Now you try it!' smiled Roxanne, turning to Dave.

'Easy!' said Dave, 'No problem!'

Dave walked off up the road in his fake leather jacket, doing his best Fonzie swagger. 'Tickets for the gig? Who wants tickets?'

Nothing happened.

'Anyone want tickets?' he repeated.

Again nothing.

'Tickets for tonight's gig!' he said louder. Too loud.

The crowd went quiet; everyone seemed to be staring at Dave. Then I realised they were actually looking behind him. Two policemen were marching up toward him.

'Oh shit!' I said.

One of the coppers tapped Dave on the shoulder.

Bugger.

Dave turned around, startled, and the officers gestured for him to follow them over to the side of the pavement. One of them was talking into his walkie-talkie. Dave looked like he was going to quite literally poo his pants then and there, on the pavement.

Alison and Roxanne started giggling uncontrollably. Dave looked like he was getting a right ticking off. A few minutes later, he walked back over, his tail firmly between his legs.

'What happened?' I said, 'what did they say?'

'Oh no big deal – they just wanted to know why I had spare tickets,' Dave said, trying to look like he wasn't bothered in the least.

'What did you say?' asked Alison, wiping a tear of laughter from her eye.

'I said my mates were ill.'

'Did they believe you?' I asked.

135

Dave shrugged. He was still trying to look cool. If he hadn't been shaking quote so much, he might have carried it off.

'They just said they'd be keeping an eye on me and asked if I knew it was an offence to resell tickets at more than face value?' he said. He faked a laugh whilst still looking tentatively over his shoulder.

'What are you going to do then David?' asked Juliette, who seemed more rattled than anyone else.

'Ah don't worry,' Dave said breezily, 'they were only trying to put the frighteners on me.'

'Put the frighteners on you? What is, this the Streets of San Francisco?'I laughed.

Alison and Roxanne were wetting themselves.

Juliette looked really frightened.

'We'll just find a new patch!' said Dave, ignoring me and still doing his best Michael Douglas impersonation.

'We won't get into trouble will we?' I heard Juliette ask Dave as the two of them walked ahead of us.

'No, don't worry doll, I know what I'm doing.'

'Doll? Did he really just call her doll?' Roxanne whispered.

'Fraid so,' I said, shaking my head in disbelief.

Dave was showing off to Juliette; walking backwards. That's when he collided with one of the largest, meanest looking Rude-boys, I'd ever seen in my life. The guy was wearing the full Two-Tone gear; a ridiculously small pork-pie hat which perched on his huge head like a a sparrow on a boulder; a Ben Sherman shirt, bright red braces, Levis that were turned up so that they stopped just above black knee-length lace-up DM's. He scowled at Dave as he looked down on him - the bloke was at least six feet six tall and about twice as wide. We all held our breath for a moment.

'Dave's dead,' I muttered.

Instead, the huge rude-boy suddenly broke into a smile, patting Dave's head, like he was a naughty puppy.

'Careful mate, you wanna' look where you're walking, there's some right dodgy geezers around here tonight!' he laughed. He winked at Juliette, who looked as if she was about to be sick and then he moved on.

'What a cool bloke,' said Dave, the colour slowly returning to his face.

By the time we reached the venue, every other person we came across seemed to be selling tickets. The air was full of fast-food smells; hot dogs, burgers and chips. There were already queues forming around the huge white Marquee that had been erected slap-bang in the middle of the common.

'Come on, we'd better start queuing!' I said.

'Hang on mate, we've go to sell these other tickets first,' said Dave, reaching in the back pocket of his jeans.

Bloody hell. We'd be all night trying to sell those bloody spares. If we weren't careful, we'd miss half the gig.

Then Dave did that comedy thing when you can't find something that you know was there in your pocket a minute ago. He dragged out two Opal Fruits and a used tissue from the rear pocket of his jeans - there was nothing else there. He checked his other rear pocket and then he started rifling through his front pockets, pulling out change and various bits of rubbish - everything but the spare tickets. Finally, he started frantically patting down his bomber jacket. A look of sheer panic came across his face.

'Fuck! Fuck! I've lost the tickets!' he said, digging his hands back into his arse pockets.

'They must be there somewhere!' I said, 'come on, stop pissing about, we'll miss the start of the show!'

'Look, I'm not joking Tim! I've lost the fucking tickets!'

'Calm down!' said Alison, 'you can't have lost them!'

'Look, you stupid cow. Watch my lips - I'VE- FUCKING- LOST-THEM!'

'Oh charming,' said Alison.

'Think,' said Roxanne, 'where did you put them?'

'IF I FUCKING KNEW THAT, I WOULDN'T BE FUCKING SEARCHING FOR THEM WOULD I?"

'Ok mate, calm down,' I said, 'losing your rag isn't going to help!'

'WHAT DO YOU MEAN, CALM-FUCKING-DOWN? I'VE JUST LOST FOUR TICKETS - THAT'S TWENTY QUID DOWN THE DRAIN!'

Someone started crying.

We all turned.

It was Juliette. We all looked at each other. Dave was still searching through his pockets, like the missing tickets would suddenly, and miraculously, appear.

'See, now look what you've done!' said Alison, 'you've made her cry!'

'How have I made her cry?...Shit, oh shit!'

'What now?' I said.

'My own ticket's gone as well - I can't even get into the bloody gig!' Dave said.

'That bloke!' said Roxanne.

'What?' I said.

'That bloke. You know, the big guy with the braces and the DM's. The one who bumped into Dave. He must be a pickpocket. He must have taken them!'

'Shit, you're right!' I said.

'I'LL BLOODY KILL HIM!' Dave said.

Everyone within ear shot stopped and looked at him.

Through the crowd we saw the big bloke. He smiled in our direction. He was the size of a small aircraft carrier.

I looked at Dave.

The girls looked at Dave.

'Shit!' he muttered.

So, Dave ended up buying a ticket from a tout.

It cost him twenty quid. As he handed his ticket to the bouncers at the door, he looked completely gutted.

'That's forty-five quid that's cost me altogether. For a five quid ticket.'

'Never mind mate, it'll all be worth it!' I told him.

'They'd better be bloody good!' he spat.

'They will be. I promise.'

'God, it's massive!' said Alison, as we squeezed into the back of the huge tent.

We were packed in like sardines. There seemed to be thousands and thousands of Police fans in there, all noisily chanting for our heroes to appear. Then a huge cheer went up and a short dark-haired man strolled out to the mike on the middle of the stage.

'That's Jools Holland,' I said.

'Who?' said Alison, who was clinging to my right arm. Roxanne stood to my left and Dave and Juliette were in front of us.

'Jools Holland. He's the keyboards player from Squeeze!' I said excitedly, 'maybe Squeeze are supporting!'

'I hope so. Blood Elvis Presley and The Beatles should be supporting for the money I've forked out!' said Dave.

'It's bound to be someone dead good!' I said.

'Ladies and gentlemen, boys and girls please welcome....Mr. Tommy Cooper!' said Jools.

'Tommy Cooper!' said Dave, 'Tommy Bloody Cooper! What the hell....?'

Sure enough, the huge TV comedian wandered on, wearing his trade-mark Fez.

Most of the the audience applauded politely, but there were a few muted boos. Everyone looked totally bemused. Tommy Cooper supporting The Police? What next Arthur Askey gigging with The Jam? The Sex Pistols on tour with Pam Ayres?

Tommy looked a bit nervous but he started with the usual sort of routine that I'd seen him doing on telly.

Tommy Cooper. I just didn't get him at all. Why did people think he was funny? Mum and Dad think he's hilarious. But then Mum's in her late forties and Dad's fifty-something; ancient. The average age of the crowd here was about nineteen. There were a few giggles but really he was dying on his arse. And to be fair, it could have been someone hilarious up there like The Two Ronnies or Lenny Henry, the result would have been the same. This audience had come to see a Rock concert, not a music hall act. It started to get embarrassing; Tommy was being really heckled. The boos grew worse. No-one was listening to him. Everyone was shouting for The Police. They started slow hand-clapping and stamping their feet. I wasn't a fan but I felt pretty sorry for Tommy. What was Sting thinking?

'Never mind,' I shouted into Roxanne's ear, 'I expect Squeeze will be on in a minute.

They weren't.

Next on was that bloke who plays Wolfie in Citizen Smith. We all looked at each other. We were all thinking the same thing. Had we come to Sunday Night at The Palladium by mistake? Wolfie started spouting on about the Tooting Popular Front. Ah, of course, Tooting. That's where I'd heard the name before. Wolfie got the hint though; after just a few minutes and a couple of clenched fisted "Power To The Peoples" he was off. And Jools Holland walked on stage again.

'For God's sake Jools, introduce the band,' I said. I feared a lynching.

139

Jools must have heard me. Without further delay, he announced the band.

The lights went down and the music to "Be My Girl Sally" started up. The crowd went mad. And then Sting waked out and for a moment I was convinced I was about to go deaf. The roar was incredible. He was wearing a white flying suit, over which he wore a teacher's gown and mortar board - like the stuff he had on in the video for "Don't Stand So Close To Me". On anyone else, it would have looked like the worst fancy dress outfit in the history of the planet; Sting looked like a God. Andy and Stewart had bounded on almost unnoticed. The spotlight was focused on Sting. And when he started singing, the entire tent seemed to move. Everyone was jumping up and down and screaming their faces off. It was mental. The whole audience was a heaving mass. Roxanne was already a few yards away, being carried away as the crowd moved backwards and forwards like the waves crashing on Brighton beach. I tried to catch her eye but she was dancing from side to side and singing at the top of her voice. Alison was jumping up and down, punching the air like a mad thing. Then she linked her arm through mine. The band sounded brilliant as they broke into "Bring On The Night".

I gazed over at Roxanne and tried to edge nearer to her, pulling Alison with me. I was yanked back from behind. Dave shouted in my ear.

'We're going down the front, come on!' he said.

Juliette was holding his hand. Roxanne was getting carried further away in the other direction.

'Coming?' mouthed Alison as she turned to follow Dave.

It was decision time. I looked at Dave and Alison, and then at Roxanne.

Mouthing an apology to Alison, I turned and started to force my way through the crowd to where Roxanne was standing. As I glanced back, the others were already disappearing towards the front of the stage. The audience went into a frenzy as the Police started playing "Can't Stand Losing You". I moved up behind Roxanne and tapped her shoulder. She smiled and without turning, grabbed my hands and wrapped my arms around her waist. She held my arms with hers.

Good decision Tim. For once.

We stayed like that, linked together through the next three songs. Then Roxanne turned and faced me during "Driven To Tears". She

140

had her arms around my neck now and we stood sideways onto the stage. Then she kissed me; a kiss that seemed to last forever. We snogged for the rest of the song and the entirety of "Fall Out", which wasn't exactly a ballad. It was probably the band's punkiest number and people were pogoing all around us; we were barged into from all sides but it didn't effect our rhythm. It was three minutes into "Man In A Suitcase" before we came up for breath.

'Maybe we should watch the band?' said Roxanne, as the audience went wild at the end of the song.

'Must we?' I laughed.

Roxanne smiled. 'Randy bugger,' she muttered.

Next up was "Message In A Bottle". We watched hand in hand. It really was pretty crammed in that tent. By now, I was dripping with sweat. I wondered how the others were getting on at the front. I noticed the bouncers down there were lifting a couple of girls out of the crowd, onto the stage. They looked like they'd fainted.

'I hope the others are OK down there!' I shouted to Roxanne over the noise, 'they could get crushed if they're not careful.'

'You don't seem to mind a bit of a tight squeeze!' Roxanne shouted, hugging me closer. Did I just imagine that or did she pinch my bum?

'That's different,' I said.

'So, is this worth a fiver?' she laughed, kissing my lips.

'A couple of quid maybe?' I smiled and leant in for another.

'Bloody cheek!' she said, punching my arm, 'you better watch it if you want a lift home!'

Why does time always go so quickly when you're enjoying yourself? There were a couple of encores. We sang along to "So Lonely". And then it was all over. The crowd started emptying out. As we emerged into the freezing night air, my damp t-shirt clung to my skin.

Roxanne was still holding my hand as we stood by a hot-dog stand, waiting for the others to appear. It was hard to believe that one marquee could have held all those people. There seemed to be a never ending supply of Police fans pouring out into the night. It reminded me of one of those Monty Python sketches where impossibly long queues of people keep coming out of a small terraced house.

141

We peered into the dense swarm of teenagers, looking for Dave and the girls. You could tell by how wet their hair was that these guys had been crammed down at the front of the stage; many of the lads were bare-chested; the girls looked like they'd been in a mammoth wet-T-shirt competition.

'Look, there's Alison!' said Roxanne.

Alison was red in the face but beaming as she came out of the tent. She spotted us in the same moment we saw her and started waving and weaving her way to where we were standing.

'How classic was that guys?' she exclaimed.

'Oh, wasn't it just brilliant?' Roxanne agreed.

'Where's Dave and Juliette?' I asked.

'Oh, they should be on their way, if their bodies haven't melted together. Maybe the bouncers are prizing them apart with a crow-bar!' she laughed, 'I'm not sure how much of the gig poor Juliette saw. Dave seemed to be performing a tonsillectomy on her.'

'You're kidding!' Roxanne screeched.

'What? Dave and Juliette?' I said.

'Yep! Like rabbits!' Alison smiled.

Great. Clarkey wouldn't be the only person Karl would be killing.

Roxanne spotted them first, still embracing as they made their way through the crowds.

'Dave! Juliette!' she shouted.

They looked like they'd been standing under a shower. Then they saw us. Juliette pulled away from Dave, looking slightly embarrassed. Soon the five of us were stood together, exchanging excited stories about the gig and how mental it had been in the tent.

As we started heading back to the car, Dave and I dropped back slightly behind the girls.

'Enjoy that?' I asked.

'It was amazing!' he said.

'How about the gig?' I laughed.

'Ha, bloody ha!' he laughed.

'So,' I said, 'how are you going to break the news to Bo?'

'No need mate. There's more than enough Dave Booth to go around!' he winked. He looked pretty pleased with himself now but there would be trouble in paradise when Karl found out.

On the journey back out of Tooting, Juliette fell asleep on Dave's shoulder. Dave smiled stupidly all the way home; like the cat that had got the cream.

Alison was unusually quiet in the back.

'You OK back there Ali?' I asked after a while.

'Fine,' she muttered.

Roxanne glanced at her in the rear-view mirror, without turning her head. For once though, Roxanne was fully concentrating on the road ahead; or at least on the endless queue of red tail-lights, which was all we could see for miles. Her left hand was resting on the gear-stick. I put my hand on hers. Her mouth curled up in a smile.

'Are you sure you're OK Alison? Only you're very quiet,' Roxanne said.

'Just tired,'Alison said.

Roxanne glanced sideway at me in the passenger seat, her eyebrows raised.

I shrugged.

Girls were so weird sometimes.

It was gone 1 a.m. when we finally dropped Juliette off at her home on the outskirts of Brighton. We'd already dropped Dave off; he and Juliette had kissed good night, before Dave finally pulled himself away and headed off up his drive, smiling like a Cheshire Cat. It had been dead embarrassing.

Alison still hadn't said much. I thought I'd heard her blowing her nose at one point and I wondered if she was crying. I listened for a while, without turning my head. Just tired and emotional, I decided.

When we dropped her off, she thanked Roxanne for the lift and headed off, pausing only to kiss me briefly on the cheek.

'You behave yourself young man!' she said.

She turned and blew us both a kiss as she put her key in her door.

Roxanne shook here head and started up the car.

'Oh dear, I don't think I'm too popular with your little friend,' Roxanne said, as we turned the corner.

'What makes you say that?' I asked.

'Come on Tim, are you blind?'

'What?'

'You do realise she's got it bad for you, don't you "young man"?'

'What?'

143

'Alison! She luuurves you!'

I laughed. 'Rubbish!'

'You boys! Just can't see what's right in front of your eyes when it comes to a pretty girl can you?'

'What are you on about? She's just upset about Humph that's all.'

'Well, trust me Timothy. I'm a girl and it seems to me that I've got a rival!'

'Well,' I said, feeling incredibly embarrassed but quietly chuffed to pieces, even if I thought Roxanne was talking complete and utter rubbish, 'you'll just have to prove you're the better deal won't you?'

Roxanne laughed out loud.

'You cocky little bugger! Well I'm not sure I can compete with little Miss Perfect. Maybe, I should leave you two to it?'

'Nah, thats OK, I'll give you another chance to show what you can do!'

When we stopped outside my house, she turned off the car-light and began to demonstrate her talents. She pulled me over to the driver's seat and we kissed for what seemed like ages, until I was starting to feel decidedly hot under the collar; and indeed under other parts of my clothing. The Mini's bucket seats were dead uncomfortable though. I whacked my knee painfully against the hand-brake and yelped in agony. A minute later I hit my head on the rear-view mirror.

Roxanne was in fits of laughter.

'I sincerely hope that's the gear stick prodding my thigh!' she said.

So did I.

She sat up, pushing me away.

'Ok, I think you have to get out of the car now Mister!' she said.

The windows had all steamed up. So had I. Slowly, I started to climb out, hesitating, not wanting to leave. I should ask to see her again. Why was I so crap at this? What should I say? Thankfully, Roxanne came to my rescue.

'Maybe we can find somewhere a bit more comfortable next time?' she laughed, kissing me on the cheek, 'assuming you'd like there to be a next time?'

Was the Pope a Catholic?

'What are you doing tomorrow?' I blurted.

'Blimey, steady Tiger!' she giggled, 'actually I'm working until six but you could always meet me after work. I'll let you by me a drink. Deal?'

'Deal!'

Half an hour later, I was tucked up in my bed, my head buzzing from the gig and the events of the evening. I couldn't sleep, so I listened to Police music on my headphones.

Bring On The Night.

I looked up at the various posters on my bedroom wall and smiled. Thanks Sting.

Thanks boys.

That was one brilliant evening.

12 - And It Would Be Ok....

It had started out so promisingly but 1980 turned out to be poxy Christmas for me.

On the Monday before Christmas, the day after The Police gig, I'd arranged to meet up with Roxanne after her stint at HMV. On the bus down to Churchill Square, I started to feel a bit dizzy. I was sweating like mad. Something clearly wasn't right; it was December - everyone was wrapped up in duffel coats and parkas - and there I was, stripping down to my school-shirt sleeves. And then I started shivering. My whole body felt like I had run a marathon; whilst the Marathon I'd just eaten was threatening to pay me a return visit, along with the packet of Salt 'n Shake crisps and the can of Fanta. I had a splitting headache. Wrapping my Parka around me as I climbed off of the bus, I walked slowly and unsteadily to the shop. Roxanne was already waiting for me, just inside the door.

'I thought we could grab a burger or something and then see if there's a film on at the ABC,' she said, as she wrapped her arm through mine.

Just the thought of a "burger" made me want to heave. I shivered again as Roxanne led me out into the shopping centre, which was still surprisingly busy, considering it was gone six o'clock.

'I'm not surprised you're cold. What on earth are you doing in your shirt sleeves? You'll catch your death.'

She sounded just like my Mum.

I shuddered. 'It was really warm on the bus,' I muttered.

'Come on, put your jacket back on,' she said, holding the sleeves out for me. As I slipped my arms in, I sneezed violently. And again. And again. And again. I thought I'd never stop.

Roxanne passed me a tissue from her bag and studied my face with concern.

'Your eyes are really bloodshot!' she said, as I blew my nose.

'I do feel a bit rough actually.'

'You look awful,' she said.

Not quite the declaration of undying love I'd been hoping for.

And then, just to prove her point, I threw up a mixture of Marathon, Crisps and Fanta, all over her favourite pixie boots.

Disgusting.

Roxanne took me back to the shop, which was still open for late night shoppers. She insisted on phoning for a taxi to take me home. I was disappointed of course, but I didn't really have the strength to argue. She took me around the back of the counter, sat me down in the stockroom and gave me a glass of water. Normally, I would have been like a kid in a sweet-shop sitting in the actual stockroom of HMV. There were boxes of records and tapes everywhere. The huge Zenyatta Mondatta poster that had been up in the shop window a while back was hanging askew from one solitary drawing pin on the wall, over a dirty looking sink.

'Cool poster!' I said.

Roxanne ignored me. She was scrubbing her shoes over the sink, with about a gallon of Fairy liquid and a scouring pad.

'I think these boots are ruined,' she muttered to herself.

'Sorry,' I said yet again.

'Not your fault,' she said unconvincingly.

She rested the boots on the top of a radiator and searched around in her handbag, pulling out a bottle of perfume, before spraying her boots.

'Smells nice.' I said.

One of Roxanne's colleagues came in, grabbing an armful of T-shirts from a shelf. The sound of music drifted through from the shop. Even though I felt like death warmed up, my feet started tapping almost involuntarily.

'Anais Anais,' Roxanne said, wrinkling her nose in disgust as she held the red boots at arms length, before pulling them back on, over her ankles.

'Pardon?'

'Anais Anais. By Cacheral.'

The music was punky. The singer female.

'Yeah they're good, aren't they?' I said, 'Cacherel did you say? Sounds a bit like Siouxsie and The Banshees.'

Roxanne looked at me blankly for a minute. Then laughed.

'The Perfume, you idiot! The perfume is called Anais Anais and it's made by Cacherel.'

'Oh right - I thought you meant the band were called Cacherel. I thought Anais Anais was an odd name for a song.'

She placed the bottle back into her bag.

'Don't Dictate.'

147

'Sorry?'

'Penetration,' she said.

'What ...here?' I laughed.

It was a bit risque but I was hoping it might break the tension. Luckily it seemed to do the trick.

'The *band* you doughnut! The song is Don't Dictate and it's by Penetration. Don't you know anything about bands except The Police?' Now she was giggling like mental.

I felt a little better.

'The taxi will be here shortly. Ring me here tomorrow and tell me how you're doing. OK?'

'OK,' I said, feeling miserable; our first proper date and typically, it had all gone tits-up, 'maybe I'll see you before Christmas?'

'Well, it will have to be in the next couple of days, I'm off home to Weybridge for the holidays.'

'Yeah and I'm off to Wales on Christmas Eve, worse luck!' I said.

'OK, well, I'm sure we can fit a quick drink in before then, provided you promise not to throw-up on any more of my best shoes!'

'OK, I promise'

'Tomorrow then? Same time, same place? If you're feeling up to it?'

'I feel better already,' I lied, 'I'll see you here at closing time.'

'And then you can give me that expensive present you were planning eh?' she laughed.

Present? Bloody hell. What was I meant to get her?

Just then, another of her workmates stuck his head around the door.

'Taxi for Miss Delaney!' the lad said, 'Bloody hell, what's that smell?'

'Anais Anais,' I said. 'By Penetration.'

'But I've already had Chicken Pox!' I said.

Doctor Huggett breathed on the end of his cold stethoscope, before sticking it to my chest,.

'I was eight - I couldn't go and see Willy Wonka and the Chocolate factory with Cheryl. I remember it clearly.'

'That was German Measles. You caught if off your cousin Joanne when we were down in Wales that summer,' My Mum said.

'But I'm sure you said it was Chicken Pox.'

Mum shook her head.

'I don't think you *can* have had it before,' said Doctor Huggett, 'because you certainly have it now. Not a very nice Christmas present I'm afraid Mrs. James,' he told my Mum, who was hovering by my bedroom door.

'Oh no!' she said, 'we're meant to be off to Pembroke on Wednesday. Will he bit fit to travel?'

'I'm afraid not - the spots are just making their appearance - he'll be laid up over the holidays. Keep him warm, get plenty of fluids down him and keep him away from anyone who's not had it.'

After much noisy debate, Dad persuaded Mum that, as Cheryl was now twenty-one and "no longer a kid", it would be perfectly safe to leave me with her and her fiance Lee. Cheryl said we'd be fine, which surprised me. I thought she'd kick up a stink about me ruining her cosy Christmas with Lee.

Mum obviously thought so too. They spoke in hushed voices, standing on the landing outside my door. I didn't exactly have to strain my ears to hear them.

'I'm so sorry love, I expect you two love-birds were looking forward to a bit of time alone for once.'

'Ah well,' I heard Cheryl say, 'at least he'll be in his bedroom. He won't be getting in our way.'

Charming.

So Mum finally agreed, albeit reluctantly, to leave me at home with Cheryl.

By now, my face resembled Ermintrude, the pink spotted cow from "The Magic Roundabout". I'd covered my blisters with bright pink Calamine. They itched like crazy but I was mindful of Dr. Huggett's advice; 'don't scratch them unless you want permanent scars.' I scratched at a particularly evil bugger that had taken up residence on my chest. Not a good move. It wept, and stung like hell.

After half an hour of trying to call HMV and getting the engaged tone, I finally managed to leave a message with some kid to tell Roxanne that I wouldn't be able to meet up with her. It was two days before Christmas and judging by the background noise, the shop was really busy. I gave the kid my number and asked him to make sure she called me. The kid said he'd give her the message. I wasn't convinced. It was a bad line and the kid sounded stressed out.

Sure enough, Roxanne didn't ring back. Why hadn't I asked for her home number? I know, I'll call Poppy - she'll have it.

Karl answered; he said Poppy was asleep - she was still feeling groggy from the pox. He didn't want to wake her up.

'She always gets really arsey when she's ill,' he said.

From what I'd seen of Poppy Bloom, she was always arsey - full stop.

'Well, If you can ask her, I'd be really grateful. Or maybe ask her to get Roxanne to call me; you know if she speaks to her.'

'Yeah, OK I suppose...,'

Karl didn't seem interested in my problems; he kept changing the subject; asking me about the gig and whether Juliette had enjoyed herself.

'Yeah, I think so.'

'So, did she mention me at all?'

'Sorry mate, I can't remember to be honest. There was a lot going on, you know. Look mate, I feel really rough, I need to get back to bed.'

Karl said he'd pop around for a visit after Christmas, maybe on Boxing Day, if I was up to it. That was one visit I wasn't relishing. By then, either he would have found out about Dave and Juliette and would be going mental, or he'd still be ignorant and I'd have to either steer clear of the subject of the gig altogether, or lie to him.

What none of us in the family knew was that Cheryl and Lee weren't talking.

They'd split up - again. They were like Humph and Alison; always breaking up and then getting back together again. It was just like Sue Ellen and J.R in Dallas; they'd had more fights that Mohammed Ali.

But they always got back together.

'Not this time!' I heard her telling someone on the phone, about ten minutes after my parents had set off.

I didn't even have to sit on the landing to hear Cheryl's conversations; she always broadcasted them so the whole house could hear. She had more mouth than the Thames that one.

'I'm telling you Stacey, he's not coming here for Christmas even if he begs for forgiveness!'

So, it was Stacey on the phone. My ears pricked up a bit.

'Go on, come over please. Or I'll be all on my own!'

Er, excuse me Cheryl, I thought. What do you mean "on your own?"

'Yeah,....well apart from my kid brother, and he's got chicken pox, so he'll be up in his room. He won't bother us! Come on, we'll get hammered on Snowballs and eat all the Quality Street. It'll be intense!'

Intense? God, she talked crap.

'What?! Oh, Stacey - you're such an old slapper!' Cheryl was guffawing like mad.

'OK, I'll tell him - he's probably earwigging anyway!' she shouted.

Who was earwigging?

'Oi Tim, Stacey says play your cards right and she'll give you a blanket bath for Christmas!' she shouted up the stairs.

'In her dreams!' I shouted back.

Bloody hell. A blanket bath from Stacey Groves?

Suddenly, things were looking a little brighter.

It was weird, waking up on Christmas morning to a quiet house. Long gone were the Christmas eves, when I used to lie awake all night, waiting for Santa to climb through the window (we had a gas fire, no chimney). I was out like a light the moment my head hit the pillow. It was probably all the paracetamol I was taking. I would have slept all Christmas day too if it wasn't for Cheryl and Chalky. It seemed hideously early when Cheryl opened the door.

'Go on boy, get that lazy so-and-so out of that smelly old bed!' I heard her say.

The dog jumped on the bed, wagging his tail and licking my face. Cheryl dumped a tray on my bed, complete with a glass of Orange squash and a burnt slice of toast.

'Merry Christmas my poxy little brother!' she said, pulling open my curtains.

I winced, covering my bloodshot eyes from the glare of the day.

'What time is it?'

'Time you were up. Santa's been! Hours ago!'

I pushed Chalky off and checked the clock. It was eleven.

'Shall I bring the pressies up to the poor little munchkin or can the little soldier manage to get down the stairs?' Cheryl teased.

'Can you bring them up?' I said, in my best pathetic voice.

'Bugger off. Get downstairs and open them. Stacey will be here in half an hour. I want you back in bed and out of our way whilst we make dinner.'

'You and Stacey Groves are making Christmas dinner?'

Cheryl glared at me, defying me to say something.

'Can I just have soup?'

The phone rang while I was brushing my teeth. I hoped it would be Roxanne; although I was a bit concerned that Cheryl would answer it and that her and Stacey would be taking the Michael all day about my new girlfriend. I hurried out the bathroom door, wearing only my pyjama trousers.

'Is it for me?' I shouted down the stairs.

'Yes. It's Mum! She wants to know if you're out of your pit yet.'

'Tell her I'm in the bathroom. I'll ring her later.'

Cheryl stuck her head around the bottom of the stairs.

'Bloody hell Mum, he's wearing a red polka dot one piece!' she laughed down the phone.

'Sod off,' I said and went back into the bathroom.

Cheryl loved her Adam and The Ants LP. It was no great surprise that she'd got me an LP too. That was all that was on the list I gave her.

'Brilliant! UB40. Thanks Cheryl!'

'You're welcome. So, are you going to open the your presents from Mum & Dad?'

Mum and Dad had said they were getting me "a surprise" this year. I'd already sneaked a look at the parcels under the tree. There were two marked for me. One was tiny, about the size of a fifty pence piece. The other was flat, but not big enough to be another LP. They were both small, compared to the huge box they'd got Cheryl. What had they got me I wondered? I hesitated for a nano-second. A nano-second too long.

'Well, if you aren't going to open yours, I'm going first!' Cheryl squealed with excitement, as she picked up the huge present, tearing open the paper. She read the gift-tab as she tore. 'To Cheryl and Lee, all our love Mum and Dad. Three kisses.'

'So, half that's for Lee then?'

'Well, he can bloody well go without,' Cheryl studied the cardboard box, beneath the wrapping. 'An electric blanket? Oh well,' she said, 'I s'pose I'll need something to keep me warm now the selfish pig's gone back to his sty,' she faked a smile as she turned her head away; she was welling up.

I didn't know what to say. There was an embarrassing pause. Thirty seconds perhaps; then I reckoned enough time had passed so that I didn't seem completely heartless. Besides, they'd be back together before New Year.

'So, my turn,' I said, 'not quite as big as yours then!'

The smallest present felt lumpy beneath my prying fingers. It was so small that there seemed to be more sellotape on it than actual paper. With my finger-nails, I managed to edge open a corner and after much impatient farting around, I finally emptied the contents into my spotty palm. Uh? it was a small, heart-shaped plastic disc, with 'The Police' logo on it.

Cheryl was now grinning from ear to ear. Her eyes were now well and truly moist.

'What's that?' I said.

'What do you think it is?'

'Is it one of those things guitarists use? It's called a lectern or something isn't it?'

'A plectrum you moron. A plectrum, not a bloody lectern.'

'But why..?'

'Why not open the other one?'

Eagerly, I tore at the second present. Inside was an A4 sized book with a glossy cover bearing the same picture of The Police as on the cover of the "Regatta De Blanc" LP.

'The Police Songbook. A guide for the guitar.'

'Cool eh?' Cheryl said.

'But I can't play. What's the point of a lectern...'

'Plectrum!'

'Ok, a bloody plectrum....and a guitar book. I haven't got a...they didn't?' I said, a lightbulb switching on, somewhere in the deep recesses of my head.

'This is where I tell you to look in the shed,' Cheryl beamed, holding up a familiar looking key on a piece of string, 'assuming the invalid can make it as far as the shed? Or shall I fetch....'

I swiped the key from her hand and was out of the door before she finished her sentence.

'FEELING BETTER ARE WE?' Cheryl shouted, as I ran down the garden.

- - -

The guitar was a proper electric one, with an amplifier and everything. It was red and white with a black neck. It was called a Squire Strat. Cheryl told me it wasn't brand new. Apparently, Dad had bought it from his mate Teddy at work. Teddy used to be in pub band called The Twisters. According to Cheryl, Teddy was going to give me a couple of lessons too, all as part of the "deal". I held it in my arms. It was beautiful. I'd never seen anything like it.

'Mum says you'll have to play it in the shed. She didn't really want Dad to get it. He had to promise you won't play it in the house.'

'But it's freezing in here!'

'That's what Dad said an' all. I think he's going to bring that old paraffin heater from the garage down here.'

'Brilliant!' I slung the strap across my shoulders and started to strum with my new Police plectrum. The amp wasn't plugged in, so there was no noise. It felt good though; a bit heavy but I couldn't wait to get started. It was bloody cold in that shed though. I shivered and sneezed.

'Right, back to bed Andy Summers! If you die on my watch, I'll never hear the last of it.'

I did feel knackered. Ah well, I would never have a number one album covered in zits. World domination would just have to wait until I was feeling better.

'Are you decent?'

Cheryl knocked at my door.

They'd been downstairs for ten minutes, laughing and gossiping. Cheryl certainly didn't sound too bothered that she'd "split up" with Lee.

'Nurse Groves is here!' Stacey shouted in her screechy voice.

I had a fleeting vision of Barbara Windsor in "Carry On Nurse".

The two of them were giggling, out on the landing. I really didn't want Stacey to see me in this state; in my pyjamas and covered head to toe in calamine. Chalky had been snoozing at the foot of the bed. His little ears pricked up at the sound of Stacey's voice and his tail started to wag furiously as he stared at the door.

I pulled the duvet up around me, just in time as it turned out. The door flew open and Cheryl came in, holding a tray with a steaming bowl on it. Chalky jumped down and started yapping excitedly.

'Hello Chalky! It's only us!' Stacey said as she came in behind Cheryl.

At least she'd got the dog's name right this time.

Stacey Groves was dressed for Christmas, in an off-the-shoulder, pink fluffy jumper and with a paper-chain garland strung around her neck. She was wearing long sparkly earrings, which caught the light as she carried some napkins and a Christmas cracker into the room. Her skirt was shorter than ever. Why did she bother wearing one at all? At least her legs weren't bare today. She was wearing black woollen tights, which looked weirdly at odds with the Womble slippers she was wearing. They were Cheryl's. One foot was Great Uncle Bulgaria, the other Madame Cholet, yet on Stacey Groves, somehow even the Wombles seemed suddenly sexy. I was definitely not well.

'Oh my God,' Stacey said, putting the napkins down on the bottom of the bed and standing back in mock surprise, 'is there a handsome young man somewhere under all those spots?'

'Well, he's certainly young,' laughed Cheryl, 'but handsome? And well, I'm not so sure about "man" either. I s'pose one out of three ain't bad eh?'

'Ha bloody ha!' I said.

Stacey turned to tickle Chalky's ears. As she leant forward, her loose-fitting jumper fell away, giving me a tantalising glimpse of flesh and a black lace bra. I averted my eyes but not before Cheryl caught me having a good gawp.

Cheryl smirked - as per usual.

I blushed - as per usual.

'So, shall I do the honours?' Cheryl asked, scooping a spoonful of soup, 'or would you prefer Nurse Groves to feed you?'

'Thanks but I'm perfectly capable of feeding myself,' I said, reaching out for the spoon, just as Cheryl shoved it towards me; our hands collided in mid-air sending the spoon - and the soup - flying across the bed.

'Careful Timothy!'

The soup splashed onto the duvet. Mercifully, it missed Stacey's legs by a couple of inches but she jumped all the same.

'Blimey, the things you'll do for that blanket bath!' said Stacey.

155

Cheryl tittered.

Chalky licked at the spillage as Stacey stroked his back. I wasn't enjoying the attention one bit. Chalky, on the other hand seemed to be lapping it up.

To my relief, after a while, the girls seemed to get bored with the game and they left me to have an afternoon nap, without any further talk of a blanket bath from "Nurse Groves".

Stacey could't resist a passing shot though.

'See you later, tiger!' she winked.

Oh bugger.

The phone rang downstairs a couple of times during the afternoon; each time, my heart skipped a beat. Each time, I heard Cheryl running to answer it. Each time, I waited for her to call up and tell me Roxanne was on the phone. I didn't even care if I got the third degree from Cheryl and Stacey all afternoon; as long as she called.

The first time, it was Mum again, phoning to make sure we'd eaten. The second time, I was in the bathroom, inspecting my blisters and applying more calamine. I put my ear to the door and heard Cheryl chatting. I waited for what seemed an eternity and when she didn't call up, I knew it couldn't be Roxanne. Probably Mum again, or Lee, phoning to make-up with Cheryl. Then, after an age, Cheryl shouted up the stairs.

'Spotty Muldoon! It's for you. A young lady!'

My heart was thumping like a hammer drill. I checked my reflection. Thank God they hadn't invented video phones. I trotted down the stairs, trying to appear casual.

Cheryl stood holding the phone with those stupid raised eyebrows of hers. Like Mr. Spock caught in a Vulcan hurricane. She'd stick like that one of these days.

'Who is it?' I mouthed.

Cheryl winked mischievously and handed me the receiver.

'Hello?'

'Hello Timmy, it's your very favourite Welsh lesbian cousin!'

'Joanne?' I said, trying to hide the disappointment in my voice that it wasn't Roxanne calling.

'Yes, of course, unless you have another Welsh lesbian cousin that I don't know about?'

'No, you're the only one.'

156

'Shame! Anyway, I hear you've got the pox. Been snogging those dirty little English girls again?'

Joanne was my cousin from Pembroke. She was a laugh. I hadn't seen her since the summer. She was gorgeous but unfortunately for me, as she herself put it, she "batted firmly for the other side".

'I wish,' I laughed.

'No joy with that Alison what's her face then?'

'Not exactly.'

'Oh, still with your mate Humph is it?'

'Sort of.'

'Ah well, there's plenty more straight fish in the English Channel! Still, fancy standing me up on our annual Christmas date.'

She was a nutcase my cousin Jo. She was always saying stupid stuff like that. She was cool though. I spoke to her for ages and then she blew me a big soppy kiss down the phone and passed me over to her little sister Emily, who also wanted to say hello. Before the call was over, I had been passed on to my Auntie Sylvia, then to my Mum and then to my Namps; then I had to pass the phone back to Cheryl, so she could speak to them all too. The phone was engaged for ages. What if Roxanne was trying to call me?

The next call would be from Roxanne, I told myself.

By the time the phone rang again, I was back lying on my bed, listening to my new UB40 album. I turned the volume down and listened. I heard Cheryl pick up the phone.

'Oh, it's you,' I heard her say. 'Well, what have you go to say for yourself?'

Lee.

I hoped she wouldn't be too long. Would Roxanne keep trying if she got the engaged tone?

Still, I had more pressing concerns right now. I urgently needed to check on the contents of my pyjama trousers.

It looked like I had three goolies.

The lumps on my arms were sore. The one on my chest, which I had stupidly scratched, stung like hell. Those on my face and in my scalp felt like little daggers digging into my flesh. However, painful though they all were, none of them compared to the sheer agony of the one that had nestled itself on my scrotum.

"Go on, scratch me, you know you want to," it seemed to be saying, as I gingerly made an inspection of my nether regions.

157

'You'll scar for life if you scratch them,'Dr. Huggett had said.

No way did I want a scar down there - on the crown jewels. Even with my luck, I was hoping that one of these days, they might just come in useful. Something had to be done to ease the throbbing though. I was holding a cotton wool-ball in one hand, and the pink calamine lotion in the other, when I heard Stacey's voice.

'Timmy! Coming up, ready or not!'

There were footsteps on the stairs, making me jump out of my skin. Bugger, the cotton wool ball fell from my slippery fingers, down between my legs. Chalky thought it was a game. He grabbed the cotton wool and scampered under the bed.

'Chalky! Give me that!' I hissed, feeling around with one hand, whilst holding the open bottle in the other. Chalky growled and wagged his tail, retreating further under the bed. I could hear Stacey on the landing. Oh sod it. I looked at the bottle and then at my balls. No cotton wool. Ah well, just cut out the middle-man. Gently, pulling the elasticated waist of my pyjamas away from the combat zone, I tipped the bottle.

Stacey thumped on the door.

'Are you awake?'

The bottle slipped from my palm. Half the contents had disappeared down the front of my pyjama trousers before I managed to grab it. My nether regions were a sea of pink.

Thump. Thump. Thump.

'I hope you're behaving yourself in there!' Stacey sniggered, 'can I come in?'

'Hang on a second!' I said, desperately stuffing half a box of tissues down my pyjamas, trying to soak up the spillage.

I heard her opening and closing doors; messing around in the airing cupboard. What was she up to now?

'Found the towels!' she announced, laughing suggestively through the bedroom door.

I saw the door handle move.

Oh God. Oh God. I fumbled with the bottle, putting it on the bedside cabinet whilst tying the cord of my pyjama trousers. A wet patch was spreading out from my crotch, right across my lap. I wrapped my dressing gown around my body and jumped under the cover.

Two minutes later, Stacey Groves was sitting on the end of my bed, holding a towel in one hand and a flannel in the other. She'd filled the washing up bowl with water. It was on the bedside cabinet, next to the calamine, under my Incredible Hulk table-lamp (bloody hell; why hadn't I stuck that in the wardrobe?)

'Cheryl's on the phone. She's going to be a while. I thought I'd better come up and take care of the patient.'

Bloody hell. Bloody hell.

Stacey patted my duvet. 'Come on, let nurse Groves have a look at you.'

She's only teasing, I thought. I knew she had a boyfriend. She wasn't really interested in me. There was no way she would *actually* go through with this and *actually* give me a blanket bath. She was waiting for me to bottle out; to scream for help or make a dash for it. Then she'd have a damn good laugh at my expense with my sister. I'd never live it down; I'd be a laughing stock all over town. Well, not bloody likely I wouldn't. Two could play this game.

'Stay cool. Call her bluff,' I told myself.

She edged up the bed, dipping the flannel in the warm water, pouting and giggling like mad.

I wasn't going to bolt for it. That would make her day. She'd have to back down first.

'Right then, you'll have to loosen that gown, if I'm going to do this properly,' she said, her eyes twinkling mischievously.

I knew her game. I wasn't playing by her rules. Reaching down beneath the duvet, I unfastened my gown. I could see the hesitation in her face. I was winning.

She reached up; unfastened the top button of my pyjama top, dabbing my neck with the flannel. She was trying to look cool and sexy, but I definitely saw her wince as she got a closer look at my blisters. Good. Serves her right.

'Does that feel nice sir?' she purred.

'Yeah, it's OK.'

'Good,' She smiled. She opened my second button. The pox on my chest were particularly raw. She tried to hide a grimace as she dabbed away with the warm flannel. Actually, it did feel soothing on my itchy skin. I think I was beginning to enjoy it more than Stacey. She would back off soon. She undid my third button, dabbing my stomach as she went.

159

I gulped again. She wouldn't go any further. I'd been watching her fingers fumbling with my buttons; she'd hesitated; she was having second thoughts. I met her eyes; a sly smile played across her lips.

'I hope you're not enjoying this too much young man!' she cackled, 'because, I'll soon find out if you are, you know!'

'You should be so lucky!' I heard myself bluff.

Don't get a stiffy. Don't get a stiffy.

Stacey giggled.

She tugged slightly on the cord at the top of my trousers; not hard enough to actually loosen them. She would turn chicken any minute now. She tugged a bit harder. The bow was open and the cord hung loose from my waist. She turned to rinse the flannel in the warm water. Ruddy hell. Had I underestimated just how much bottle she had?

'Er, is Cheryl still on the phone?' I blurted.

Stacey laughed. 'Think so; why, do you need saving?'

'No, not at all. Just wondering....'

Stacey fixed me in the eye, pulling at the top of my trousers.

Stay calm Little Tim, stay calm.

She pulled back the duvet. The wet patch now extended right across my lap.

'Oh - My - God! Oh - My - God! You're all wet! You haven't? You didn't...? You dirty little bugger!' she jumped off of my bed, screeching at the top of her voice.

'What? Eh? Oh.....no, no, you don't understand, that's just...'

It was too late. She'd freaked out. She was heading for the door.

'Oh God! Oh God!' she said, her hand across her mouth. She flung the flannel on the carpet in disgust. 'I was only having a laugh. Oh, that's just so embarrassing. I'm sorry, I'm sorry!' Stacey was practically hysterical now.

'Hang on, it's only.....,' I started to get out of bed; grabbing at my dressing gown, stumbling clumsily after her. She was out of the door now, I could hear her running down the stairs.

'Stacey, Stacey come back....I can explain...'

The front door slammed behind her.

'Tim! What the hell have you done to Stacey?' Cheryl shouted from the bottom of the stairs, still holding the telephone receiver to her shoulder.

I stood helplessly, at the top of the stairs. My dressing gown had fallen open, revealing my sopping wet trousers.

Cheryl looked horrified. She was staring straight at my crotch. 'It's only bloody calamine lotion!'

13 - ...On Any Other Day

'If Mum calls, don't say anything to her!'

'OK.'

'And don't worry, I'll explain everything to Stacey; I'll ring her tomorrow.'

'Who's worried?'

It was an hour since Stacey had stormed off. Cheryl was less angry with me now. I'd finally managed to convince her that the whole thing had been a massive misunderstanding. She'd even managed a chuckle when she'd realised what a divvy her mate was.

Now she was fretting about leaving me to meet up with Lee, now that they'd obviously made up. Frankly, I was more than happy to see her go; I was exhausted; I needed a kip. And besides, I was still hoping Roxanne would call.

'So, I'm off now. You'll be OK yeah?' Cheryl finished putting on her coat and opened the door.

'Yes!'

'Remember, if Mum calls; just say, I'm doing the washing up and I can't get to the phone.'

'OK.'

It was blowing a gail - shut the bloody door.

'Whatever you do, don't tell her I've gone out and left you, OK? She'll only do her nut.'

'OK, OK – I understand!'

'I won't be long.' Cheryl said.

'Fine, you said that already' I wished she'd just go.

'I'll be half an hour, tops.'

'Take as long as you like,' I muttered.

I spent the next forty minutes, privately doing something in my bedroom, that I'd been doing up there once a week for the past few years.

It was all Jacko's fault that I'd started doing it.

John Lennon had a posthumous number one that Christmas. "Just Like Starting Over". He'd prevented the most hideous crime in recent music history by holding off St. Winifred's School Choir from the top spot. At least until tomorrow anyway; Sunday was when the new Top

162

40 would be announced. I had a horrible feeling that "There's No-One Quite Like Grandma" would topple John from the pinnacle.

But neither John or the school kids had any chance of being Number 1 in the Tim James "Festive Top Twenty". My own personal charts were compiled religiously every Saturday, based on my very own current favourites. Jacko had started doing his own chart in the third year. I told him it was stupid; childish. He didn't seem to care.

He used to show me his charts when I went round his place. At first, I just though it was hilarious, but eventually it started to get under my skin. I found myself looking forward to seeing the Martin Jackson Top 40 for the week; and then, after a while, I began to find them really irritating. I mean The Stranglers were always number one in his bloody charts! I think that's why I started doing mine, as a rival to his. I mean The Stranglers were OK; but number one every week? He was mental. At least, I varied things a bit; The Police weren't always number one. They'd even had fewer number one hits than Elvis Costello.

John Lennon's song was OK but it only made number eighteen in my top twenty. St. Winifred's wouldn't have made my top thousand. Blondie's "Tide is High" was number one in *my* Christmas chart; true it wasn't a very Christmassy song; but then most Christmas songs were rubbish. An exception was Squeeze's "Christmas Day", which had been my number one last year, but on the whole Christmas Songs were really cheesey. Wizzard, Slade, Greg Lake; more cheese than the deli counter at the local Fine Fare.

No one knew about my charts. Mum and Dad just wouldn't understand. Cheryl would take the piss. So would my mates. I couldn't even admit their existence to Jacko; not after taking the piss out of him so much when he'd told me about his. It was just a bit of fun. And anyway it was harmless. It didn't make me a saddo. Much.

I was trying to decide between The Vapors "News At Ten" and Devo's "Whip It" for Number nineteen, when I heard the hall clock chime.

It was nearly nine o'clock. Cheryl still wasn't back.

I still hadn't heard from Roxanne. Why hadn't she called?

I bet that idiot at HMV hadn't told her I'd called. Surely Poppy would have given her my message though? Always assuming Karl had remembered to tell Poppy of course. All the way through a re-run of an old Christmas George and Mildred, various scenarios went through my

163

mind - I ended up convincing myself that Roxanne hadn't got my number. She wouldn't know how to get hold of me. That was it. She was probably expecting me to call. She'd probably be dead worried about me.

I phoned Karl.

'I *did* give Poppy your message!' he said.

'Well, did she pass it on to Roxanne?'

'I don't know! Ruddy hell, hang on a minute, will you?'

Karl sounded cheesed off with me. So much for the Christmas spirit. He put the phone down; as I waited, I heard the sound of Poppy's sarcastic voice, as well as Heidi squealing, in the background. My name was mentioned at least twice, although I couldn't really make out which of the sisters was talking about me. Then, a few moments later Karl came back to the phone.

'Poppy *thinks* she gave Roxanne your number - she can't really remember.'

'What do you mean, she can't remember?' '

'Well, when Roxanne came around last night...'

'She did what? Did you see her? Did you give her my number?'

'Well, not really, I only saw her for a split second and then they disappeared up to Poppy's room.'

'Bloody hell Karl! You saw Roxanne and you didn't ask her to ring me? Thanks a lot mate!' I fumed.

'Well, they stayed up there all night, drinking Vodka. They both got pretty pie-eyed. Roxanne was smashed by the time she went home! She had to get a taxi.'

'I bet Poppy didn't even mention me did she? Well, thank your flipping' sister for nothing for me!' I said.

'It's hardly my fault Poppy's such a dizzy bird-brain is it?'

'Bloody hell Karl, she'll be off up to Surrey now, thinking that I stood her up.'

'Well mate, you know what they say about being mean and keeping them keen!' he laughed.

'Yeah, that might be alright if you're Steve McQueen or Robert Redford. But my name is Tim James. Believe it or not *mate,* gorgeous red-heads don't come my way that often!'

'S'pose not,' Karl sniffed, sounding completely disinterested.

'Does Poppy know her number up in Surrey?'

'I don't know do I?'

'Could you ask her?'

'Bloody hell Tim, I'm trying to watch The Two Ronnies! Can't you wait until after Christmas?'

'I don't want her spending the entire holiday thinking I blew her out! Come on mate, just ask her will you? Please? Just this once?'

A couple of minutes later, I'd scribbled down a number on an old Christmas card envelope that I'd retrieved from the bin.

'Are you still coming over tomorrow?' I said,' you can see my new guitar...'

'Look mate, I'm missing Little Ronnie's joke routine, I'll speak to you later,' Karl said, and put the phone down on me.

'And a Merry Christmas to you too mate!' I said to an empty line, as the front door opened behind me.

Lee and Cheryl came in. They were laughing, They'd obviously made up. What a surprise.

'Hi Lee.'

'Hi mate, merry Christmas and all that.'

'Yeah, merry Christmas,' I muttered.

'What are you doing down here? You should be fast asleep by now!' Cheryl said, clearly expecting me to make myself scarce, now that her and Lee had all that stored up, unused Christmas saliva to exchange.

'Ok, I get the message!' I snapped, taking a couple of steps towards the bottom of the stairs. The phone rang again. I made a grab for the receiver but of course, Cheryl beat me to it.

'Tim? Yes, he's here. Who should I say is calling so late on Christmas day?' Cheryl said, sarcastically, pulling a face. She held one hand over the receiver, 'it's a young lady for you, said to say it's "a friend'!'

At last. Roxanne. Poppy must have given her the message after all.

'Hi, Roxy?'

Cheryl and Lee were still having a good beak - I waved at them to go into the living room.

'No, it's Heidi!'

'Oh, right, hi Heidi, alright?' I said, trying, but singularly failing, to keep the disappointment out of my voice.

Lee had gone into the living room. Cheryl was still standing there, gawping. I lifted up my foot and gave her backside a gentle shove. She reluctantly followed Lee.

'I asked Karl to pass the phone over but he hung up. He's such a jerk!' Heidi said.

'Oh right, yeah. Well, happy Christmas,' I said, looking at my watch.

'I told him; I only wanted to say hello and to see how you are.'

'Oh, yeah, I'm fine thanks...' I said.

Nearly ten past nine.

'....just a bit spotty and a bit itchy but I think I'm over the worst.'

'Yeah, me too, the spots are dying - I'm not so itchy anymore. I'm feeling a lot better now. Thanks for asking!' she laughed.

'Oh, sorry, yeah, that's great.'

'Well, anyway, what I was asking Karl to ask you when you were on the phone - only he forgot...'

'Yeah, he's good at forgetting..'

'...was that...well, would it be OK if I come around with him to see you tomorrow?'

'Well, yeah, I s'pose..'

'Oh great, thanks, only otherwise I'll have to go with Mum to visit Aunt Lucy. She's not really my Auntie; she's just a neighbour,' she whispered, 'she's dead boring! She always makes me eat her horrible cooking....'

Heidi went on for what seemed an eternity about her horrible Aunt Lucy, whilst I anxiously watched the clock.

'So,' I said, finally getting a word in edgeways, 'I'll see you both tomorrow then?'

'Great, I'll bring the mistletoe!' she giggled.

She would too.

'Ho ho ho!' I said, in my best Santa voice.

It was nearly twenty five past nine by the time I eventually got her off the phone.

I looked at the scribbled number on the back of the envelope. I looked at the clock. Was it too late to call?

'So, who's Heidi?' said Cheryl, sticking here head around the door.

'Yeah,' said Lee, peeking over the top of her head, 'and not only that, but who's Roxy?'

Half an hour later, I was still staring at the crumpled envelope. I should really call her and explain myself. Pulling the cord as far as I could from the door and my eaves-dropping sister. I sat on the bottom

166

step and started to dial the number. I'd give it four rings and if there was no answer, I'd leave it. I took a deep breath; imagining Roxanne and her family, all sitting around the TV or playing board games. It was a bit late really; the phone rang; once, twice, three times..

'Hang up,' I muttered, 'call tomorrow instead...'

'Hello?'

It was a male voice. There was loud music playing. Kool and the Gang. "Celebration". My heartbeat pounded to a funky disco beat.   'Oh, hello, is that Mr. Delaney?'

The music was deafening. Kool and The Gang sounded like they were having a whale of a time.

'Mr. Delaney? You want Mr. Delaney did you say?'

'Er no, ...I...'

'No, he's not here at the moment mate, can I take a message?'

A young bloke. Roxanne's brother? I could hardly hear what he was saying. It seemed he was having the same problem.

'There's a party going on right here...'

'Oh hi,' I said, sticking my finger in my ear, 'er.. is that ..Patrick?'

'Patrick! My man! How the devil are you?'

'Sorry?'

'Pat?'

'No, this isn't Pat. I thought you were...'

'Sorry, who is this? You'll have to speak up, it's a bad line....'

'Sorry, I thought you were Roxanne's brother?'

'Roxanne's brother did you say? Did you want Gerard? Hang on..'

'Gerard!'

'I heard footsteps; a door closing. The music grew quieter.

'Hello?' another voice said, 'this is Gerard. Who's that?'

'Sorry, I was after Roxanne. Is she there?' I said.

'Roxanne?' the voice sounded puzzled, 'Er yeah I guess so, who shall I say is calling?'

'Oh, it's Tim...her...friend.'

'Roxy!'

There was a brief pause. Kool and The Gang got much louder again; someone had opened a door. Then they went quiet again. I could hear a male voice, followed at last by Roxanne's.

'Some kid for you. I think he said, Tim?' the male voice said. There was another brief pause; I could hear them talking but couldn't make out what was being said.

167

'Tim? Is that you?'

'Yeah, hi Roxanne. It's me?'

'What's up?' she said, sounding a bit strange, 'is something wrong. It's a bit late for a social call isn't it?'

'I just wanted to say hello and wish you a Merry Christmas!'

'What, at ten o'clock at night?' she sounded narked, just like Karl had done earlier.

'Well, I wanted to make sure you got my message.'

'Message?'

'Yeah, I was a bit worried in case you thought I'd sort of, you know, stood you up or something the other day...'

'No, don't be silly. Charlie from the shop told me you'd called. I knew you were poorly.'

'Oh right. That's OK then. I suppose he didn't give you my number then?'

There was a pregnant pause.

'Actually, to be honest, I think he did, but the last few days have been so manic, I sort of...mislaid the bit of paper. I tried to find it when Poppy reminded me yesterday.'

Oh well, perhaps Poppy Bloom wasn't so bad.

'..we got a bit bladdered and then I had to drive up here with a hangover and well, it's been a bit mad here. Sorry.'

'Oh, right, I see....,' I said, feeling a little hurt. Still, I suppose she had been a bit busy by the sounds of it. 'Sounds like a bit of a party going on?'

Kool and the Gang had finished celebrating. Now it was the turn of the Bee Gees; either that or Roxanne's brother was castrating the family cat.

'Er, yeah, we've got a few people round.'

'Was that your brother?'

'What? oh yes, Gerard. Patrick's still touring Europe. We thought that might be him calling. Mum's going ape-shit that he hasn't rung us.

'Oh, right I thought that was him answering the phone.'

'Oh, no that was....my cousin Rob.'

'Your cousin?'

'Yeah, my...cousin Rob.'

'Oh right, well, like I say, I was a bit worried that's all....so, I just thought I'd...'

The music got louder again.

168

'Shut the bloody door! I'm still on the phone!' Roxanne shouted.

"How deep is your love?" Hairy Gibb was screeching.

An appropriate enough question. Roxanne wasn't giving me any real clues.

I didn't think much of her family's taste in music.

'So,' I said, not really knowing what else to say now that I'd called, 'I haven't gone to Wales after all.'

"....living in a world of fools,"

How *do* they reach those high notes?'

'You're in Wales?' she said; she was barely audible.

There were two voices again now; Roxanne sounded muffled. The other voice was male.

Roxanne said something but I couldn't make it out.

'Sorry. What was that?' I said.

'What? Oh no, I wasn't taking to you Tim. Look....'

'Er excuse me mate,' someone had grabbed the phone. It sounded like her cousin again. 'Sorry, but it's a bit late and I'm expecting a call. Can you call back when it's not Christmas?'

'Christ Rob, you're pissed!' I heard Roxanne shout, before she came back on the phone. 'Listen Tim it's a bit awkward at the moment - maybe I'll call you tomorrow OK?'

'Ok, that sounds great ....'

The phone went dead.

I sat down on the stairs.

No matter how long I stared at the phone, it wasn't going to ring. She wasn't calling back.

'Everything OK out here?' said Lee, as he came out to get another can from the kitchen.

'Are you still up?' Cheryl shouted from the living room, 'isn't it about time you got some sleep?

'Yes Mum!' I shouted sarcastically.

'Less of your lip. Get you're arse up those stairs!' she said.

'Night mate,' Lee said, carrying his lager back to the TV; closing the door behind him.

After a couple of minutes, I finally traipsed upstairs, feeling utterly miserable.

My blisters hurt like hell.

Roxanne had been really weird. What had happened? What had I done?

Women! I'd never understand them if I lived to be thirty-five.
And that bloke on the phone. What was all that about?
Rob.
Her Cousin.
Wasn't her ex-boyfriend called Rob?
Robert. Rugby playing Robert. Was that rugby playing Robert?
And if so, what was he doing around Roxanne's house at Christmas?
Something stank; and it wasn't just the calamine.
A poxy end to a poxy Christmas.

14 - I Burn For You

"I'm still here, I'm not going anywhere".
Thomas Hardy's *Far From The Madding Crowd* was taunting me.

That was the thing about homework; no matter how much I tried to ignore it or put it off, it wouldn't go away; it never did itself. It always, but always, required my input. The only exception to this rule over the years, had been on the couple of occasions when Gary Hurst had been persuaded to do it for me. And even then, there had been input from me, in the form of appropriate remuneration. Since we'd been in the sixth form however, Gary (who was now studying Commerce as one of his A-levels), had finally wised up. He had put his prices up. Even with the combined incomings of my weekly pocket money and paper-round salary, his fees were now out of my league.

At some stage over the next two weeks, I had a date with the man with the impressive moustache who stared at me accusingly from the back cover of my dog-eared paperback.

"You'll have to face me sometime."

'Not tonight matey.'

I covered Hardy's face with a plate of Bourbon creams.

'There's always tomorrow.'

Even though I knew I was only putting off the inevitable, I really couldn't raise the enthusiasm.

Unfortunately for Hardy, that afternoon, Jacko had presented me with Volume 6 in his series of now legendary "songs for Tim" mix-tapes. One giant of English Literature versus the assembled heroes of, what I assumed would be, the contemporary punk and new wave scene. No competition - sorry Thomas.

To be fair, even without the delights of Jacko's latest TDK C90, there were already too many other tasty distractions available to me; there was Christmas TV to watch, my new guitar to play around with; and countless board games to be played. Tackling homework on Boxing Day wasn't the smartest idea that I'd ever had. But then the idea hadn't actually been mine to start with. It had been Cheryl's.

'Haven't you got homework to do?' she said, as I beat Lee at Connect Four yet again. I'd only just finished my tea.

Cheryl was gesturing towards the stairs with her head and giving me a funny look. I knew what she was getting at but I wasn't giving in that easily.

'I'm not well.'

'Yeah, I could tell that from the way you polished off that second barrel of Twiglets!'

Lee chuckled and went off to get yet another lager from the fridge.

Cheryl moved across to sit next to me on the sofa, as I put the game back in it's box. She placed her warm little hand on my arm, leant over and whispered in my ear.

'A quid?'

'Disney time is on in a minute!'

She shook her head and pulled some money from the pocket of her Wranglers.

'One pound fifty and that's my last offer,' she slammed a note and a coin down on the coffee table.

'Deal.'

I'd quite fancied watching Disney-time, followed by *"Earthquake"*, but it was always a smart move to stay in Cheryl's good books, especially when she was prepared to throw hard cash my way. So, as Cheryl and Lee settled down to some serious snogging in front of ITV's Big Christmas Movie, I found myself up in my room, quite definitely not doing my essay. I laid back on the bed, pressed the 'play' button on the music centre and prepared myself for an evening of musical delights, courtesy of Martin Jackson.

Jacko had been the first of a small parade of friends who turned up to "visit the invalid" on Boxing Day. And he'd certainly been the least problematic. He arrived that morning, unannounced, looking decidedly nervous.

'I'm on my way to Fay's place,' he explained.

'Really?'

'Yeah, I've had the big summons to meet the folks.'

'Isn't it a bit soon? You only rediscovered each other a couple of weeks back! Isn't it a bit early to be asking Mr. Carpenter's permission for his daughter's hand in marriage?'

'That's pretty much what I told her, but apparently "they've heard all about me" and "can't wait to meet me."

'Really? Are you sure she's told them all about the right person? I mean, surely, if they've "heard all about *you*", the last thing they'd want to do would be to *meet* you?'

'Watch it sunshine, just because you're a bit spotty don't think I wouldn't give you a camel bite!'

Jacko's "camel bites" were the stuff of nightmares. The procedure involved him grabbing, really hard, on the flesh of your inner thigh until you pleaded for mercy. I cringed at the thought; the camel-bite was bad enough at the best of times but if he caught one of my blisters between those evil finger-nails of his, I knew I'd howl like a baby.

'It *is* a *bit odd* though don't you think?' I said.

'Yeah, definitely. Do you think they're going to warn me off their daughter?'

'Maybe. Perhaps money will be involved? They might make it worth your while!'

'How much do you reckon?'

'A couple of quid?'

'Well,' he said, rubbing his stubbly chin, 'Fay is quite tasty but every man has his price. If they make it a fiver, I'll think about it!'

Jacko laughed, but I could tell he was bricking it. His leg was doing that St.Vitus-dance thing.

'So, to what do I owe the pleasure?' I said.

'Well, I thought I'd just bring a pen around and play join the dots!' he laughed, drawing an imaginary line in the air in the front of my face, 'God, you're a spotty sod aren't you? I thought your acne was bad enough but really, this takes the biscuit!'

'So, you just came around to take the piss then?'

'Oh yeah and to deliver this,' he reached into his parka pocket and pulled out the tape.

'Oh, classic!' I said, 'cheers mate.'

'Well, I was doing one for Fay - she absolutely loved it by the way - never fails, a mix-tape I tell you - and well, I thought I'd run you off a copy too.'

Oh well, it's the thought that counts.

Half an hour after I'd finally persuaded Jacko he should be biting the bullet and heading for his future in-laws, the phone went. As usual, Cheryl did her Alan Wells impression and sprinted to the phone before I could even put my guitar down and get out of the armchair.

'Tim? Yes, who is this? Let me guess, Heidi? Roxanne?'

She was really asking for a dead leg that Cheryl.

'Oh right! Hello, how are you? Tim! It's Alison.'

Bloody hell. Now what? I snatched the phone and glanced in the hall mirror. It was nearly one o'clock in the afternoon. I was still wearing my pyjamas and I hadn't brushed my hair.

'What the hell do they all see in you?' Cheryl said.

'You've either got it or you haven't!' I said.

'Well if you've got it,' Cheryl smirked whilst wrinkling her nose, 'it needs a wash; it smells like a dead thing.'

'So, did you have a good Christmas?' I asked Alison.

It was weird. If Alison Fisher had rung me on Boxing Day last year - or in fact, any previous year since I'd first met her, I'd have probably wet my trousers. Today, I actually felt irritated. She wasn't Roxanne.

'Yeah, fine thanks...you?'

'Well, I've had better Alison. Chicken pox is no barrel of laughs.'

'No, I remember. Sorry.'

'I look like the spotty dog from The Wooden Tops? Do you remember, 'the biggest spotty dog you ever....'

'It must be terrible,' she said, interrupting my meaningless twaddle, '...I was just wondering, if you've heard from Chris at all?'

Her concern was overwhelming. And Roxanne reckoned Alison had the hots for me! Like hell. She was still potty about Humph.

'Not a dicky bird, you?'

'No, not a thing,' she sounded gutted.

'Well, not to worry. He'll be in touch - as soon as he gets fed up with Waldorf and Statler's company.'

She laughed.

'Yeah, that's them! Pete and Doddsy. At last! *That's* who they remind me of!'

'Exactly. They're right Muppets, those two.'

There was another pause. I heard her breathing; I couldn't think of much to say - as usual.

'So, anyway, what I was going to ask was, are you up for a visit this afternoon?'

'Well, not really, I can't leave the house..'

'No, stupid, can I come over to you? I could do with getting out of the house for an hour.'

174

'Well...'

'Don't worry, I've *had c*hicken pox.'

'Yeah but...' I glanced at myself in the mirror again. Did I really want Alison Fisher to see me looking like this?' '...Karl and Heidi Bloom are coming over.'

'Karl?'

'Yeah, and Heidi...'

'Karl? Really? What time?' Alison sounded perkier all of a sudden.

'Not sure, this afternoon sometime...'

'OK, great, I'll see you after lunch then.......oh and Tim, I've got a little surprise for you...,' she giggled.

'What?'

She'd hung up.

I'd never washed so quickly in my life. It took me less than ten minutes; and that included washing my hair, splashing on some of my Dad's Old Spice and re-applying calamine lotion to every spot I could find; carefully - I wanted no repeat of the Stacey Groves fiasco.

Then, I took ages deciding what to wear. After much debate, I settled on my old school rugby shirt. Not that I ever really played rugby - but it was one of the things that your parents had to buy for their kids when you started in the second year. The shirt was much too small now and it smelt musty. I probably hadn't worn it for two years, but it did have one major advantage. I could pull up the collar - blokes in bands were always doing that - that way I'd look pretty cool *and* hide the blisters on my disgusting neck. It was tight and only came down to my belly button but the collar was huge; you could hardly see the zits on my neck at all. I was just in time. The front doorbell rang. I started racing down the stairs.

As usual, Cheryl beat me to it. She grinned stupidly at me, as she pulled open the door.

'Chez!' said Stacey Groves as she came bounding through the door, throwing her arms around my sister.

'Alright darlin'?' Cheryl said.

They hugged and kissed as if they hadn't seen each other since the Beatles split up.

My momentum carried me to the bottom step, before I realised my mistake.

Stacey had seen me. Too late to turn back. There was a brief awkward silence as our eyes met. Then she started giggling. And so did Cheryl.

'Oh Timmy' Stacey blushed, pouting, 'are we still friends?'

'Of course,' I shrugged. I was dead cool about it.

'Sorry about yesterday. Cheryl explained. I felt so silly!'

'Forget it,' I said.

'So what do you think?' Stacey asked, twirling in order to show off her frock. It was black, very tight fitting. She looked amazing; it was a very different look for her. For one thing, it came all the way down to her knees.

'I love it!' said Cheryl

'Yeah, Mehmet's such a sweetie, he chose it all by himself!'

Mehmet. That must be the boyfriend; the good looking middle-eastern bloke. It reminded me of that night in the Peds. I hoped Stacey hadn't realised I was there.

Stacey beamed, looking at me expectantly. Was I expected to comment on the dress too?

'Very nice,' I muttered.

'Well, thank you kind sir! And you look....' she looked me up and down, '....interesting.'

'Is that seriously what you're wearing for your girlfriends?' said Cheryl, 'you must have something smarter than that?' she tutted, shaking her head.

'Girlfriends?' shrieked Stacey.

'Yeah, he's got them flocking after him. God knows why!' Cheryl smirked.

'Well, I'm not that surprised. I did say he was a cutie!'

I stared at my feet.

'Well, I can't see it myself but he must have something. They've all been on the phone. There's an Alison, a Heidi, a Roxanne. I can't keep up with it - and they're all coming around to visit today!'

'Not *all actually!*' I said, feeling flustered.

Roxanne wasn't coming. She hadn't even called.

'It's really nice, don't you think Karl?' Heidi said, as she sat on the end of my bed.

'Yeah it's not bad mate - for a first one like, you know.'

176

Karl sat on the floor, plucking a tune on my amp-less guitar. I was sitting at the head of the bed, resting against the wall; my hair brushing against my "Regatta De Blanc" Poster.

'Love the poster!' Heidi said, 'I can't believe we missed the gig. Was it as great as Juliette said?'

Karl looked up at the sound of Juliette's name.

'Yeah, it was fantastic,' I said, 'would you like another mince-pie?'

I was trying to steer the conversation away from the dangerous territory of The Police gig; and of bloody Dave and Juliette. There was no way I could avoid it all afternoon.

Heidi munched her third mince-pie, spilling crumbs onto the floor, where Chalky gratefully hoovered them up.

'Blimey, you don't half knock the food back!' I laughed.

'I know, I am so fat aren't I?' Heidi said, holding out her tiny stomach. It was like an ironing board.

'She ought to be the size of her mate Glenda!' Karl smirked.

'Oh, don't be wicked about Glenda!' said Heidi, 'you know she loves you to bits.'

'Worse luck,' Karl muttered, playing a little tune that sounded a bit like "Hey Jude" - but only a bit.

'So, have you heard from Boothie at all?' Karl asked, 'he hasn't been in touch since the gig. He's petrified.'

'Of what?' I said, almost choking on a mouthful of Mr. Kipling's.

'Of catching the pox of course. He's a right chicken, if you excuse the pun!'

I laughed; breathing a sigh of relief. There would be hell to pay when Karl found out about Dave and Juliette. Ah well, it wasn't my fault that Dave chased anything in a skirt.

'So,' said Heidi, 'did you hear from Roxanne? Juliette said you two were getting on like a house on fire at the concert.'

'Er yeah, she's gone back home for Christmas but I spoke to her yesterday.'

'Oh, great,' Heidi said.

'So, does that mean you two are...you know..,' Karl looked at me, then at Heidi. He was obviously embarrassed talking about such things in front of his little sister.

So was I.

'Are you "doing it" with Roxanne? That's what he wants to know,' Heidi said, shaking her head in disgust.

My cheeks were burning now.

'That's not quite what I was going to ask *actually*!' Karl laughed.

'No comment,' I said, throwing my pillow at Heidi.

The doorbell came to my rescue. We heard Cheryl gallop down the hallway.

'TIM!!'

For once, I was actually glad to hear Cheryl's voice. I got up and stuck my head around the door.

'Two more young ladies to see you!' Cheryl said in her most sarcastic tone.

Two?

'I told you I had a surprise for you!' Alison said. She took her coat off and threw it on the bottom of the bed, next to Heidi.

'Don't I even get a kiss hello then?' said Collette Fisher, Alison's cousin from Solihull.

She stood over me, offering her cheek. I gave her a peck and felt myself flush.

'You look.....spotty,' she said, eyeing me up and down, 'I think you may have shot up a few inches since the summer!'

'Really?' I didn't think I'd grown at all.

'Yeah, judging by that top you're wearing!' she laughed.

Ouch.

'Off to play rugby are you?' she said sarcastically.

She hadn't changed much.

'Heidi, Karl, you both know Alison, and this is her cousin Collette,' I said.

It was getting crowded. My little bedroom wasn't really designed for five people and a lunatic dog. Chalky was going bananas, lapping up all the fuss. Alison manoeuvred herself so that she was sitting cross-legged, next to Karl on the floor. Chalky instantly curled himself up in her lap, wagging his tail furiously. Karl was cradling my guitar like his life depended on it.

Collette Fisher sat herself down on the bed between me and Heidi. It was the first time I'd seen her since she'd gone back up north. We'd had a holiday fling in the summer. Collette was older than me, the same age as Roxanne. I must have a weakness for older women. Collette was dark and pretty. I used to think she looked like Kate Bush; then she sent me a photo. She'd had her hair cut short. I'd realised that she didn't look much like Kate at all and, possibly as a result, I didn't really fancy her that much.

'So you're the local rock star that Alison's been telling me all about then?' Colette said to Karl.

'Hardly,' smiled Karl. His adams-apple bobbed up and down. He was suddenly fascinated by the guitar strings.

'What are the band called again?'

'The Morbid Morsels,' Heidi said proudly.

'Sounds like a bundle of fun,' said Collette. She stared at Heidi liked she'd only just noticed her, 'and which of these lucky boys are you attached to?'

Heidi giggled and went bright red, 'Karl's my brother and Tim's a...Tim's Karl's mate.'

'Oh right. So, do you always follow your brother to his mate's houses?' Collette teased.

Poor Heidi.

'Ah, don't blush, I'm only joking,' Collette said in her Solihull accent, 'you want to watch this one though,' she said, jerking her thumb at me, 'he's a bit of a heartbreaker.'

'Honestly Collette, you're such a wind-up merchant! Leave them alone will you?' Alison grinned.

'Anyway Collette,' I said, suddenly rediscovering my voice, 'how's what's-his-face?'

'Greg? OK I expect.'

'Still driving his Cortina is he?'

'Ooh, Cortina driver eh?' laughed Karl, 'furry dice? Leopard-skin interior?'

Alison burst out laughing, a little too much. It wasn't that funny.

'Ha ha!' said Collette, 'actually Greg drives a Dolomite these days..'

'Wow a Dolomite Karl, fancy that!' I scoffed.

'Well....as far as I know,' Collette continued, 'he's seeing some air-stewardess from Heathrow these days. Her name's Chloe.'

'Oh, sorry,' I said.

'That's OK, there's plenty more fish in the sea Timbo! Are you seeing anyone?' she winked.

I gulped. Not for the first time, I had the distinct feeling that Collette Fisher would eat me alive if I let her.

'He's seeing a very pretty young lady, aren't you Tim?' said Alison, 'her name's Roxanne and she works in HMV.'

'Roxanne? Roxanne?' spluttered Collette, 'what? Roxanne as in "Roxanne" by your favourite band The Police? Bloody hell Tim, how long did it take you to find someone with that name? Or did you get her to change her name by deed-poll?'

The others were all laughing now. Even I was struggling not to.

'Roxanne is her bonafide, real, honest-to-God name!' I said.

'Only, be honest Tim, you do seem to make a habit of falling for girls based purely on songs by your heroes, don't you?' said Collette, trying to suppress a stupid grin.

'What?'

'Well, didn't Elvis Costello do a song called Alison?'

'Collette! Behave yourself will you?' Alison said. She picked up the pillow and whacked her cousin.

Karl and Heidi started giggling.

I'd walked straight into that one.

All through her last visit, Collette had teased me about the fact that it was "obvious" to her that I had a crush on Alison. She'd also told me that Alison wasn't my type. At the time, I'd been so impressed with this confident, exotic newcomer that I'd instantly started to agree with her. Now, I was starting to wonder what I'd ever seen in Collette. There was a thin line between confident and cocky.

'You're so wicked!' Alison said to her, 'just ignore her Tim, she was on the Snowballs before we came out. She doesn't know what she's saying!'.

'What I'm saying is that unless Paul Weller writes a song for The Jam called "Collette", I've got no chance of rekindling our little relationship!'

Karl and Heidi thought she was hilarious.

I just shook my head, sneaking a furtive glance at the clock. Gone three o'clock. No call from Roxanne. When were this lot buggering off home? Should I call her? Would that seem too desperate?

Thankfully, the pick-on-Tim session seemed to be over as quickly as it had started. Alison and Collette started asking Karl about his band. They were both flirting like mad. I don't know what Karl had that made girls go all doe-eyed but whatever it was, for the moment I was glad of it.

They asked him who his favourite guitarists were. Karl talked about someone called Barney Sumner.

'Is that Sting's dad?' laughed Alison.

'Barney Rubble? Isn't he in The Flintstones?' winked Collete.

'Joy Division,' Karl said, 'you know, "Love Will Tear Us Apart"?'

'Isn't he dead?' said Heidi.

'No! That's Ian Curtis, their singer, thicko!' I said. I'd never heard of Barney Sumner but everyone knew Ian Curtis was the singer.

Heidi leant over and slapped me on the leg, 'Oi, don't call me "thicko"!' she laughed.

'Don't know him,' said Collette, her eyes twinkling like she'd just switched them on for Christmas, 'who else? Anyone we might have heard of?'

'How about The Edge. You must have heard of The Edge?'

'Are we still talking about guitarists or has he moved onto trigonometry?' Collette asked Heidi, who giggled right on cue.

'U2? The Edge from U2?' Karl said.

And so it went on; the Fisher girls bombarding Karl with questions. Karl looked seriously flustered; he might need rescuing soon, I thought. Well, for the moment he could bloody well tread-water - I wasn't about to throw him a lifeline; I was relishing the breathing space. I was wondering if I could sneak out under the radar and make a call to Weybridge.

There was a knock on the door.

Lee stuck his head in. It was the first time I'd ever known him come to my room. I looked at the three attractive teenage girls lolling around my bed and wondered whether this was a sheer coincidence.

'The girls downstairs have made mulled wine and hot sausage rolls. Are there any takers?' Lee announced, smiling for the ladies.

Smarmy git. He'd be dead if Cheryl saw him.

'Brilliant!' said Karl, seeing his chance for escape and grabbing it with both hands. He leapt to his feet, dumped the guitar on the bed next to Heidi and headed for the door.

'Yeah, thanks, that sounds great!' said Alison, following suit.

'Wait for me!' Heidi got up too and followed her brother.

'Get me some Ali, will you?' shouted Collette, 'I'll stay her and look after the invalid.'

'So, have you spoken to Dave since the concert?' I heard Karl ask Alison, as they walked down stairs together. Oh bugger.

'ALISON!' I shouted, leaping to my feet.

The door slammed shut in front of me. Collette stood with her back to it, barring the way.

'So, alone at last...' she said.

'But I really fancy a sausage roll while they're still hot...,' I protested.

'I'm sure the others will bring some up,' Collette said.

She had that look back in her eye; like Bruce Banner, just before he gets angry and turns into The Hulk. Something told me I wouldn't like her if she got angry. I sat back on the bed and waited for her to start turning green.

'So, you and this Roxanne, is it serious?'

Bloody hell, she didn't mess around.

'Er, depends what you mean by...'

'And is that why you stopped writing to me?'

Stopped writing to her? What did she mean? I'd never bloody written to her.

'Sorry? What?'

'You didn't write back to me; when I sent you my photo.'

'Er, no, well, you were with Greg and his legendary Cortina,' I said.

Was she accusing *me* of terminating our relationship? *She* dumped *me. Didn't she?*

'There didn't seem much point...' I said.

'Well, that's just it, I wasn't still with Greg was I?' she said, 'not after I told him about you...'

'You said he was fine with it...'

She did, I distinctly remember her saying so.

'Well, yeah, so I thought!' she said. She sat heavily on the bed next to me, her head on her chest. 'And then, lo and behold, two weeks later, he goes off with a trolley-dolly.'

'Oh. Right. Well, sorry, but what's that got to do with me?'

'What do you mean, what's that got to do with you? It's got everything to do with you! He only dumped me because I told him about you. It's obvious isn't it?'

'Is it? Maybe he just met this..Cleo.....'

'Chloe.'

'Chloe...and ...'

'...and what?'

'Well....he just preferred her?'

'Oh, lovely, thanks for that vote of confidence Timothy. As if being dumped by two different blokes in two weeks isn't bad enough! Kick a girl while she's down why don't you?'

'Maybe you shouldn't have been seeing two blokes at the same time then?' I heard myself say. It sounded much harsher than I intended.

'Oh, that's bloody rich. You didn't seem bothered when your tongue was in my mouth!' she said. There was real anger in her voice now.

Blimey, where was all this coming from? She looked furious. Were those tears in her eyes or was this just another part of her Incredible Hulk transformation?

'I didn't even know....'

'Well, fuck you!' she said. And then, she stormed out of the room.

'Uh?....' I said to the door as it slammed behind her. The door didn't answer.

'What on earth did you say to Collette?' asked Alison, as she came back into the room, two minutes later. 'She's in the kitchen, in floods of tears!'

'Nothing. I don't know. Is she ...hormonal or something...?'

'Well, she's been a bit upset since she split up with Greg, but she's been fine the last few days...until now!'

I shook my head. Alison shrugged. She sat down on the bed and offered me a hot sausage roll. We sat there and ate in silence.

'So, are Karl and Heidi keeping her company down there?' I asked as I chomped on the last mouthful.

'No...er I think I might have put my foot in it there. Karl said they had to go. He seemed really ....odd, all of a sudden.'

'You didn't...'

'I forgot!'

'How could you forget? You knew Karl was besotted with Juliette!'

'It just sort of came out...'

'What? What did you say?'

'That the last time I saw Dave, he was examining Juliette's fillings..'

'You said what?'

'It was a joke. The sort of thing Collette's always coming out with...'

'Bloody Collette! She's bad news.'

'You've changed your tune!' she smiled.

I laughed.

What a day.

'Sorry about Karl. He'll get over it,' she said.

'After he's killed Dave, maybe.'

'Oh God, do you think we should warn him.'

'I think we should stay out of it from now on, don't you?'

Alison shrugged. 'Christmas does strange things to people doesn't it?'

'I suppose it does,' I said.

Alison laid back on my bed, studying the sleeve of my new UB40 album. She had really long legs. Her foot was resting on my thigh. The leg of her jeans had ridden up and I could see an inch or two of perfect, pale skin above her pumps. Damn. Alison Fisher even had sexy ankles.

'Tim?' she said.

'Yeah?'

'What do you think Chris is up to today?' she gazed at me. She looked miserable. Her eyes were welling up. Oh bloody hell.

'I really don't know Alison. Sorry, but you'll have to excuse me. I really must just go to the loo.'

Women. They were so emotional!

I must have been in the loo for ten minutes - just sitting there. If I waited long enough, would Alison and Collette get fed up and go home? Didn't they know I was ill? Couldn't they just leave me alone?

After a while, I heard strains of UB40, floating through the wall from my bedroom. I think that answered my question. They were happy to wait. They were making themselves comfortable by the sound of it. Forcing myself to my feet, I spoke sharply to my reflection.

'Come on, Tim, be a man. Get back in there. Tell them it's been great to see them but you're tired and need to lie down.'

Was that the phone?

I pushed open the door.

'Tim, it's Roxanne!' shouted Cheryl.

184

At last.

'So, that was quick. How's Roxanne?' asked Alison, as I got back to my room. At least she'd stopped crying; she was jigging around to UB40's "Food for Thought", admiring herself in my mirror; dry-eyed and back to as-near-perfection-as-it-was possible to be. Collette had come back up too; she'd passed me in the hall, as I talked on the phone with Roxanne. She'd given me a look. Now, she sat on the floor; she was uncharacteristically quiet, my new guitar resting on her lap.

'OK,' I said, defensively.

I didn't want to talk about it.

'So, when are you two love birds getting together again then?'

'Not sure really. I don't think she wants to risk catching the dreaded pox,' I said, casually.

'She's blown him out,' Collette muttered.

'Ho ho,' I said.

'She hasn't!' laughed Alison, 'she hasn't has she?' she said, studying my face.

'No, of course she hasn't!'

'So, you're seeing her for New Year then?' asked Alison.

'Er...no, not really.'

'Told you, she's blown him out,' Collette strummed on my guitar, looking pleased with herself.

'If you *must* know, Miss. Know-it-all, she's staying up in Weybridge for a few days. Her Dad's not very well.'

'Huh!' Collette said, 'the old sick-relative ploy eh?'

Alison gave her cousin's feet a swift kick; looked at her daggers.

'Oh dear, nothing serious I hope?' she said.

'Not sure really, she sounded...a bit weird,' I said, picking up my Thomas Hardy; feigning interest in the back cover blurb.

'What exactly did she say?' Asked Alison.

'She just said her Dad wasn't well - he's having tests done.'

I remembered the sound of Roxanne's voice.

"They think it might be..."

Her voice had trailed off.

"I'm going to stay up here and see how things pan out."

On reflection, I realised, I hadn't handled the news as sensitively as I could have.

'Really? How long do you reckon that will take?'

185

'How do I know Tim? Not too long I hope. A couple of weeks maybe?' she'd said, irritation in her voice.

'Fine,' I'd said, sulkily. I was still thinking about her so-called cousin. What the hell was going on?

'Well, I'll call you when I get back OK?' she'd said.

'OK, hope your Dad is ...' I tried to say. To be fair it was a bit of an after-thought.

She'd already put the phone down.

'Well,' she's just a bit worried about her Dad, isn't she?' Alison said. 'Things'll be fine when she comes back to Brighton. You'll see.'

'Do you think so?' I said.

'Of course, trust me, I'm a girl!' said Alison, tousling my hair.

'Yeah, don't worry Tim,' Collette said to my complete surprise.

'Thanks,' I muttered begrudgingly.

'She probably just *"prefers"* Weybridge,' Collette grinned.

I thought they'd never go. I yawned; closed my eyes; lay on the bed; asked Alison to get me some Aspirin; basically feigned being as near to death's door as it was possible to be, without actually keeling over. Eventually, thank God, they got the hint. They went home for tea. Alison kissed me on the cheek and said she'd see me soon; Collette didn't and wouldn't. She'd said her piece; I didn't think I would be hearing from her again any time soon. I wasn't too upset. Nutter.

I was exhausted. I went downstairs and collapsed on the sofa with Chalky. Cheryl and Lee were washing up as I watched some Survival special on ITV all about Penguins. Then Cheryl made me some toast and marmite and we played Connect Four.

That was when Cheryl 'suggested' I have an early night and so, reluctantly, I climbed the stairs for an evening with Gabriel and Bathsheba. Or, as it turned out with Sting and Joe Jackson.

I lay on the bed; Jack's mix-tape in one hand; Hardy in the other. The track-listing for Martin Jackson's latest masterpiece made interesting reading.

"It's Different For Girls" by Joe Jackson.

Fair enough. Good choice.

"My Sharona" - The Knack.

OK, if you like that sort of thing.

"Dance Away" - Roxy Music.

A bit schmaltzy. But classy with it.

"The First Time Ever I Saw Your Face" - Roberta Flack.

What?

"I'm Not in Love" - 10cc.

Sorry?

"Kiss You All Over" - Exile.

Eh?

The track-list, all written out in Jacko's unmistakeable scrawl, contained no fewer than seven "loves", two 'kisses", and three "hearts".

Bloody hell. What was going on? Talk abut a musical departure. Jacko was a punk! Or was he a mod? Anyway, whatever he was, this music wasn't Jacko.

I picked out the earlier volumes of "Songs for Tim" from my dusty cassette box and studied the contents.

Volume 1

"Wasted Life"- Stiff Little Fingers,

"I Feel Like A Wog" - The Stranglers,

"F**k off"- Wayne County and The Electric Chairs,

"Liar" - The Sex Pistols.

That was Jacko; angry, offensive, a bit nasty.

Volume 2

"Hateful" - The Clash,

"Borstal Breakout" - Sham 69,

"Killing An Arab"- The Cure.

Pretty much more of the same.

Volume 3

"Homicide"- 999.

"Orgasm Addict" - The Buzzcocks,

"The Winker's Song (misprint)" - Ivor Biggun.

A bit of humour thrown in, fair enough - but still pretty punky.

And now I studied side two of his latest;

Volume 6

"Without You" - Nilsson?

"Bridge Over Troubled Water" - Simon and Garfunkel?? -

"D'ya Think I'm Sexy?"- Rod Stewart???

187

No, I bloody well don't think you're sexy Jacko! There were no two ways about it; "Songs for Tim, Volume 6" was definitely a surprise. "Songs for Fay, Volume 1" more like.

'You wait until I see him,' I muttered to myself, 'he's gone all lovey-dovey

And then I saw it, tucked away there; last track, side 2. Like he'd hoped I wouldn't notice.

"I Burn For You" - The Police (bootleg)

The Police on a Jacko compilation? Now I knew things were getting serious.

"I Burn For You" was probably the closest thing to a ballad that I'd ever heard Sting sing. Jacko had given me a "bootleg" live LP of a Police gig last year. He'd got it for me at some record fair he'd gone to up in London. It was great.

Jacko dismissed it of course. He'd told me he had only played the LP once. He said it was rubbish; couldn't wait to get rid of it. He wouldn't take any money for it, that he'd feel like he was "robbing me".

Well, it can't have been that bad can it? I mean he must have bloody taped it before he'd given it to me.

Blimey. "I Burn For You" by The Police.

The story, according to the NME, was that it was a really old song that Sting had written for the jazz band he'd been in, before he was in The Police. I loved it. I wished they'd record it properly. It would be massive. And now, here it was, tucked away on 'Songs For Tim Volume 6".

Fancy Jacko doing a loved-up mixtape for a girl. So much for Punk. Mind you, he said Fay had loved it. An idea was forming in my mind. Cheryl's new hi-fi had a tape-to-tape deck. I could do another copy. Yeah, definitely. Why not? If it worked for Jacko, maybe it could work for me too?

I pressed fast-forward and found the start of the song. Throwing "Far From The Madding Crowd" on the floor, I kicked off my slippers and laid back on the bed. A voice cut in, pure and unaccompanied.

'Now that I have found you....'

Sting was burning for his lover.

Sting 1 Thomas Hardy 0.

15 - Be My Girl

'You were absolutely bladdered!'

'Oh and you weren't I suppose?'

'Not as bad as you mate! Me, Pete and Doddsy had to carry you out of the pub!'

'I'm surprised you can even remember, the state you were in!'

'It was a great night though eh?'

'Totally!'

It was a week into the New Year, 1981, and Humph and Jacko had come around to cheer me up; which for some reason they'd decided would be best achieved by going on about what a brilliant time they'd had, out and about in Brighton on New Years Eve, whilst I was stuck at home, still recovering from bloody chicken pox, watching Juliet Bravo and the Two Ronnies with my Mum and Dad.

'So where did you actually end up?' I asked. 'Did you get into any of the clubs?'

'No, we didn't bother. Too much hassle with all that crap about dress codes and needing to show ID,' Humph explained.

For a group of young blokes, getting into one of the Brighton Discos was never easy - especially if some of the group were under age.

'We gate-crashed a party upstairs at the Sea-House,' explained Jacko.

'Yeah, we were there at slinging out time and Doddsy gets chatting to this woman his sister sort of knows,' Humph explained.

'And it turns out that this woman is a friend of a girl who was related to the bloke whose party it was....' Jacko continued

'No, the woman's mate used to go out with his sister.....'

'Oh right, did she? Oh, I thought....'

'So, you got in there then?' I interrupted, cutting their incredibly long story short.

'Yeah, so we all piled up there and it was a really good laugh, as it turns out. There was a DJ, free grub, subsidised bar, the whole lot. We were dead lucky. We'd never have got into Sherry's,' said Jacko.

'Well, *you* wouldn't, *you* were already well oiled by then,' Humph said.

And so it continued.....they prattled on endlessly about what an amazing time they'd had.

This was the first time I'd seen Jacko since Boxing Day. I hadn't seen Humph since the Christmas party and his very public bust-up with Alison. I'd almost forgotten what either of them looked like. Jacko had become permanently attached at the hip to Fay Carpenter - frankly, I was surprised to hear he hadn't gone out without her on New Years Eve. He was totally under the thumb. Still, at least Jacko had bothered to arrange this visit. He'd phoned a couple of nights ago and asked if it was alright to come over. We'd chatted about Christmas, TV, his mix-tape - the usual sort of stuff and then suddenly, as if from nowhere, he asked me when I was seeing Roxanne again.

'Your guess is as good as mine,' I said, 'why do you ask?'

'Oh, er nothing,' he said, his voice sounding a bit weird, '...Fay was asking, that's all.'

'Really?'

'Er yeah...she said something about going out as a foursome, you know?'

'A foursome? What, like The Beatles?'

'Well, more like Abba technically speaking, you know - two ugly blokes with two gorgeous girls.'

I was sure there was something going on. Jacko had sounded odd when he asked about Roxanne. Maybe he was just still totally astonished that someone like Roxanne was interested in someone like me. I wasn't surprised he was surprised. I was pretty gobsmacked myself.

'I'll try and get Humph to come over too shall I?'

'Huh,' I'd said sulkily, 'I won't hold my breath.'

'Eh?'

'Nothing. Yeah, ask him. It would be good to see him,' I said, 'just as long as he doesn't bring Pete and Doddsy.'

'They're not that bad!'

'Yes they are.'

'Yeah, fair point, they are, you're right.

So, to my complete surprise, Jacko had somehow dragged Humph away from the clutches of his mates and here he was. Not that I could think of anything to say to him; it was like I hardly knew him anymore.

I tried not to pick at my crusty arms, as I listened to their tales of the drunken revelries. Most of my spots had now dried up and formed scabs. Dr. Huggett told my Mum that I should be able to go back to Denton in a week. I couldn't wait. I was sick to death of being stuck at home.

'So how was your Christmas?' asked Humph after what seemed like an age of him sitting quietly, playing with the guitar.

'I've had better.'

'Yeah, bad time to get the pox eh?'

'But you had visitors didn't you?' asked Jacko, 'other than yours truly I mean?'

'Well, after you on Boxing Day, Karl came over with his kid sister; we compared spot stories.'

'Gross,' Humph said.

Should I mention Alison's visit with Collette?

Humph hadn't mentioned Alison at all; I didn't know the state of play there. To play safe, I decided not to mention that she'd been round. Something told me it was best to let sleeping dogs lie.

'Karl can play you know,' I said gesturing to the guitar. 'Apparently he's in a band.'

'What? Like our pretend-punk band?' laughed Humph, 'what were we going to be called?'

'Arse and The Arsonists,' said Jacko, 'I still think it's a great name!'

'Ridiculous,' Humph laughed, shaking his head.

'Actually, his band can really play by all accounts. Heidi was telling me they'd done gigs down the Alhambra. They've supported all the big local bands; Peter & the Test Tube Babies, Nicky & the Dots, even The Piranhas.'

'Wow, big time Charlie!' said Jacko sarcastically, 'let us know when he's going to be on Whistle Test!'

I did what I always did; ignored him.

'Apparently, he has to lie about his age; they won't let him play if they realise he's under eighteen. Heidi reckons he's playing down the Northern sometime in February. They're supporting The Manic Depressives. We should all go and see them.'

'So what are they called then this band of Bloom's?'

'The Morbid Morsels. And it's Grimm, not Bloom.'

'What?' said Humph.

'Karl Grimm, that's his stage name.'

Humph and Jacko burst into laughter. Soon, they were rolling around my bedroom floor in hysterics. Humph had tears streaming down his face before they'd finished. Jacko had snot bubbles blowing from his nose. I had to give him a tissue.

'So, what do you reckon then? Do you fancy going to see them?' I said when they'd stopped taking the piss.

'Yeah, why not? I'm up for it. You Humph?' said Jacko, blowing his nose noisily.

'The Manic Depressives supported by The Morbid Morsels? Sounds like a really fun evening that does!' said Humph, 'do they supply the razor blades to slit your wrists or do you have to take your own?'

'Ignore him Tim, he's still into Brotherhood of Man,' laughed Jacko.

Humph really should never have admitted to liking "Angelo" back in the second year.

'Go on, mate, let's go along, the beer's cheap in the Northern if nothing else.'

'Leave it out Jacko. An evening in that skanky pub, watching some smelly school kids doing Undercocks covers? No thanks!'

Humph knows that the proper names of the bands are The Undertones and the Buzzcocks. He just refers to the "Undercocks" to try and wind me and Jacko up. He's never liked punk. He's never had any taste in music at all, come to think of it.

'Karl says that if I'm any good, he might get me into the band!' I said.

'Bloody hell, they must be crap!' said Humph, 'definitely count me out!' Humph strummed on the guitar and whirled his arm around in the air like Paul Weller.

'Well, they can't be worse than you!' I said.

'Karl bloody Grimm? He loves himself that one! Big blonde poseur,' said Humph.

'Sod off. He's OK is Karl' I said.

'Mind you, talking about the Blooms. That reminds me - we saw Poppy Bloom and that mate of hers down in the Sea House at New Years,' Humph said.

Jacko shot him a look; shook his head. Then he saw me looking at him, and he smiled, like nothing was wrong.

'What?' Humph said, 'I was just saying....'

'So, when exactly are this band of Karl's playing then?'

'What friend of Poppy's?' I asked Humph.

'What sort of music do they do? Isn't Karl a bit of a shoe-gazer? Is it all that cheerful Joy Division stuff? Jacko continued.

'You know, the red-head from HMV, the one you used to fancy. Nice looking type. She was at that Denton party at Christmas. You know, what's her name?'

'Do they do covers or their own stuff?'

I gave Jacko a look.

'Roxanne? You saw Roxanne on New Years Eve?'

She was supposed to be up in London. She told me she wasn't coming back for a couple of weeks because her Dad was poorly.

'Yeah, it was her wasn't it Jacko?'

'It did look a bit like her..,' Jacko said, 'but weren't you saying she was up in London or something Tim?'

Jacko was looking daggers at Humph.

Humph was oblivious.

'Yeah it was definitely her, I never forget a face, especially not one like that. Don't you remember that time we all went into HMV to get a look at her. Tim was shitting himself wasn't he? He used to have a massive hard on for her, didn't he?'

Humph's choice of phrase had gone right down hill since he'd started working with Pete and Doddsy.

'Yeah, I didn't update you on that did I?' said Jacko meaningfully.

Humph looked at him blankly.

'So was it just the two of them?' I asked casually, you know Poppy and Roxanne?'

'Actually,' Jacko sighed, still glaring at Humph, 'she was with a whole group of people mate.'

'Yeah, but there was one particular bloke...'

'I wouldn't say one *particular* bloke,' Jacko corrected him, 'just a group of friends..'

'Yeah, you remember, Jacko, there was that huge ape, she kept dancing with. A right Hooray-Henry type he looked, you know, all muscles and corduroy trousers. Brainless rugby type. A right Bill Beaumont....they were dancing together all night.'

'I don't think she danced with him that often,' said Jacko, who was now clearly wriggling, as he sat on the end of my bed.

'Well, she certainly didn't seem to be fighting him off. I bet old Bill scored a try that night...and a conversion!'

Bloody Robert. It had to be.

'So, what did you think of my mix-tape then?' asked Jacko, a fixed grin on his face.

Just the day before, Roxanne had finally called.

She was on her lunch break and said she couldn't talk for long. She spoke in a high-speed whisper; like she was worried about getting caught. Apparently, her manager didn't mind her making the odd private call, as long as she didn't "take the piss".

'Sorry I haven't called before. Dad's been having tests. I had to stay up there.'

I didn't have time to say I understood, or to ask how her Dad was doing, before she was off again.

'So, maybe we should meet up? If you're up to it?' she'd asked, completely taking me by surprise.

I'd told her a white lie.

'Yeah, the Doc says I'm OK to see people now. I'll be back at school, *college,* tomorrow.'

'Really? Oh, great. Well, are you free friday evening?'

'Yeah, great..'

'Eight o'clock in The Shades bar?'

'Where's that?'

'You've never been to Shades?'

The way she asked made me feel like a kid. A stupid one at that.

'Oh *Shades,* of course! I've never heard it called The Shades *Bar*; that's what threw me!'

'See you there then. Must go; really busy!'

'Ok, see you...'

'And Tim...don't forget my Christmas present!' And with that she'd hung up.

Christmas present? Oh God. I hadn't had a chance to get her anything. Now, I'd have to persuade Mum and Dad that I was well enough to go down to the shops tomorrow *and* go out with Roxanne on Friday night. Bloody hell. Oh well, I was a lot better. I'd just have to convince them.

The phone conversation with Roxanne had been too brief to decipher anything; after the last two conversations I'd had with her, I

194

still couldn't really fathom whether I was in her good books or not. Well, at least she'd called.

I'd felt guilty for the past couple of weeks, waiting for her to call. I'd been pretty insensitive about her Dad. I felt I couldn't really call her in the circumstances, although I'd felt tempted on more than one occasion. And now, according to Humph and Jacko, she'd been in Brighton less than a week after we'd spoken and she hadn't called me. A further week had passed since New Years' Eve before she'd got around to calling; what had she been up to?

I'd gone out that afternoon and spent most of my meagre savings on her present.

Covering most of my remaining zits with calamine, I'd dressed in my best jeans and denim jacket; in the breast pocket of which nestled a copy of Jacko's infamously lovey-dovey mix-tape, which I'd decided to hold in reserve and present her with, if, and only if, the evening went well.

I'd asked Jacko where the pub was; I knew he'd know.

'The Royal Pavilion Tavern - bottom of North Street,' he said,

'Are you sure? Roxanne said it was called The Shades Bar?'

'Everyone calls it Shades,' Jacko sighed. It was like I'd asked the most stupid question ever.

'Are you sure it was Roxanne on New Year's Eve?' I'd asked again, after Humph had gone to the loo, leaving me and Jacko alone.

'It was her,' he'd nodded.

There'd been an uncomfortable pause.

'I wouldn't read too much into it though, if I were you,' Jacko had said, 'I'm sure it was all perfectly innocent.'

Jacko's words were still ringing in my ears as I'd nervously walked into The Royal Pavilion Tavern, aka Shades. *Perfectly innocent* it may have been but why had Roxanne had been out in Brighton with her 'cousin' Rob, when she'd told me she was up in London, nursing her sick Dad? I needed an answer.

Shades was dimly lit. It took my eyes a while to adjust. Still, at least the low level lighting helped to hide my nervous smile as I approached the bar. I'd braced myself for a blunt refusal, or at the very least a request for ID, when I ordered a pint of Stella, but I was pleasantly surprised when the trendy looking barmaid served me without even flinching. Stella was the only beer they had that I'd actually heard of. It was bloody expensive; and bloody strong. Before I'd drunk more than a couple of sips, I already felt light-headed. I hadn't eaten my tea; I hadn't had any appetite. Jacko was always saying you shouldn't drink on an empty stomach. Now I was beginning to understand why.

Roxanne was late.

I had the jitters, sitting there on my own in the dark, smoky bar with its mysterious little alcoves. I'd found a table in a dark corner, where I could barely be seen by the growing crowd of drinkers. It made me feel slightly less self-conscious; but only a little. I sat there cradling my gift for Roxanne and trying not to look too-obviously seventeen. I had to keep standing up, poking my head around the corner of the alcove, in case I missed her. About the fourth time I did this, she was standing right there. I almost jumped out of my skin.

'Sorry, did I startle you?' Roxanne laughed, pecking me on the cheek. She sat down opposite me. She was wearing a long raincoat and had her long red hair, piled up in a bun on her head. She was holding a huge Christmas present. Some sort of long tube.

'I'll have a G and T, thanks for asking.'

I hadn't.

'Oh yeah, of course,' I said, fumbling for change in my pocket. I hoped I had enough money to last the evening. I'd only left home with a couple of quid. 'Er, what was it again?'

'A G and T?' she said.

I smiled, trying not to look thick.

'A gin and tonic?' she explained.

'Oh right, of course,' I said.

'So, how's your Dad doing?' I asked, as I sat down, placing her drink in front of her.

I'd been served by a young bloke this time; and for one moment I thought he was going to ask me for proof of age. He'd definitely given me the twice-over but he hadn't said anything; just told me the price and watched as my chin hit the carpet.

'Yeah, he's OK thanks. Still waiting for test results, but he seems perkier.'

'Great,' I said, already wondering how I could bring the conversation around to New Years Eve, without sounding too accusatory.

'Here, I got you this,' she said, handing over the tube-shaped package.

'Thanks a lot!' I said, 'And this is for you!'

'Oh, you shouldn't have done. Can you afford it?'

'Not really!' I laughed.

She smiled.

And I can't really afford to buy you any more drinks either, I thought.

We opened our presents, neither of us speaking as we tore at the wrapping paper. She'd opened hers long before I'd even got purchase on a stray bit of sticky tape and started to tear pathetically at one edge of the tube.

'Ah, how sweet! Anais Anais, you remembered!' she said, holding the bottle of perfume I'd bought her. She seemed genuinely pleased. She leant across and gave me a proper kiss - on the lips and everything.

Encouraged by her reaction, I decided the moment had come and blurted it straight out.

'So, a couple of my mates reckoned they saw you in Brighton on New Year's Eve,' I said, still pulling at small pieces of wrapping. 'I told them it must have been another gorgeous red-head, because you were up in London.'

I might have had more success with the parcel if I was actually looking at it; but I found myself studying her face intently for a reaction. I didn't know what I was expecting; confirmation of a case of mistaken identity or some quickly concocted excuse maybe? I got neither.

'Oh yeah, that's right. My cousin's friend was having a party. Rob insisted I should go; and Dad said it would do me the world of good, so we drove down at the last minute; we crashed at my place; Jackie was up at her folks.' Roxanne spoke matter-of-factly; she didn't seem phased at all by my sudden question.

'So, it was just you and this cousin...er Rob is it?'

'No, there was a whole group of us from back home. Poppy, Jake - that's Rob's mate- he's sort of based down this way now- he's a bit of a party animal - always throwing parties wherever he goes - mind you, he's worth a bob or two is Jake. His Dad's in textiles or something - Jake's dating a girl called Yvette from a place called Ditchling I think it was? Do you know it?'

'Er yeah, it's nice, I've been there,' I said.

Never mind all that I was thinking; I want to know more about this "cousin" of yours.

'Yeah, anyway, it was an OK party actually. So, mates of yours were there were they? Anyone I know?'

'Er, Jacko and Humph, they were at the Christmas bash.'

'Humph? isn't that Alison's ex? How is Alison? Did you see much of her over Christmas? I bet she got you something nice eh?' Roxanne nodded towards my half-opened present.

I wished she'd stop changing the bloody subject.

I tore the rest of the paper away. Inside was a cardboard tube - my first thought was that she'd bought me the longest loo roll in history. There was a round white plastic cap at either end. I opened one, pulling it off off. There was a roll of glossy paper inside. I started to yank it out.

'You might not want to open that...'

Too late.

' ...Poppy and I had a devil of a job of getting it in there in the first place.'

'Oh, Excellent!' I said. I should have guessed. It was the massive Zenyatta Mondatta poster I'd seen in the stock-room at HMV.

'I put it aside for you!' said Roxanne, beaming.

'Oh, it's brilliant, thanks!' I said, really chuffed, even if it had occurred to me that she hadn't technically *bought* me anything, whilst I'd spent a fortune on her sodding perfume.

'So glad you like it. I'll get another round in shall I?'

Bloody hell, she'd finished that gin and tonic quickly. I'd better be careful; I wasn't used to drinking at this pace.

'Great, thanks. A pint of Stella please,' I said absent-mindedly, still studying the poster.

Leaning forward to take a sip of my beer, I felt a sharp corner digging into my left nipple. The mix-tape. I'd forgotten about that. Things were going really well. Was now the time? I thought of the tunes that Jacko had copied. "I Burn For You". It was a great tune but would she take it the wrong way? After all, it was pretty in-your-face as declarations of love went. And as for Rod and "D'ya Think I'm Sexy?', well maybe that was just asking for trouble. There was no hurry; gauge the temperature Tim, don't rush it.

When Roxanne came back from the bar, I was in such a good mood that I didn't want to spoil it. So, I decided not to pursue the subject of New Year. Like the mix-tape, it could wait till later - maybe even until another evening, if indeed there was to be another evening. For the moment, things were going well; why make waves? However, we got talking about her family a little later.

'Dad's from Ireland; hence the name. He runs his own small business, imports and exports. he's got a few lorries.'

'Is your Mum Irish too?' It was weird, it was hardly the most fascinating topic of conversation but I really wanted to know about her folks. I could listen to her talk all night.

'No, she's a Londoner; she used to be a secretary. That's how she met my Dad; he was delivering furniture to the firm she worked for. Mum says it was love at first sight. Dead romantic eh?' she laughed.

'And you've got two brothers?'

Could I keep asking, going through her entire family one by one, until we got around to cousins?

'Patrick's still in Europe - he phoned from Bucharest on Boxing Day.'

'Blimey, that's Hungary isn't it?' I asked, trying to show off my less-than-encyclopaedic geographical knowledge.

'No, you're thinking of Budapest. Bucharest is Rumania.'

Same thing. Oh well, History was really more my subject.

'And what about your other brother? Is he off travelling the world too?

'What, Gerard?' she snorted through her lovely lips, almost choking on her G&T, 'the furthest he ever travels is to the fridge. Lazy bugger. He's about your age actually. Sixteen.'

'I'm seventeen,' I pointed out.

'Yeah, he's seventeen in March. Still acts like a big kid though,' she chortled.

'Really?'

'Yeah, not half. He spends all his pocket money on records; he's got no decent clothes, he never goes anywhere or does anything......,'

Ouch.

'...he never gets out of that bedroom of his, just sits up there listening to his records all day and night.'

Double ouch.

'He should really get a life!' she laughed, 'he's such a loser.'

199

'Yeah, sounds like it,' I laughed. He sounded perfectly OK to me.

'Do you know, every Sunday evening, he listens to the chart rundown on the radio...'

Yeah, so?

'...you're not allowed in the room right? He sits there with his finger on the pause button, taping all the songs and making ridiculous mix-tapes. Blokes are really funny with mix-tapes and stuff aren't they? Poppy's ex used to give a mix-tape every birthday and every Christmas. That was his idea of a present. Can you imagine?'

'No, really?'

Nervously, I fingered the button on my jacket pocket. Good, it was done up. Was the lump too obviously tape-shaped? No, it could be anything - a wallet - a packet of fags.

'Anyway, the thing is, Gerard gets really cross if the DJ speaks over the song; it's hilarious..,' she laughed.

Well? It *was* annoying - you didn't want ruddy Tony Blackburn prattling on all over your songs.

'You're joking!' I said.

Gerard sounded like a pretty regular bloke to me.

'And not only does he spend ages and ages making his pathetic tapes..' she smirked, '..but you'll never believe this...' she leant in like she was about to disclose something incredibly shocking, 'he makes up his own charts based on his favourite songs!'

'No!?'

I studied my hands, my legs, the ceiling, our empty glasses - looking everywhere to avoid her smirking eyes.

'Yeah, seriously. He writes them out every week; he keeps his charts in this book in his underwear drawer - my Mum found it when she was tidying up his room. She told me all about it.'

'Really?' I shook my head as if it was the weirdest thing I'd ever heard.

'He should really get out more, eh?' I said.

Note to self - put all Tim James' Top 30 charts in the bin as soon as you get home.

And lose the mix-tape.

'Ah, I suppose Gerard's harmless,' she said, 'but I wish he'd get himself a part-time job or something whilst he's at sixth form; he can't sponge off Mum and Dad forever. That's the trouble though - youngest child you see? Spoilt rotten. Patrick and I always had to get Saturday

200

jobs when we were studying, but not our kid brother, oh no. You work don't you?'

Bloody hell, don't mention the paper round.

'I...work at the local Newsagent - just on Saturdays you know.'

'Well that's something. Are you working tomorrow?'

'Yeah, why?'

'I fancy another. But if you've got to get up early...?'

'No, that's fine. I'll be ok.'

In the words of Dave Booth, we were both well and truly Brahms ("Brahms and Liszt" is cockney rhyming slang for "pissed" according to Dave Booth. Dave says he gets "Brahms" most weekends - which, of course, is crap - he's almost as much of a fantasist as Jacko).

When the pub called last orders, Roxanne's head was resting on my shoulder.

'Walk me home?' she slurred, making the proposition sound incredibly suggestive.

'My last bus will be going soon,' I said, checking my watch.

Roxanne giggled.

'Well if you'd really rather go home than come back to my place...'

'Really?' I said.

Thanks to the beer, it took a few seconds for what she was saying to hit home; then my heart started missing beats.

'Walking? Won't it be freezing?'

Good old ever-sensible Tim James.

'You can keep me warm,' she whispered; breathing out alcohol fumes that could have felled a small herd of buffalo.

We left by a back door, finding ourselves in a dark side street. Alison pushed me up against a wall and with her hands either side of my face, started to kiss me, long and hard, forcing her tongue in between my teeth, pressing her soft, warm body hard up against me. I placed my one free arm around her waist; I didn't want to drop my poster after all. My head was spinning - this was all happening pretty fast. OK, the evening had gone pretty well; we'd made each other laugh and as we talked she'd casually touched my leg several times (eight actually - but who was counting?); but I really hadn't been expecting this. Maybe I was just incredibly naive but as far as I could tell, there had been no advance notice that she was about to jump on me.

Her tongue tasted of gin and tonic. She was a brilliant kisser, right up there in my top three. Although, as I'd only ever kissed two girls previously, perhaps that wasn't such a great accolade. A group of tanked-up lads wandered past, jeering at us. One of them wolf-whistled; another shouted.

'Get in there my son!'

'Neanderthals!' Roxanne said, giving them the finger.

They jeered some more but moved on.

Roxanne grabbed my arm and we marched off in the opposite direction.

At the junction with East Street, she stopped, embracing me again. She kissed me some more. Softer, warmer little kisses; much nicer - I felt myself responding. There was a queue of people at the taxi-rank. They were gawping, but I didn't really care. The poster tube dropped to the pavement. We both stooped to pick it up; our heads colliding with a thud. Ouch. We both laughed, rubbing our heads theatrically.

The street lights seemed to be spinning. She had to grab me to stop me falling over. We walked off towards the seafront, both holding one end of the tube and giggling like mad.

As we neared the ABC cinema, Roxanne stopped. We were staring down a dark alley-way. I recognised it instantly.

'Quadrophenia!' we both said.

This was the actual alley where Phil Daniels and Lesley Ash had hidden from marauding crowds of Mods and Rockers in the Who film. It had been filmed right here in Brighton; some of the older kids at Denton had been extras in the fight scenes.

'Have you seen it?' asked Roxanne as we stood looking up the alley.

'Er yeah. Sting was great in it, wasn't he?'

Sting had played Ace Face, the coolest mod of all. Ace was Jimmy's hero (that's Phil Daniels character) but he turned out to to be a bell-boy at the Hotel Metropole, or was it the Grand?

'Well, he's not exactly Al Pacino is he?' laughed Roxanne, 'but he did look quite cool in that long leather coat.'

Al who?

'Yeah, dead cool.'

'Didn't you think Lesley Ash looked amazing in it too?'

'Yeah, I suppose....' I started to say. I stopped myself. Was it a trick question? Of course I liked Leslie Ash; that went without saying. She was a bit of alright, but was that the right answer in the circumstances? I had to be careful; this was a no-win situation. I could easily say the wrong thing. I wasn't falling into that trap.

'Well, she's not here right now, so will I do instead?' Roxanne gave me a knowing smile. She looked up and down East Street, 'come on, no-one's watching!'

It looked dark and cold down there. The street lighting was rubbish. All you could see was a pool of light illuminating some large puddles left behind by the recent deluges.

I felt light-headed as Roxanne started to drag me along; a mini air-squadron was doing loop-the-loops in the e pit of my stomach.

I told myself I should try to sober up - I might want to remember this in years to come.

And as it turned out, I was unlikely to ever forget it.

Unfortunately.

16 - No Time This Time

'Tim, honestly, it could happen to anyone.'

'But that's the second time it's happened when you've been around. I don't want you to think I make a habit of it. I'd just had far too much to drink...'

'Tim, just forget it, it was an accident. It's no big deal.'

I checked my reflection in the shop windows, as we walked up St. James Street, making sure that my sweatshirt was hidden under my leather jacket. There wasn't much I could do about the wet arse of my jeans. I was certainly sobering up pretty quickly now.

Roxanne's flat was in Kemptown. We walked in silence for the rest of the journey. As it cleared, my head started to throb. The more it cleared, the more it throbbed and the more the memories of what had happened came back into sharper focus.

So embarrassing.

Even though I was curious to see Roxanne's flat, as we turned up into Upper Rock Gardens, I really wished I was somewhere else.

'Come on, here we are,' Roxanne announced, as we stood in front of a tall town house, 'this is me,' she said, pointing to the concrete stairs, which led down to the basement flat,'let's get you cleaned up and I'll make us some coffee.'

'Is Jackie home?' I said, suddenly remembering she had a flat-mate.

She shook her head, as we reached the bottom of the stairs.

'She's a night-owl, she won't be in yet.'

Roxanne turned the key and soon, we were standing in a ridiculously small hallway, which was made to look even smaller by the two push-bikes resting against one wall. There were two doors on the other side. She led me through the first. The room was in darkness but you could tell this was Roxanne's place; Anais Anais filled my nostrils. She hesitated in the doorway, leaning across to switch on a lamp. The lamp was one of those tall, floor-standing affairs, with an old-fashioned red shade, complete with tassels. It was totally not Roxanne. I'd been expecting modern style decor - the lamp was like something out of "Great Expectations".

Once lit up, it revealed a sparsely furnished room that seemed to be a lounge-cum-kitchen. Besides the Miss Haversham lamp, there was an old leather two-seater sofa, a small table supporting a tiny portable TV, a rickety looking book-shelf crammed with paperbacks, and a couple of huge, polka-dotted bean bags. The "kitchen" was basically a work-surface down one wall, with an old fridge and a small, antique cooker. Roxanne glanced over her shoulder and caught me taking it all in.

'It's not the Ritz, but it's home!' she said.

'It's....great,' I said.

'Liar,' she laughed, 'still, Mum and Dad bought me one of those new microwave ovens for Christmas. That'll make a lot of difference. That cooker's a death-trap.'

'Aren't they dangerous those microwaves? Can't you get radiation poisoning or something?' I said.

My Mum was really keen to get one but Dad said they were "cancer boxes".

'Well, I doubt that Tim. Practically everyone's got one in the States. They're amazing, they cook things really quickly. Dad reckons no-one will be using conventional cookers in ten years time.'

'Shame, you haven't got it now,' I said, 'maybe we could use it to dry off my jeans!'

'Oh sorry, I'd almost forgotten. Here, let me show you the bathroom, you can take off those things and hang them up to dry-off, before we get this coffee down you.'

She led me back into the hall. We clambered over the bikes and she pushed open the door at the end of the hall. Behind the door, was possibly the smallest bathroom I'd ever seen in my life. Somehow they managed to cram in a bath, a WC and a wash-basin into what was essentially a large cupboard. Over the wash-basin was a full colour poster of a topless, muscular man cradling a new-born baby in his arms. The man's biceps were wider than my chest. I bet he'd be good at rugby, I thought to myself. Perhaps Roxanne liked the more muscular man? If that was the case, I might as well go home right now.

'I'll leave you to it. Don't be too long, the coffee will be cold,' Roxanne said, closing the door behind her.

I sat on the end of the bath and took off my denim jacket; my knees were pressed up against the loo. The bum of my Levis still felt damp. The stain on my grey sweatshirt looked huge.

'Pretty impressive Tim,' I thought to myself as I ran water over the rancid patch and scrubbed at it with my fingers. I was only making it worse. The stain was spreading; my hands were wet and reeked of puke. I had a sudden flashback to that alley. I shivered and pulled the offending top off over my head.

Oh God, I'd never be able to watch Quadrophenia again.

I bent to take off my shoes, hitting my head twice on the wash basin in the process; then I undid my belt and let my jeans drop to my feet. There was a washing-line running the length of the room above the bath; a damp pair of tights and a Sussex University scarf, which I guessed must be Jackie's, were draped over it at one end. I threw my shirt and jeans over the line next to them and looked around for something to wipe my hands on. There was no towel. Bloody hell, there was no towel. What kind of people had a bathroom with no towel? Students, of course. Ask a stupid question...

Ah well, I wiped my hands on the nearest dry thing I could find - the Sussex University scarf. I sniffed at it; not surprisingly it stunk now too. I panicked; I had to hide the evidence. I stuffed it into my jacket pocket. I caught my reflection in the mirrored tiling. Above my head loomed the picture of the bloke and his baby. The guy flaunted his muscles and his fertility in equal measures. His tanned torso rippled with health. My own torso was covered in pasty white flesh, with intermittent scaly red chicken pox blisters. My rib-cage poked through beneath a pigeon chest. My eyes panned down to the baggy pair of navy blue y-fronts.

'You Sex God,' I muttered.

How could Roxanne resist?

There was no way I was going back out there dressed like that. Why on earth had I put those bloody big baggy y-fronts on? I put the denim jacket back on, buttoned it up and looked for something to throw around my waist. No bloody towels! Not even a face flannel? Surely, there had to be something I could use? Then I spotted the pedestal mat on the floor. I grabbed it up and held it against my waist. It was pink and fluffy. Not really my colour but beggars couldn't be choosers. I tried pulling the two edges together at the hip but it wasn't wide enough. I needed something to tie it with. Then I saw the scarf, hanging from the pocket of my jacket. It would have to do.

Taking a deep breath, I pulled the door open and stepped out into the hallway - wearing only a denim jacket, socks and shoes - and a

206

pink pedestal mat, tied around the waist with a Sussex University Scarf. The whole natty ensemble stunk of drying puke.

And in a perfect example of sod's law in action, right on cue, a young woman I'd never seen before in my life, but who simply had to be Roxanne's flatmate, chose that precise moment to walk through the front door.

She was tall and slim, wearing one of those figure-hugging, silk, oriental type dresses. It clung to her like cling-film. She had long black hair and lots of eye-make up; she looked slightly oriental herself. A sort of slightly more English-looking version of Wei Wei Wong from The Golden Shot. Very pretty.

It was obvious that neither of us were expecting this particular encounter. We both stood there with our mouths open. Given my own wonderfully exotic outfit, I imagine hers was open widest. But not by a lot.

'Ah, you must be Jackie?' I said, casually, 'Hi I'm Tim, Roxanne's...friend,' I offered my hand.

Bad move.

The bath mat instantly fell to the floor.

At least the scarf stayed in place. My goolies were emblazoned with the legend 'Sussex University'.

'Er, is that my scarf?' Jackie said, pointing at my scrotum.

I glanced down to where she was gesturing.

Woolly tassels were hanging down my naked leg.

Bloody brilliant.

'Maybe.' I said; a stupid grin on my bright red face.

'Tim had a little accident, Roxanne explained. She made it sound like I'd wet myself or something.

The three of us shared coffee and ginger-nuts, perched around the leather sofa. Roxanne had leant me her dressing gown; white towelling, with a pattern of small red roses around the collar; nice. Still, it was better than wearing a pink pedestal-mat kilt.

Jackie hadn't said much; she kept eyeing me suspiciously from the other end of the sofa.

'I'm really sorry about the scarf. I'll get it cleaned and let you have it back,' I said.

'No problem, I understand,' said Jackie, pulling a face.

Clearly she didn't understand at all.

I preyed that Roxanne wouldn't offer any further clarification of my 'accident'.

'He fell over,' she said.

Great. Thanks a bunch. No, really.

'Oh,' Jackie looked concerned.

I smiled my best puppy-dog smile.

'Sat in a puddle....' Roxanne said, smirking.

'Ah...' Jackie smiled

'And then he threw-up all down his sweat-shirt.'

They fell about laughing.

'Sorry Tim,' Roxanne said between sobs,' but it *was* funny!'

Marvellous.

'Where was this?' asked Jackie.

'In that alley. The one in Quadrophenia,' Roxanne, said matter-of-factly.

'What?' Jackie exclaimed, bursting into laughter, 'what the hell were you doing down there?'

Roxanne raised her eyebrows.

Realisation dawned on Jackie's face.

My face was burning; my humiliation complete.

'Ah,' Jackie said, her spare hand over her mouth, trying to suppress further laughter, 'films eh? Never quite the same in real life is it?'

She could say that again.

After a short while, Jackie said her goodnights and left us to it. We finished our coffee in silence, with Roxanne trying very hard, but in vain, not to laugh at me in her rather fetching dressing-gown. After a couple of minutes, she stretched and yawned.

'I'm all in,' she said, 'I need my bed.'

'Oh, yeah...er right, I suppose my clothes will have dried out a bit by now. I'd better be making a move,' I started to stand.

She laughed. 'And what are you going to do? Walk all the way back to the other side of town, in damp clothes, at this time of night? Don't be stupid; you're staying right here.'

I looked at the sofa. It looked bloody uncomfortable. And far too short.

'Don't worry, you can sleep in mine....'

What? The shock must have registered on my face.

Roxanne grinned.

'Don't go getting ideas now. I've got one of those fold-up beds in my room. It's not exactly Silent Night but it's better than the settee.'

'I can't get over how big it is!'

'I know, I've seen some really big ones but that is a monster'

'I'm not really sure what I'm going to do with it.'

'Well, don't take it out again now, we'll never get it back in again.'

Suddenly, Roxanne put her hand to her mouth, 'Oh God!' she said and then started giggling uncontrollably.

'What?' I said, 'what is it?' I stood at the foot of her bed, holding the poster tube.

'I've just realised,' she said, screeching into the palms of her hands, 'what we've been saying,'

She sat on the end of her bed, rocking backwards and forwards as she laughed.

'Uh? What's so funny?'

'These walls are paper thin!' she sniggered, 'I just hope Jackie can't hear us! What on earth will she be thinking?'

'Sorry?'

'You know, *"I can't get over how big it is"*, she sobbed, *"it's a monster"*, she hissed.

The penny dropped. 'Oh God, *"don't take it out again, we'll never get it back in."*

Roxanne guffawed. She was crying into her hands.

'Shh,' my face breaking into a stupid smile.

She cuffed her hands around her mouth and pretended to shout through the wall, 'we're only talking about a poster Jackie! A huge poster!' she screeched in a throaty whisper.

I was giggling too now.

'You've got a filthy mind!' I said, waving the tube at her like a lightsaber. I whacked her softly across the head.

'Put it away! Put it away!' she screamed, still doing her best hyena impersonation,'Oh God! that sounds even worse!' she roared.

'Well, where should I put it?'

'Shhhh!' Roxanne laid back, holding her stomach as she laughed and laughed.

209

It *was* a problem though. I looked around the poky room. There was hardly room to swing a proverbial cat, and certainly not to leave a six-foot poster tube lying around, where no-one would fall over it.

'Stick it under the bed,' she said, sitting up and wiping a tear from her eye as she finally started to clam down, 'keep that monstrous thing away from me!'

I shook my head, 'you're terrible you are!'

Such a filthy mind.

She was so great.

Perhaps I should have taken my chances on the sofa. The room was freezing and the thin spare blanket she had thrown me smelt musty and was nowhere near long enough. My feet stuck out at the end every time I tried to pull it up around my neck. The bedroom was pretty cramped with a too-large wardrobe, a chest of drawers, a bookcase, a bedside cabinet and a pile of LPs propped up under the only window - all jostling for space that didn't exist. There was barely room for both Roxanne's single bed and the foldaway. The two were crammed right up next to each other but any hopes I might have had about snuggling up to her were dashed by the fact that the foldaway was roughly six inches lower than her bed; plus we were sleeping head to toe. All I could see from my vantage point were the heels of her bed-socks.

As I laid there with my head throbbing and my teeth chattering, I kept having flashbacks to that bloody alley.

It had all been going so well. I'd felt really randy when Roxanne kissed me outside the pub. It felt like there was a small volcano going off in my head - and another in my pants. She'd grabbed me by the hand and dragged me up there; not that I was kicking and screaming exactly. Scenes from Quadrophenia raced through my mind.

It was one of my favourite movies of all time. Jacko, Humph and I had tried to bunk into see it at the ABC when it was first released; it was an "X" ; we were under age. Jacko got his ticket but then Humph and I were both asked for proof of age. We didn't get in. And do you know what that bugger Jacko did? He only went in on his own. Not only that, but for months, he rubbed it in; going on and on about how brilliant it was.

Humph and I finally got to see it at the Duke of Yorks about a year later. They were less strict about age; Alison and Sara Potts came with us too; you always had a better chance of getting in to an "X" at the

Dukes if you had girls with you. Jacko came too. He said he wanted to see it again. He was a right pain in the arse all the way through it; he kept saying things like "Oh this bit is great" and "Oh this bit coming up is totally epic". He was spot on though; it was brilliant. I'd seen it twice more since then.

As Roxanne led me up the alley, I could almost see Jimmy and Steph running away from the riot. Roxanne looked nothing like Leslie Ash mind; she didn't have the blonde hair or the leather coat - but I wasn't complaining. Just like Jimmy in the film, I was about to get the girl I'd been fantasising about for weeks. I could picture the scene quite clearly; the two of them running towards the door at the end of the alley; Jimmy kicking it open.

It was all Phil Daniel's fault.

I could have broken my ankle.

'Yeah, why not,' I thought, taking a run up and kicking the gate as hard as I could with the heel of my shoe. It was locked. I lost balance; fell backwards; managed to find the biggest rain-puddle in the whole of Brighton and sat down plum in the middle of it.

Roxanne's face was a picture. Her mouth formed a perfect 'O' . Then she laughed. Not a little snigger, not a mild titter, a great big, right-up-from-the-pit-of-her-stomach, belly-laugh. She had to rest her hands on her knees she was laughing so much.

I put an arm out to steady myself; trying to stand up. My poster tube was rolling towards another puddle. What happened next was like an action replay on The Big Match. Reaching out to grab the poster, I slipped and fell into the puddle-cum-lake for a second time. Just like the first time, Roxanne made her 'O' face. And then she laughed even harder. The tears were running down her face. She offered me her hand and pulled me up.

'Come here you!' she said. It was exactly what Steph had said to Jimmy, except that I couldn't recall Leslie Ash wetting herself with laughter at Phil Daniels.

She pulled me over to her and as she leant back against the most famous alleyway-door in Sussex, she started kissing me. Even with a sopping wet arse, I kissed her back. Just like Jimmy and Steph, when Sting and his mod mates were fighting with coppers in East Street.

We were snogging; Roxanne's hand was heading south - from my chest to my stomach. And then just like Steph, she started to use her

211

tongue - in and out of my open mouth with little darts. She was breathing really hard too.

A stupid, unwanted, thought entered my head. Was she trying to inflate me? I had to fight the urge to laugh.

It was a different urge that proved my undoing. The urge to gag. That alley stank. Those foul aromas stayed with me long after that evening. The stink of fag smoke on our clothes, courtesy of the Royal Pavilion tavern, the smell of piss from where the alley had obviously been used as a makeshift urinal by all manner of tramps and pissheads, and the stale waft of fried food from the nearby fast food shops. That's what set me off. I started to feel a bit odd; my head was swimming. I felt sick.

Roxanne was oblivious to my problems. She was like a woman possessed. Her fingers were on my belt now, and she was tugging it open. Ruddy hell; she was going for the full alley-experience. But for me, the moment had passed. It was weird, just five minutes ago, my Levis had been the home to a small quake registering pretty high on the richter scale - now the only seismic activity was in my grumbling stomach.

Little Tim didn't want to play out.

Roxanne had my belt open now and was fumbling with the button on my jeans. Oh God, she was going straight for the big prize and all she was going to find was a major disappointment.

And then it happened. I was hot; sweaty, light-headed. And then I retched; just managing to shove Roxanne away from me in time before I turned and puked up five pints of Stella Artois; projectile vomiting straight into the puddle I'd been sitting in just two minutes before.

Oh, excellent.

As Phil Daniels had said so succinctly on his second visit to the alley in Quadrophenia, "Fuck it."

What a bloody disaster.

Wide awake and freezing, I thought about getting out of bed, putting on my wet jeans and my smelly sweat shirt and getting out of there. That's when Roxanne proved yet again that life is indeed full of surprises.

At first I thought I'd imagined it; something prodding at my ribs; but then it happened again. Roxanne was kicking me.

'Are you still awake?' she whispered.

212

'Yes,' I whispered back.

'I'm freezing, are you?'

'Yes. Totally.'

'Well, why are you still over there then?'

'Sorry?'

'You heard; get over here will you?'

Pulling back the duvet, I climbed in, snuggling up to her back. Oh that scent. Anais Anais.

She pulled my arm around her waist. I jumped slightly as my bare legs touched hers. All she had on was a long T-shirt, which barely covered her bum. Her legs felt like ice.

'No wonder you're so cold! Have you ever tried wearing pyjamas?'

She laughed. 'This is my winter outfit. I don't usually wear anything.'

'Chanel No.5 and a smile eh?' I said.

'What?' she giggled.

'Marilyn Monroe. That's what she said she wore to bed,' I said.

'Huh, I wish.'

'Me too.'

'Oi, watch it!' she laughed and elbowed me, 'I don't suppose Marilyn would be inviting you into her bed after your performance this evening.'

'I sincerely hope not. She's been dead twenty years!'

'Well, she'd be even colder than me then, wouldn't she?'

'Not a lot!' I said, 'ruddy hell, you're like a block of ice.'

She laughed again. 'Well,' she said, turning to face me 'you'd better warm me up then, hadn't you?' Her T-shirt caught on my jacket. My hand felt naked flesh. She wasn't joking; she really didn't wear much in bed, there was nothing under that T-shirt.

'And will you get that sodding jacket off. It stinks!'

'Oh bloody hell. Yes Ma'am!' I joked, climbing out of the bed and out of my jacket, 'and will there be anything else for Madam?'

There was a glint of light shining through the gap in the curtain and for the first time I could make out her face. She was lying on her side smiling up at me, her red-hair tousled around her face. She looked beautiful, even without her make-up.

'And whilst we're on the subject of getting things off - don't forget those manky socks!' she said, pointing to my feet.

Self-consciously, I threw my socks on the floor. I was down to my sexy Y-fronts. Should I take them off too? She was smirking.

'You're not even going to turn around are you?' I said, reluctant to get bollock-naked in front of this gorgeous girl.

She giggled. 'Steady on tiger, I don't think we're quite ready for the experimental stuff yet, do you?'

'Oh, no... I didn't mean...'

Now she was really laughing again.

Sod it. I climbed into bed, still in my pants. As soon as I was under the covers, I wriggled them down over my feet and tossed them into the air. Then I cuddled up to her back.

'Don't you go getting any ideas. I just wanted a cuddle.'

'Oh right, well, yeah...I just thought you know, after the alley-way, we sort of had unfinished business...'

'Well, I think the moment passed don't you? Besides, I'm all-in and I've got to get up for work in the morning,' she patted my hand.

'Goodnight Tim, sweet dreams.'

'Yeah, you too.'

I lay there, tracing the outline of her neck with my eyes.

Sweet dreams? Huh, some hope. I had the feeling I wasn't going to get much sleep at all.

So, there I was.

My cherry was still intact; the cork still in the bottle, but who was I to complain? I was actually lying in bed, with a real-life, flesh and blood hottie. What would my mates say if they saw me now? Blimey, what would my old Dad say? What would Mum say? Bloody hell, Mum and Dad. I hadn't told them I would be staying out for the night.

Oh shit. I checked my watch, straining to see the illuminated arms in the gloom of Roxanne's room. It was gone one o'clock. Mum would be really worried. Dad would go mental.

'Roxanne!' I said, shaking her shoulder with my free hand, 'Roxy, wake up!'

'What?" she said with a start.

'Have you got a phone?'

'Bloody hell Tim, I was just nodding off, I thought there was a fire or something!'

'Sorry,' I said.

I explained about my parents. I felt dead embarrassed.

Roxanne sat up, 'do you want the good news or the bad news?'

214

The tips of my fingers were blue and I could see my own breath, as I traipsed up the road to the phone-box. My jeans were still damp around my bum and I was wearing just my jacket on the top half. Roxanne's good news was that she did indeed have a phone. The bad news was that it only took incoming calls. Bloody typical. Roxanne explained that they couldn't afford to pay the bill for outgoing calls. Apparently Jackie used to call her family in Singapore all the time. That's in Asia. I knew she looked oriental.

Roxanne was not amused when I told her I didn't have any change for the phone box. She looked dead stroppy, rifling through the clothes in her wardrobe, looking for two-pence pieces.

The phone box was a good ten minute march away in Queens Park Road. My fingers were so numb, I could barely dial the number. And then I got a proper bollocking from my Dad.

'Do you know what time it is? Where have you been? Do you know your mother's been half out of her mind with worry?'

'Sorry Dad, I had a bit too much to drink and decided to crash at... a friend's place.'.

'Well, you could have bloody phoned! Mum wanted me to call the coppers out!'

I could hear Mum in the background.

'Ask him where he is. Does he want us to go and pick him up?'

'I'm not bloody picking him up at this time of night!' I heard Dad's muffled voice say.

I pictured him standing there in the hallway, his hand over the mouthpiece, trying to calm my Mum, who'd probably been pacing up and down. I felt a pang of guilt.

'But is he OK? Where's he calling from?' Mum said.

I didn't fully catch Dad's reply.

'Which friend?'

'I don't know which friend! Which friend are you with Tim?'

I hesitated, wondering whether to say I was at Dave's or at Jacko's. But then I knew I'd only get caught out if I lied. My Mum was like Sherlock bloody Holmes when she got going.

'You wouldn't know....her,' I said.

'He's with a girl,' I heard Dad say.

'Oh,' I heard Mum say.

There was a long pause. I thought I heard muffled laughter.

215

After a while Dad said, 'Your Mum's says it's not a school night, so that's OK.'

Not a school night? Was that all she had to say?

'But next time you get lucky,' Dad added, 'make sure you bloody phone us first OK?'

'OK Dad!'

Yeah right, next time I had a gorgeous girl's hand down my trousers, I'd be sure to phone home and tell them.

Roxanne had given me her spare key and I let myself back into the flat. Desperately trying to be quiet so as not to wake her, I undressed in the dark, stumping my toe on the bed. The yelp had left my mouth before I could stop it.

'Were your folks OK?' I heard a little voice say.

'Yeah, of course. Like I said, I just hadn't told them I'd be staying out.' I said, 'they're never bothered as long as I tell them.'

Like this sort of thing happened all the time.

I was a crap liar.

I fumbled for the duvet and climbed back into bed.

'Christ, you're freezing!' she said, almost jumping out of her skin as my cold body touched hers, 'I thought you were meant to be warming me up not the other way around!'

'Well, I'm sure we could find a way to warm up,' I said, amazed at my own bravado.

'Nice try Tiger. No chance, I'm whacked. Let's see what happen in the morning.'

Ruddy hell. Now, I knew I wasn't going to be able to sleep a wink.

The morning turned out to be another anti-climax.

I'd laid there awake for ages and only finally dropped off in the early hours. And of course, then I was fast asleep and missed my big chance when Roxanne had woken up.

I'd been dead to the world; how she'd climbed out of bed without waking me, I'll never know. When I finally did come around, my head felt as if it had been hit by a cattle stampede.

Roxanne was nowhere to be seen. It took me a while to make sense of where I was. It was only when I heard laughter and voices from the next room, that everything fell into place. Maybe if I waited, she would come back to bed? I lay there, staring at the unfamiliar ceiling.

It wasn't possible to make out exactly what they were saying next door. Jackie's voice was the loudest; I heard Roxanne "shush" her a couple of times. Listening carefully, I managed to make out a few snippets of their conversation.

'...a bit young?'

'...seventeen..'

'...cradle-snatcher!'

Laughter.

'....what do you mean a bit of fun?'

'....shhhhh....'

'....just what Rob said....'

'....different....'

'.....how is that different!...'

'....shhh, you'll wake him up.....'

Rob. There was that name again.

A couple of minutes later, the bedroom door opened. I pretended to be asleep; waiting for her to climb in. She was moving around by the bedside cabinet, leaning over the zed-bed. It creaked under her weight. I opened my eyes and smiled, like I'd just woken up.

'Just made you a coffee,' she said, pointing to a steaming cup on the cabinet. 'How are you feeling?'

'A bit rough, you?'

'Terrible. I'm not looking forward to work.'

Work. Crikey. The paper round. Old Cyril would be going mental by now; he'd kill me. People would be phoning up; moaning they hadn't had their Daily Mirror.

'What time is it?'

'Half eight.'

Oh crap. Ah well, too late now. I just hoped Cyril hadn't bothered Mum and Dad. I was going to get the riot act as it was.

'You didn't wake me.'

'You were well away, besides, I slept late myself. Wasn't time for...well, what you had in mind!'

'Mind-reader are you?'

'Don't need to be psychic to read your mind, you randy little bugger!'

I sat up and made a grab for her. She kissed me on the forehead and shoved me back down on the bed.

217

'No time, this time ok?'

'That's a Police song!' I said.

'I know, mastermind! That's why I said, it was a joke!'

She was amazing.

'See you soon. Let yourself out,' she said, 'don't be late for the newsagent. She kissed me again, this time on the cheek and ruffled my hair, 'sorry Tiger Tim, but time and HMV wait for no woman!'

'Shall I see you later?' I said, instantly regretting lifting my head from the pillow. My eyes ached and my mouth felt like I'd been eating too many cream crackers.

'Oh, I'm sorry, I can't tonight - I've...got plans,...maybe in the week?' she said breezily, opening the bedroom door.

How did she manage to look so immaculate; hair in place; make up perfectly done? I felt like a half-dead zombie. She looked back and blew me a kiss and then she was gone. "Just like that" as The Police's warm-up act might have said.

'I'll call you!' I said but the door had already closed behind her.

So, there I was lying as naked as the day I was born in Roxanne's bed. I glanced around her room; the wardrobe full to bulging, the chest of drawers containing untold secrets, the pile of LPs all waiting to be explored. The whole room smelled of her. It was curiously cozy. I was tempted to go back to sleep. Then I sat up with a start as the door opened.

Roxanne put her head around the corner and breathlessly asked me what I was doing tomorrow.

'Sunday? Not a lot. Why?'

'I've had an idea - do you fancy a trip to Surrey?'

17 - Someone To Talk To

It'd happened overnight.

I'd turned into a two-headed alien overnight.

Or at least, that's how it seemed.

Ever since I'd got home that Saturday morning, Mum and Dad had been acting really weird.

'Alright son?'

Dad hardly took his eyes away from Grandstand when I walked into the room. That wasn't unusual in itself. The Russians could invade our street and Dad would still be glued to Frank Bough. But this was different; it was like he was too embarrassed to look at me.

'Have you had breakfast at your...friend's?' Mum asked, without looking up from her magazine.

'Yes, thanks.'

Jackie had made me some toast when I'd finally dragged my sorry arse out of her flat-mate's bed. She'd been much friendlier in the morning than she'd been the night before; but then I was no longer wearing her puke-ridden scarf as a belt or her toilet mat as a makeshift skirt.

Once home, I'd gone straight to my room, changed my clothes, put my puddle-stained jeans and the sweat shirt that still stank of puke in the wash-basket and hung up my jacket in the wardrobe. It was only when I felt the lump in my jacket pocket that I'd remembered Jacko's mix-tape. I threw it in the bin, before opening my bottom drawer and removing my 'charts' file from beneath the pile of t-shirts. I put that in the bin too.

After a couple of minutes, I retrieved the file and the tape and put them back in the bottom of the drawer.

Laying down on my bed, I'd felt exhausted. My body craved sleep but my mind wasn't having it. I was still buzzing from my date with Roxanne, still running through the events of the night, over and over. I'd closed my eyes but couldn't sleep. I was hungry and although I hadn't wanted to face my parents, I was only putting off the inevitable. Eventually, I'd got up and gone downstairs to face the music. There hadn't been any; just an eerie silence.

I sat down on the settee next to mum. She shuffled in her seat; looking dead uncomfortable, staring at the same page of her Woman's

Own for what seemed like an eternity. Dad barely blinked, let alone spoke. He got up to flick channels to Saint and Greavsie. Ian and Jimmy were the only ones doing any talking. Parents - it was a funny old game. Greavsie was cracking his usual jokes; Saint was in hysterics. Dad laughed along a little too loudly. Like everything was normal; except it wasn't. I'd stayed out for the night. Stayed out with a girl. Everything had changed.

I yawned.

'Are you OK son?'.

'Just tired,'

Mum and dad exchanged smirks.

They were pathetic.

'Ooh, I almost forgot,' Mum said, 'one of your friends called this morning. David I think he said his name was? Seemed like a nice boy. I told him a little white lie. I said you weren't up yet. I wasn't sure whether you'd want him knowing...you know....anyway, I jotted his number down on the pad.'

Thank God for Dave Booth. An excuse to be somewhere else other than that living room with the alien invaders that had replaced my parents. For God's sake, I'd only spent the night at a girl's house, you'd have thought I'd been convicted of murder or converted to Buddhism; or both.

'I'll just go and give him a buzz then,' I said, heading out through the door.

'Tim!' Dad shouted as I was on the bottom stair.

'Yes?' I said, failing to keep the irritation from my voice.

'Don't forget Teddy Upsons's popping round later for your guitar lesson. You better have recovered your strength by then!'

Mum and Dad chortled.

'Shh!' Mum said.

Really pathetic.

Dave sounded agitated.

'*Someone*,' he said with accusing emphasis, 'has said something to Karl.'

'What do you mean?' I said, innocently.

'He's been really weird with me all week.'

'In what way?'

220

'Well, take Monday morning, I walk into the common room; he's sitting there, reading a text book....'

'That *is* weird,' I said, trying for a joke.

'....I say "Hi, how was you weekend",' Dave continued, ignoring my comment, 'and he just plain snubs me. Acts like I wasn't there. Gets up, puts his books away, walks out of the room.'

'Maybe he's worried about that gig coming up?'

'And then Tuesday, we're in photography, developing some film. He's standing right next to me all through the lesson; doesn't say a word. Forty minutes of the silent treatment.'

'Bizarre.'

'Same thing happens on Wednesday. So, I've started thinking, "he knows", you know, about me and Juliette? Someone must have said something.'

'Perhaps he saw you together at school.'

'No, that's just it. We agreed like, Juliette and me, we agreed to keep it quiet, pretend nothing was going on. You know, until I've had a chance to tell Karl. Juliette knows he likes her - apparently she knew all along. Heidi told her.'

'So, doesn't she like Karl?'

'Well, she said that her mate Glenda loves him to bits, so she couldn't do anything, even if she did like him....'

'So, *she's* got some scruples then?' I said, unable to resist a dig.

'What do you mean by that?' he said testily.

'Nothing....so I take it you haven't told Karl then? About you and Juliette I mean?'

'I didn't need to did I? Someone's obviously beaten me to it.'

'Are you sure? Maybe you're just imagining it?'

'Yeah, maybe I'm just imagining that my best mate told me to "go fuck myself" when I offered him half of my Twix on Thursday?'

'I think he prefers a Crunchie...'

'And maybe I ignored the fact that when I tried to talk to him on the bus home yesterday, he told me to stay well away from him if I wanted to keep all my teeth?'

'Ah, yeah, that does sound a bit dodgy I suppose....'

'Bloody hell Tim, how did he find out?'

'I don't know. I haven't said anything.'

221

It wasn't a lie. I hadn't. It was Alison who had the big gob. But I wasn't about to drop her in it. Besides, part of me felt that Dave had it coming to him. It served him right.

'So what are you going to do?' I asked.

'I don't know what to do. He's really hard is Karl. '

I thought about pointing out that perhaps he should have considered that before he copped off with Juliette but I decided that whilst that was undoubtedly true, it wouldn't be particularly helpful under the circumstances.

'I'm sure he'll be alright once he's calmed down.

What did Dave expect me to do?

He asked me if I would talk to Karl, to see if he'd calmed down since the previous day. I thought it was a pretty ridiculous idea but in order to get him off the phone, I told Dave I would ring Karl later; see if I could "talk some sense" into him. All of a sudden, I was expected to be the diplomat. How had that happened?.

'I'll pop round later, on the way back from Juliette's - see what he said.'

Reluctantly, I said 'OK' and he hung up.

Bloody hell; how did I get myself into these things?

Jacko telephoned just as Teddy Upson was leaving. Mum asked him to wait; explained I was just showing Teddy out.

I guessed that Teddy was roughly Dad's age, yet he was as different from Dad as you could imagine. Dad would never wear a Led Zep T-shirt, or have tattoos of naked women on his arms. Dad uses Brylcreem and he's always clean shaven; Teddy had a permanent five o'clock shadow and his grey hair was brushed back into a ponytail. Dad wore cufflinks, Teddy had a huge gold loop earring in his left ear. Chalk and cheese. How on earth did Teddy work in an office, looking like Robert Plant's dad?

'Well, it wasn't a bad start, but you must master that plectrum,' Teddy said, hoisting his guitar case onto the back of his van, the back of which stank of cigarettes. Teddy was a chain smoker; he did the coolest thing when he was playing. He attached his fag to the neck of the guitar.

'Do you want a good tip on the very first thing to remember though?' he smiled, blowing a smoke-ring into the air.

'Yeah, what?' I said, eager to please the maestro.

222

'Stop calling it a lectern!'

'OK,' I blushed. He must think I'm such a dick.

Teddy was an unbelievable player. I'd never, ever, be that good, even if I practised twenty-four hours a day, seven days a week. What was Teddy doing working in an office with my Dad? He should be on the road; making a fortune.

'See you next Saturday - same time then? And remember I want you to study those chords between now and then, OK?'

He gave me a thumbs up and climbed into his Transit. He was dead cool - for an old bloke.

'So, is Andy Summers losing sleep yet?' Jacko said, as I picked up the phone

'I don't think Sting will be giving him the bad news just yet.'

'So how's it going?'

'Slowly. It's all chords and scales and something called 'licks' according to Teddy. Don't know when I'll actually start playing the bloody thing.'

'Well, you'll get there. In the meantime, what are you doing this evening? My folks are out. I've got some Woodpeckers in, do you fancy coming over and watching a film?'

'Yeah, why not. What's on?'

'Your favourite is on BBC2. The Magnificent Seven.'

'Brilliant. What time?'

'Six thirty. Just come over when you're ready.'

'OK.'

Bugger. I suddenly remembered Dave.

'Actually mate, I'm not sure I can.'

I explained to Jacko that his old primary school mate was popping over.

'Well, bring him with you; it'll be good to see the cocky git!'

'Really?'

'Yeah, why not. And hey, Tim, why not bring the guitar over too. If we get a chance, I'll show you a thing or two.'

'I didn't know you could play guitar.'

'I can't but I can't be any worse than you, can I?'

'Piss off Jacko,'

It wasn't until later that I remembered my promise to Dave about speaking to Karl.

Bloody hell. Why was it down to me to call him? Why hadn't I just said 'no" for once?

'So, why didn't you say something?'

Dave was right; Karl sounded really narked.

'What?' I was a bit taken aback. Why was he having a go at *me*?

'You could have told me. I thought we were mates? You're as bad as him!'

That was out of order. I wasn't standing for that.

'How do you work that out? I didn't have my tongue down Juliette's neck did I?'

'You obviously knew though and you didn't say anything. If Alison hadn't blurted it out, I'd be none the wiser now, would I?'

'Well, true, but I didn't think it was any of my business really. It's between you and him isn't it?'

I was trying to keep a lid on my own growing anger, whilst hoping to appeal to Karl's sense of reason.

'Well, if that's how you feel, why are you ringing?'

Charming.

'Well, I just thought I'd try my hand at diplomacy,' I said, trying to lighten the mood.

'Yeah well don't give up your paper round just yet.'

There was a nasty edge to his voice.

'Look mate,' I said, taking a deep breath, 'I know you really liked the girl but it wasn't as if you and her were, you know, an item or anything was it?'

'And that makes it alright does it?'

'No, but....Dave's your mate. You shouldn't fall out over this.'

'Yeah, right, some mate.'

'He's alright is Dave. You know he's a good bloke at heart. I don't think he got off with her deliberately; it sort of ...just happened. Ask Alison..she'll tell you.'

'Yeah, a lot of things *just happen* with Dave. And Alison wouldn't think he was a such a good mate if she knew about the photos.'

'Photos? What photos?'

Karl hesitated for a moment; then I heard him take a deep breath at the other end of the line.

'The photos. The ones with her top off. Who do you think it was who circulated them? Your precious mate, Dave Booth of course.'

'Eh?'

'Haven't you seen them?' he cackled. 'You must be the only bloke at Denton who hasn't. They're all over the school.'

'Do you mean the photos of her on holiday?'

'Yeah. So you've seen them then?'

'Er, well...not exactly.'

Bugger, I'd walked into that.

'What do you mean they're all over the school?'

'They are! Everyone's got a copy. Dave found these photos in the canteen. He was going to keep them but we persuaded him to give them in. He posted them through the office door; but only after he'd nicked a couple of the negatives. The ones of her with her tits out.'

'Bloody hell.'

'Yeah, he ran loads of copies off in our photography class. We were meant to be developing shots of our field trip - The Royal Pavilion or the Pier or something. Now, Dave runs a couple more copies off every time we're in there. They sell like hotcakes.'

'He's selling them?'

'Yeah. I can't believe he hasn't offered you a copy.'

I could. He knew I'd go mental.

'So, thanks for ringing mate.' Karl said. 'Oh yeah, and tell Dave I look forward to seeing him on Monday!'

And with that, Karl hung up.

Well, that went well.

Bloody Dave.

'Just how many copies have you made?'

'Only the odd one or two,' Dave said sheepishly.

I'd been waiting for him. I'd put my coat on and dragged him up the path, as soon as he'd arrived. The moment I'd answered the door, he'd started asking about what Karl had said.

'I'll tell you what bloody Karl said!' I'd said, slamming the front door behind us, 'follow me!'

As soon as we were out of earshot of the house, I'd laid into him about the photos.

'Why didn't you tell me?'

'Er excuse me? Why didn't I tell you? This is precisely the reason. I knew you'd go bonkers.'

'Too right. Bloody hell. If she finds out, she's bound to blame me.'

225

'Why, because everyone knows you've got the hots for her?'

'I do *not* have the hots for Alison!' I said.

'Yeah right.'

One of my neighbours passed by. A little old lady pulling a poodle on a long lead. We exchanged smiles. I dragged Dave further down the road.

'I do *not!*' I repeated.

Dave smirked.

'Ae you sure?'

'Ok, I might have done, once upon a time. But not now, she's a mate.'

'And she's got great tits,' he laughed.

I wasn't going to laugh. I was angry. I bit my lip.

'Anyway,' Dave said, 'Why would she blame you? You're her best bosom buddy; if you excuse the pun.'

'Yes, and I was the one she was showing her photos to, when they went missing.'

'Really? Did she show you the topless...'

'No!'

'So, you've never seen them? Are you sure you don't want a copy? They're amazing. Both of them. The photos that is, not her...'

'OK, I get the picture!'

'It can certainly be arranged. Ten pence to you. Usually they go for twenty.'

'Very generous of you,' I said, trying not to laugh. It wasn't funny. Alison would probably never speak to me again if she ever found out.

'You need to get them back before she finds out.'

'What? You must be joking. I've spent most of the money.'

'What?'

'New Devo LP. It's brilliant. You can borrow it if you like.'

'Dave. I'm not joking. Get them back. Or we're both dead men.'

'There's no way, can you imagine people like Jez King and Frank Little giving them back for nothing, after they've handed over their dosh?'

'Jez King and Frank Little? Bloody hell Dave!'

'Yeah, and the rest of the football team.'

'All of them?'

'Pretty much. Well except Gavin Pitt of course,' Dave winked.

'Is he?'

'What do you think?'

I smiled. Pretty much.

'Look, don't change the subject! We've got to get them back. How much have you made?'

'About four quid altogether.'

'Four quid? Bloody hell!'

'Sorry mate.'

'Bloody hell.'

'I've got some of it left but if you really want to get them all back, I'm going to need some serious spondoolies,' Dave said, rubbing his fingers together to signify hard cash.

I thought for a moment. I needed a loan. I needed to find someone with some spare cash. I knew just the person.

'Well, we're almost there.'

'Almost where? Where are we going? And you haven't told me what Karl said yet.

'I'll tell you when we get to Jacko's.'

'So, you did the dirty on Karl then?' Jacko asked Dave; as tactful and sensitive as ever.

'Well, not really,' said Dave, 'I can't see what all the fuss is about. OK, it was common knowledge that he had a bit of a crush on Juliette but it's not like he ever did anything about it, was it?'

'All's fair in love and war and all that eh? Is that your philosophy?' Jacko grinned.

'Yeah, I s'pose so,' Dave shrugged.

I wasn't sure he was convinced by his own argument. One thing I did know though; he had bugger-all chance of convincing Karl.

The three of us sat around Jacko's bedroom, drinking cider and listening to UB40. The film hadn't started yet; we were killing time.

'Well, hopefully, it will all blow over eh?' I said, more out of something to say than anything; hoping to make Dave feel a bit better. He looked thoroughly miserable.

'Yeah,' said Jacko, 'after Karl's pummelled you into next week, things will get back to normal.

Dave laughed nervously; supped on his Woodpecker.

I felt a little sorry for him; but only a little. After all, he had made a pass at a girl that his best mate was mad on. And then there was the whole thing with the photos.

227

I'd decided to say nothing about that in front of Jacko. I didn't want it getting back to Humph and I couldn't trust Jacko to keep his big gob shut. But I needed his help financially. The lull in the conversation gave me my opportunity. I had to think fast. Which is probably why I came up with such a lame excuse.

'Jacko, can you do me a favour?'

'Here we go. I get an ache in my wallet every time you say that.'

Dave laughed on cue. They were as bad as each other. Comedians.

'It's Roxanne's birthday coming up.'

It was the first thing that came into my head. It wasn't true of course. Not as far as I knew at least. I realised I had no idea when her birthday was, except she'd told me she was eighteen and three quarters. Her birthday had to be relatively soon.

'And the wallet goes into cardiac arrest,' Jacko said, tipping his can to his mouth, raising his eyebrows at Dave.

'It would only be for a while, I'd pay it back.'

'From your paper round or has your old man won the pools since I last saw you?

'Well, if you're going to be like that about it...'

'How much?'

'Four quid,'I told him.

'How much?'

'I want to get her something special.'

Jacko shook his head.

Dave laughed.

I gave Dave a look. I saw the penny drop.

'I'd make it five mate,' he said.

'What?'

'Jewellery you said didn't you?' Dave gave me a knowing look, 'that doesn't come cheap you know, you might need a bit *extra?*'

I stared at him. He just shrugged

'Go on Jacko, be a mate,' Dave said, winking, 'he's on a promise.'

'OK, but if you haven't got your leg over by this time next month, I want my money back!'

Jacko went to his wardrobe, to get the money from his jacket.

Dave gave me a thumbs up.

'*All* of them!' I mouthed, behind Jacko's back.

Dave just shrugged.

'So, anyway where's this Juliette tonight then?' Jacko asked.

228

'At home, I should think.' Dave shrugged, acting casual, like it was no big deal to him either way, 'we're not joined at the hip you know.'

'Not for the want of trying though mate eh?' laughed Jacko.

'Give over mate, she's barely sixteen. It's snogging and action above the waist only at present.'

'Ah well, hang in there. You'll be heading south for winter!'

Dave almost choked on his cider.

We sipped our drinks; listened to UB40's lilting reggae. I surveyed the room. Originally, there might have been wallpaper; it was hard to tell. The walls were completely covered with a collage of posters from the NME, Sounds and Melody Maker. Jacko's favourite bands - The Stranglers, The Jam, Blondie, Talking Heads, Patti Smith - surrounded us on all four walls; punk and new wave dominating the theme, with only one exception. The centre-piece, above his bed, was a poster of a girl playing tennis. She had her back to the camera, walking away from the net as the sun was setting behind her. In one hand, she held her racquet. In the other, she was scratching her bare arse, which was pretty peachy. She was wearing no knickers. My eyes were drawn to the thought-bubble that someone had drawn coming from her head.

"New balls please" it said.

'I don't get it.' I said, pointing at the picture.

'Oh right,' Jacko nodded, 'our Trevor's idea of a joke.'

Jacko's older brother was in the Army. He was stationed somewhere called Belize. We never saw him.

'New balls?'

'Trev reckons I'll need new ones, 'cause I'm always jerking off to that poster.'

Dave and I sniggered.

'Not now you've got the lovely Fay though eh?' Dave said.

'Yeah, where is she tonight then?' I asked.

'How come you've got a night off?' Dave laughed.

'Well, you know how it is?' Jacko smiled.

No, I didn't.

'Obviously she wanted to see me but these women can get too much of a good thing, you know.'

'Blown you out has she?' I laughed.

'Out with her parents. Theatre or something,' Jacko conceded.

'And what about you? How are you getting on with Roxanne?'

'She's invited me up to her place in Surrey tomorrow. She's driving me up there.'

'Bloody hell,' Dave said, 'getting serious all of a sudden isn't it?'

'Is that the sound of wedding bells I hear?'

'Piss off Jacko,' I muttered.

'I don't think you need to buy her an expensive birthday present mate,' he smirked, 'you're well in there already,' Jacko laughed.

'I wish. She just wants a hand bringing back some stuff - her folks have bought her one of those microwave things.'

'So, you're just a glorified furniture remover; like one of those Chimps on the tea adverts,' Dave sniggered.'

'Coo-ee! Coo-ee Mr. Shifter!'

'Dad, do you know the piano's on my foot?'

'You hum it son, I'll play it.'

The two of them thought they were Morecambe and Wise.

I smiled, humouring the idiots.

'It's six-thirty,' I told Jacko.

'Uh?'

'The film; you know the one we came over to watch. The Magnificent Seven?' I said.

Jacko got up from his chair.

'Can you imagine?' he smirked, looking at Dave, 'Tim dumping her fancy new microwave down the stairs?'

He lifted the stylus from UB40. Now, I was the one getting the needle.

'Just drop it will you?' I snapped.

An unfortunate choice of phrase. They fell about laughing.

I made out like I'd meant to say it.

Afterwards we wandered down stairs to the living room. Jacko switched on the TV. Just in time. The familiar music to The Magnificent Seven started up at last. I'd never been so relieved to see Yul Brynner. At least now, they would shut up, surely? Apparently not.

'Why, *exactly*, has she asked *you* to help her?' Jacko chortled as he sat back down and resumed his cider swilling, 'I mean you're not exactly Charles Atlas are you?'

'What she really needs is a *man* to help, not a *boy*!' Dave flexed his biceps, like he was Mohammed Ali. They were barely bigger than mine.

'Well, we'll see *exactly* how much of a man you are when you see Karl on Monday, won't we?' I laughed.

That took the smile off his face; the colour drained too.

'I think I feel a cold coming on,' he said, 'possibly even flu'.

'You better not have,' I said, 'you need to do that *thing* for me, remember *mate*?'

'Not getting you to do his homework for him, is he Dave?' Jacko said, looking from me to Dave and back.

I darted Dave another look.

'Something like that,' I said.

18 - Deathwish

It was a cold, crisp Sunday morning as we drove up the A23 in the rickety old mini.

I wasn't sure if it was the half-dozen cans of cider I'd drunk at Jacko's, the hurried slices of toast for breakfast after I'd overslept, or just the fact that I was shitting bricks over meeting Roxanne's family, but if Roxanne didn't stop at the next available gents, we were both going to be in big trouble.

'We've only just left Brighton, can't it wait?'

'Not really, sorry!' I said.

It *really* couldn't.

'Sweet Jesus, it's like having a toddler in the car!' Roxanne sighed.

She shook her head in disbelief, as she scrunched the gearstick up into fourth. She wasn't a happy bunny. Not a great start to the day.

My stomach felt like it was hosting a re-enactment of the D-day landings and Roxanne's less than casual regard for safe-driving didn't help.

'There's a Little Chef a couple of miles up the road, you'll just have to hang on until then.'

You try telling my guts that.

According to The Eagles, who were playing loudly on the Mini's cassette player, there was *"plenty of room at the Hotel California"*. Well, I hoped we came across it soon; and I hoped they had a toilet in reception.

The choice of music wasn't helping my mood. It had been our first disagreement of the day.

'You know I love The Police as much as anyone but we're not playing them every time you get in the car Tim!' she'd said.

'Ok, but haven't you got something a bit...less...dull?'

'What do you mean dull? This is a classic album. Perfect for a Sunday morning drive. Give it a chance, you'll love it,' she'd said.

I had and I didn't. It was so.....American. If my head wasn't aching so much, it would have sent me to sleep.

My stomach felt awful. I shifted uncomfortably in my seat, trying to regulate my breathing like I was going into labour. I couldn't help myself, I uttered those immortal words of childhood passengers everywhere.

'Are we nearly there yet?'

It broke the tension at least. Roxanne giggled, removing her left hand from the wheel to dig her long manicured nails roughly into the flesh of my thigh.

'Nearly,' she said, 'do you want to play I-spy to take your mind off it?'

'I don't think that's going to do it,' I grimaced.

After ten minutes that seemed like an eternity, we pulled into the Little Chef car-park.

'Lock the door!' shouted Roxanne, as I slammed the car door behind me, making an ungraceful dash for the cafe entrance. I waved an apology over my shoulder. There was no way I was turning back.

The doorway to the Little Chef was blocked by a queue of hungry travellers; I tried to push my way through but one of them, an elderly man in an Albion blue and white bobble-hat, glared at me, pointing at a sign that read *"Please wait to be seated"*.

'Sorry but I really need the loo.'

He pointed to the far side of the room. I'd never been so relieved to see a *Toilets* sign in all my life.

'Thanks,' I muttered to the old man, without looking back. I made my way past the queue, mouthing my apologies and receiving numerous scowls in return.

My jeans came down in a new land-speed record. The relief was instant and immense. The whole exercise can't have lasted more than thirty seconds. It was the type of evacuation that only six cans of cider can produce. A cold sweat had broken out all over my body and for the first time that morning, with the pressure taken off my poor aching guts, I realised how much my head was throbbing. Resting my arms on my knees, I hung my head low between my legs and let out the biggest sigh that had probably ever been heard in that part of Sussex.

My guts were not good. The cubicle stank like a disused abattoir. My lungs cried out for fresh air. I needed to get out of there fast. I reached for the toilet paper. The holder was empty. Bloody typical. What the hell was I meant to do now? I sat there like an idiot, my pants and trousers around my ankles, preying for divine intervention.

Nothing happened.

There must be something to wipe my bum on, surely? Gingerly pulling my pants and trousers up, I stuck my head out of the cubicle. Thankfully there was no-one waiting to use the loo. As quickly as I could, I grabbed a handful of blue paper towels from the dispenser above the wash-basin and took them back to the cubicle, closing the door behind me. The blue paper towels weren't exactly soft or absorbent but I didn't have much choicc. Having done the necessary, I dropped the used paper down the loo, allowing myself another sigh of relief as my heart-rate started to return to normal.

Job completed, I stood up adjusted my clothes and turned, pulling the old-fashioned loo-chain which hung from a rusty-looking lever. Water gushed down. The mound of soiled blue towels stayed put, refusing to budge. Water swilled around it, filling the loo to the top, almost to seat level.

'Bugger it.'

I yanked on the chain again; it creaked noisily but nothing happened; apart from a very slow trickle of water, adding to the whirlpool below me. Patience Tim, wait till it fills up and try again. I glanced around as I waited for the tank to fill again - and that's when, for the first time, I noticed the sign; hand-written in huge letters on the back of the cubicle door.

'PLEASE DO NOT FLUSH BLUE PAPER TOWELS DOWN THE TOILET'

Sodding hell! What did it mean, "do not flush the blue paper towels down the toilet'? What the bloody hell else was I meant to do with them? Stick them in my pocket? I mean, they could have told me that *before* I'd wiped my ruddy arse on them couldn't they?

I looked around for some alternative solution; like the rarely-spotted, shitty-blue-towel-fairy was going to appear from out of thin-air and grant me three wishes. Oh sod it, they would never know. A little bit of soiled paper couldn't damage the bloody loo could it? Then I saw the second notice, directly above the cistern. In even larger, angrier, letters than the first, they screamed at me;

'DO **NOT** FLUSH BLUE PAPER TOWELS DOWN THE TOILET. THEY WILL BLOCK THE CISTERN'

How the hell hadn't I see that before? The answer was obvious of course - I'd been too desperate to notice. There could have been neon lights flashing over my head and I wouldn't have noticed.

Oh God, Oh God. What was I meant to do?

The cistern had stopped it's noisy refilling. I pulled on the chain again and watched in sheer horror as the churning water level rose and rose, until it started to seep over the sides, creeping under the seat and

234

dripping onto the linoleum below my feet. The submerged paper mountain hadn't moved a fraction of an inch but what seemed like at least half a gallon of foul soiled water had spilled all over the floor, splashing my trainers and the bottoms of my jeans.

'Damn, damn,' I said - or words to that effect.

Submersing my hand deep into the maelstrom of soiled water, I snatched frantically at the mound of soggy paper and pulled it all out; instantly relieving the pressure in the WC. The water level started to drop slowly as it started to drain.

This was just brilliant; there I was, en route to meet my new girlfriend's parents, stood in a Little Chef toilet cubicle, my feet and lower legs dripping with sewage and cradling a huge armful of soggy, soaking, soiled paper towels in my hands.

Life didn't get much better.

Somehow, I managed to open the toilet door. Out of the corner of my eye, I noticed the elderly Albion fan I'd encountered in the queue, minding his own business as he stood over a urinal, head back, whistling some tuneless ditty to himself.

I looked around for somewhere to deposit the soggy mound of paper. Then I spied the rubbish bin. It was one of those swing-top efforts, sitting below the wash-basin; ridiculously small and already pretty full with discarded paper.

A third sign stood sentinel above the basin.

'DO NOT FLUSH PAPER TOWELS DOWN TOILET. DISCARD THEM IN BIN PROVIDED'

'Great.'

By now, I'd just about got the message.

Moving as quickly as I could and without looking around at my peeing companion, I stuffed my pile of putrid papier mache as far into the bin as I could, which, at a rough estimate, was precisely two thirds of an inch. Some of it fell out onto the floor, the remainder stuck to the now no-longer-swinging lid like it had been super-glued there.

Conscious of the eyes of the elderly gent on the back of my neck, I joined in with his casual whistling, quickly washed my hands and dried them on yet further blue paper towelling, which I nonchalantly let fall, to join the growing pile below. And then, without looking back, I strolled out of the loo and back into the cafe area.

The place was packed. I scanned the queue for Roxanne but there was no sign of her. Then I saw her waving from a corner-table by the

235

window. I strolled across the cafe, leaving wet footprints on the red carpet.

'What do you fancy?' she started to say.

'Er, nothing really,' I said.

Her eyes dropped to my wet feet. Her mouth fell open.

'I'm feeling a bit peaky, mind if we make a move? I think the fresh air will do me good,' I said, turning towards the door and walking away, without waiting for her answer.

'But I only just got this table!' I heard her say.

Glancing back, I saw her grab her hand-bag and shrug apologetically towards the closest waitress, as she hurried to catch up with me.

Over her shoulder, I noticed the elderly man, coming out of the loo, looking in my direction; a look of pure disgust on his face. He said something to the nearest member of staff, a spotty lad sporting a natty line in Little Chef hats. The man pointed and they both stared at me as I pushed my way through the exit, turning my head away from their gaze, as I held the door open for Roxanne to follow me out.

'Are you OK?' she said.

'Never been better.'

19 - Roxanne (I Won't Share You With Another Boy)

Life in the fast lane.

Roxanne was taking the Eagles literally, foot through the floor.

I'd never drink again.

Looking past Roxanne's left ear, I still couldn't quite get used to the peculiar sight of my socks trailing in the wind from the driver's window. That had been Roxanne's idea.

'We'll get them dried off in no time,' she'd said.

We'd used her window, which was closed, holding the soggy socks in place. Despite the freezing January wind, I had the passenger window down. The fresh air made me feel a little less nauseous and also helped to hide the unpleasant aroma emanating from my dripping jeans. My trainers were propped up against the Mini's heater, which Roxanne had turned up to full blast.

I sat there in my bare feet, feeling extremely silly.

Whenever I glanced in Roxanne's direction, she appeared to be smirking.

Finally, after half an hour of listening to nothing but soft rock and traffic noise, Roxanne broke her silence.

'At least you didn't claim a hat-trick,' she chuckled, a smile playing across her lips.

'Uh?'

'You didn't throw up for a third time in front of me. A girl could take offence you know?'

'Yeah, I suppose I've been making a bit of a habit of that haven't I?'

'So come on, come clean - if you excuse the pun; what was all that about back there? What took you so long in that loo? And why are you so wet?'

'Sorry, I...er..just felt a bit rough, so I splashed water on my face to freshen up.'

'I've some news for you; you missed!' she smiled, nodding at my jeans.

'Yeah, the water came out a bit quickly.'

When she'd stopped chuckling, she squeezed my knee.

'Are you sure you're OK? If you're not feeling too good, we can go back you know? Do you want me to take you home?'

Ooh, it was tempting.

'No, really, I'll be fine.' I attempted a grin.

She saw right through it.

'They won't eat you, you know. They'll be fine.'

'What? I'm fine, honest.'

My stomach was still doing cartwheels. And that wasn't the worst of the side effects of my night on the cider. Bit by bit, I felt like I was slowly deflating. I shifted uncomfortably in the seat, in an attempt to hide the fact that I was farting like a trooper. I don't think the subterfuge was working. Roxanne kept wrinkling her nose. After one particularly foul blast, her tolerance finally reached it's limit and without thinking, she reached down to wind down her window.

'Don't!....'

Too late. My socks sailed off, over a passing hedgerow and into the green fields of leafy Surrey.

'Brilliant.' I said.

We were still laughing, when fifteen minutes later, we arrived at our destination.

'You....live....*here?* ' I said.

'Yes, of course,' she said, 'why?'

'Oh, nothing. It's very.....nice,' I said, struggling for the right word. I couldn't believe my eyes.

We'd left the main road some way back and having turned down an endless number of ever-greener, less inhabited minor roads, we'd eventually passed a sign that said "private road". This turned out to be the Delaney's driveway.

Roxanne stopped the mini in front of a a large pair of iron gates, hung between two stone pillars which were topped with two reclining stone lions. Either side of the pillars were six foot high bushes, blocking the view of the house from outside. From what I could make out from peering through the gate, Roxanne's family appeared to live in a slightly smaller-scale version of Buckingham Palace. And not *much* smaller at that. I'd never actually seen a house like this before - well, maybe on the telly, but certainly not in real life. Did places like this really exist?

'Be a star and open the gates will you?'

'OK.'

238

I pulled on my trainers; they were warm - still damp, but at least *warm* and damp.

Climbing out of the Mini, I tied my laces, before standing up and staring in amazement.

Behind the gates I could make-out a sweeping gravel area, where three cars were parked - a Landrover, a family saloon and a little red sports car. Beyond the drive stood the house, stone steps leading up to a round porch area, surrounded by more stone pillars, which ran along the full length of the ground floor.

There seemed to be two upper floors; where all the windows led out on to their own little balconies. There were even more windows built into the roof. It was a house and a half. You certainly wouldn't find anything like it on the Mellor Park Housing Estate.

I must have been in a trance. I heard Roxanne saying something but it wasn't really registering.

'Pardon?' I muttered, as she wound down her window.

'Push the button! Next to the gate,' she pointed.

'Oh, right, yeah of course...'

A minute later, I climbed back into the car as the gates swung slowly apart, revealing my first proper view of "Delaney Mansions" in all it's glory. It was even bigger than I first thought.

'Is there something you've forgotten to tell me Roxanne?'

'Like what?' she said, as we drove up on to the gravel.

'Well, you're not like fourteenth in line to the throne or something are you?'

She laughed, tossing her red hair back over her shoulder. 'Twenty-third I think!'

'Which wing is yours?

'Oh shut up! It's not that big!'

'It's bigger than my entire street!'

'Nonsense. Don't exaggerate!' she laughed.

'Roxanne?'

'What?'

'You don't have corgis do you?'

'Ho, bloody, ho!' she said, pulling a face, as she turned off the engine.

She started to get out.

I sat there. I couldn't move. She stuck her head back in.

'Come on, what are you waiting for?'

239

'You know what you said earlier?'

'No, what?'

'About turning back?'

She smiled. 'Come on, you'll be fine!'

'Really?'

'Just leave the talking to me. You'll be fine.'

What did she mean by that? Did she think I was going to embarrass her?

Oh well, I was so nervous, that arrangement suited me just fine.

It was only after she'd introduced me to her family, that I realised she'd obviously been doing a fair amount of talking already.

'Think nothing of it,' said Roxanne's Mum *("please call me Sandra"),* 'Gerard won't mind.'

The grey tracksuit bottoms were about five sizes too big for me. Gerard obviously wasn't as petite as his sister. Thank God for elasticated waists.

'I'll just stick those damp jeans in the spin drier and we'll have them back to you in no time. Are you sure we can't get you some socks?

'No thanks,' I said.

'Tim's trying to start a new fashion,' Roxanne tittered.

Her Mum frowned; clearly she had no idea whether her daughter was joking or not.

It was Jackie and the flat all over again. Yet again, I was meeting Roxanne's nearest and dearest, minus my trousers. This was becoming a bit of a habit. One that I could do with breaking, given that I only owned two pairs of jeans. My best ones were already in the wash, following the alley incident. Oh, that alley. It still made me shudder just to think about it.

'And, as I told Roxy on the phone, I think this is extremely kind of you Tim,' said Sandra, 'after all, it's not everyone who'd give up their day off to help a work colleague like this, is it Bryan?'

Day off? Work Colleague?

'It is not!' said Mr. Delaney ("and this is Bryan"), 'you're obviously a top man young sir, good on you.'

Bryan Delaney sounded as if he were doing a particularly exaggerated impersonation of Terry Wogan off of the radio. My mum loves Terry Wogan. I don't. His voice makes the hairs stand up on the back of my neck. Mr. Delaney even looked a bit like Wogan, with his black hair and ruddy cheeks.

'Yeah, he's a real sweetie, aren't you Timbo?' said Roxanne, winking at me, 'everyone at the store loves Tim, he's always so helpful!'

The store? What?

I narrowed my eyes in Roxanne's general direction.

She blushed a little and winked in a way that said "just play along ok?"

'Well, can I get you a coffee before you get started?'

'Er, could I have tea please Mrs...er Sandra?'

Get started with what?

'Oh, of course. Don't tell me, you look like a "milk and two sugars" lad to me?'

'Er, one sugar please?'

What exactly did a "milk and two sugars lad" look like then? I wasn't entirely sure, but I had an uneasy feeling that I might just have been patronised.

'Super. On it's way! And after that you kids can load up the old jalopy.'

Load up the old jalopy? What was she on about? Did she mean the car? As far as I knew, Roxanne was picking up a microwave oven. What exactly had I let myself in for? Well, whatever it was, it couldn't be too bad could it? I mean, how much stuff could we load into a Mini?

'It really is very kind of you Tim,' she said again, 'and afterwards, you really must stay for some lunch, I absolutely insist!'

Blimey. Lunch. They were dead posh in Weybridge.

We had dinner and tea in Brighton, we never had lunch. Was Sunday lunch more like dinner or tea? I hoped it was dinner. It was nearly one o'clock - dinner time in our house. Sunday roast time. Mum, Dad, Cheryl and Lee would just be sitting down to chicken and all the trimmings. Despite my nervous stomach, I'd started to feel hungry as we drove into Weybridge. I quite fancied a nice roast.

'We're having bagels today. I hope that's OK?' Roxanne's Mum said, as she filled a space-age white container that I think might have been their kettle.

'Oh great,' I said.

I had no idea what bagels were.

241

'Cinnamon and raisin, Roxy's favourite.'

'Oh raisins....lovely,' I said, seizing on a word I actually recognised. Raisins were a bit like currants. I hated currants. They reminded me of dead flies.

'So, Roxy my sweetheart,' said Bryan Delaney, 'I've left everything in Mum's garage.'

Every-what-thing? Wait a minute...they had *their own* garages?

'Lovely, thanks Dad. Come on Tim, we'll get the car loaded up and then we'll eat.'

'Uh?'

Exactly how long could it take to load a microwave oven into a mini?

'Shall I get that lazy toe-rag Gerard to come down and give you a hand?' Bryan said.

'Er, no that's OK, I'm sure we can manage,' I said, following Roxanne who was already out of the door and on her way down the front steps, as I called after her.

'Roxanne? Just how big *is* this microwave?'

'Ah, actually there's a few other bits and bobs as well.'

She headed off across the drive towards one of three garages, which were each about the size of my house. The little sports-car was parked in front of the one she headed for. When she lifted the garage door, I stood there open-mouthed. A few other bits and bobs?

In Sandra Delaney's garage, we found a tea-chest packed with pots and pans, a large cardboard box, which judging from the picture on the front, contained Roxanne's new microwave and three smaller boxes, each crammed with everything you could possibly want to stock up a very large kitchen - or a small chain of restaurants.

'So, were these all Christmas presents? Just how many relatives do you have exactly?'

'No, don't be silly. Mum and Dad have just re-kitted out the second kitchen..this stuff would have all been thrown out, so I said I would have it...'

'*Second* kitchen?'

'Yeah, the one in the granny annexe. It's round the back, behind the paddock. It's where Patrick hangs out when he comes home.'

'Granny annexe? Paddock? Next thing you'll be telling me you've got tennis courts.'

'No.'

'Oh right, that's OK then,' I smirked.

'Dad had them demolished to make space for the pool.'

Oh of course, how silly of me.

'Pool? You've got a pool?'

'Yeah, just a small one. It's not Olympic size or anything. It's only one of those small outside ones.'

Only?

'It's all covered up this time of year, otherwise I'd show you.'

I shook my head again as I looked back through the open garage door and gazed back at the Delaney pile.

'It's cool isn't it?' Roxanne said.

'Yeah, it's cool alright.'

'It's Georgian. In the revival style.'

'Really? Funny that - ours is ex-council estate. Stone cladding style.'

She just pulled a face; lifted one of the smaller boxes and passed it to me.

'Can I ask you a question?' I said.

'Sure, what is it?'

'What was all that about in there? Why does your Mum think I work at HMV.'

'Well, I had to tell them something didn't I?

'Did you? And what's wrong with the truth?'

'Nothing. It's just well....they might wonder why I'm hanging around with someone who's...'

'Still at school?'

'Someone who's Gerard's age.'

'So, how old do they think I am?'

'Nineteen.'

'Really?' Wow, I actually felt rather flattered. I was so shallow.

'Yeah, and by the way, if it comes up, you're also studying journalism at Sussex.'

'What?'

'Well, it's what you want to do isn't it?'

'Well maybe... not necessarily at Sussex though.'

'Well, I could hardly say you were working part-time in Brighton HMV whilst studying in Newcastle could ?'

'I s'pose not.'

She picked up another box.

243

'So, mind if I ask you another question?' I said as I stood there, counting the number of windows I could see on the front elevation (eleven).

'Of course, what?'

'Where does she stay when she comes to stay? Which room?' I said, pointing up at the second floor windows.

'Who? When who comes to stay?'

'You know,' I whispered, placing my finger to my lips, 'Lady Diana Spencer.'

'Oh, you think you're so funny don't you?'

It took us three quarters of an hour to cram everything into the Mini. Try as we might we couldn't fit the tea-chest in. We had to empty it out and pile all of of the contents, which Mrs. Delaney (or, I suspected, a footman or a butler) had carefully wrapped individually in brown paper parcels, into the spaces behind the front seats. The box containing the Microwave oven was massive; you could have housed a couple of kids in it, quite comfortably; it wouldn't fit on the back seat.

'It'll have to go in the front. You don't mind sitting in the back do you? You can make sure none of the crockery gets broken if I go over a pot-hole.'

Brilliant.

Most of the pots and pans went into the Mini's ridiculously inadequate boot. We had to tie the handle of the boot to the rear bumper with some old rope. Then it was time for lunch. I was starving. I really hoped bagels came with roast spuds.

A bagel turned out to be a currant bun with a hole in the middle.

I actually didn't mind the raisins - I couldn't really taste them after Mrs. Delaney crammed the bagel with smoked-salmon and something called 'Philadelphia'', which tasted like cream-cheese to me, except that it came in a box and not in foil triangles. I could have murdered for a decent roast potato.

I finally got to meet Roxanne's brother. He certainly looked like he'd sunk a few roast potatoes in his time. And he could certainly demolish a bagel.

'Nice trackie bottoms. I've got some just like them,' Gerard Delaney laughed, shaking my hand.

'Yeah, thanks for that. I had a bit of an accident.'

'Don't worry, I know what it's like. I always wet myself whenever Roxy drives me anywhere.'

Gerard winked, his fat face full of salmon and cream cheese.

'Don't talk with your mouth full,' Roxanne said, giving him a look.

'Police fan eh?' he said, ignoring his sister and gesturing towards my T-shirt.

'Yeah, do you like them?' I asked

'More of a two-tone man myself.'

Yeah, I thought. Two-tones. Pink and blubbery.

'Have you heard The Specials album. It's fantastic.'

'No, but I really like the singles.' I said.

'I love the whole scene,' he said.

The boy was a git. No-one actually used the word "scene" unless they were Tony Blackburn.

'Yeah, I might get myself one of those pork-pie hats.'

'Cool,' I said. I wondered if he realised they weren't *actually* edible?

'I'll run you off a copy of the album if you like, you know, before you go.'

'Oh, great! That's would be cool!'

What a nice bloke.

'So, you're going to be a hack?' Bryan Delaney said, sipping a glass of red wine.

'Sorry?'

'A journalist,' Roxanne prompted, 'I told Mum and Dad about your degree subject.'

'Oh yeah, that's right.'

'I know a man in newspapers,' he said.

So did I. I delivered them six days a week.

'Really?'

'Yes, I have a couple of contacts in Fleet Street. You must remind me to let Roxanne have the details.'

'Excellent, thanks Mr. Delaney.'

'Bryan!'

'Bryan.'

'I bet Tim would rather be a Music journalist wouldn't you Tim?' Gerard smiled, 'NME, Sounds, Melody Maker, something like that?'

'Maybe,' I said.

245

:kets, backstage passes. I fancy that myself!' Gerard said,
other chunk of bagel into his fleshy gob.

a surprise,' Roxanne muttered.

Sandra Delaney shot her daughter a look.

'And what is Sussex Uni like?' Sandra said, 'would you recommend it to Roxy for next year?'

'Yeah, it's brilliant!' I said, 'Roxy should definitely...'

'Ah well, we've got our heart set on Leeds really haven't we? Robert was really happy there wasn't he dear?' Sandra said, pushing her empty plate away.

'Robert?' I said.

'Yes, Roxanne's boyfriend. Or should I say ex?' Sandra said, glancing at her daughter.

'Let's not go there, eh Mum?' said Roxy, picking up her plate. 'Are Tim's jeans dry yet? We should probably be making a move.'

'Let's check,' Sandra said, heading towards the kitchen. 'And if you think you're going anywhere, without helping me clean up, you've got
another think coming young lady!'

Roxanne shrugged and got up to follow her.

'I'll shoot upstairs and do you that tape,' said Gerard, still stuffing food into his face.

'Great.Thanks Gerard.'

'So, Tim, can I get you a proper drink?' said Bryan, emptying his glass.

'Have you got a lager?'

As we sat, waiting for Roxanne to come back with my jeans, Bryan Delaney handed me a can of Heineken and told me about the haulage industry.

'I built the business up from scratch. When I got off that boat from Dublin, back in the fifties, I hardly had two farthings to rub together.'

He went on and on. He talked about how many lorries he had; how many men he employed; the different countries he had travelled to. My attention started to waiver. I was more interested in the hi-fi that dominated one corner of the room. It looked like something from the space age. It was housed in a purpose-built cabinet and was about as tall as Gerard was wide. It was the swankiest piece of equipment I'd ever laid eyes on.

After a while, I stopped listening to Bryan's descriptions of German Autobahns and CB radio. The bluesy music he'd put on was so laid-back, I could hardly stay awake. Plus, I couldn't help catching snippets of conversation drifting in from the kitchen, over the sounds of clanking crockery. It was impossible to catch the full conversation, as Bryan droned on about the price of shipping freight, but I caught the odd phrase here and there. My ears were burning.

'He seems nice...' I heard Sandra say at one point.

Roxanne was making her shushing noises again. 'A bit of fun...' I heard her say. *Again.*

My ears also pricked up when I heard the name "Rob" mentioned, at least twice. I hoped Bryan wouldn't notice as I inclined my head further towards the door. No, I told him distractedly, I didn't really know anything about the rising price of diesel. I was more interested in this Rob and what Sandra was grilling Roxanne about in the next room.

'Here you go Dad,' said Roxanne, carrying a tray through the door a few moments later.

'Ah you're a good sweet girl!' her Dad said, 'cheese and biscuits, my favourite. The perfect accompaniment to a glass or two of Merlot. Here Tim, help yourself to some cheese.'

Roxanne smiled encouragingly and disappeared back to the washing-up.

So, I tucked into the cheese and crackers, whilst half-listening to Roxanne's Dad and half-straining my ears to listen into the conversation in the kitchen. Sandra talking and Roxanne shushing. I knew I shouldn't be ear-wigging, but I couldn't resist.

'You need to make your mind up...'

'Shhh....'

'....won't wait forever...'

'Shhh....'

'...two wrongs don't make a right you know....'

'Mum, just leave it!'

'Just taping side two now; it might be done before you've gone,' announced Gerard, wobbling into the room.

Through the ceiling, I could hear the faint sounds of Ska competing with Bryan's easy-listening.

Gerard dive-bombed onto the couch; only to struggle back up again when he spotted the cheese.

'Ooh did you do that to the Brie?' he said, pointing to the wedge of soft cheese I'd been tucking into, 'better not let Mum see that, you'll never hear the last of it.'

Gerard and Bryan exchanged knowing glances, chuckled.

I had no idea what they were on about. Bryan was obviously feeling very mellow by now; he'd kicked off his slippers, head back in the armchair, lighting a cigar.

'Oh, I love this one!' he announced, singing along with the woman singer to a song that I vaguely thought I recognised.

'Billie Holliday,' Bryan said, 'voice of an angel.'

The words sounded familiar and soon I found myself singing along, trying to work out how I knew them. I'd never consciously heard Billie Holliday in my life. I had heard the name - but I thought Billie was a bloke, like Billy Idol from Generation X. The song reached it's chorus.

'Strange Fruit!' I said, finally identifying the song, 'this is a UB40 song!' I told Gerard.

'Oh, they're great aren't they? Gerard said, giving me a thumbs up. The rest of his fingers were busy cramming brie and grapes into his fat face.

'You be who? I doubt it!' scoffed Bryan, 'T'is a famous Billie Holliday number is this. All about the deep south and the KKK. A classic.'

'It's a UB40 song, it's on their LP. I've got it at home.'

'And when did they record it?' Bryan smirked.

'Oh ages ago..last year I think.'

'Ages ago?' he laughed, 'well Billie recorded it in 1939. So, I t'ink theirs may be a cover version.'

Cover version? UB40 didn't do cover versions. They were dead political were UB40. There must be some mistake. 'Ah well,' I said, 'it's better by UB40.'

'Now yer talking complete bollocks!' Bryan slurred.

'Well that makes a change!' said Sandra, as her and Roxanne came into the room, 'usually you have the monopoly on that!'

'So what are you boys arguing about?' Roxanne smiled.

Bryan told her what I'd said about UB40.

'Well, let's be honest Tim, if it's not The Police, you don't know the first thing about music!' Roxanne laughed.

'Well, he must know something, if he's working in that record shop during his time off,' Sandra pointed out.

It was a good point. Or at least it would have been, but for the fact that the job was a complete fabrication.

'Yeah, I must know something, *working in HMV,*' I muttered, smirking in Roxanne's direction.

'So, Tim is the Police song the only reason you're knocking around with my ugly sister then?' asked Gerard, breaking into a high-pitched wail, which he clearly regarded as an impersonation of Sting singing Roxanne's name.

'Must be I suppose,' I laughed.

'You know her real name's Muriel don't you?'

Gerard laughed like a drain.

I laughed too. He was a funny guy was Roxanne's brother.

'Good one,' I said, acknowledging the joke.

'It was my Mother's name,' Sandra Delaney said, giving me a filthy look.

What? I looked at Roxanne. She was blushing.

'Roxanne's my middle name,' she said, 'I've always been called that though.'

'And that was my choice!' Bryan smiled drunkenly, raising his glass in mock toast.

His wife shook her head. I think we'd touched a nerve.

'Muriel!' screeched Gerard, to the tune of Roxanne. Then, he winched himself up out of his seat, 'you don't have to wear that dress tonight! Doesn't quite go does it?' he said, winking as he headed upstairs.

Muriel?

'Who cut the nose off the cheese?' Sandra said, looking around the room.

I blushed now. I sensed I'd done something badly wrong.

'Sorry love, that was me,' Bryan said, casting me a wry smile,' you know what I'm like when I'm on the Merlot.'

Muriel Roxanne Delaney leant over and kissed her Dad on the cheek.

'Thanks Dad,' I heard her whisper.

'Muriel? Muriel?'

249

I repeated the name for the umpteenth time for comic effect. It was hard to get a clear picture of Muriel / Roxanne's reaction from my viewpoint; sitting diagonally behind her, carefully cradling a box of crockery on the back-seat; whilst we drove down the A23 later that afternoon. Considering she clearly thought she was James Hunt, I should have known better than to distract her really. After all, the more I wound her up, the more inclined she was to lift her eyes to glance at me in the rearview mirror. The corner of her mouth flickered but couldn't really tell if she was smiling or frowning.

'Muriel Delaney. Muriel Roxanne Delaney!' I continued teasingly.

'Muriel Roxanne *Aisling* Delaney actually!'

'Aisling? Sounds like you're ill.'

'My other granny's name.'

'Blimey, what a mouthful!'

'Mmm.'

'Muriel!'

'Sod off or I'll tell Mum you cut the nose off her precious cheese!'

'Yeah, and what was all that about? I never knew cheese *had* a nose!'

'It's etiquette, you shouldn't cut the nose off of the cheese. It's bad form! Don't you know anything, you oik!' she laughed.

'Fine, next time, I'll go for the ears.'

Roxanne grudgingly let me play the Specials tape that Gerard had knocked-up for me, which meant I didn't have to put up with any more "Hotel California". I put it away, taking the opportunity to look through her tape collection. The Eagles fitted into the gap between 10CC and Meatloaf's Bat Out of Hell. Alongside Regatta De Blanc, there were also tapes by The Clash, Barbara Streisand, Steely Dan and someone called Charlie Parker.

'Interesting choice,' I commented.

'It's called having eclectic taste.'

'Isn't that an illness? Do you have fits with it?'

'Ho ho. It means I don't just like one band, to the exclusion of all others.'

As well as having 'eclectic taste', I noticed that she didn't have one handwritten inlay card

'Don't you ever copy stuff. These are all pre-recorded.'

'Why bother. I get staff discount.'

'Huh, I bet they're still still expensive.'

'Not that bad. And don't forget what Andy Summers says. "Home Taping is Killing Music".'

'That's alright for Andy. He doesn't have to survive on pocket money. You don't believe all that rubbish do you?'

'Well you are depriving them of royalties you know. It's like stealing really.'

'Now you're talking crap. If the record companies didn't rip people off by over-inflating the price of LP's, people wouldn't have to copy them.'

Roxanne shrugged.

'I mean, £3.50 for an LP? It's taking the piss isn't it?'

'If you say so,' she said, pretty condescendingly.

'Well it is. It's ridiculous. I saw one going for £3.99 the other day!'

Roxanne was laughing now.

'What?' I said, feeling more than a little narked. 'What's so funny? We're not all bloody rolling in money you know!'

She sniggered.

'Oh, go on then, have a good laugh at the school-boy's expense,' I snapped.

'Do you want to know what's funny?'

I shrugged, staring out of the window.

'I've known you five weeks now and that's the first time I've ever heard you get annoyed about anything. Never mind nuclear disarmament or third world poverty, all Tim James cares about is the fact that LP's are over-priced!'

She was giggling away now.

'It's not true. It's not the *only* thing I care about,' I muttered, refusing to laugh along.

'It's absolutely true and you know it!' she said, laughing even louder.

'It's not,' I said, indignantly, 'I think singles are over-priced too.'

She screamed at that one.

I folded my arms; bit my lip.

'Oh shut up,' I said.

It only made her laugh even more.

Roxanne seemed to be in a pretty good mood. Things were going well. So, why did I have this nagging sensation? I kept re-running the snippets of conversation between Roxanne and her Mum in my head; trying to fill in the blanks. I had to know.

251

'Can I ask you a question?' I said.

'No, we aren't invited to the Royal Wedding and no, we don't spend the summer in Balmoral!' she laughed.

'Good but I wasn't going to ask about that.'

'OK, what?' she glanced in the mirror again - at seventy-five miles per hour, according to the little speedo, which I kind've hoped was faulty. 'Fire away.'

'You won't mind?'

'Now you're worrying me.'

'You won't get annoyed?'

'I will if you don't ask whatever it is *soon*!' The car wobbled slightly as she turned her head through forty-five degrees.

'About Robert...'

'Oh,' She glanced away from the mirror.

I sensed she'd stopped smiling. Her fingers clenched the steering wheel. But I wasn't going to be put off.

'Do you still see him?'

Silence.

'Only isn't your cousin - the one I spoke to at Christmas at your place - isn't he called Rob as well?'

There was a brief pause and she changed gears, pulling over into the slow lane and glancing back at me again.

'So, we're having this conversation *now* are we?' she sounded sulky, 'you really want to spoil a good day do you?'

OK, perhaps it wasn't great timing but then again, was there ever going to be a good time to talk about this?

'Well, it's just been playing on my mind a bit that's all....'

'Yes Tim, Robert my ex and Robert my cousin are one and the same,' she said, sitting upright in the driver-seat and brushing the hair from her eyes as she checked the rear-view mirror and pulled out to overtake a young lad on a moped.

'So, you were .....' I struggled to find the least confrontational description for what I wanted to ask, '....going out with... I said, (*"sleeping with"* I meant), ...your *cousin*?'

'Well, he's not *really* my cousin. That's to say, not strictly speaking. He's my Uncle John's step-son. John's my dad's brother. He married Rob's mum when Rob was a toddler. We grew up together. Rob and me. We were always around each other's houses. We were best friends all through school. It's...sort of... complicated.'

'Go on,' I was sitting upright too now, watching her ear get redder as she spoke.

'Well, it sort of went from friendship to ...well, you know...we were sort of childhood sweethearts, from when we were fourteen or something. He was my first real boyfriend... hell, my only real boyfriend!'

'So what happened?'

She took a deep breath. 'He went off to Uni up in Leeds. I used to go and see him every weekend at first but it was too expensive to keep catching the train up there and we agreed I'd only go once a month.'

'And?'

'And I got lonely; I was missing him. I decided to pay him a surprise visit. Except that it was me who got the surprise. Walked into his halls and found him with some tart from Manchester. Beverly. Huge tits and legs up to her shoulders - well, his shoulders actually.'

'Oh, right...that must have been...awful.'

'You think?'

Roxanne pulled the mini back into the inside lane, changed down to third; cruising again.

'But you still see him?'

'Well, it's pretty difficult not to isn't it Tim? I mean, he's family. And he knocks around with all the same people that I do. I couldn't just ignore him forever, could I?'

'Er, no I suppose not,' I said.

What I was actually thinking was "hell, yes actually - and have nothing more to do with the cheating bastard!"

And then she said it.

'Worst thing is that I think he wants to get back with me. He's been apologising ever since it happened. He's really trying hard to make it up to me....' she went quiet, staring at the road ahead.

'And, what do *you* want?' I asked, I felt perfectly reasonably, 'do you want to get back with him?'

'I don't know, OK Tim? I just don't bloody know!'

I stared into the mirror, tilting my head, trying to see if my suspicions would be confirmed. They were. Even from the back seat, I could see that her eyes were welling up.

'Look, I didn't mean to..,' I said, 'really...don't get upset.'

To be honest, I was probably as concerned for my safety as I was for her feelings at that precise moment - her driving was scary enough at the best of times, let alone when her eyes were full of tears.

'Why don't we pull over and talk about it?'

She shook her head, her left hand wiping a stray tear from her eyes. 'Like I said, it's complicated...can we just leave it there, OK?'

We didn't speak another word until we passed the pylons that marked the boundary of Brighton. The silence had been almost physically painful.

'Roxanne?'

'What happened to "Muriel"? Not so funny anymore?' she muttered.

'Something else I was wondering about...'

'Oh Jesus, can we not go over this again?'

'No, not that. I was just thinking - where the hell are you going to put all this stuff? There's barely room in your kitchen for a kettle and a toaster, let alone all this gear!'

'Well, I won't be living there for ever will I?'

'No, but...'

'Hopefully, I'll get a bigger place soon.'

'Really? What, when you go to college?'

I felt suddenly sick at the prospect of her moving away. Sandra's comments about Leeds being their favourite hadn't been encouraging.

'Maybe.'

'Aren't most student places just as poky as yours?' I said.

'Well, yeah but...well, it depends who I share with doesn't it?'

And most students don't have parents living in a palace in Surrey, I thought.

'Anyway, surely that won't be until September will it?' I pointed out.

Her shrug was barely noticeable. She said nothing.

'That's like eight months away. Where are you going to put it until then?'

'There's a loft space that Jeff said Jackie and I could use.'

'Jeff?'

'My landlord. He says it's empty. No-one ever uses it.'

'A loft? And how are you going to get it all up there...?'I started to say.

'Well, if you're offering, that's really kind. It shouldn't take too long and then as a reward I'll take you for a Kentucky. Deal?'

What was I going to say?

Fried chicken and red-heads. I was such a sucker - for both.

20 - Behind My Camel

Of course, once I knew about the photos, it became glaringly obvious. How I hadn't noticed before, I'll never understand.

After just five minutes of sitting in the canteen with her that Monday lunchtime, I'd seen at least three groups of lads nudging each other, behind Alison's back. Of course I was used to that to a certain extent. With the way she looked, Alison had always been the subject of a lot of attention from the boys at Denton. But now I knew about the photos, I could see this was a different kind of attention. These lads were laughing too much, making too many rude gestures. I'd seen it for the past few months but I'd failed to put two and two together until now. Now, it was all adding up. I didn't like what I was seeing. It was out of order and I felt guilty. If only I'd done the decent thing and taken the photos back to her when I found them.

All morning, I'd been nervously waiting for Dave Booth to update me on his campaign to retrieve all the copies of the photos that were circulating around DSFCL6. During the break between History and English Lit, I'd collared him by the vending machines.

'So, how many have you managed to get hold of?'

'Flippin' Nora Tim, it's only twenty past ten, give me a chance. I've been in classes all morning, what did you expect me to do, get a message out on the jungle drums?'.

He had a point. Maybe I was being a bit impatient.

'Besides,' he said, looking around nervously and lowering his voice, 'I've got my own problems you know?'

'Oh, right, sorry, How *was* Karl?'

'Blanked me all morning.'

'Really?'

'Sat on the other side of the class; wouldn't even acknowledge me.'

'He'll come around. Give him time.'

'I think I'd rather he just got it over and done with, and clobbered me one. Maybe we'd both feel better.'

'Be careful what you wish for.'

'True.'

Dave started to walk away.

'So, hang on a minute. Have you got *any* of them back yet?'

'One, from Clarkey...,' Dave turned back, digging his hands in his Adidas bag.

'Clarkey had one? Ruddy hell, I didn't think he was...interested in girls.'

'You thought Clarkey was a shirt-lifter? I'll tell him that, he'll be dead chuffed.'

Dave handed me a copy of the photo of Alison lying topless on a Florida beach. I snatched it from him, stuck it in my jacket pocket before anyone saw.

'No, I knew he wasn't, you know, ...but... he's never seen that....bothered.'

'Still waters run deep my friend. The quietest ones are always the worst,' Dave said, tapping the side of his nose.

'Well, thank you for that pearl of wisdom Dr. Booth. Never mind the amateur psychology, when are you going to get my photos back?'

'*Your* photos? Since when were they *your* photos? Are you planning to keep them all for yourself you crafty little perv?'

'You know what I mean. I've paid for them..'

'Well strictly speaking, Jacko paid for them, so they must be his.'

'...and when I get them back, I'll personally destroy them all...'

'Oh yeah, good one.'

'...and the negative. You *do* still have the negative don't you?'

'It'll cost you.'

'Sod off.'

'What? You may have coughed up for the photos, but you didn't say anything about the negative. That'll be...ooh let me think....another quid?'

'Or maybe I'll just tell Alison you nicked it?'

I was bluffing of course but I managed to keep a straight face.

'OK, I'll let you have it back at lunchtime.'

'Good. And the rest of the photos OK?'

'I'll see what I can do?'

Alison wasn't herself. She looked tired; she hadn't bothered with make-up.

'I know it's none of my business...'

'I'm not ringing him,' she said, holding up her hand as if to shut me up, 'end of discussion.'

'OK, enough said.'

I looked over her shoulder. Two lads from our common room, Matthew Trent and Philip McCain were still tittering, looking in 's direction. Trent saw me staring at him and quickly looked away. I wondered if Dave had spoken to them. They'd clearly seen the photos. Probably both had copies.

'So, has he been in touch?'

For a moment I thought she meant Dave.

'What? Who?'

Then I realised what she meant.

'Oh, Humph. No sorry.'

'Bastard,' she said.

A bit harsh.

Then she got up and walked off, without so much as a goodbye.

I waited another twenty minutes. My Social Studies class was over the other side of the campus. I had to go. Bloody Dave. He was avoiding me.

It was Tuesday before I remembered the poster.

If it was an Outlandos D'Amour poster, or even a Regatta De Blanc poster, I'd probably have noticed sooner. Both those albums had been played to death, when I'd first got them - there was no way I would have gone two days without seeing the LP covers, which in turn would have jolted my memory and made me realise I'd left the poster under Roxanne's bed. But it wasn't; it was a Zenyatta Mondatta poster.

The third Police album hadn't become a permanent feature on the platter, like the first two. Don't get me wrong, it wasn't all bad - in fact it was great in places, but it also had some clunkers that, for me, really didn't work. For every classic like "Don't Stand So Close To Me" there was a stinker - an "Other Way Of Stopping" for example. "Man in A Suitcase" was great, "Bombs Away" sucked. I loved "Canary in a Coalmine" but "Voices Inside My Head" had got boring pretty quickly.

As hard as it had been for me to admit, the album just wasn't as good.

What had happened? Had Sting, Andy & Stewart got complacent? Had all the number one hits, the screaming fans and the blanket media overage gone to their heads? I'd read somewhere that the album had been written and recorded in just four weeks, whilst the band were doing gigs and preparing for a world tour. It had only just been finished in time. Maybe that's what it was. They'd just been too rushed. It seemed to me that they'd recorded half a dozen great tracks, before throwing a handful of half-completed instrumentals into the

258

mix, just to finish the album. One of the instrumentals was called "Behind My Camel". Apparently it was an in-joke within the band, which they explained by asking what you always got behind a camel? The answer? Yep - a great big pile of...

Well, at least they were able to joke about it I suppose - whereas I, for one, was not impressed. Maybe it served them right then that this particular fan had found himself deserting them and listening to other bands' LP's in preference to Zenyatta. UB40's "Signing Off", Joe Jackson's "I'm The Man"; The Clash's "London Calling" - they were all getting more airplay than Zenyatta on the Tim James Hi-Fi. That would simply never have happened with Outlandos or Regatta.

Putting away "Talk, Talk, Talk" by The Pyschedelic Furs, caused me to thumb through the P's in my collection - yes OK, my LPs are stored in alphabetical order - is there anything wrong with that? That's when I saw the sleeve to Zenyatta staring back at me and that's when I remembered.

Bloody hell. The poster! It must still be at Roxanne's flat. All her talk of going up to Weybridge with her had made me completely forget it. Immediately, I jumped up off the bed. I should call her; arrange to go over and pick it up. But hadn't she said *she* would call *me*? I hesitated; I didn't want to seem too keen; too desperate, to hear her voice; even if I *had* been thinking about her pretty much non-stop since the weekend. I put The Jam on and sat sat back on my bed. 'Be cool Tim,' I told myself. 'Be patient. She'll call'.

Kevin Clarke X
Peter Allen X
Graham Everett X
Phil McCain X
Luke Watson X
Mark Bennett X
Greg Jones X
Trevor Tiler X
Martin Yates X
Glen Newton X
Matt Trent X
Billy Gregory X
Reuben Hilyard X
Max Burgess X

Stu Tucker X
Me X (plus negative!)
Jez King
Frank Little
Karl Bloom
Almost there mate!!!
Paul Weller rools.
Dave woz ere

Dave Booth had left me the list, with a scrawled footnote, in an envelope marked *"For the attention of Dog Breath - private and confidential"*. I assumed I was *Dog Breath*. I found it when I went to get my Chaucer from my locker on Wednesday morning. I really should get into the habit of locking it. Not that I ever kept anything of value in there. Nobody would nick Chaucer - worse luck.

"Almost there mate" was true, judging by the names he'd put an "X" against, but it was the three he hadn't, that I was most worried about. Frank Little and Jez "Kong" King were tough guys to do business with without receiving a good pummelling; whilst I envisaged trouble from the last name on the list. Ruddy Karl. And what's more, there was no sign of the photos, or of the promised negative and I still didn't trust Boothie further than I could throw him.

I was still studying the list, when Alison and Sara Potts wandered past. Alison had the locker next to mine. I'd chosen my first. It wasn't like I was stalking her or anything, I'd chosen number 14, because it was the number Johan Cruyff always wore - Cruyff was my favourite footballer of all time. Alison had locker number 13 - no one else would go near it but Alison always said superstition was stupid.

I scrunched the list up and put it in my trouser pocket but not before Sara saw me.

'Secret love letter?' she said, nodding to my pocket.

'Shopping list,' I lied, 'from my Mum.'

'Ah, what a sweetie!' Sara said, tousling my hair.

Alison still looked miserable. Still no make up; hair a mess. I had a feeling a current photo might not sell twenty copies.

'Alright Ali?' I said.

'Not really,' she muttered, throwing her books into her bag and marching off.

Sara and I watched her walk away.

'I wish you'd speak to that bloody mate of yours,' Sara said.
Why not? It had to be worth a try.

These days, when Humph wasn't out on the lash with Pete and Doddsy, he was either playing football or training to play football. He played for one team on a Saturday afternoon; another on a Sunday morning. He went to training two or three times a week. So, I hardly expected him to be home on a Wednesday tea-time. But I popped around on the off chance, whilst taking Chalky for his evening constitutional. I got lucky.

'Hello mate,' he said, as his Mum called him downstairs. He was eating a slice of toast; a pair of rolled up football socks in his spare hand.

'This is a rare pleasure. I can't stop though, I was just packing my bag for training. What can I do for you?'

Humph's Mum was making a fuss of Chalky.

'Can I have a word?' I said, gesturing upstairs, in the direction of his room.

'Go on, you go on up. I'll take care of this little chap. I s'pect you'd like a nice biscuit wouldn't you boy eh?' Mrs Humphreys said, leading Chalky through to the kitchen.

'So, don't tell me, you need a loan for some gig or other, is that it?' Humph said, closing his bedroom door behind us.

Bloody hell, why did everyone always assume I was on the scrounge?

'No, it's.....about Alison.'

'Oh,' he said, the friendly smile disappearing from his face, 'sent you round to do her dirty work has she?' He stuffed the crust of toast into his mouth and the socks into his Arsenal bag.

'No, she doesn't even know I'm here,' I said, twiddling my thumbs.

'I'm not pleading with her to take me back, if that's what you think. Not after what she said about my mates.'

I stared at the poster of Frank Stapleton above his bed.

'She's really unhappy you know mate.'

'And who's fault is that?'

'I'm not saying it's anyone's fault. I'm just saying, you know, that she obviously still...you know....misses you.'

'Maybe she should try apologising then?'

This was going well.

261

'Couldn't you just...I don't know...giver her a call. Just say "hello" and ask her how she's doing?'

'What and get another bollocking? Not likely mate. If she's regretting giving me the elbow, *she* needs to call *me.*'

'And if she did, would you...make up with her?'

Humph shrugged.

'You do still...fancy her don't you?'

'Maybe.'

'So, if I could get her to call you, you'd speak to her?'

'If I wasn't doing anything else I might I suppose.'

Ahh. And they said romance was dead.

'OK, I'll see what I can do.'

I'd had an idea.

It had been a stupid idea at the time but maybe I could turn it to my advantage now.

Back in the second year, when I'd first set eyes on Alison Fisher, and before it dawned on me that I had about as much chance with her as I had of being handcuffed to Deputy Dawg, I'd thought of all sorts of cunning ruses for winning her affections. You know the sort of thing; stuff that twelve year old boys think will impress twelve year old girls, like showing off my brilliant cartwheel skills in the corner of the gym, whilst the girls were doing gymnastics; or doing my best Columbo impression in the canteen (this basically involved me half-closing one eye, pointing my finger and saying "just one more thing" over and over again). As wooing techniques went, they were the pre-teen equivalent of the mix-tape I'd decided against giving Roxanne. Lamer than a one legged ostrich.

When I'd first seen the card in the shop in the lanes, during one of my first "adult" forays into town with my new mate Martin Jackson, it struck me as the basis of a really romantic gesture. One of the first things I'd ever discovered about Alison was that she loved John Travolta in the film Grease, which was massive in the cinemas at the time.

The card ("left blank for your own message") bore a still from the film; Travolta and his co-star, in a loving embrace, smiling for the camera in a brilliant display of teeth and Brylcreem, beneath the legend "You're The One That I Want".

I know; I *know*. It was naff, even by my pathetic standards.

262

Telling Jacko I was buying it as a birthday card for my cousin Joanne, I paid over my 49p and stashed the card away in the deep pocket of my fake M&S parka pocket. By the time I got home, I'd realised that I'd never actually have the balls to actually give it to Alison in a million years. I thought about posting it to her anonymously, signed only with a huge question mark and a couple of kisses. But even that, I decided, was too cheesey for words.

Putting it down to a rush of blood to the head and cursing myself for wasting my perfectly good pocket money, I put the card away in a drawer and sort of forgot all about it. Occasionally, whilst looking for an elastic band or hiding my 'top twenty charts' file, I'd catch a glimpse of Travolta grinning back at me from beneath my socks, with his impossibly square chin, but somehow, I could never bring myself to put it in the bin. After all 49p was 49p.

It was whilst talking to Humph that I'd had the brainwave. The card might not be a total waste of time and money after all. If I could somehow pass it off as a grand gesture of apology from Humph, maybe, just maybe, I could get Alison to call him and things would be back to normal.

I had plenty of examples of Humph's handwriting. That was the advantage of being a hoarder. I never threw anything away - postcards, birthday cards, ten-pin bowling score-cards - you name it, I kept it - all under my bed in an old shoebox.

After a couple of practice attempts on a scrap of paper, I was satisfied that I'd got his scrawled writing and signature off to a tee and wrote *"please call me, love Humph xx"* in red biro.

Now all I had to do was pass it to Alison and *Bob's Yer Uncle,* or at least, hopefully, *Humph's Yer boyfriend.*

I suppose I could have just given it to her. That was my original intention. But then, just as I had way back in the second year, I chickened out. I'd never be able to keep a straight face; or avoid going crimson and giving the game away. So, instead, I decided to leave it in her locker. As ideas went, it was right up there with the cartwheels and Peter Falk. And of course, it was far from straightforward. Alison, like most normal people, was in the habit of locking her locker whenever they left anything in it. Unlike me - I didn't even know where my key was these days. Alison wore hers on a silver chain around her neck. I knew that all too well. It was a fairly long chain, which meant that the key nestled in an area which I'd spent half of my school-life trying, and failing, not to gawp at too obviously, whenever I spoke to her.

Three times that Thursday, I'd accidentally bumped into her at the lockers and tried in vain, to distract her long enough to slip the card in without her noticing. I'd have needed to be David Nixon or Ali Bongo to get away with it. The opportunity never knocked. So, I had to bide my time.

Due to a spate of break-ins last term, the headmaster had put round a memo in September, to advise students not to leave valuables in their lockers overnight, as the school couldn't accept responsibility. For Alison, who's middle name was "sensible", this meant leaving absolutely *nothing* in her locker overnight. Her daily ritual, come the end of her last lesson, was to empty the contents of her locker into her large straw bag and lug all her books home with her. What's more I knew that when it was empty, she always left it open.

'That way,' little Miss Sensible had explained to me one afternoon, 'no-one will be tempted to break in.'

I couldn't fault her logic, even if it kinda felt that it made having a locker fairly pointless in the first place. Anyway, for my sneaky purposes, her common sense principles played right into my hands. I needed to find an alternative way of getting the card to her; preferably one which didn't involve me having to face her as I handed it over. So, waiting until she went home and then hanging around until after everyone had gone, was no big deal.

Except of course, I hadn't counted on Dave "Romeo" Booth and his Juliette, having pretty much the same plan, but for their own purposes.

I'd just sneaked the card into number 13, when I turned around and walked, quite literally straight into them.

'Blimey mate, what are you still doing here?' Dave said.

Juliette looked embarrassed,

'Oh, just getting something from my locker.'

Dave looked behind me.

'Number 13, eh? Unlucky for some!'

'Er, yeah. How about you two? What are you doing sneaking around here so late?'

'Just, er off to the library, you know,' Dave winked.

Juliette was squirming.

'OK, well don't work too late,' I said. 'And Dave, we'll speak tomorrow eh, about those...things?' I said knowingly.

'Oh, yeah, of course, righto Tim, see you in the morning.'

Thursday evening. I was still waiting for Roxanne to call. I decided four days was long enough - and after all, wasn't the poster a legitimate reason to call her without sounding too needy?

Jackie answered the phone. She sounded a bit "off".

'She's not around I'm afraid. I haven't seen her much this week. I've been out and about.'

'Oh, OK. Have you see a poster lying around? It's in one of those special poster tubes..it might be under her bed?'

'Can't say I have. But then I don't really have much reason to go in there to be honest.'

I waited for her to offer to have a look. There were a few moments of silence. She clearly wasn't going to offer.

'You couldn't just....'

'Look, I'm sorry lovey, but I'm in a bit of a hurry to be honest; I'm just off out myself. I'll tell Roxy you called.'

'Oh, OK, thanks...'

'Oh and by the way Tim?

'Yes?'

'Have you still got my scarf?'

'Er, yeah, it's in the wash. I'll give it back to Roxy when I see her.'

The scarf. That had put the cat amongst the pigeons at home. I'd stuck it in the wash basket, hoping Mum wouldn't ask any questions. Some hope.

'So, this girlfriend of yours is at the Uni is she?' she asked, as we were all eating dinner on the Monday evening.

'Er, well, not exactly....'

'Only, I was thinking, if she's at Uni, she must be quite a bit older than you?'

'Crikey, he's pulled an older woman!' said Dad. Him and Lee cackled like Sid James. Dirty old men.

'Well that figures, I mean most of the residents at St. Dunstans *are* pretty old!' Cheryl said.

St. Dunstans is a home for blind people out near Rottingdean. She's hilarious my sister; about as funny as anal warts.

I gave her a look. 'You should be on the stage. Marti Caine must be really losing sleep,' I said.

265

'Well, older or not, I don't suppose she was too chuffed with you, if that's what I think it was on her scarf - and on your sweatshirt!' said Mum, 'I had to hand-rinse them before I could put them in the machine.'

'What did they stink of?' laughed Lee.

'I can't tell you whilst we're eating....' said Mum.

Dad and Lee laughed again; Cheryl glared at me, pulling a face, 'God, you're disgusting,' she said, 'what does an older girl see in you?'

It was a fair question.

After my conversation with Jackie, I went back up to my room. I'd begun to feel so guilty over my neglect of Zenyatta Mondatta that I decided to give it another chance. Maybe I'd just need a break from it.

I lay on the bed, wondering what I'd done wrong. Why hadn't she called? I hadn't seen or heard from her since Sunday evening. After we'd shifted her boxes into her landlord's attic, we'd walked into Brighton and she'd treated me to a slap-up meal of three pieces and chips with extra coleslaw. She'd really pushed the boat out - I'd had a large Coke too. I was gutted when she didn't invite me back. Mind you, it was a school night and I was bushed after humping all those bloody boxes up three flights of stairs. I was almost falling asleep by the time she dropped me off. She pecked me on the cheek and as I closed the Mini door behind me, she said she'd call me. I'd been kind've hoping for something a bit more concrete - like a specific day or time but, as usual, instead of pushing my case, I decided to act cool and left it at that. Now of course I was regretting that I hadn't taken the proverbial bull by the horns.

My heart wasn't in Zenyatta Mondatta.

What did you get Behind A Camel?

That's exactly what I felt like.

21 - Bombs Away

Dave caught up with me on the Friday morning.

'The news is like that film; The Good, The Bad and The Ugly, which would you like first?'

He stood over me as I was sitting in the Library. I wondered if he'd been there all night with his Juliette.

At this rate, I'd never get far with The Canterbury Tales.

'I think I'd like some good news for a change.'

And just for a change, it was raining outside. It promised to be another grim, wet weekend.

'Well, the good news is that I've managed to get you two of the remaining three photos back. I finally persuaded Frank and Jez to see reason.'

'So, I should have some change for Jacko then?'

'Ah, that's the bad news. I had to offer them an incentive.'

'How much?'

'A quid.'

'A quid?'

'Each.'

My lips formed an F.

'So *you* owe *me*.'

'So, what's the ugly news?'

'Karl.'

Karl was not playing ball. He wouldn't even talk to Dave, so Clarkey had been left with the job of trying to convince him to give up the last copy of Alison's infamous photo still circulating Denton. Even though Clarkey hadn't been sent to Coventry with me and Dave, he'd had no joy. Clarkey conveyed his message back to Dave – it consisted of two words; the second being "off".

Karl had given me the same treatment that he'd dished out to Dave.

'Hi mate!' I'd said breezily on the Monday morning. He was making a coffee with the grotty old kettle we'd been provided with in the common room. He glanced around, saw it was me and turned back to his pouring without so much as a grunt. I'd tried again later in the day as we passed in the corridor. He looked right through me. He'd obviously decided that I was guilty by association. He was being bloody childish. Well, sod you, I'd decided.

Now I needed to try again. Almost a week had passed and I hoped he would have started to calm down; thought he might have stopped sulking. I had another think coming.

Consigning Chaucer to the bottom of my bag yet again, I went looking for him. As expected, he was in the common room, reading an old music mag. I sat down next to him; it took him a second to realise who I was; he shifted uncomfortably, focusing even more fiercely on an article about Lemmy and Motorhead.

'He should really try using Clearasil.'

It was a cheap joke; and perhaps deservedly, it didn't raise so much as a chuckle.

Plan B then. I opened the Curly Wurly. Hit him in the weak spot.

He pretended not to notice. I took a bite and chewed noisily, making exaggerated 'mmmm' sounds.

Karl tutted.

I took the second one from my bag and held it out in from of him. He ignored it for precisely ten seconds. Then he snatched it out of my hand, resting the magazine on his knees and opening the packet without a word.

'Don't mention it,' I said.

He went back to studying lyrics to "Ace of Spades".

'No, you can't have the photo,' he said, without looking up.

'Oh come on mate..'

'You're wasting your time.'

'Don't be like that.'

'Why should I help Dave out? I think it would be best all round if Alison knew what a great friend he really is, don't you? I'm thinking of posting it to her. Yes, I think I might just do that - tell her the whole story of how her mate Dave sold topless photos of her all around Denton.'

'Bloody hell mate, I know you're angry at Dave, but why hurt Alison just to get back at him? She'll die of embarrassment.'

I thought I saw the first flicker of some reaction in his face. The first chink in his armour. I decided to go for it.

'And besides, she'll probably blame me.'

'Why you?' Karl turned around; looked at me for the first time. Ruddy hell.

I explained how I'd been there in the canteen, when she'd left them behind. How I'd sneaked a look; how I'd thought about handing them back to her, how I'd chickened out; how I could have avoided all this in the first place, if only I'd done the right thing. For the first time since Boxing Day, Karl laughed.

'You sneaked a look? You little perv!'

'You can talk! At least I didn't bloody buy a copy!'

'Only 'cause you weren't offered one,' he said, still grinning, 'Dave knew you'd do your knight-in-shining-armour routine and do your crust if you found out!'

At the mention of Dave's name. The smile disappeared from his face. There was an awkward silence.

'So, can I have the photo back?'

'I'll think about it.'

First thing that morning, I'd hidden in a classroom doorway, along the corridor. From that vantage point, whilst I couldn't see the girls at all, I could clearly hear their reaction.

'Is it from Chris?' I heard Sara say.

'I think so, it looks a bit like his writing. But how did it get here? said Alison.

A bit like his writing? It was spot on!

'Well, no prizes for guessing that. It must have been Tim. Who else do you know around here who would leave a message from Chris in your locker?'

At the sound of my name, I shrunk back into the doorway. I'd already checked it was open and that the classroom was empty. My escape route was well planned.

'So, aren't you going to open it?'

'Do you think I should?'

'Unless you've got x-ray vision, yes.'

It went very quiet for a few moments. I imagined, rather than saw, Alison opening the envelope. I also imagined the smile on her face when she saw the card; imagined her delight on reading the message within.

'So, what does it say?'

'Here, see for yourself.'

s trying to work out from the tone of her voice whether Alison was excited, surprised, sceptical. It was impossible. I'd resisted the temptation to peak my head around the corner.

'Ah, I suppose that's sweet.'

Alison laughed. 'Don't you mean cheesey?'

Damn it. I knew it was cheesey.

'So, what are you going to do?'

'I don't know. It's a bit....odd, don't you think?'

'Well, yes, if he wants to speak to you, why doesn't he just ring?'

Oh shut up Sara.

'Because he's too proud?'

'Or too chicken?'

There was the sound of lockers being closed, followed by footsteps going away from me, back down the corridor. I stepped out of the doorway, just in time to see their backs; one slinky, one wide, turning the corner.

'Nice job Tim,' I congratulated myself.

Later, after lunch, I stood for ten minutes outside the canteen door, waiting for my chance to bump into Sara on her own. I finally collared her on her way out; after Alison had gone off to her Art class.

'Hi Sara!' I said casually, 'what's new?'

Sara smiled. 'Like you don't know.'

'What?' My face was a picture of surprise.

'Oh, Mr. Innocence. Planted anything interesting in anyone's locker recently?'

'OK, it's a fair cop,' I laughed, holding my hands up in surrender.

'So what was in the envelope? I asked, giving Sara my very best puzzled expression, which wasn't a million miles from my Columbo impersonation.

'You must know,' he grinned. narrowing her eyes.

'Humph wouldn't say.'

Sara gave me an appraising look. She didn't seem convinced but nevertheless, she told me all about the card.

'No?' I said, shaking my head in shock.

I should be on Coronation Street; I was that bad an actor.

'Grease eh? That was their first date wasn't it?'

'Yeah, cheesey eh?'

'*Dead* cheesey,' I agreed

'You went and saw Chris then?'

270

'Yeah. I think he wants to get back with Alison.'

'So, what exactly did he say?'

'He said....well, he obviously misses her.'

'Did he actually say so?'

'Not in so many words.'

'That's a "no" then?'

'Well, no, but he gave me the card.'

'And why didn't he just deliver it himself?'

That was, of course, a reasonable question.

'I suppose he thought I'd be seeing her before him.'

Phew. Good one Tim.

'And when was this?'

'Oh, last night.'

It was only a white lie.

'Huh, sounds like he's getting you to do his dirty work if you ask me. The coward.'

'Yeah, what a coward.' I shook my head, like I really couldn't believe what a total coward Humph was.

'Right, well, OK. Let's hope it's good news.'

'It is. I mean, I'm sure it will be.' I smiled.

'Ok, see you later,' she said, turning to walk away.

'Tim?'

'Sara?'

'By the way, I meant to ask, 'how are things with you and Roxanne?'

'Yeah fine thanks,' I answered as brightly as I could.

She still hadn't called.

Maybe I'd pop up to HMV after school. But maybe not. I had my pride after all.

I still hadn't made up my mind when History, my final lesson of the day, had finished that afternoon.

'So, did you get the envelope?'

Dave had wandered over to me as I was in the corridor, digging in my bag for the half - empty bottle of 7 Up that I'd tossed in there earlier. I'd had to have a ridiculously hurried lunch after my encounter with Sara. I hadn't even had enough time to finish my fizzy drink. I was starving and parched.

'What envelope?' I said, still searching underneath my text books.

271

'The one I put in your locker,' Dave said.

'What? When was this?'

'About half an hour ago. Sorry I couldn't give you them earlier with Juliette around.'

'Dave, what are you talking about?'

'The photos. All of them - and my negative. All yours. All you need to do is get the last one from Karl and your dirty little secret is safe forever.'

'*My* dirty little secret? I'm not the David Bailey of Denton, you are!'

'No, OK - *our* dirty little secret then. Anyway, they're in the locker.'

'*Your* dirty little secret, David. And why did you stick them in my locker? You do know it doesn't lock don't you?'

'Well, I guessed that, by the fact that it was open. But anyway, I couldn't carry them around with me all day. What if I got caught with them - you know, by Juliette?'

'Oh thanks, so its OK, if I get caught with them?'

'Well, they'll be safe there. Who's going to look in your skanky little locker?'

'Thanks.'

'No problem. Still unlucky for some though?'

'What?'

'Number thirteen. Like I said last night, unlucky for some.'

'Number thirteen? You put them in locker number thirteen?'

'Yeah, that's yours isn't it? I saw you in it last night.'

'Number thirteen?'I repeated, hoping I'd misheard him.

'Yes.'

'Half an hour ago?'

'Yes Tim. Why are you repeating everything I say?'

'Was it open?'

'Of course; how else would I have put it in there?'

'You put the envelope in locker thirteen, which was open, half an hour ago?'

'Bloody hell Tim, yes, that's what I said. Why, what's wrong?'

Oh shit.

Please let her have gone home.

272

Please let her have emptied her locker, finished for the day, and gone home.

Please God.

My first thought was to check the crowds of kids walking down to the bus stop. Alison was nowhere to be seen.

Don't panic Tim, she'll have gone home. Why else would her locker be empty? Calm down, everything will be OK.

My heart was pounding, despite my best efforts at reassuring myself, as I started hurriedly heading back towards the common room and the lockers.

Clarkey was ambling down the school driveway towards me; he was playing around with his Sony Walkman.

'Clarkey! Clarkey!'

'Oh hi Tim,' he said, pulling the headphones down from his sweaty ginger head.

'Have you seen Alison?'

'Oh yeah, she just went that way,' he said nonchalantly pointing in the direction I was heading.

'What?'

'Yeah,' he chuckled, 'she was cursing Sara and her gluttonous appetite. Sara was dragging her all the way back to the common room. Said she'd forgotten her late afternoon snack or something. Left in ...'

Don't say 'locker', don't say 'locker'.

'...her locker.'

I was no athlete but I must have broken the land speed record getting over to the common room, on the other side of the campus, sprinting across the hockey pitch and splashing through ankle deep puddles as I went. I scrambled up the the muddy, grass embankment hurtled through the staff car-park and around the back of the tennis courts.

Sweat was dripping from my brow as I stopped on the forecourt to catch my breath. Then with my second wind, I burst through the back door to the building, almost knocking over two second year girls in the process, raced up two flights of stairs and through the door to the sixth form corridor. As I passed the very doorway in which I'd taken refuge to spy upon Alison and Sara only that morning, I caught sight of the two girls, standing in front of the lockers. My heart sank as I came to an abrupt halt fifteen feet away from them. My breath was coming in bursts. My hair was sopping wet and my black trousers were splashed with streaks of mud, right up to the knee. In short, I must have looked a right state.

The girls stood with their backs to me. Sara Potts had her arm around Alison's shoulder; a tupperware lunch-box cradled in her other hand. Alison's head was down and as I slowed to a deliberate stroll, I caught the sound of sobbing echoing down the corridor.

'Who would, sob....do something, so....horrible?'

My heart lurched.

For once, even Sara Potts seemed to be speechless. I saw her comforting arm squeeze Alison tighter.

'We should report this,' she was saying, 'someone must have stolen your negatives.'

'I knew....sob, there was something going on....sob. Oh God! All those comments.'

My momentum had carried me within a few feet of them now. Every fibre in my body screamed at me to turn around and walk away, before they saw me. But it was too late. Sara must have heard my footsteps. She turned her head towards me. She had tears in her eyes but she didn't look upset, she looked angry. Really furious.

'What's happened?' I managed to say.

Alison noticed me for the first time. She let out a heartbreaking sob.

Sara shook her head, pulling Alison towards her.

'What is it?' I repeated. My heart was pounding. I felt terrible.

'Someone's left a horrible ....package in Ali's locker.'

'The card?' I said stupidly, 'it wasn't that bad was it?'

By now, Alison was in floods of tears - inconsolable.

'Not the card,' Sara said, shaking her head.

Alison buried her face in Sara's shoulder.

Her voice sounded muffled but absolutely distraught.

'They....*sob*....stole my....*sob*.....holiday photos. It's so horrible!'

I put my hand on her shoulder. 'I'm so sorry Alison.'

'What sort of a bastard would do something like that?' Alison said, her distraught face streaked with mascara and lipstick.

'And then to put them in her locker,' Sara said, 'that's just despicable.' She looked me up and down, only now noticing the mess I was in.

'What's happened to you?'

'Oh, right,' I said, 'I forgot my homework. Just came to get it.'

274

Instinctively, I reached over and pulled open the door to locker 14. My actual locker.

Sara saw it first. Her face looked like she'd been prodded up the backside with a red hot poker. I followed her gaze which had fixed onto something over my shoulder. Then I saw it too. A photo had been sellotaped to the inside of my locker door. A photo of Alison, lying on a Florida beach, wearing only a very skimpy pair of bikini bottoms. A scrawled note had been taped next to it, in what I instantly recognised as Karl Bloom's handwriting.

"Here's your precious photo back! Enjoy! You owe me 20p"

Then I heard another terrible shriek of pain from behind me.

Alison had seen it too.

22 - Bombs Away (Part 2)

'So, did you explain to her?

'I didn't get the chance did I? She was hysterical. The language she used! You should have heard it Clarkey!'

'Bloody hell Tim, you do get yourself into some embarrassing situations mate.'

'But that's just it. I don't get myself into them, other people get me into them!'

Clarkey had come around to my place again that Saturday. He'd brought along his new video of David Bowie live on his "Scary Monster" tour. Mum and Dad had got a video player for Christmas. It was brilliant – it could tape stuff off the telly and everything; but we didn't have many tapes yet. I wasn't a huge Bowie fan like Clarkey, but it was a pretty good gig; the lighting was cool, and I enjoyed the songs I recognised like "Ashes to Ashes" and "Fashion". Other bits were a bit dull. I couldn't concentrate anyway, I had too much going on in my head. Women! I was waiting for two phones calls, neither of which had materialised.

Roxanne still hadn't been in touch. And now I was expecting a call from Sara Potts too.

'So why did you call Sara?' Clarkey asked, 'why didn't you just ring Alison?'

'You didn't see her, she was like that girl out of The Exorcist. I thought her head would explode. I've never seen anyone that angry or upset.'

'And what did you tell Sara?'

'The whole story of course!'

I had phoned Sara at home the previous evening. I'd thought she might not want to talk to me and at first, she was pretty angry. I'd had to plead my case – get her to listen to my explanation for the photos.

'The whole story?'

'Well, I may have left out the bit about finding the photos that day in the canteen. And I didn't say I'd sneaked a look at them of course.'

'So, did you tell Sara who had copied them?'

'Not exactly. I just said that I'd found out that somebody was handing copies out around school and that I'd tried to get them all back so that Alison wouldn't have to know.'

'What did Sara say?'

'She said I should have told her. I told her I didn't want Alison to have to face the embarrassment. I mean, ruddy hell, I had to pay out a lot of my own money to get them back didn't I?'

'Your own money?'

'Well, Jacko's.'

'So how did you leave it?'

'Sara said she would tell Alison what I'd said. I asked her to let me know if she was OK. Sara said she'd call me back – that was...' I checked my watch, 'over fifteen hours ago. Do you think I should call her?'

'Maybe you should let the dust settle eh mate? See how the land lies on Monday.'

Mum came in with coffee.

'Here you go Kevin, two sugars. That's right isn't it?'

'Yes, lovely – thanks Mrs. James.'

'Oh and Tim, that scarf is dry now if you'd like to return it to your lady-love,' Mum said, grinning stupidly at Clarkey.

Lady-love? Where did my Mother get these sayings? I knew she was fishing for information again and as usual, I wasn't taking the bait.

'Thanks,' I grunted.

When Mum realised she wasn't getting any more information from either me or Clarkey, she went back to her housework.

'What was that about a scarf?' Clarkey asked as he sipped his coffee.

'Long story.'

After three quarters of an hour of Bowie, Dad came in, saying he wanted to watch Grandstand.

Clarkey and I went up to my room. We talked about doing our History homework – an essay on the Treaty of Versailles. We opened my text book and compared notes for about a minute and a half, but it was obvious our hearts weren't really in it. We got talking and the subject came around to Christmas presents.

'So did Roxanne get you anything?' he asked.

'Yeah, she gave me this huge Zenyatta Mondatta poster that was up in the shop.'

'Oh, cool, let's have a look!' said Clarkey.

'I left it at her place,' I said.

'Her place eh? Something you want to tell me?'

277

I laughed, 'I'll leave it to your imagination.'

His imagination would be a lot better than the reality.

'Ah well, you lucky dog, you can pick it up next time you're there.'

Next time? Was there going to be a next time?

My face must have been transparent.

'I mean, I assume there is going to be a next time is there mate?'

Who knew? Not me.

Sod it. Maybe it was about time I found out.

'Look, sorry mate, I need to pop out for a while. We'll have to do that essay another time.'

'She called in sick,' Christian, the Terry-Hall-lookalike told me, in a huff.

As ever on a Saturday, the shop was really busy. Christian did not seem happy. He was re-stocking the shelves with armfuls of cassettes.

'What's wrong with her?'

'Your guess is as good as mine mate,' he said dismissively, placing a Dr. Feelgood tape next to Dr. Hook.

'Didn't she say?'

'Well, she put on the old at-death's-door-voice, you know, like we all do, but...'

'But what?'

He shrugged.

'Dunno,' he tapped the side of his nose, 'bloke-trouble if you ask me.'

I wished I *hadn't* asked.

'Why do you say that?'

'Look mate, I'm busy right? All I know, is she's hardly been in all week...' he walked off.

'Is Poppy around?' I said to the back of his head, thinking that Poppy might know a bit more about what was going on.

'Lunch,' he said, without taking his eyes from the display of cassettes.

He looked stressed out; I decided not to push it any further.

What was going on?

It was like Roxanne had disappeared off the face of the earth. I thought about hanging around outside the shop for Poppy to get back but after a few minutes I grew restless. By the time I'd finally managed to find a phone box that wasn't vandalised, I found myself

278

half way down North Street. Then, when there was no answer from her phone, I made a decision. I would go up to her place; see if she or Jackie were home and hopefully pick up my poster. To be honest, I'd known that was my ultimate destination from the moment I'd left Clarkey at the end of our street. Why else would I have stuffed Jackie's scarf into an old Fine Fare bag on my way out?

There was no answer when I rang the doorbell. Jackie's scarf wouldn't fit through the letter box, as it had one of those stupid brush things on the inside. I'd have to leave it somewhere. Looking around, I noticed a large terracotta pot to the left of the door, containing some very dead daisies. The idea was to stuff the bag containing the scarf behind the pot, leaving a note to say I'd called. Why I bothered fumbling in my pockets I'll never know, it's not like I actually ever carry a pen. But I did find something else I'd forgotten was in there. Roxanne's key. The one she'd given me when I'd got up to ring Mum and Dad in the middle of the night. I hadn't given it back to her. I turned it in my hand, debating whether letting myself in would constitute "breaking and entering". I decided it wouldn't; after all, she'd trusted me to have it and I was just returning it. And I could return the scarf and get my poster. It all made sense.

Even though I told myself all this, I still called out her name as I opened the door, and then again as I scrambled around the bicycles in the hallway. There was no answer.

The living room looked exactly as I remembered it, except messier. Dirty dishes were piled up around the sink area and cigarette stubs spilled out from an ash-tray on top of the TV. Throwing Jackie's scarf down onto the sofa, I crept over to Roxy's bedroom door. I was sure she wasn't in but I knocked all the same, before slowly pushing it open. Her bed was unmade and to my surprise, the foldaway bed was still out too - they both looked like they'd been slept in. Both beds were unmade and there were items of clothing strewn around the floor.

I didn't need to search under the bed for my poster. The tube was propped up in the far corner and as I made my way around the bed, I stubbed my toe again, just as I had that night. Except not on the bed but on something that was sticking out from underneath it. Looking closer I was baffled to see a bright red motorcycle crash-helmet. I stooped and picked it up. There was a smaller, second helmet under it. The smaller one was pink, with fluffy leopard skin ears sticking out of the top. My guts were churning now; my mind was doing the sums and I wasn't liking the results.

Peering out of the window and down the street, I spotted a bloody great Harley Davidson sitting in the road just a few yards away - I hadn't noticed it when I came along Upper Rock Gardens - but then why would I? I hate motorbikes - bloody noisy monstrosities as my Mum always calls them. I looked around the room; some of the clothes were definitely not Roxanne's, unless she had developed a sudden liking for denim waistcoats and leather biker-gloves. My brain was working over time as I sat on the end of her bed, twirling the pink helmet with the fluffy ears around in my hands. There was a noise at the front door. Throwing the crash-helmet on the bed and picking up my poster, I hurried out of the room, closing the door behind me, just as the living room door was pushed open from the other side.

She jumped out of her skin.

'Bloody hell, what are you doing here?'

'Hi Jackie, sorry...'

'Sorry? You almost give me a ruddy cardiac and all you can say is "sorry"!' she said with real anger in her eyes, as she stood in the doorway, hands on hips.

'Sorry,' I muttered again.

'How the hell did you get in?'

'Roxanne leant me...,' I fumbled in my pocket with my spare hand and pulled out the key, '....this!' I held it up for her to see.

'Why the bloody hell would she do that?'

Jackie was red in the face. A small vein was throbbing in her temple.

'It was that night I stayed over,' I said, a tremor in my voice, 'I needed to go to the phone-box; she gave me it so that I could get back in...you know without ringing the bell.'

'I don't suppose she meant you to keep it though did she?'

'Maybe not...'

'And I don't suppose she knows you're using it to prowl around her flat when she's not even here!'

'Prowling? No, but...'

'And I certainly don't think she wants to come home and find you rifling through her things!' Jackie's gaze fell on Roxanne's bedroom door, which was slowly opening behind me, with an accusing creak.

'I wasn't rifling through her things, I was just looking for my poster.

We stood there, staring each other down across the back of the sofa.

'Well? You've got it now. I think you should go, don't you?'

'My eyes fell on the Fine Fare bag on the arm of the sofa.'

'Oh yeah,' I said, 'and I brought your scarf back.'

Like that explained everything.

'Thanks,' she muttered grudgingly. Then she held out the palm of her hand. 'Key please!' she said. I got the impression she wasn't in the mood to argue, so I handed it over.

'I'll tell Roxanne you ..''called'',' Jackie's eyes were cold. There was no humour there like the time I'd met her in the hallway dressed in her bathroom mat. She was obviously angry at my uninvited intrusion, which I suppose was understandable but I hadn't really done anything wrong. Why should I feel guilty? Shouldn't I be the one who was bloody angry, given what I'd just discovered?

'Ok, I'm going,' I said, walking past her and heading back through the living room door. I stopped and turned.

'Jackie, just a couple of things?'

'What?'

'Where the hell *is* Roxanne and whose bloody crash helmets are those in the bedroom?'

23 - Bombs Away (Part 3)

I don't really know what made me call her. I needed to speak to someone. And I was fed up feeling like the one in the wrong, when I'd only been trying to do the right thing.

Her Mum picked up the phone. She sounded pleased to hear from me. She asked me whether I was enjoying sixth form and how my studies were going.

'Fine thank you Mrs. Fisher...'

'You really should come around for tea again, we'd all love to see you...'

I'd been to Alison's for tea a few months back. Mrs. Fisher had treated me like a hero. All I'd done was stupidly rescued Alison's brother Adrian from getting a beating from some school thugs. For my pains, I was rewarded with a black eye from Steve Andrews and vol-au-vents and fondant fancies from Mrs. Fisher.

'Thanks, I'd like that.'

After a few moments, I heard footsteps and then Alison picked up the receiver.

'Hello, Tim?'

'Hi Alison, how are you?'

'Oh Tim, I'm so sorry. I was going to call you later. Sara called me. I feel terrible; I was so horrible to you. Can you ever forgive me? I acted like a total....'

'That's OK, I understand....'

'No, really, I thought.....'

'Alison, it's OK, don't....'

'Sara told me that you paid out all that money, just to get the photos back. You're so kind. And I was so nasty...'

Afterwards, I couldn't have said why I'd said what I did. It just came blurting out.

'Would you go out with me? For a drink I mean. Tomorrow evening?'

'Sorry?...'

'Don't feel obliged. Only if you're free...you know... I was just thinking, that's all...if you're not already doing something.'

'Where did you have...'

'I mean, you know, I know it's Sunday and we've got school the following day....'

'That's OK...'

'And you know, only if you've not already made plans with Sara or anything...'

'No, that's fine...'

'It's no big deal, you know, I was just thinking it would be nice...'

'Tim!'

'Sorry, yes?'

'Yes.'

'Yes what? Sorry?'

'Yes, that would be really nice, I'd love to go for a drink with you tomorrow. Where shall we meet up?'

Shades wasn't quite as busy as the last time I was there. It was still surprising just how many people went for a drink on a Sunday evening though.

'So, do you come here often?' Alison asked, giggling, as she glanced around the bar.

We were sitting at the very same table I'd shared with Roxanne a couple of weeks back. Was it only that long? It seemed like ages.

'Now and then,' I said, trying to sound casual, 'you?'

I looked around the bar. Had I really expected to see Roxanne here? Was that why I'd suggested we meet here?

'Nope, this is my very first time. I'm officially a Shades virgin.' Alison laughed, brushing a stray red hair from her forehead. She still had the dyed streak through her otherwise blonde hair, which she'd tied back behind her head in a girlish pony-tail. She looked lovely. I just hoped that Humph and his mates didn't frequent the Shades bar on a Sunday. What was I doing? Now that we were here, I had no idea why I'd asked her out.

'A penny for them?' Alison said, snapping me away from my thoughts.

'Sorry, I was miles away.'

'HMV by any chance?'

'Am I that obvious?'

'So, I assume by the fact that you're sitting in a pub with me tonight that things are not going too well with Roxanne?'

'Can't a boy ask a friend out for a drink?'

'To...friends,' she said, raising her glass of Coke.

'Friends!' I said, returning her toast.

283

Alison studied the bar. I studied Alison.

She was wearing a purple satin blouse, loosely buttoned. Each time she leaned forward, she gave me a tantalising glimpse of the gently sloping flesh that I remembered only too well from those bloody photos. Alison had perfect skin. I found my eyes focusing on the nape of her neck. It was so smooth and soft and not for the first time, I found myself wondering just what it would be like to kiss that neck. Humph would know of course. Note to self - *don't* ask him. Instead of the locker key that she wore around her neck at school, I noticed that Alison was wearing a thin gold necklace with a small gold heart pendant hanging from it. Humph had brought if for her last Valentine's day.

'So, did you call him?'

'I did.'

I felt a sudden panic.

'You didn't tell him about the photos did you?'

At the mention of the photos, Alison frowned for a moment. There was still real pain in her eyes.

'Not likely. He'd have gone nuts.'

Yes, he would.

'So, how did it go?'

'Good!' she smiled mischievously, 'but do you know what was strange?'

'No, what?'

'He sounded really surprised to hear from me.'

'Really?'

'Mmm, really. And what's more, he didn't mention anything about any card he'd supposedly sent me.'

'Oh?'

She laughed.

'Did you really think I'd fall for that?'

'Fall for what?'

'It was quite a good attempt at the handwriting I suppose, but you did make one pretty stupid mistake.'

'What do you mean?'

'Tim, just remember in future - Chris never, ever, signs himself "Humph" when he's addressing me.'

'Oh.'

God, of course I knew that. Sometimes, I was so thick.

284

'Oh, indeed,' she laughed, 'still it was a really sweet thing to do.'

Alison leant across the table. She kissed my cheek.

'So, if you knew the card wasn't from him, why did you call him?'

'Because I needed to, after the day I'd had on Friday, I mean.'

'Oh right, yeah, of course.'

'And what happened? Are you going to see him?'

'Maybe,' she smiled coyly.

'What does that mean?'

'Well, I must be sizzling hot this weekend. Including you, I've had three offers of dates!'

'Really? Mind you, I wouldn't say this really counts as a .....'

'Yep, Chris asked me if I wanted to see The Morbid Morsels with him at the Northern next Saturday.'

'You're joking?'

'What do you mean? I'm not that much of a toothless hag am I?' she laughed.

'No. Your teeth are fine! Not so sure about the rest of you...' I said, pretending to look her up and down. Never a chore.

She leant over and whacked me playfully around the head.

'The Morbid Morsels though?' I said, 'Humph interested in seeing Karl Bloom's group. I can't believe it!'

'Do you know what I think?'

'No, what?'

'I think he reckons I've got a thing for Karl Bloom.'

'And why would he think that?'

'Possibly because Sara Potts told him I did?' she smiled.

'Any why would Sara do a thing like that?'

'Who knows? I can't possibly think why my best friend would tell my ex-boyfriend something like that, can you?' she laughed.

'What?'

'Oh come on Timothy, keep up!' she chuckled. Then she winked.

'Ahh!' I said, the penny dropping. 'Devious!'

'I thank you kindly sir!' she gave a mock bow; her blouse fell even further open. Oh God, Black Lace. Focus Tim, focus.

'And what did you say?'

'I told him "thanks but no thanks", I couldn't go with him as I was already going with someone else!'

'You didn't! You're not?'

'Uh-huh,' she nodded.

'With Karl?'

'No! Karl would never ask me out would he?'

'No?'

'Of course not, he's worse than you!'

'What do you mean he's worse than me?'

'I'd be an old maid before either of you ever made a move!'

Harsh. But probably true.

'So, you haven't really got a date for the gig then?' I asked, feeling like I'd lost the plot again.

'Of course I have!' she said, like I was missing the bleeding obvious.

'Who?'

'Wait and see!'

Whilst we made small talk, I was conscious of several pairs of male eyes watching us; all thinking the same thing - what the bloody hell was a girl like that doing with a jerk like me? I felt strangely proud of myself, which was probably more than a bit sad in the circumstances.

'Anyway Mr. James, it was neatly done but don't think you've thrown me off the scent!' she said a few minutes later.

'Uh?'

'I asked you how things were going with Roxanne and somehow you got me talking about Christopher and my date for next weekend! Nicely done!'

I shrugged; took another gulp of beer.

'Tim?'

Five minutes later, I'd finished telling her the whole sorry story.

'Well, if you want my opinion....'

'Am I going to like it?'

'....if you want my opinion!'

'Sorry, go on.'

'I reckon she's confused.'

'Why do you say that?'

'Well, speaking as someone who's recently been in the same boat, I reckon Roxanne probably doesn't know whether she wants this Rob back or not.'

'And..?'

'And, well, what she probably wants is a version of this Rob that no longer exists - the Rob that she knew before he cheated on her.'

'Well, that's not possible is it? He did cheat on her. Nothing can change that, can it?'

'Well, no but...'

'I mean, how would you feel if you knew Humph had cheated on you?'

'Why? What do you know that you're not telling me?'

'Nothing! I'm just saying, would you, if he had?'

'I suppose it depends.'

'Depends on what?'

'On what else was on offer, of course. Does she have an alternative on offer that is better than taking another chance on the love-rat?'

'And by "an alternative" I assume you mean yours truly?'

'Uh-ha,' she nodded.

'And what would you do in her position?'

Alison shifted uncomfortably in her seat. She shrugged her shoulders; swilled the dregs of Coke around the bottom of her glass.

'I'm not Roxanne though, am I?'

'No, but if you had a choice between taking Humph back after he'd cheated on you or seeing someone else, what would you choose?'

'Depends on the "someone else" doesn't it?'

She put down her glass and absent-mindedly began to fondle her pendant - the one Humph had given her. I think I knew what her real answer would be, regardless of the "someone else".

'Can I make a really obvious observation?' she asked.

'If you must.'

'You need to tell her how you feel about her.'

'If I could actually find her, I might just do that,' I said.

And then again....

24 - Driven To Tears

Scrubbing very half-heartedly, I lifted the windscreen wiper from the glass. The dirty smears moved from one side of the windscreen to the other, refusing to budge.

Sting was singing about being *Driven to Tears*.

I wasn't going to let it happen, no matter what.

I leant in through the car window and defiantly, turned the volume dial up a couple of notches; drumming my fingers on the bonnet in time with Stewart Copeland. Then I pushed the dirty old chamois back down into the bucket, pulled it out and threw it back onto the windscreen.

Driven to Tears.

Huge soapsud-teardrops fell onto the bonnet. Alison's voice was on "repeat" in my head.

'You need to tell her how you feel about her.'

I had wanted to but somehow, the opportunity never presented itself.

I'd waited until Wednesday. It was a whole week and a half since I'd seen or heard from Roxanne. Maybe I should have called sooner? But then, even if I had, who's to say she would have been there to answer?

The phone rang for ages. I was about to give up. Then someone picked up. I hadn't even waited for her to speak.

'Hello, is that you Roxy?'

There was no immediate reply. I thought I heard breathing.

'Roxy?'

Definitely - a small intake of breath.

'It's me, Tim.'

At last she seemed to recognise my voice

'Oh, hi Tim, how are you?'

She hadn't completely forgotten me then?

'OK thanks - long time, no see eh?'

'Yeah, I'm sorry about that. And after all that help you gave me with the kitchen stuff; I must seem a really ungrateful bitch eh?'

'Not at all.'

Well, a bit actually.

'Yeah, well, anyway, I was going to call but things have been a bit....complicated. Jackie said you'd popped round. Thanks for bringing her scarf back. And the key. That was really thoughtful. Did you find your poster OK?'

'Yeah, thanks.'

'Great,' she said.

Was that a motorbike revving up in the background?

There was a pregnant pause. Before I'd finally dialled her number, I'd made up my mind that I was just going to ask her out; to tell her I needed to talk to her. If I could get her on her own then maybe, just maybe, I could do what Alison had suggested. It seemed relatively straightforward, but of course the reality was different.

"You need to tell her how you feel about her."

Now that she'd answered the phone, I wasn't so sure. She sounded odd; really...uncomfortable.

'So,' she said, another deep breath, 'you must have wondered what the hell had happened to me I suppose?'

'Sort of, yeah,' I said, trying to sound as cheerful as I could.

'Jackie said you were asking about the helmets?'

'Well, yeah, I was...curious, I suppose...'

'Yeah, well, as you may have guessed, I had an unexpected house-guest.'

'Oh, really?'

Here we go, I thought - this should be good.

'Yeah, Rob turned up on the doorstep one morning, completely out of the blue. Typical Rob!'

She laughed.

I didn't.

'Woke me up; woke Jackie up, hammering on the door; probably woke the whole street up! I could have murdered him as you can imagine!'

Well, yes, I could certainly imagine wanting to murder Rob.

'He just stood there looking pathetic. I had a right go at him - told him to sling his hook.'

'But he didn't? I mean I'm just guessing - you know from the crash helmets and the y-fronts on your bed?'

Oops, did that sound *too* sarcastic? Tough.

'Er no,' she laughed nervously. 'He just stood there on the doorstep.'

289

'Yeah, so you said...'

'Well, I could see all the curtains twitching, so I couldn't just stand there having a slanging match with him, could I?'

'No?'

Why not exactly?

'So, I let him in, made him a coffee and then he tells me all about it.'

'All about what?'

'About Uncle John - that's his Dad - how he'd thrown him out.'

'Really? Why?'

'Whacky Baccy'

'What?'

'You know, weed? Hash? Marijuana?'

Oh right.'

Was that one drug or four? I knew nothing about drugs. I didn't want to ask though. I didn't want to sound like a right idiot.

'Yeah, Auntie Annabel - that's Rob's Mum, she found his private little stash in his sock drawer.'

'He keeps drugs in his sock-drawer?'

'It was only a bit of weed. Hardly enough to roll a single joint!'

'Right.'

Joint? I had absolutely no idea what she was talking about.

'So, she told Uncle John and he went absolutely mental. Told Rob he wouldn't have junkies living under his roof. Threw him out there and then. Rob didn't know where to go.'

'Doesn't he have any mates up in Surrey?'

'Sorry?'

'It seems a bit odd that he rode his bike all the way down to Brighton, you know, rather than going to a mate's place or something.'

'Yeah, that's exactly what I said. Apparently, he rang around a few people but none of them could put him up. He said I was the only one he could think of who had a spare bed.'

Good one Rob. I had to applaud his ingenuity.

'A spare bed? You mean the foldaway in your room?'

'Yes, that's the only spare bed in the flat,' she said, sounding slightly tetchy, I thought.

'He couldn't have slept on the sofa?'

'On that old thing? Hardly.'

'So he slept in your room?'

'Yeah. Well, it's not like I've got anything he hasn't seen before is it?'

Oh great. That made me feel a whole lot better.

'Right.'

The next pause was so pregnant I could almost hear the waters breaking.

'Look, I know what you're thinking but nothing happened OK? Not that it's really any of your business.'

Very tetchy.

'Rob knows he's got no chance in that department,' she said.

'Does he?'

'Yes.'

Super tetchy.

'OK.'

There was that pause again. It was fully dilated and the head was engaged.

'So, anyway,' she continued eventually, 'I let him stay here for a couple of days. I told him he needed to go and see his Dad. I said he needed to apologise. I told him he couldn't stay indefinitely.'

'And?'

'Well, of course - he's a typical bloke. He was far too chicken to actually face Uncle John on his own. I had to take him back up there didn't I? I had to smooth-talk Uncle John - I've always been his favourite niece.'

'So you went up there with him?'

'Yeah, we took the Mini.'

'And that's where you've been all week?'

'Well, sort of...'

'Only I popped into HMV and they said you'd been off all week.'

'Bloody hell Tim, what are you, Columbo or something?'

Funny she should say that. *There's just one more thing.*

'No, I was just trying to get hold of you that's all.'

And I wasn't the only one by the sound of it. Sounded to me like Rob was trying to get hold of her too. Chucked out on his ear? What a load of cobblers.

'Well, Mr. Detective, as it happens, if you must know....'

Really, really, quite tetchy.

'...when I got up there, it turned out that Dad's been really poorly again, so I hung around for a few days, to look after him, while Mum was at work, OK?'

She emphasised "OK" with such ferocity, I could almost feel the spittle on my face, all the way down the line.

'OK,' I said.

"Keep your bloody hair on." I thought.

Had I touched a nerve? I pictured Mr. Delaney. Her Dad had looked in perfect health when I was up there - he was certainly knocking back the vino without too much of a problem. Maybe it was cirrhosis of the liver?

'Well?'

'Well what?' I said.

'Yeah, Dad's feeling a lot better now Tim. Thanks for asking.'

She could be really stroppy when she wanted.

"You need to tell her how you feel about her," I heard Alison saying.

Did that mean I should tell her she was a stroppy cow? Probably best not.

Well, nothing ventured...

'So, are you around tomorrow night?' I said, hearing the catch in my voice; preparing myself for another verbal onslaught.

'Tomorrow?' she said sulkily, 'er, sorry, no, not really...'

'Don't tell me,' I said, not letting her finish her sentence, 'Rob?'

'No, as it happens, I've got some old friends...*girlfriends*...coming down. They're staying for the weekend.'

'Oh *really?*'

'Yes *really.* Is that OK with you? Or do you want to get a few witness statements Inspector Clouseau? Maybe I could take a lie-detector?'

Blimey, talk about touchy. I was trying not to bite back but I just couldn't resist a little nibble.

'So, that's a "no" then? You're not free this weekend then? How about next week?'

'I'm not sure...'

Suddenly a nibble wasn't enough, I needed a ruddy great gouge.

'Let me guess, your third cousins twice-removed are over from Outer Mongolia?'

I regretted it the moment the words left my mouth but by then of course it was too late. This time there was no mistaking the sharp intake of breath at the other end of the line.

'No,' she said coldly, 'but I shall be having my period.'

'Oh.'

Well, that explained a lot.

'And do you know what Timothy? It will be a lot less painful than this shitty conversation!'

She slammed the phone down so hard, I had to jerk my head away from the receiver. My ears were ringing for ages afterwards.

That hadn't gone quite as planned.

Three days later and I was still regretting it. But I hadn't called Roxanne back.

Washing Dad's car was a welcome distraction. But Sting didn't want to let me forget.

Driven to Tears.

OK Mr. Gordon Sumner, I admit I could easily let it happen. But I won't - just for once, you're not getting inside my head with your lyrics.

25 - Peanuts

'Tim, it's for you!' Cheryl announced, poking her head around the door, 'oh, sorry I didn't realise you had company.'

'Hang on Clarkey, put it on pause!' I said, getting up from the sofa. My heart missed a beat. Please be Roxanne, please be Roxanne. Yeah, it had to be. I knew she'd phone. I knew she'd apologise.

I shut the living room door behind me as Cheryl handed me the receiver.

'If you didn't have that telly on so loud, you might have heard it yourself and I wouldn't have had to run downstairs,' Cheryl said in a strop.

'Ah well, you could do with losing a few pounds.'

She clouted me round the head.

'Ouch! Bloody hell Cheryl, I was only joking,' I shouted at her back as she climbed the stairs, taking two steps at a time. I waited for her to go back into her room, before I took the call.

'Hello?'

'Timbo!'

'Oh, it's you.'

'Don't sound so pleased. Were you expecting someone else?'

'Not really,' I lied.

It was Saturday. Clarkey had brought his David Bowie Scary Monsters video around again. Dad was watching the Albion play Liverpool, so we had the telly and our shiny new video recorder all to ourselves. Not that I was that bothered about seeing the concert to the end to be honest but Clarkey kept going on about how brilliant the encores were, so I agreed we could watch it again, just to shut him up. Besides we still didn't have any decent tapes at home; they were far too expensive for me to buy, so it was a good opportunity to play with Dad's new toy whilst he was out. After twenty minutes, during "Up The Hill Backwards", I was stifling a yawn and wondering what excuse I could find to suggest we do something else without offending Clarkey. That's when the phone went.

'Actually Jacko,' I said, lowering my voice, 'I'm relieved it's you. I need rescuing.'

'What're you doing?' he asked breathlessly on the phone.

'Watching a video.'

'Great minds think alike, so are we. I'm at Wilf's.'

'Wilf's got a video player?' I said, shocked.

From the way Jacko had described his colleague from the bank, I'd formed this image of Wilf as an old hippy. I was surprised he'd be up with new technology.

'Yeah of course, Wilf had a video before most people had even heard of them. He got it in Hong Kong when he was back-packing. He's got some *brilliant* tapes too. Do you want to come over?'

I hesitated. I'd heard a lot about the legendary Wilf, but I'd never been invited to meet him until now. He'd always sounded a bit mental. And anyway, what was I meant to do with Kevin?

'Can I bring Clarkey?'

'The Dog?'

'Not Chalky! Clarkey! Kevin Clarke!'

'Same difference,' Jacko laughed, 'if you must I suppose. Yeah, why not? I'm going to call Humph too - it'll be a right laugh.'

Clarkey wasn't at all keen at first. Even though I pointed out that he'd probably already seen it a dozen times, he still moaned about missing the end of the Bowie gig. So, I told him a little white lie.

'Jacko reckons Wilf's got loads of bootleg LPs. He's sure to have some Bowie stuff.'

I had no idea if Wilf even liked Bowie but the way Jacko told it, Wilf owned just about every record ever made, so I thought there was probably a fair chance I was right.

Wilf's flat was in an old converted building, down a side-street off the Hove end of Western Road. We jumped on a bus and by the time we arrived, not only was Humph there but much to my disgust, so were Pete and Doddsy.

'Sorry mate, Humph insisted on bringing them,' Jacko explained in the tiny kitchenette, as we collected beers from Wilf's surprisingly well-stocked fridge. Jacko was putting snacks into some unhygienic-looking tupperware. He asked after Roxanne.

I gave him an abridged version of my uninvited visit to her flat, including the fact that Jackie had arrived home unexpectedly, which he thought was hilarious. When I repeated Roxanne's explanation for the crash helmets and for her subsequent disappearance back up to Weybridge, he was pretty sceptical.

295

'Sounds like bollocks doesn't it?'

A harsh assessment – but one I couldn't entirely disagree with.

'So, do you buy all that about her family?'

'Who knows what to believe Jacko? It's weird; Roxanne blows hot and cold.'

'You wish...,' Jacko started to say, smirking suggestively and sticking his tongue in his cheek.

I wasn't amused.

'Piss off Jacko.'

'Oh come on you miserable sod!' he said with his usual degree of sympathy, 'come and have a look at Wilf's tapes, that'll cheer you up.'

To Clarkey's disappointment, Wilf's unique collection of "movies" did not feature David Bowie - or indeed any other actor that I actually recognised. Presumably the budget for the particular genre that Wilf favoured didn't stretch to Hollywood A-listers - or David Bowie.

Currently playing at the Wiffy Wilf picture-house was an hilariously entitled parody of Star Wars, called *"Star Whores."* As Jacko and I returned with the refreshments, the mini-epic was already underway. All the best seats in the house had already been commandeered, so I settled on the floor, with my back against the sofa.

It took me a while to catch up with the "plot" of the movie but right from the off it was clear that the so-called actor playing the part more famously portrayed by Harrison Ford, was putting his light sabre to some pretty unusual uses. I certainly didn't remember that in the original. There again, the Ford and Carrie Fisher characters weren't called "Handy Solo" and "Princess Layer' in the George Lucas version either.

Pretty early on, and certainly by the time Handy's sabre had dimmed, I'd decided that this was one particular film I wouldn't be recommending to my parents. I'd never actually seen an "adults only" film before. I just kept wondering how they'd persuaded the actors and actresses to take part; I mean weren't they embarrassed? Wouldn't their parents recognise them?

For the want of somewhere else to look, I found myself studying the infamous Wiffy Wilf. The reason for his nickname had become pretty obvious, as soon as he had bounded over to shake my hand. His breath was horrible. Like something had died a slow and lingering death in his mouth.

I was never good at ages; Wilf could have been anywhere been twenty one and thirty five by my reckoning. All I knew was that he worked as a post-room clerk at Jacko's bank. I say "Jacko's bank", what Jacko did there wasn't entirely clear to me either; from what little he had revealed, Jacko seemed to be something the rest of the staff referred to as the 'office gopher', from which I guessed he wasn't exactly running the place.

Wilf's hair was dyed jet black. It looked as if it had never seen either shampoo or a comb - the style reminded me of a sort of dark haired, grimier version of the TV character "Catweasel".

Black was Wilf's favourite colour. He wore black laced-up Dr. Martens, skinny black jeans, and a plain black T-shirt - plain that is apart from the coffee stains down the front, and the large, unsightly green stains under his arm-pits. The only contrast to his colour-free outfit was the wide leather belt slung around his waist, which bore a huge silver buckle in the shape of an eagle's head. Wilf seemed pretty uninterested in Star Whores. He was sitting on the arm of an old armchair, rolling a fag. I'd never seen anything like him.

Wilf's flat was a bit of a first for me too. For starters, there was the smell. A sort of sweet, musty odour like someone had mown the lawn and then set fire to the clippings. Then, there was the decor. One of the bright purple walls was covered with a wall-length, hand-painted mural of some American-comic characters that I didn't recognise. On the opposite wall were two huge posters; one I instantly recognised as a picture of the famous guitarist, Jimi Hendrix; the other was of a painting of a swarthy looking bloke with long dark hair and a beard. Underneath the painting, a single word was printed in gothic letters. 'Che'. I had no idea who he was, but he looked a bit like Jesus. Except that, at least as far as I was aware, Jesus never wore a back beret.

The furniture consisted of two deckchairs; presumably nicked from Brighton beach, a sofa that may have been rescued from Sheepcote Tip and two battered old armchairs with the stuffing hanging from the arms. I was beginning to wonder what the hell Jacko had in common with this guy, when my eyes rested on the fabled Wilf record collection. You couldn't miss them really - they were propped up against the length of the wall behind the TV; there were literally hundreds of LPs. I'd never seen so many records in one place, outside of HMV or Virgin.

'This is a good bit,' Wilf suddenly said, without looking up.

Pete and Doddsy studied the screen as a seven foot Wookie got more closely acquainted with the Princess. They were pressed up so close to the set, I had to crane my neck just to see past their thick heads.

'I suppose that's why they call him Chewy eh?' said Wilf.'

Pete and Doddsy roared with laughter.

Frankly, I found the plot pretty thin, and as for the appalling acting – well the stars wouldn't be troubling the Oscar judges this year, put it that way.

The boys certainly seemed to be enjoying it though. Pete and Doddsy were so close to the action, I thought they might join in. They were in their element; making all sorts of lewd comments. Humph and Jacko seemed to think it was hilarious; Clarkey was bright red in the face and looked like he was about to die of shock. As for me, I didn't know where to put my face. This was definitely a long way up the scale from my previous encounters with the world of pornography - which essentially consisted of sniggering at the saucy seaside postcards on the Palace Pier, or perusing the underwear section of my Mum's Freemans catalogue.

It was partly my complete lack of porn-etiquette that led me to making my stupid remark, and partly a desire to prevent an ugly scene developing between Clarkey and Humph's mates.

'Blimey that Princess Layer's pretty tasty isn't she?' Doddsy observed, 'I wouldn't mind boldly going somewhere with her!'

Clarkey snorted; shook his head.

Doddsy looked over.

'What? Did you want to say something?' he said.

There was an ugly little pause.

'That's Star Trek not Star Wars,' Clarkey remarked. He said it with such derision that he might as well have added "you complete imbecile".

Doddsy clearly wasn't impressed. He scowled.

'What did you say?'

Please shut up Clarkey, I thought to myself, looking from one to the other. Doddsy was about twice Clarkey's size and was a mean looking son-of-a-bitch when he was angry. Keep you mouth shut Clarkey, please, please, keep your mouth shut.

Unfortunately, I hadn't quite mastered the art of telepathy.

'Actually, "boldly going" is a quote from Star trek, *not* Star Wars,' Clarkey pointed out. He might as well have tattooed the word "smug" on his forehead.

You could have heard a pin drop. I prayed for someone to say something that might diffuse the situation.

'He's right actually,' said Wilf, puffing on his roll-up.

Maybe I should pray more often; those weren't exactly the words of divine intervention I'd been hoping for.

The vein in Doddsy's neck was doing the pogo. He gritted his teeth, ignoring Wilf and focusing his growing annoyance directly at Clarkey.

'*Actually,* I couldn't give a toss,' Doddsy sipped on his beer and looked around the room, before muttering sarcastically 'who invited the nerd?'

Clarkey's face flushed almost as crimson as his hair.

I couldn't tell if he was angry, embarrassed or shit-scared - possibly a mixture of all three. I was really hoping the deckchair he was sitting in would open up and swallow him.

'Blimey, she's got an impressive pair of storm-troopers!' Humph said; clearly trying to change the subject.

We all laughed nervously; all except Doddsy and Clarkey that is; they were a picture of silent menace.

Doddsy was still glaring at Clarkey, who seemed to have suddenly realised, and frankly not before time by, that he was playing with fire and that there wasn't a fire extinguisher anywhere to be seen. He was now desperately trying to avoid making eye contact by staring fixedly at the screen.

'So, Timbo, are you and your little ginger mate old enough to be watching grown-up films?' said Doddsy, trying to drag me into the conversation and clearly intent on provoking Clarkey into making some other rash comment.

I tried to laugh. It sounded like I was having a choking fit.

Jacko and I exchanged nervous glances.

Jacko, bless him, tried to lighten the mood.

'Is that the Princess's backside or R2D2's little cousin?' said Jacko, admiring the Princess's shapely rear and trying his best to head a potential bloodbath off at the pass.

I laughed rather too obviously and much too loudly.

Doddsy was still staring at Clarkey; daring Clarkey to even *look* at him.

Clarkey was sinking further and further into his deckchair.

Doddsy turned his attention back to "Star Whores" and for a split-second I thought that we'd managed to avoid armageddon.

But my sigh of relief was premature.

Doddsy hadn't finished with Clarkey. He picked up a handful of peanuts and one by one, started to throw them directly at Clarkey's head. The first one narrowly missed its target, hitting the wall with a resounding ping. The second was a direct hit, bouncing violently off the end of his nose. Clarkey flinched. To his credit, he tried to ignore it. The third peanut-missile him in the ear.

The others turned their attention away from the film, waiting for Clarkey to react.

He was either going to start sobbing or retaliate - either way, he was going to end up in tears, unless someone intervened – quickly.

Only Wilf seemed blissfully oblivious to the tension in the room. He casually blew a smoke-ring into the air, as he watched the Princess roll-up her tunic to reveal a shapely pair of legs.

'Great pins eh?' he observed.

'Say something Tim, say something' a little voice in my head said. 'Distract their attention.'

'Cor yeah!' I said over-dramatically.

Everyone looked at me expectantly.

Clearly, I was expected to comment further on the action but I could think of absolutely nothing sensible to say. So I settled for something stupid instead.

'She's got...'

What exactly had she got? Come on, think of something...

Boobs? Already mentioned. Bum? Jacko had covered that. Legs? Wilf had highlighted them. Come on, what else could I be admiring about the lovely Layer?

'....fantastic....*knees* too.'

Knees? Fantastic *knees*?

Everyone burst into laughter. Pete almost choked on a peanut. Even Doddsy snorted.

'Great what?' Doddsy said. .

'Knees. She's got great *knees*! Don't you think?' I repeated, now aware of six pairs of eyes looking at me.

'Great knees?' Humph spluttered.

'Yeah,' I said, the heat rising in my cheeks, 'blimey, I wouldn't mind....er, *licking* those knees!'

It was the first thing came into my head and possibly the most stupid thing that anyone had said in the history of the world. But what else could I have said? I mean the others had already commented on the key parts of the Princess's anatomy; they hadn't really left me with many body parts to enthuse about.

'*Lick* her *knees*?' said Pete, almost sobbing with laughter '*lick* her *knees*?'

'Licking knees? Is that what you're in to then mate is it?' Humph sobbed.

Even Clarkey was laughing now.

'So, have you licked Roxane's knees yet mate?' asked Humph.

Pete and Doddsy fell about laughing.

We all laughed.

Tears were running down Jacko's face.

'Stop it! Stop it! It hurts!' said Wilf, holding his stomach.

'I'm sorry mate!' said Jacko, wiping a tear from his eye, 'but no wonder she's off with that Robert bloke, if that's the sort of kinky stuff you are into!'

Great. Why did I never learn? Why the hell did I ever confide in Jacko?

'She was fed up with wet knees I expect!' said Pete.

They were all having a good old laugh now, unfortunately at my expense. Ah well, at least my stupid remark seemed to have broken the tension for a bit.

But the reprieve was only temporary; Doddsy wasn't going to be distracted from his prey that easily. He wasn't finished of course. Bullies like Doddsy never are.

Slowly, he picked up a whole handful of peanuts and then suddenly, still laughing, he lobbed them at me, really hard. Several hit me in the face. One hit me right in the eye.

'Ow!' I shouted, 'Bloody hell Doddsy, that fucking hurt!' I said, clutching a hand over my eye.

Pete howled like a hyena.

Everyone else went quiet.

301

My eye stung like hell.

'That could've blinded me!' I said, feeling myself getting angry at last. Everyone has their breaking point and Doddsy had just found mine.

I stood up, grabbing the first thing that came to hand. The video case. Without thinking, I hurled it at Doddsy. It missed by a mile of course. I've always been crap at throwing. It landed with a thud on the corner of the coffee table. However, from the way Doddsy reacted, it might as well have hit him square on the jaw.

He leapt to his feet and made a lunge at me, grabbing the collar of my shirt and yanking me up off the floor.

Humph leapt up too. Throwing himself between me and his workmate, Humph grabbed Doddsy's arms and pulled him off me, almost taking half my shirt with him.

'Hey come on mate, calm down will you?' he said, 'things are getting out of hand!'

Doddsy let go of my collar, still glaring at me.

My hands were shaking. There was an awkward hush. For a moment, everyone seemed frozen in time.

Clarkey was the first to move. Getting up from his chair, he grabbed his blue anorak from the floor and calmly turned to Humph.

'Do you know the difference between your new mates and two sacks of shit?'

'What?' Humph said. His face was a mixture of puzzlement and amazement. He was still restraining Doddsy with both arms.

'The sacks!' said Clarkey, as calm as you like.

And with that, he strolled casually towards the door, 'cheers Wilf, nice meeting you.'

Wilf was covering his mouth, trying not to laugh.

Pete and Doddsy's mouths fell wide open.

'Think you might have to explain that one,' I whispered to Jacko, gesturing with my head towards the sack-less shits in question. Then, I picked up my jacket and followed Clarkey out of the room.

As we were running up the stairs from the basement, we heard a commotion behind us. It sounded like someone was wrestling with the door.

'Leave it Doddsy! Just let it go will you?' I heard Humph say.

'Do you think someone explained?' I said.

302

What a turn up. Clarkey. The worm that turned.

He was alright was Clarkey. There was more to him than a Bowie obsession and an unfortunate penchant for hair gel. He had balls.

When we finally stopped running - and laughing, we got talking.

'So, all that about Roxanne and another bloke. What was all that about?' he asked, as we walked back along Western Road into Brighton, through throngs of late afternoon shoppers.

So, for the second time that day, I found myself relaying the details of my dates with Roxanne and my visit to her flat. By the time we reached Churchill Square, I'd told him the whole story.

'Do you want to know what I think?' he asked.

'Will I like it?'

'Possibly not.'

'Fire away.'

'You're the rebound.'

'Eh?

'The rebound,' he repeated, 'it's a classic case isn't it?'

'Is it? How do you mean?'

'Well, I know this sounds bad, but maybe she just sees you as a bit of fun until such time as she decides to take him back or not.'

'Oh, I dunno though, she says it's complicated....' I said, suddenly feeing defensive.

'Only because she's choosing to make it that way.'

Bloody hell, mate don't mince your words will you?

'Anyhow, how come you know so much about affairs of the heart all of a sudden?'

'I watch Crossroads - every day!'

We'd reached the bus stop outside Marks & Spencer, opposite Churchill Square.

'Is she working today?' asked Kevin.

'She *should* be, but who knows?'

'Want to know where you stand with her?'

'Of course.'

'Follow me, I've got an idea.'

As ideas go, it was pretty simple.

Despite the fact that HMV was packed with Saturday shoppers, we spotted Roxanne straight away. She was carrying a box of 45's and filling up the racks of the Top 40 display. Before I could attract her

303

attention, Clarkey grabbed me by the arm and dragged me up the elevator to the first floor, where he took off his blue anorak and handed it to me.

'Here, put this on.'

'What?'

'Trust me. Just do it, ok?'

Clarkey was one of the few kids in our year who was even smaller than me. The anorak was a snug fit but I put it on. He zipped me up, as if he was my Mum. Then, he told me to put the hood up.

'Right, stand here, pretend you're looking at the easy-listening tapes and whatever you do, don't turn around and don't say a word.'

'Why? Where are you going?'

'To get your lady-friend.'

So I stood there, like a dick in a life-size blue condom, looking at tapes by Val Doonican, Matt Monroe and Gene Pitney. This wasn't good for my street-cred. What was Clarkey up to?

Finally, having waited for what seemed like an eternity, I glanced over to the top of the elevator and saw the tops of two red-heads gliding into view. Clarkey and Roxanne. I turned back towards the cassettes and hastily grabbed a tape. Barry Manilow. Please God, don't let anyone see me here.

'So, what sort of thing does your pen-pal like?' I heard Roxanne say to Clarkey.

Pen pal?

'That's it - I just don't know really - she said she's into Country music but it's really not my bag. I was hoping you could suggest some stuff?'

Blimey Clarkey was dead good at lying.

'I mean, she's mentioned people like Kenny Rogers and Tammy Wynette - and I know Johnny Cash is her all time hero but I'm trying to impress her; so something a bit more..."now" would be good.'

'OK, well I shouldn't really say this, I might get the sack,' laughed Roxanne, 'but....,' and then I heard her whisper... 'it's not exactly my scene either to be honest!'

They both laughed.

'But I can show you what other people have been buying I suppose.'

'Great, thanks,' I heard Clarkey say.

They were pretty close to me now, probably only a few yards away.

304

'So are you local?' asked Roxanne, 'only you look familiar, like I've seen you somewhere before.'

Clarkey laughed slightly nervously, 'you're not trying to pick me up are you?' he said.

It was a good line. He certainly was a ballsy bugger was Kevin Clarke.

Roxanne was giggling now; an embarrassed, slightly girly giggle, 'No, really, I'm sure we've met somewhere?'

I guess this was precisely the "in" that Clarkey was looking for.

'Go on, I bet you say that to all the boys!'

Roxanne giggled.

'What would your boyfriend say if he knew you flirt with the customers when you're working?'

God, he had some nerve.

I was really blushing myself; I was desperate to look at him, to see whether he looked as calm as he sounded. But I remembered Clarkey's warning. *"Whatever you do, don't turn around and don't say a word."*

'Huh, he probably wouldn't mind even if he did!' Roxanne said.

I bloody would mind. I *did* mind! I mean, it was obvious she was only doing her job but did she really have to be that flippin' flirty? Clarkey was an ugly little ginger bugger; what would she be like if a good-looking bloke was really chatting her up?

'What about this? Do you think she would like Crystal Gayle?'

'Sounds like a glass blower,' Clarkey snorted.

'You know, she did that *"Don't it make your brown eyes blue"* song a few years back. This is her new one, I've heard it's had pretty good reviews.'

'What in, "Cowboy Monthly?"' laughed Kevin.

'Or "Rodeo Mirror?",' Roxanne suggested.

God. Gorgeous and funny with it.

Clarkey laughed out loud. Come on mate, it wasn't *that* funny! And besides, how was all this flirting meant to be helping me exactly?

'I know. You've been talking in your sleep.'

'Pardon?' I heard Roxanne say.

What was he talking about?'

'Didn't she do that too?' He started to hum a tune, which I vaguely recognised. Roxanne clearly recognised it too.

'Oh yeah, that's right. That's her! Crystal Gayle...or there's The Bellamy Brothers, they're pretty popular too.'

There was a pause, presumably whilst Clarkey studied the tapes.

'So, you *do* have a boyfriend then?' I heard him say.

Bloody hell, he was persistent I'll say that for him.

'So, now who's chatting who up exactly? Do you think your Canadian pen-pal would be impressed if she knew you were trying to pick up shop-girls in the UK?' laughed Roxanne.

'She's a few thousand miles away and I've never actually met her. I can't imagine she's too bothered can you? Besides, who's going to tell her?'

'Well, my boyfriend isn't that far away and I just might tell *him*!'

Bloody hell had she rumbled me? Almost involuntarily, I glanced around. Fortunately, Roxanne had her back to me.

Clarkey caught my eye over her shoulder, and shot me a warning look. I turned back around and started fumbling with Olivia Newton-John. In my dreams.

'What does he do then?'

'Do you really want to buy some Country and Western music or is this all a ruse?'

There was the first hint of irritation in Roxanne's voice.

I don't know how Clarkey was doing, but I was starting to feel pretty shaky.

'No, I was just interested...' Clarkey said, starting to sound a little flustered for the first time in the conversation.

'Well, if you really must know, my huge, rugby-playing boyfriend is a motor-cycle courier.'

What? A bloody courier? A rugby-playing courier? She was talking about bloody Robert. Bloody hell, she was describing Robert as her boyfriend.

'...it's his own business actually....'

Bloody heck, she sounded like she was proud of him too.

'....and actually, forget what I said earlier, he would mind if he knew customers were hitting on me. He can get pretty jealous.'

I hoped she hadn't mentioned *me* to him then.

'OK, OK, you win...I'll take the Bellamy Brothers. No offence intended.'

'That's quite OK sir, none taken,' Roxanne said, easily flipping back to her professional charm,'follow me and I'll take you back to the till.'

'OK, you carry on, I'll be down in a minute, I just need to have a quick look at the Reggae section....I've got another pen-pal...in Jamaica.'

It went quiet; I didn't dare move, although frankly I was too stunned to move far.

'Did you hear that then mate?' Clarkey whispered; making me jump.

'Yeah,' I said, glancing around to make sure Roxanne had actually disappeared back to the ground floor, 'but it didn't mean anything necessarily did it? I think she was just trying to scare you off.'

'You think?'

I shrugged. I didn't really know what to think. All I knew was that I wanted to be as far away from bloody HMV as possible.

'So?'

'So, what?'

'Shall we make a run for it or do you fancy trying out the Bellamy Brothers?'

'How fast can you run?'

26 - When The World Is Running Down, You Make The Best of What's Still Around.

Roxanne didn't ring that weekend.
She didn't ring again on Monday.
Nor on Tuesday, Wednesday or Thursday.
On Friday I decided that the Mod band Secret Affair were right; It was Time For Action.

All week, there had been just two topics of conversation after class, in the common room, in the canteen and on the bus home. The two big events of the coming Saturday; the big match and the big gig.

The first burning issue of the week was whether Denton could beat arch-rivals Thatcham in the Sussex Sixth Form Cup. Since my eventful trial, I'd become what Mr. Beattie referred to as a "regular squad member". Translated into plain English, this meant I was regularly a substitute; one of three permitted. And sure enough, when I'd checked the P.E. notice board earlier that week, there was my name printed in Beattie's familiar handwriting. Warming the bench again. I could't raise an awful lot of enthusiasm for the "big match" after that.

The second subject on everyone's lips was the upcoming appearance of the by-now near-legendary Morbid Morsels at The Northern public house in London Road. "Legendary" that is, within the confines of the DSFCL6 Common Room, and more particularly in the head of their guitarist, Karl "Grim" Bloom. The hyped-up status of the band was based purely, one hundred per cent, on hearsay and gossip. Very few people at college, other than the band members themselves, had even heard them play. According to Clarkey, who was basing his prediction entirely on what he had been told by the not-totally unbiased Karl, they were the "next big thing". Depending on who you listened to, they were on a par with Joy Division, The Buzzcocks and the American band Television. It seemed a tall order and even though I'd heard Karl play my guitar, and had to accept he could play a hundred times better than I probably ever would, I was pretty sceptical that he and his band-mates could actually live up to their billing. Besides, things between me and Karl were still frosty, so even up to the day before, I wasn't even sure that I would go, despite Clarkey's urgings.

'It'll be triple ace!' he said, as we rode home on the school bus that Friday evening.

'It was going to be "double ace" yesterday,' I pointed out, 'and just plain "ace" the day before that.'

'Well, it will. It'll be quadruple ace!'

'Yeah, you've said.'

Forty-three times. Was there even a word for forty three multiples of "ace"?

'Hey wasn't that your stop?'

'Maybe.'

Clarkey gave me a knowing smile.

'What?'

'Remember what I said, 'rebound.'

Yet again, I stood outside looking in.

It was closing up time.

Christian, the Terry Hall lookalike came out first. I watched from my vantage point, under the canopy of BHS, across the square from HMV. Christian slung his Gola bag over his shoulder and walked off toward the bus-stops. More staff left; a small group of girls I vaguely recognised, laughing and joking as the door swung behind them.

Then Roxanne came out, with Poppy Bloom. They stopped outside the shop, Poppy digging into her bag, handing something to Roxanne. Lipstick. Roxanne started applying it to her lips.

I took two deep breaths, composed myself for one very long second, then forced myself out of the doorway. They were chatting; Roxanne studying her lips in a vanity mirror; they hadn't seen me yet. Trying to appear as casual as possible, I sauntered across the walkway, my heart thudding like a pneumatic drill. It was Poppy who spotted me first. Her face dropped slightly, then she checked herself, nudged Roxanne with her elbow and broke into one of the falsest smiles I'd ever seen. Roxanne looked questioningly at her friend, then followed her gaze and saw me too. The frown she wore, before returning to the serious task of applying her lippy, was hardly encouraging; but it was too late to turn back.

'Oh, hi girls!' I said breezily, 'Is the shop still open? I was hoping to get the new Stiff Little Finger single.'

'It's not out 'til next week,' Poppy said.

I knew. Mike Read had told me.

'And the shop's closed anyway.'

'Oh right, bummer.'

Just as I planned. I didn't have any money to buy anything anyway.

Poppy shuffled her feet. Roxanne closed the compact and handed it back.

'So, Roxy, how are you?'

'OK thanks, you?' Her voice was icebox cool.

Two can play at that game. Play it cool Tim. Play it cool.

'So, I just wanted to say sorry about...'

'Tim, I'm sorry...'

We both stopped talking at the same time; laughed.

'Look, I'd better be off,' said Poppy, 'have a good time this evening love,' she kissed Roxanne's cheek, 'bye Tim, see you soon,' She started to walk away.

'See you tomorrow?' I called after her.

She glanced around, a puzzled expression on her face.

'The gig? Karl's gig?'

'Oh yeah, right. Maybe,' Poppy waved her hand vaguely in the air and walked off.

'So,' I said, turning back to Roxanne, '"have a good time"? Are you up to something special tonight?'

'Er, not really...'

'Sorry,' I said, putting my hand up in a gesture of surrender, 'none of my business eh?'

Roxanne studied my face, narrowing her eyes, trying to work out if I was being sarcastic. I wasn't as it happened but she could have easily heard it that way.

'I'm just meeting a friend for a quiet drink. You?'

'No plans. Big football match tomorrow. Got to be bright eyed and bushy tailed.'

After all, I might even get on the pitch for the last five minutes.

'Oh right, good luck with that.'

'Thanks.'

We both studied the dirty Churchill Square paving slabs.

'You need to tell her how you feel about her.'

'Well, I'd better be going too...'

'What are you doing *tomorrow* night?' I blurted.

'Er, I'm out with the girls,' she said.

She'd hesitated a second too long.

310

'Oh right.'

'Why?'

'Karl Bloom's band are playing. The Morbid Morsels. They're on at the Northern in London Road. I expect Poppy will be going. I just wondered if you fancied....'

'Sorry Tim, like I said, girls night out.'

'Oh, right, yeah, of course.'

'Maybe we can get together for a drink and a chat sometime?' she smiled.

'Ok, when are you...?'

'I'll call you OK?'

'Right. Fine.'

'Now this bloke's the real deal,' said Dad, pressing 'play' on his new video recorder, 'just watch and admire real footballing skill Timothy; never mind your Kevin Keegans or your Trevor Brookings, those guys are not fit to clean this bloke's boots!'

It was Dad's birthday and Mum had bought him a new video tape all about his hero, Georgie Best.

'This must be that match that he turned up for then?' I said, teasing.

'Ho ho. You can laugh if you like, but just you watch this. The bloke's a genius!'

George Best? Get over yourself Dad, you're so stuck in the seventies.

But then I watched the video.

All I knew about Georgie was what I'd heard on the news over the last few years; boozing, clubbing, going out with Miss World and failing to turn up for training at Man United. Once, I remember, he went missing for weeks. More recently, he'd been playing in the USA and then last year for Hibs, up in Scotland.

'He's not as good as he was,' my Dad was always saying.

It was hardly surprising. I mean the man's ancient. Must be in his thirties if he's a day.

Whenever he was in the news, coming out of a nightclub, they'd show footage of Georgie Best in his Man United days. He'd had really long hair and was dead good looking - more like a rock star than a footballer. And I knew he was good; everybody knew that. I didn't need Dad rubbing it in my face every five minutes to know it. But it

311

was like the thing with Elvis Presley or The Beatles - everything Dad liked was better than anything I liked.

'Tragic,' Dad muttered, 'what a waste of talent. He's let it all slip away.'

'Made loads of money though I expect?' I said.

'Yeah and spent it all on booze and birds. Like I say, tragic.'

Loads of money; gorgeous women. What was tragic about that? Blimey, I wish I could be half as tragic.

The video was made up of bits of pieces of different matches; some were filmed in black and white, others, filmed later, were in colour. This was Georgie's heyday. His hair got longer as the years passed and he grew a beard. There were interviews with ex team-mates and people who knew him - everyone was saying much the same as Dad; what an amazing player and what a shame that he'd given up playing for United when he had. The football footage spoke for itself. And of course, as much as I hated to admit it to his face, Dad was right; Georgie Best was simply amazing. The ball seemed to be glued to his feet. There was one mesmerising clip where Georgie was playing for Northern Ireland against Russia. Someone gave him the ball straight from the kick-off and instead of passing it back, like everyone else I'd ever seen do, in every other single match I'd ever watched, Georgie just ran at the Russians with the ball, taking them all on - and beating most of them.

'Good eh? See what I mean?' Dad purred.

'Yeah, he wasn't bad I suppose,' I said, my tongue firmly in my cheek.

'Not bad? Not bad? He was bloody brilliant.'

I just shrugged, smiling to myself. I loved winding Dad up - it was so easy.

But the more I studied George; the more I got it. The way he dropped his shoulder and went into another gear, sending defenders sprawling in his wake. Fantastic. I'd have to try that out myself, if old Beattie would actually let me get onto the pitch for once.

'So, are you running the line again today Tim? You were brilliant last week.'

Coming from anyone else, I would have taken this comment as a complete piss-take but with Glenda Craven, I knew it was just her way of trying to be nice. However, judging by the way that they tried to

312

stifle sniggers, it was obvious that Karl and Heidi Bloom saw the funny side of her comment.

'What?' said Glenda.

Poor Glenda. Mocked by her best friend and the boy she worshipped. Life was so unkind sometimes. Hurt flickered in her eyes as she turned on them.

'He is! He's really good!'

'Yep, best linesman in Sussex school football, that's our Tim!' laughed Karl, turning around from the passenger seat to wink at me. At least he was speaking to me now, which was more than you could say for Dave Booth. Karl still refused to acknowledge his existence, which was not ideal, considering the two of them were team-mates. Dave had taken to avoiding Karl completely - he'd been off ill the last few days. Apparently it was sickness and diarrhoea. I didn't know about the sickness, but I was pretty sure Dave was still shitting himself.

'Ah, never mind, maybe you'll get a game today Timmy,' said Heidi, who, as ever, was sitting a little too close to me on the back seat of Mrs. Bloom's car.

I had been running the line during every match for the past couple of months; being linesman was the dubious honour bestowed on the substitutes from each team; those poor souls who weren't quite good enough to get in the first eleven. I had spent many wet afternoons or freezing Saturday mornings running up and down the line, waving my little orange flag half-heartedly and being shouted at by Dave Booth or Jez King for ruling them 'offside'.

'Well, you must be good at it, if Mr. Beattie keeps asking you to do it Tim,' added Mrs Bloom from the driver's seat.

'No, Mum, it's because none of the other substitutes ever turn up!' explained Karl.

He was spot on. For the first match, I'd been one of three subs selected - alongside Clarkey and Jason Chapman. It had absolutely chucked it down. Jason had got soaked as he ran the line in the first half whilst Clarkey and I had sheltered in the Denton minibus. Mr. Beattie asked Clarkey to swap with Jason for the second half and there was a hailstone shower - Jason spent the second half shivering in his wet kit in the back of the bus and Clarkey finished the match half-frozen to death and cursing Mr. Beattie under his breath. The team won easily and none of us subs got on to play. We'd all ended up bored stiff and freezing our balls off. The others hadn't been seen at

313

any of the matches since. Word got around. Every time Mr. Beattie tried to select another loser as a substitute, they mysteriously failed to materialise on the day. So, I was now officially the one and only "super-sub"; like Liverpool's David Fairclough, except without the ginger hair or, more significantly, the goal scoring talent. I'd actually got on to the field of play three times in twelve matches. I was pretty cheesed off with it but I couldn't let Mr. Beattie down, could I?

'You will turn up on Saturday, won't you Tim?' he'd said during our PE lesson that Friday morning.

As with every previous match, I'd been racking my brains for possible excuses for ducking out. But I couldn't do it to him.

'It should be an easy match - hopefully you'll get at least half a match.'

Gee, thanks sir, that makes me feel really special.

So, there I was, in the back of the Bloom's car with super-fans Glenda and Heidi, on my way to Thatcham High, heading for my latest bout of running up and down, waving my flag and being shouted at.

It was the Saturday morning of The Morbid Morsels' gig at The Northern. You could tell Karl was excited; he spent most of the journey telling us about the new numbers the band had been rehearsing. But he went quiet after Mrs. Bloom asked Heidi where Juliette was that morning.

'It's most unlike her to miss a match,' Mrs Bloom observed.

'She's been off sick all week,' Heidi explained.

'Oh, just like David?' Mrs Bloom said, 'is there something going around?'

'Must be,' I muttered.

I caught Karl's eye in the rear view mirror. He scowled at the mention of Dave's name.

'Ah well, at least you've got a bit more room in the back today eh Tim?' Mrs Bloom laughed, 'no excuse for Heidi to sit on your lap today!'

'Mum!' Heidi said, giggling. She was practically on my lap anyway.

'So, if David doesn't turn up,' said Glenda, 'maybe you'll be playing Tim?'

Blimey, I hadn't thought of that. And Dave was the main striker. The Centre Forward.

Dave Booth was Centre Forward. He'd phoned in sick that morning. I was replacing him in the team. At left back.

'OK,' explained Mr. Beattie as we sat in the dressing room before the game, 'we're going to reshuffle the team. Karl Bloom moves from Midfield to Centre Forward, Graham Everett from left back to Midfield and Tim James will be playing at left back.'

Left back? Left back? I'd never played left back in my life - didn't Beattie remember that great goal I'd scored in the trial? I was a natural born striker; a poacher; a Tony Woodcock, a Karl-Heinz Rummenigge, a David Fairclough. Bob Paisley wouldn't play Fairclough at left back. Left back? What was Beattie thinking?

Bloody Dave Booth; it was all his fault. Sick? My arse. He was just avoiding Karl. He was such a chicken. And now, thanks to him, here I was making my long awaited full first team debut; at bloody left back.

From the dressing room, there was a long walk around Thatcham's playground and through a leaf-strewn tennis court, in order to get to the playing fields. The studs of our footie boots clattered on tarmac and echoed back of the walls off the building. There were butterflies in my stomach. Graham Everett and Miles Gilmore were having a long discussion about the merits of screw-in studs. All the cool boys had screw-in studs; apparently you could change them - choose the appropriate length of stud for the conditions of the ground. I'd watched enviously as Graham, Miles and others in the team had used these fancy little spanners to tighten their studs in the changing rooms. My studs were of the fixed variety. I had a cheap pair of boots that my Dad had bought me from Marks & Sparks. All the boys got their boots from Swift Sports in town. They all had Gola or Adidas written on the tongue; mine used to say St. Michaels. I'd got a lot of stick about that the first time I wore them. When I got home, I went straight to the garden shed and took out my house-key. It had taken me bloody ages to scratch the gold lettering off that tongue.

'Blimey, look there's that bird of Frank Little's!' said Miles Gilmore, turning to Karl.

The girl was standing at the side of the pitch. I recognised her from the Christmas party. Even wrapped up in a woollen scarf and an unflattering duffel coat, the other boys in the team noticed her too.

'She's a bit of alright isn't she?' said Graham.

Karl just shrugged. He was still sulking about Dave and Juliette. He turned to me and muttered.

'What do you think then Tim? Like to lick her knees would you?'

I grimaced.

'Ho ho. Been talking to Clarkey have you?'

Me and my big mouth.

Miles and Graham started doing keepy-uppies in front of the girl, trying to impress her. She didn't seem bothered. She was pacing up and down trying to keep warm. Then Frank came running past in his green goalie's shirt and tracksuit trousers. He gave her a peck on the cheek as they stood talking on the touchline. The rest of the team looked on in envy.

'Who is she?' I asked no-one in particular, 'I've not seen her around Denton.'

'Her name's Jasmine, she goes to the Art College,' one of the boys said.

'And she works in The Pizza Palace at the weekends,' said another, 'that's where Frank chatted her up.'

'Lucky bugger,' I muttered.

'I know,' said Miles Gilmore, 'he gets free garlic bread.'

It must have taken all of ten minutes for Mr. Beattie to realise the error of his team selection. Playing at left back preferably required at least a basic ability to tackle. I couldn't tackle for toffee. The other team had this really quick lad playing on the wing, who skinned me every time he got the ball. First he went one way, then the other and then to cap it all he "nutmegged" me before whacking the ball past Frank Little.

The opposing team were celebrating their second goal a few minutes later, when Mr. Beattie helped me off of my arse and called Graham Everett over.

'Tim, I think you should swap with Graham. You play midfield.'

I didn't do much better there. The bloke I was up against was the size of a small battleship - he looked like he was in his mid-twenties, instead of seventeen - he had sideburns, two inches of stubble and his upper legs were the size of my waist. Every time I got the ball, he just stood in my path and I rebounded off him like I was running into a wall.

Twenty six minutes. Three- nil.

316

Thirty three minutes - Four-nil.

Somehow though, we held fast for the next seven minutes and managed to keep the score down to four-nil at half-time. We trudged over to the touchline. Mr. Beattie was red in the face.

'Well boys, that wasn't great was it?'

Nobody spoke. The lads were subdued; shivering and chewing the orange segments that had been handed out by our travelling support - i.e. Jasmine, Heidi and Glenda.

I accepted a slice of orange from Heidi and sat on the grass with my head down, hoping no-one would notice me. Then I saw a shadow looming over me. I didn't look up; I'd guessed what was coming.

'Tim,' hissed Mr. Beattie, 'what's wrong with you? This is your big chance to shine. You've waited long enough for an opportunity. I know you can do better than that! That wasn't the Tim James that scored that cracking goal in the trial is it?'

He remembered that? He was alright was old Beattie. I felt ashamed. There was a weird lump in my throat. I had to bite my lip.

'No sir,' I muttered, a catch in my voice.

'I'll tell you what; how about staying out on the wing in this half. You're pretty fast - let's give them a taste of their own medicine, OK?'

Blimey, a left-back, a midfielder and now a winger; I hadn't realised I was so versatile.

Beattie wandered off. I rubbed my eyes with my knuckles. There was another shadow across my legs now.

'You're playing well!' said Heidi.

'Yeah, you're doing great!' agreed Glenda.

I didn't look up. They meant well of course but neither of them were exactly Jimmy Hill when it came to football punditry. My eyes drifted over to where Jasmine was standing with Frank. She had her arm around him. She kissed him on the cheek. Frank shrugged her off like he was embarrassed. Bloody hell, she could comfort me anytime; the ungrateful sod.

Heidi saw me watching them. She smiled and ruffled my hair with her hand.

'Hey cheer up. It's only a game.'

Girls. They just didn't understand.

'Hey, it's Karl's gig tonight. That's something to look forward to.'

Big deal.

'It should be really good!' Heidi said.

317

'Are you going then?' I asked, somewhat surprised that a fifteen year old should be going to a rock gig in a sweaty pub.

'Are you asking?'

Was she thick? Of course I was asking. I'd just asked hadn't I?

'Yes...'

'Oh brilliant. Of course I'd love to go with you. I'll have to check with my Mum, but thanks...'

'What....?'

Heidi was already disappearing along the touchline, whispering to Glenda as they walked away. They both looked back at me and giggled. What the hell had just happened?

We all ambled back onto the pitch for the second half. No-one looked like they were really up for it. When I glanced over at Mr. Beattie, he gave me an enthusiastic thumbs up. I remembered his words of encouragement.

'You're pretty fast - let's give them a taste of their own medicine, OK?'

Jcz King was clapping his hands furiously, as he walked towards the centre circle with Karl to take the kick-off.

'Come on boys, we can do this!' he shouted.

Some of the Thatcham boys actually laughed out loud; the arrogant sods. As I took up my position, their left full-back gave me a look of complete contempt. My direct opponent was a tall, skinny lad with bad acne and one of those lop-sided hair-cuts that were all the fashion thanks to bands like Human League and Spandau Ballet. He he looked me up and down; smirking dismissively. He was clearly thinking to himself that he was going to have the easiest forty minutes of his miserable life. Well, whether it was Mr. Beattie's words, Jez's encouragement or the sneers of our rivals that had rattled my cage, I'll never know; maybe it was a combination of the three, but whatever it was that did it, I suddenly felt pumped up. I would show them a thing or two; the cocky buggers.

Pretty soon, Karl got the ball and I found myself hurtling down the wing hell-for-leather, with the momentarily stunned left-back trailing in my wake. Karl, looking equally shocked that it was me who was shouting for the ball, passed it almost instinctively, before he'd had a chance to decide that his better option would be passing to just about anyone else in the team. Amazingly, I took the ball in my stride and

318

even as I heard my team-mates bellowing at me to shoot, something hit me from behind and my legs were taken away from under me.

'Penalty!' numerous voices shouted and to my complete and utter disbelief, a whistle sounded. As I pushed myself up onto my knees, I saw the referee pointing to the penalty spot. The zitty Spandau Ballet fan had clobbered me. As he dragged his long legs from under me, it was my turn to smirk. He was clutching his shin where I'd landed on him.

'Shame,' I muttered under my breath.

The boy's floppy fringe fell over his eyes. Tony Hadley looked like he was about to cry. I couldn't help thinking it was a good job he wasn't wearing his eye-liner; it would be getting pretty smudged by now. My opponent limped away gingerly, as Karl picked up the ball and placed it on the spot.

'Well played mate!' he said as he strolled past me.

Blimey. I was still pinching myself as Karl took the penalty; blasting it high to the goalkeepers's right. Four-one.

'You alright mate?' I asked Spotty Hadley, offering him my hand, as he hobbled towards me a few moments later.

He ignored my gesture of sportsmanship, refusing to offer me his hand in return. Instead, he just glared.

I smirked and returned his glare, imagining him at home, in his full New Romantic clobber; the kilt and the frilly shirt. I wondered if he actually did wear make-up in his spare time? Well, with those zits...

Our tails were up now. Straight from the re-start, we surged forward again and Karl had a shot which their goalie saved. The ball went out for a corner. I started to amble towards the penalty area, already dreaming of somehow fluking another goal.

'Tim, where are you going? You're the winger. Take the corner!' Beattie shouted.

I'd never taken a corner in my life. Stevie Coppell, Man United's winger, could swing the ball over into the box and onto a striker's head like it was the easiest thing in the world. I doubted whether I could even lift the thing off of the ground, let alone kick the bloody thing that far.

I took a run up, hitting it as hard as I could. To my amazement, the ball sailed over in the right direction. Not only did it reach the penalty area, but it zoomed towards the goal. Thatcham's goalie came hurtling out to try and catch it but misjudged it completely. It flew over him. And then something else amazing happened.

Jez King must have smuggled a trampoline onto the pitch. All of a sudden, he was head and shoulders above the others. There was a thud as skull met leather and the ball flew off his head into the back of the net. There was a brief pause and then suddenly pandemonium broke out. The rest of our team mobbed Jez. They all ended up in a big heap on the grass like we'd won the cup or something; and we were still losing four-two. I still couldn't quite believe I'd kicked a ball that far - and in the right direction - as I wandered back towards the half-way line.

'Great corner Tim!' shouted Beattie.

'Yeah, well played Tim!' Heidi hollered.

My team-mates were all giving me the thumbs up. Karl ran up and put his arm around me. 'Brilliant ball mate!' he said.

I could feel a stupid grin spreading across my face.

'Come on, we can do this boys!' Beattie shouted.

The Thatcham boys didn't laugh this time. Spotty Hadley looked really cheesed off. Thatcham's PE teacher was having a right go at them.

You could almost see the adrenalin pumping through the Denton boys now. A few minutes later, one of the Thatcham boys tackled Jez. As they fell in a heap, the ball rolled towards me.

'Go Tim, use that speed of yours!' Beattie shouted.

Was he confusing me with someone else?

I started running; the ball at my feet. Spotty Hadley and I were face-to-face. Bloody hell what now?

That's when I remembered my Dad's video. I could see Georgie Best swivelling his hips and dribbling one way then the next. I'd probably do myself a damage if I tried it but hey, what the hell? Imitating Georgie, I dropped my shoulder as if to go to my right and instead went to my left. Spotty seemed to tumble, losing balance. I dropped my other shoulder and went to my right. Spotty fell on his zitty arse. There were roars of encouragement from all around me. Heidi and Glenda were screeching like tom-cats. I tried my Georgie moves again as another defender came towards me. He fell for it too. Blimey, it was working; I was like a man possessed. Looking up, I saw their goalie hesitate, before running out to the edge of the penalty box. He was only a few feet away from me.

320

'Hit it!' Beattie was shouting.

And so I did. I hit it as hard as I could. The goalie dived as I let fly and the ball hit him smack in the stomach. He crumpled in a heap.

I winced.

That must have hurt.

The ball rebounded straight into the path of Karl and he whacked it into the empty net. He was mobbed just like Jez had been moments before.

It was four-three.

The girls were all jumping around like mad things on the touchline. Beattie was running up and down shaking his fists and cheering like a loony. I'd never see anything like it.

'Brilliant play boys!' he shouted.

I felt seven feet high as I walked back past Spotty Hadley; he looked daggers.

'Come on Thatcham!' their sports-master was shouting, 'last five minutes, let's give it everything, we're still winning!'

The tackles were flying in thick and fast now. Both sides were really pumped up. I saw Beattie anxiously looking at his watch. He gestured to me as I looked over; two minutes left.

As we pushed for an equaliser, a Thatcham defender desperately whacked the ball clear. It fell to me on the wing.

'Cross it!' somebody shouted.

Spotty Hadley was facing me; a determined look on his stupid, pimply face; like he was daring me to take him on again. I ran straight at him and dropped my shoulder like before. He lunged wildly at me as I flew past. The ball span off at an angle but I managed to stay upright, jumping over his flailing legs. Pressing on, I found myself, once more with the goalie bearing down on me.

'Tim! Tim!' yelled Karl as he ran up alongside me, 'square it, square it!'

Of course I should have passed it to him - he was unmarked and would have had a simple tap in. We'd have been all square at four-all. But in that fleeting moment, I had just one thing on my mind. I'd seen the way Jez and Karl had been mobbed when they scored - now I wanted a piece of that action. If the Georgie Best approach worked with defenders, why shouldn't it work with a goalie too? Just drop my shoulder, feign to hit it one way, then hit it the other. The goalie would dive the wrong way, the ball would flash into the net. Tim James, instant hero.

Except of course, it didn't pan out like that at all.

'Tim! Tim!' Karl's pleading voice seemed to have taken on a hysterical pitch as he yelled at me to pass the ball to him.

I dropped my shoulder; feigned to shoot to the goalie's left and as anticipated, he started to dive in that direction. Then I whacked the bloody thing to his right with all the strength I could muster. I could almost hear the sound of the bulging, rattling net and the cheers of the capacity crowd of six as it flew through the air.

But there was no rattling net, no wild applause; instead there was an almighty thwack as the ball thudded against the goalpost and shot back over my head.

My momentum carried me forward, lunging over the goalie's outstretched legs. I hit the net alright - with my head and my arms; my entire body ending up in a tangled heap in the back of the goal. As I struggled to untangle myself, the ref blew the whistle. There was an outbreak of cheering and just for a second, I assumed that one of my team-mates had scored; that Karl or Jez had picked up the rebound and fired that all important equaliser. Until I managed to free my head from the net and look around behind me.

The Thatcham boys were hugging and giving each other high-fives. The game was over; we'd lost.

Karl was striding towards me. I managed a rueful smile and held out my hand for him to help me up. He just glared at me, his face glowing scarlet, as he leant over me, his arms down by his sides, his fists clenched.

'You stupid selfish bastard!' he shouted, 'I was on a hat-trick, you should have passed!'

Then Jez King stood over me. 'Well done mate,' he said, 'you just lost us the bloody match. I hope you're really proud of yourself!'

Graham Everett was standing with his hands on his hips, shaking his head. A couple of the other lads just stared. No-one offered me their hand. They all walked away.

Eventually dragging myself to my feet, I walked slowly back to the dressing room, feeling utterly dejected. The rival PE teachers shook hands as I sloped past. I sensed Mr. Beattie walking behind me. Then I felt his hand on my shoulder.

'Bad luck Tim. You played really well,' he said.

He was a good bloke was Beattie. I felt tears pricking at the back of my eyes.

Then as he stepped up a pace to catch up with the others, he looked over his shoulder and added, 'but you should have bloody passed!'

The atmosphere was like a morgue back in the dressing room. No-one said anything. They didn't need to. Their looks said it all.

Undressing slowly, I waited until everyone was out of the shower, before I went in. I stood there for ages, until the water went cold and the skin on my hands was wrinkling. Only then, when I was confident they'd all gone, did I sneak out. The dressing room was deserted, I dressed in silence, with only the rattling of the radiators and the pitter-patter of the rain on the windows for company. After a while, Mr. Beattie stuck his head around the door and told me to get a ruddy move on.

I'd hoped that they wouldn't be there; that Mrs. Bloom would have given up waiting. I hadn't given any thought as to how I would've actually got home, right across the other side of Brighton in the rain, but at that moment, I just wanted to be on my own. Maybe there was a back exit out of Thatcham? Of course, I didn't know my way around, so I had to leave by the front door.

'Tim, we were getting worried about you!' said Heidi, who was standing with Glenda under a pink Barbie-doll umbrella.

'Mrs. Bloom was telling Karl to come and find you,' added Glenda.

I could see Karl sitting in the passenger seat of his Mum's Cortina. He was staring through the windscreen at nothing in particular, intent on ignoring my very existence.

Heidi's eyes followed my gaze. 'He said his ankle hurt too much,' she explained.

Yeah, right.

The car park was almost empty. All the other boys had disappeared. Only Mr. Beattie was standing by his little red Triumph Spitfire.

'OK then Tim?' he asked.

I nodded, feeling far from OK.

'Right, see you Monday,' he said, climbing into his sports car.

I sat directly behind Karl as his mum drove us home.

The girls chatted about the game and said how well we'd played in the second half.

323

'Two goals love! Well played,' Karl's Mum said to him.

He just grunted, turning his head to stare at the roadside. Our eyes met in the wing mirror; we both looked away.

'And what about Tim eh Mum?' said Heidi, 'wasn't he brilliant?'

'Yes, you were super Tim!' agreed Mrs. Bloom, 'and so unlucky to hit the post right at the end there. Don't you think so Karl?'

'S'pose,' muttered Karl.

It was the last word either of us spoke during the journey.

'Thanks for the lift Mrs. Bloom,' I mumbled as we reached home.

'You're welcome love,' she smiled as I started to climb out.

'See you tonight then Tim!' shouted Heidi.

'Oh, right...'

'Are you sure it's not an imposition, taking Heidi along to this concert of Karl's?' Mrs. Bloom asked.

An impo what?

'Of course its not Mother!' Heidi protested, 'you asked me didn't you Timmy?'

'Er...yes, ..er no, ...of course,' I said, ducking my head to talk through the open door.

Frankly, looking after Heidi at Karl's gig was the last thing I wanted to do that evening.

'And you'll be picking her up from our house I understand?' Mrs. Bloom said, 'at about seven thirty?'

Would I? Had I said that? I glanced at Heidi, who was staring back at me with her cutest Dana-all-kinds-of-everything eyes.

'Sure,' I nodded, like the prize sucker I so obviously was, 'from your place,' I told her Mum.

'Good, I can give you all a lift in to town,' Mrs. Bloom replied, 'that'll be..."cool" as I believe you youngsters say?' she laughed.

'Oh, God! Mother, you're so embarrassing!' Heidi screeched, 'OK, see you tonight then Timmy!' she added, beaming up at me, as I closed the car door behind me.

All through this, Karl said nothing.

Great.

It promised to be a marvellous evening.

That afternoon, I soaked in the bath, nursing my injured pride and listening to Zenyatta Mondatta on Cheryl's new Sony Walkman. Sting was doing his best to comfort me as usual. *"When the world is running down, you make the best of what's still around."*

Make the best of what though?

Maybe taking Heidi to the gig wouldn't be so bad, I thought as I dried myself off.

'Timothy!' Mum shouted up the stairs, 'phone!'

'Miss Sussex University 1981?' she whispered as she handed me the receiver, looking me up and down.

I was wrapped in the bath towel, water still dripping down my legs. 'What?'

'Your young lady,' Mum whispered.

Then I twigged. Mum was still under the impression that I was seeing someone from the Uni.

I shook my head. It was bound to be Heidi.

'And don't be long, you're dripping water all over my carpet!'

I gave Mum a look as she trudged off back to watch Grandstand.

'Hello?'

'Tim, hi, it's Roxy!' she said, sounding really breezy.

Roxy? My heart started to thud. I almost dropped the towel.

'Oh, hi,' I said in my coolest voice, holding the towel over my privates.

'You OK - you sound poorly?'

So much for cool.

'Yeah, I'm fine, just ...a bit damp - I was in the bath.'

'Oh, sorry. Look, I won't keep you long. I just wanted to check that you're still going to Karl's gig tonight? Poppy told me you're taking Heidi?'

'Well, yes I'm going but I'm not really taking....'

'Good, so you'll definitely be there then?'

'Yes. Why? Have you changed your mind about coming?'

'What time will you be there?'

'Oh, I'm picking up....er, meeting Heidi and Karl at their place at around half seven.'

'Excellent, so you'll get there at about eight?'

'Yes, I expect so. What time will you...?'

'OK Tim, I've got to rush now.'

'See you later then.'

'Bye.'

And she was gone.

Bloody hell. What a turn up.

Maybe it wouldn't be such a waste of an evening after all?

I started singing to myself as I leapt up the stairs two at a time.

"When the world is running down, you make the best of what's still around."

As usual Sting was spot on.

27 - The Other Way Of Stopping

'I really love you, you know?'

I'd almost forgotten just how beautiful she was.

'I know you do, and I love you too,' she said, 'and now lets get you home to bed.'

They were the very words I'd hoped would be spoken to me at the end of that evening; words spoken by the beautiful girl who was holding my hand and who was about to take me home.

The wrong girl.

The wrong home.

The wrong reason.

She pulled me up to my feet. The ground beneath the bench was still doing that twirly-twisty thing, but more slowly than it had been half an hour before. The clock on St. Peters church sounded a lonely, solitary chime.

'Come on, everything will feel better in the morning.'

I sincerely doubted it. I gave the clock a rueful glance. If only I could have turned it back to seven thirty.

'And you will make sure she's outside at eleven on the dot?'

'Oh Muuuuum!' Heidi wailed.

'Yes Mrs. Bloom,' I said, conscious of Clarkey standing beside me, trying hard not to snigger.

'And you will make sure she doesn't touch alcohol?'

'Mummmmmmm!'

'Yes Mrs. Bloom.'

'And Timothy?'

'Yes Mrs. Bloom?'

'You will try and remember she's only fifteen, won't you?'

'Oh God! Muuuuuum. Shut up, will you?!'

Remember she's only fifteen? Hadn't I just promised that I'd make sure Heidi was ready for her lift home at the right time and that I wouldn't let her drink. What did she mean by *remember she's only fifteen?*

By now, Clarkey was desperately trying not to laugh, as I stood there with my mouth open.

Mrs. Bloom stood with her hands on her hips, clearly waiting for an answer to what I'd had assumed was a hypothetical question.

Clarkey came to my rescue.

'I'll make sure he remembers Mrs. Bloom.'

'Thank you Kevin. Don't get me wrong; of course I trust you all, but then I know what it's like when boys have had a drink or two. Kissing's fine. Holding hands is fine. We just don't want any shenanigans, OK?'

'Oh mother! You are so embarrassing!' Heidi squirmed.

'Sorry? Shenanigans?' I said, shrugging. I turned towards Clarkey, wondering if he had any clue what she was on about.

Clarkey just raised his eyebrows; smirked knowingly.

Then the penny finally dropped and I felt myself going an acute shade of purple.

'Oh no, you don't understand...,' I started to say something about meeting Roxanne, but Mrs. Bloom wasn't listening.

'Oh, but I do understand Timothy. I may look old and decrepit but it might shock you to know that I was your age once - and not that long ago either. Mr. Bloom was pretty free with his hands when he was your age. Dr. Octopus I used to call him...'

'Oh yeuck! Mother!' Heidi gestured shoving two fingers down her throat.

'Yes, well, that's all every well but these things have to be said young lady...'

'No mother, they *really* don't,' Heidi shook her head and pointed to the driveway, 'please can we just get in the car now?'

I'd been kind've expecting Poppy to be coming with us - maybe even that Roxanne might be meeting her there at the Blooms. So far, there had been no sign of either of them.

'Oh, isn't Poppy coming with us?' I asked.

'Oh no dear, she went out a long time ago - I think she was meeting up with her friends from the shop.'

'Oh, right,' I said.

'Come on, we'll be late!' said Heidi, climbing into the back of the Cortina.

All the way into town, Mrs. Bloom kept up her constant chatter. She'd win a gold medal if talking was ever made an Olympic sport. Clarkey had got her on the subject of music. Apparently, she thought

Karl was a "competent" guitarist but she "didn't much care" for his band, or for the type of music the Morbid Morsels played.

'Frankly, it's a ferocious din,' she explained.

Trying really hard to keep a straight face, Clarkey asked her what sort of music she liked.

Apparently Mrs. Bloom "favoured classical" but when pressed, she admitted to liking some "modern bands".

'Oh, really? Who's your favourite?' Clarkey said, casting a sly grin to Heidi and me in the back.

'Oh, I don't know, people who sing songs with harmonies - like The New Seekers or The Dooleys.'

'Yeah, good choices,' said Clarkey straight faced.

Heidi sniggered.

I was biting my lip.

'So here we are then,' said Clarkey, as we rounded St. Peter's and pulled up in front of The Northern. 'I think I can hear them warming up already.'

'What a racket!' laughed Mrs. Bloom. Then she put her hand to her mouth. 'Oh, that sounds awful doesn't it? Don't tell poor Karl I said that!'

As we stepped onto the pavement, we could all-too-clearly hear the rehearsal. Clarkey and I exchanged grimaces. Tuneless electric guitars and epileptic drumming. What was it Mrs. Bloom had said? Ferocious din? That pretty much summed it up. Perhaps they should call themselves that. I imagined John Peel introducing them on his show "And these are The Ferocious Din" - yeah, as a name it definitely had something.

'Well, have a good time and behave yourselves!' shouted Mrs. Bloom, as she wound up her window and drove away.

'Blimey. I thought she'd never go!' said Heidi, pulling bright orange lipstick from her little handbag and applying it to her pouting lips. She was wearing a matching orange ra-ra skirt with a black denim jacket.

Try as I might not to notice, I had to admit that she looked a lot older than fifteen. Thankfully, the bouncers on the door seemed to think so too. As, they gave me and Clarkey the full once over, we both braced ourselves for a request for proof of age, or even a straight rejection but then ironically, they took one look at Heidi, who was two years younger than either of us, and waved us all in.

329

'Come on, lets get in and get a good place up front by the stage,' Heidi said, grabbing me eagerly by the arm, as soon as were through the door.

I'm not quite sure what Heidi had been expecting, but we had absolutely no problem at all getting near to the stage. The Northern wasn't exactly Wembley Stadium. The main entrance led into a small, dimly-lit bar with a raised seating area in one corner, from which a couple of middle-aged drinkers in jeans and donkey jackets watched our uncertain progress from across the room. My initial reaction was that we'd come to the wrong place. You could easily count the punters who were scattered around the shabbily decorated pub, on the fingers of one hand. And this was Saturday evening. It made the Pedestrian Arms look like Piccadilly Circus.

'It's early yet,' Clarkey said, as if reading my mind.

There was no obvious sign of an impending gig but the less-than-melodious strumming we'd heard from outside seemed to be emanating from somewhere behind the bar.

'We're here for the band,' Clarkey said to the barman, an ageing punk-cum-teddy-boy hybrid, with with an enormous beer gut, Brylcreemed hair, wall-to-wall tattoos and a fag seemingly super-glued to his lower lip.

'Round the back,' he muttered, without dislodging the fag.

Following his jerked thumb, we spotted a narrow hallway. The "music" grew steadily louder as we walked along the darkened passage; Heidi holding me by the arm as if terrified for her life.

We emerged in a slightly larger bar with a tiny stage situated against the back wall. There were a few more people in there. I needed both hands to count them all - but that did include the four band members themselves.

The self-named Karl Grim, sat cross-legged on the stage. Despite Heidi yelling his name and waving like a demented banshee, he pretended not to notice us. He was far too busy plucking at his guitar and practicing his best rock-star-lost-in-his-muse look. Idiot.

There were three others in the group; like Karl, they were all trying far too hard to perfect just the right level of effortless cool. The lead singer was a very skinny guy with a mop of hair like Robert Smith from The Cure. He seemed to have had trouble predicting the likely weather conditions in a dark, centrally heated pub in the middle of

March. To be on the safe side, he'd opted for both a pair of sunglasses and a full-length coat. Perhaps he should have consulted Michael Fish.

The bassist and the drummer were also warming up; murdering a tune that sounded like a cross between The Funeral March and a child running its finger-nails down a blackboard. The bass player was a tall skinny lad, dressed in a similar trench coat; he looked as if he hadn't had a decent square meal in months. Maybe the drummer had eaten for them both? He was as fat as the bass player was thin. He had long, greasy hair and wore a leather biker jacket. I wondered whether the jacket was just part of the image or whether he actually had a bike. A quick getaway could come in handy if his warm-up playing was anything to go by.

'Cool aren't they?' said Heidi, admiring her sulky brother and his bandmates.

'Must be freezing, judging by the size of that singer's overcoat,' I quipped.

Heidi laughed like it was the funniest thing anyone had ever said. Sweet kid. She put her hand through my arm and rested her head against my shoulder. *Clingy* sweet kid.

'Aren't you going to get me a drink then?'

I tried to ignore the puppy-dog eyes.

Clarkey grinned, noticing my discomfort.

'Yeah, Tim, why haven't you got your date a drink yet? Call yourself a gentleman?'

I gave him a Paddington-bear hard stare.

'And I'll have a Guinness,' he winked.

'What would you like then Heidi?' I asked, fumbling in my pocket for change.

'Rum and Coke?' she smiled innocently.

'Nice try. One Coke coming up.'

'Aw, Tim!'

'I'm not getting on the wrong side of your mum. You heard her; she'd have my guts for garters.'

'But Tim!'

'Coke.'

She was still whingeing as I walked to the bar. By now, a few more fans had arrived for the gig and there was a small crowd of thirsty punters waiting to be served. I leant across a soggy Carlsberg bar towel, my pound note held out, hoping to attract the attention of the barman. It didn't look promising. After what seemed an age, I was still waiting. Jacko came to my assistance.

'Blimey, I must be seeing things,' a familiar voice said from behind me, 'for one minute there, I actually thought I saw Tim James getting a round in?'

I turned to find Jacko's ugly mug smiling at me. He was with Fay Carpenter and Wiffy Wilf.

'Don't look so panicky. I'll get them in, tight-arse!'

'Thanks,' I said, putting my precious pound note back in my pocket, 'Heidi wants a Coke and Clarkey's is a Guinness.'

'Chancer,' Jacko said, shaking his head.

'Yeah, cheers Jacko, mine's a pint too.'

We all turned.

'Bloody hell, look what the cat dragged in,' Jacko said.

It was Humph; and what's more, he had my favourite comedy duo in tow.

'Well, well, well if isn't the phantom knee-licker of ol' Brighton town!' said Doddsy.

Pete laughed; gave him a congratulatory high-five.

'Funny,' I said.

Tossers.

I hadn't seen the Three Musketeers since that afternoon at Wilf's. Clearly, they hadn't forgotten my stupid comments about Star Whores. I just preyed their memories weren't so good when it came to their little spat with me and Clarkey.

Whilst Humph and Jacko were greeting each other in time-honoured fashion; by play-punching each other's arms as hard as they could, Pete and Doddsy pushed their way to the bar and before I knew it, they were being served before anyone else.

Glancing behind them, I exchanged smiles with Heidi.

Pete noticed and gave Doddsy a nudge. They both looked from me to Heidi and smirked stupidly at each other.

Great.

'I thought this wasn't your scene?' I said to Humph.

'Well, we've had a hard week at work, we thought we could do with a laugh. I thought I'd surprise you!'

'You've certainly done that, hasn't he Jacko?'

Jacko wasn't listening. He was facing the door with his mouth gaping. I followed his eyes across the room.

'Buggering hell,' I muttered.

'Talking of surprises,' Jacko said.

I looked over to Humph. He'd already noticed. So had his mates.

'Isn't that your bird?' Pete asked.

'Was,' muttered Jacko.

It was Alison. And she was with Jez "Kong" King, plus his mate Frank Little and Frank's gorgeous girlfriend, Jasmine.

'Blimey,' said Doddsy, 'who's her pet gorilla?'

Kong was oblivious to the attention he was attracting, as he wrapped his arm around Alison's waist.

Humph wasn't amused. His eyes met Alison's and they glared at each other across the room. Then he stormed off to the loo.

'Did you know?' Jacko said.

'Definitely not,' I said.

So, Jez King was Alison's mysterious date. How had that happened? I couldn't help thinking about the quid I'd had to give him to get that photo back. I suppose he must have liked what he'd seen.

'This could be a fun evening,' Jacko muttered.

More people started appearing from the other bar. The night's surprises just kept on coming. I couldn't believe my eyes.

Dave Booth had some neck. He walked in as bold as brass with Juliette on his arm. Karl had obviously seen them too. His guitar let out a particularly frenzied howl and then went silent. Clarkey caught my eye. He was shaking his head in disbelief as Heidi greeted her friend with a noisy shriek, followed by a girly hug. Dave nodded slightly uncomfortably as our eyes met. Karl had disappeared behind the curtain at the back of the stage, followed by the rest of the band.

So, pretty much everyone I knew was here now. With one noticeable exception. There was no sign of Roxanne.

Jacko finally got served just as the lights went down, prompting a less than deafening ripple of applause around the room.

We were all walking from the bar towards the stage, when I noticed Pete and Doddsy were sizing Heidi up and grinning stupidly. Here we go, I thought.

'Here you go love,' said Pete, holding out the Carlsberg bar-towel to a bemused looking Heidi, 'you might need this to dry your knees later!'

Doddsy snorted in his beer. They went through their high-five routine again.

Absolute tossers.

'What was all that about?' asked Heidi.

'No idea,' I shrugged.

With my pint in my hand and Heidi clinging to my elbow, I wandered over to where a small crowd had gathered around the foot of the stage, ignoring the raised eyebrows as my friends drank in the sight of my fourth-year date.

Clarkey looked nervous as I handed him his Guinness.

'Don't worry - Karl will be fine!' I said.

'Who's worried about Karl?' he hissed in my ear. He nodded over my shoulder towards Pete and Doddsy. They were both glaring menacingly over the tops of their pint-glasses. Unfortunately for Clarkey, it seemed that even Neanderthals had pretty long memories.

Just then, the tattooed punk-ted took to the stage and coughed into the microphone.

'Ladies, Gents and clientele of other persuasions, please give a big Northern welcome to our first band of the evening, Brighton's own ...,' he looked down at the scrap of paper in his hand, 'Morbid Morsels!'

There was polite applause and a couple of ironic screams as Karl and his band-mates ambled onto the stage.

'Hello Brighton,' yelled the lead singer, a tad theatrically I felt, given the paltry size of the audience, 'we're The Morbid Morsels!'

Yeah, we got that already.

The hairy drummer clapped his drumsticks in the air and with that, Karl and his mates instantly burst into action. The opening number was played at such an impressive volume that it was hard to tell if there was an actual tune involved.

Heidi started jumping up and down excitedly. One or two people gave her bemused stares, before taking a step or two sideways.

It took a couple of minutes, but when they reached the chorus, I finally identified it as a rather too-fast version of Joy Division's hit, Love Will Tear Up Apart.

Pete, Doddsy and Humph were all pulling faces. Doddsy put one of his fingers in his ear. They all laughed. Still, at least they seemed to have forgotten about freaking Clarkey out; for a while at least.

'Great aren't they?' Heidi said, standing on tiptoe and breathing in my ear. I smiled, before grimacing, as I turned to face Clarkey, who was giggling into his Guinness. It promised to be a long evening.

Thankfully, The Morsels didn't just murder cover versions; they had some pretty horrendous songs of their own to slaughter too. One particularly notable dirge had the lyric "Die you lying cow" spat out by the singer repeatedly, with the same three chords repeated over and over. It was a tune that sounded like it had suffered a slow and painful death. People were openly laughing now. Even Heidi had stopped jumping up and down.

It was just as this potential chart-topper was coming to it's cringeworthy end that I felt a tap on my shoulder.

It was Poppy Bloom, standing there, dressed up to the nines. And completely alone.

'Hi, Tim,' she said, unsmiling.

'Hi Poppy, where's Roxanne?'

'Can we have a chat?...in the other bar.'

'Hi sis!' said Heidi, suddenly noticing her big sister, 'you've missed some great songs. Where have you been?'

'I'll explain later. I just need to borrow Tim for a couple of minutes.'

Having followed her through to the other bar, I stood there with a sinking feeling in my stomach as Poppy rummaged through her handbag.

'Here,' she said, holding out a pink envelope, 'Roxy asked me to give you this.'

I studied Poppy's face for clues but she was wearing her best poker face. I looked at the envelope in her outstretched hand.

'Take it,' she said gently, pushing it towards me.

'What's going on Poppy?'

Poppy looked embarrassed but said nothing. Instead, she did something pretty out of character. She leant over and kissed me on the cheek.

'Sorry,' she muttered. And then she turned and walked out of the pub.

The saloon bar was empty; everyone had either wandered through to the stage area to find out what was making that horrendous noise or had been driven out to find another drinking hole. I sat down at an empty table and stared at the envelope for a few moments. The sinking feeling had descended from my stomach to my lower intestines.

In the other bar, The Morsels had started to torture a Cure song.

The envelope was plain pink - no writing on either side. I ran my fingernail along the still-moist flap and prized it open. Inside was a single sheet of lined paper, which I pulled out. My name was scrawled on one side. Roxanne's writing. My heart was beating furiously. I looked around the room, half expecting Heidi or one of the others to appear from the narrow passage between the bars. To be on the safe side, I took the letter into the gents, where I locked myself into a cubicle and sat trembling, urging myself to get it over with and turn over the page. Taking a deep breath, I turned the sheet over.

There was still no-one in the Saloon bar. The barman was reading The Sun, as I wandered over.

'Heineken,'

'Pint?'

I nodded, staring into space.

'Hey, there you are! We've been looking for you!'

Heidi emerged from the hallway with Juliette.

I managed a thin smile.

'Where's Poppy?'

'Gone.'

'Gone where? She's missing Karl's gig!'

'She didn't seem that bothered.'

Clarkey was next to appear around the corner, grinning from ear to ear.

'Jesus wept. That has to be the worst pile of...' he stopped mid-sentence when he saw the look on my face.

'You OK? Your face looks like a slapped arse.'

'Don't you like the band?' asked Heidi, rubbing my arm.

I shrugged her off - a little too forcefully.

'What's up?' she said.

'Nothing,' I said, giving the barman his fifty pence, 'I'm going back through.'

I wandered back through to the stage bar; lost in thought and only vaguely aware of the others following behind.

The Morsels had finished off The Cure and had now started on Siouxsie and The Banshees.

"This is a Happy House," Talk about taking the piss.

Humph and his mates had given up on the band and were standing as far from the stage as they could; propping up the far corner of the bar. Wilf and Fay were chatting over to one side. Alison and Jez wandered past with Frank and Jasmine, heading for the saloon bar. Soon, Heidi and Juliette were dancing again. Clarkey stood by my side.

'You sure you're OK mate?'

I felt like getting very drunk; I gulped down my lager.

'What did Poppy Bloom want?' Clarkey was persistent, I'll give him that.

I nodded towards the saloon.

'Buy me another beer?'

'Sorry mate,' Clarkey said, folding the sheet of paper and handing it back to me.

'Well, I suppose I should have known after your oscar-winning performance in HMV.'

Clarkey took a swig of his Guinness; said nothing.

'Aren't you going to say I told you so?'

He shook his head. 'Well, at least you know now.'

I buried my face in lager.

'And without wishing to quote too many cliches at you in your time of need, there *are* plenty more fish in the sea.'

'If you've got the right tackle, I know, Jacko's always saying.'

'Well, it's true. I mean a lot of lads would be happy to have Heidi Bloom trailing around after them for starters!'

'If they were fifteen perhaps.'

'Tim mate, you're only seventeen yourself! The age gap isn't massive. It's hardly Charlie and Lady Di!'

'She's a kid,' I said.

'Yeah, a pretty one though.'

'Still a kid, all the same.'

There was a lot of laughter coming from the elevated corner table. We glanced over.

'Now, that's one fish I wouldn't mind landing,' Clarkey said, supping his third Guinness of the evening.

Blimey he was a dark horse was Clarkey.

337

'Alison?' I said, 'I think Kong might have something to say about that. Not to mention Humph!'

'No, not Alison; the other one. The one with Frank.'

'Oh right, yeah, Jasmine. Yeah, she's OK I suppose.'

'OK? OK? Have you had a good look at her? She'd do alright in Miss World that one!'

'Who would do alright in Miss World?' Heidi said, appearing at Clarkey's elbow, 'are you talking about me again Kevin?'

'Yes of course Heidi,' lied Clarkey, 'Miss Denton-fourth-form 1981, that's you, eh Tim?

'Well would you like to buy Miss Denton another Rum and Coke?' she said, waving her empty glass under his nose.

She had some front did Heidi, I'll give her that.

'A Coke maybe,' Clarkey smirked.

'Oh, sweet Jesus, get her a rum,' I said.

'You've changed your tune!' Heidi smiled.

'You're only fifteen once eh?'

Over Heidi's shoulder, Jasmine was laughing at one of Frank's jokes. She looked over. Our eyes met. She smiled. Clarkey was right. Miss World. I returned her smile and then remembered the size of her boyfriend. I went back to my lager.

After Clarkey got his round in, we ambled back to the stage bar. The Morsels were between songs. Then the bass guitarist started thrumming away. The beat seemed familiar. Then Karl started playing a reggae riff over the top of it.

Oh my God, they weren't were they?

The singer lifted the mike and sang the opening lines.

They were.

They were doing "Can't Stand Losing You".

Karl had kept that addition to the set-list pretty quiet. Mind you, on hearing their version, I couldn't really blame him. The Morsels were committing first degree homicide on one of my favourite songs.

Clarkey clapped me on the shoulder and smiled.

Heidi grabbed my hand and started jigging about like a mental thing.

'Dance!' she mouthed.

I held up my pint, pointing out that it was impossible to dance with a drink in your hand but Juliette snatched my glass before I had a chance to protest any further. Alison and Jasmine appeared at the back of the room, doing that Sting dance; the one that looks like he's walking in very slow motion with chewing gum stuck to the soles of his feet. Alison waved and blew me a kiss. Heidi had both my hands now and was pulling me across the floor. I wasn't nearly drunk enough for this. I started to move my feet but they felt like they were ankle deep in treacle. I really wasn't in the mood.

The familiar words just made me think of Roxanne and her note. I could feel a stinging sensation at the back of my eyes. Heidi looked really hurt when I yanked my hands away from her but I had to get away. I bolted for the refuge of the Gents.

Safely back in the locked cubicle, I stared at the note again. Already, the words were as ingrained as those of "Can't Stand Losing You".

Dear Tim
This is the hardest letter I have ever had to write.
Why write it then?
I know I've treated you badly. I've acted like a total bitch.
Well, at least there was something we agreed on.
I've been really confused since we met.
She's been confused?
I really like you. It's been fun. You're such a good laugh.
Yeah, I feel like a right laugh just now.
But I've realised I still have feelings for Rob.
Yeah, I've got a few "feelings" for him myself too.
I know he's been a total prick in the past.
Really?
But he's been different recently. He's been really making an effort. He says he loves me and he's really sorry for the way he treated me.
What a guy.
We've been spending some time together and I've come to a conclusion.
That he really is a total knob?
I think I'm still in love with him too.
Great.
Believe it or not, he's asked me to marry him.
Wonderful news.
We're engaged.
Congratulations.

339

Please don't think badly of me.

Of course not Roxanne, I think you're the Dogs Bollocks.

I know this will have come as a bit of a shock.

Mmm, yeah, you could say that.

I'm sorry if I've hurt you.

No, that's fine, I love feeling like my guts have just been ripped out; and twisted around my neck for good measure.

You're a lovely lad Tim James. I'm sure you will find someone really special.

Excuse me whilst I throw up.

All my love, Roxy xx

Not quite *all* your love though eh?

There was a banging on the door.

'Tim, are you alright in there?' a voice shouted.

Jacko.

'Tim? Are you OK?' he shouted.

I flushed the chain and opened the door.

'You OK?' he repeated, more quietly this time.

'Hunky Dory,' I said, 'why shouldn't I be?' I started washing my hands in a filthy looking wash basin.

'Clarkey told me about Roxanne. I'm sorry mate.'

'No skin off my nose. Come on, I fancy another drink.'

The Morsels finished their set, taking the polite applause as an excuse to squeeze in an encore. "One of our own tunes" the singer had announced. I was still waiting for the "tune" when they finished three minutes later. I'd knocked back a fourth pint and was already half way down my fifth. I was sat at the saloon bar on my own; the others were through in the stage bar awaiting the arrival of the headline act; and no doubt the news of my sudden single status was spreading like wild fire.

Someone sat down on the stool next to me.

'Knocking those back a bit aren't you?' Alison said.

'Oh, hi,' I slurred, turning to face her.

She was dressed in a long flowery skirt and a denim jacket over a very tight T-shirt. Her hair was tied back in a ponytail. She looked effortlessly gorgeous as ever, although she had far too much make-up on for my liking. She certainly had no problem attracting the barman's eye. It took all of a nano-second as she held out her pound note.

'Vodka and Lime and a pint of Carlsberg please.'

The barman smiled lecherously.

'I'd offer you one too,' she said, watching the barman pour Kong's Carlsberg, 'but I'm not sure it would be a good move. Is that the fifth?'

'You keeping count?' I snapped.

'Just might want to take it easy a bit. Haven't you got to take care of your little girlfriend?'

'She's *not* my girlfriend,' I said, spitting beer.

'Would you like to spray that again?' Alison said, wiping her arm.

'So, what's with you and King Kong then?' I said. Even to my half pissed ears, my voice sounded sulky.

'What's it to you?' she snapped back.

'Got over Humph quickly didn't you?'

Her face went crimson. She scowled at me.

'Grow up Tim, no wonder Roxanne dumped you.'

Bloody hell, was someone sending smoke signals across the pub?

Alison took her drinks and walked away.

The barman's eyes never left her shapely backside. He saw me looking at him and just winked. Then there was a sudden, muffled shout from the passage-way.

'Watch it!'

That sounded like Clarkey, I thought.

Heads turned. Everything went quiet. As I stepped down from my stool, the ground seemed to wobble. As I swayed across towards the commotion, the jukebox was playing Madness' "Baggy Trousers". It was appropriate, given the slapstick scene which now confronted me.

Clarkey was on all fours, surrounded by a pool of Guinness.

'You want to watch where you're walking when you've got a glass in your hand,' Pete was saying as he looked down at him.

Clarkey slowly picked himself up off the ground. A large pool of drink had spilt from the glass he had obviously dropped as he fell; or more likely, as he had been tripped, judging by the way Doddsy was smirking.

Pete leant against the wall, laughing like a drain, as Doddsy stood over his victim.

Doddsy glanced at me as I approached; an evil glint in his eye. Then he turned his attention back to Clarkey, who was now kneeling. The black liquid dripped from his jeans.

'He's right you know, you need to be careful with glasses,' Doddsy sniggered at Clarkey, 'you could easily get wet!'

Then as his growing audience looked on, Doddsy slowly tipped his own glass, until a large drop of beer splashed directly onto the top of Clarkey's head.

I'm not sure what came over me. Under normal circumstances, my instinct for self-preservation would have quickly kicked in, ensuring I steered a wide berth away from the fracas. Maybe it was the booze, maybe it was because I was still reeling from Roxanne's note. Whatever the cause, I felt uncharacteristically reckless. The rage just seemed to creep up on me.

'You are such arseholes!' I heard myself shout.

The whole pub went eerily silent. Suggs had even stopped singing.

'You what..?' Pete said, almost choking on his beer.

The hairs were standing up on the back of my neck. I'd gone past the point of no return now. In for a penny....

'You heard. Clarkey was dead right. You're a couple of complete shits.'

'And what exactly are you going to do about it school-boy?' Doddsy snarled.

He lunged for me and, before I knew what was happening, made a grab for my neck. Unfortunately, as well as making me stupidly mouthy, the booze had also made my reactions ridiculously slow. Before I could move, he had me in a head-lock.

'Eh Doddsy, maybe he wants to lick his ginger mate's knees!' laughed Pete.

'Of course!' said Doddsy, shoving my head downwards.

'Piss off Doddsy!' I tried to say.

Doddsy's huge biceps muffled my voice. All I could see were Clarkey's legs, a pool of Guinness and a grubby looking skirting board. I wrestled and wriggled but couldn't move. I'd forgotten just how bloody strong he was.

Then I heard shouting, chairs scraping back, a door flying open; and the sound of at least two pairs of running feet. Doddsy let me up, though still with his arm draped loosely around my neck, as if we were the best of mates. Clarkey got to his feet, brushing his wet legs, as the two bouncers from the main door came hurtling over.

'Here come the cavalry', I thought. Great. Serve the bastards right.

Doddsy pulled his arms away from me, holding them out-stretched in a display of innocence.

'Hi guys,' he said to the bouncers, 'just having a bit of fun with our two young friends....'

To the complete amazement of us all, the two burly bruisers didn't bat an eyelid in our direction. Instead, they hurried straight past, towards the gents. We all watched as they dived in through the door. Suddenly, we were aware of an even louder rumble coming from that direction. There was yelling and swearing and as I walked closer, for a better view, I saw someone was lying on the floor. The bouncers disappeared momentarily and then one of them reappeared, manhandling a lad, forcing him up against the urinals; before folding the miscreant's arm painfully behind his back.

'Bloody hell,' I said, 'it's Karl!'

The second bouncer was picking another boy up off the floor and placing him in a similar hold. It was Dave Booth. As the bouncer bundled him to his feet, Dave was swearing and protesting his innocence.

'Dave?' said Clarkey, now standing by my side; his wet clothes dripping Guinness on the tiled floor, 'what's going on?'

'He bleeding started it!' Dave was saying as he was led towards the side door. His face was blooded; a scarlet smear running from his mouth to his chin.

'And I'm bleeding ending it, OK?' the second bouncer said.

'But I'm in the band!' Karl said, as the first bouncer opened the door onto the street.

Juliette appeared in the doorway, she was crying. Heidi had her arm around her.

'Yeah and good riddance to that bloody racket too!' the bouncer said.

With that, both Kevin and Dave were flung out unceremoniously.

'And another thing,' the second bouncer shouted after them, 'I recommend your crappy little band finds another venue; you're both barred!

The two bouncers came strolling back past us, congratulating each other on a job well done. For once, Pete and Doddsy looked like perfectly behaved little lambs.

'Come on mate, let's get you cleaned up,' I said, taking Clarkey by the arm and leading him towards the wash basin.

'See you later,' Pete sneered as we walked away.

Juliette was still sobbing five minutes later, when Clarkey and I emerged from the loo. Clarkey was dabbing his wet clothes, clutching a handful of bog-roll.

'What happened?' I asked a tearful looking Heidi.

She shrugged, wiping running mascara from her face with her sleeve.

I was having trouble focusing; Heidi seemed to be a multi-armed octopus. I was beginning to feel a bit queasy.

'Juliette said she saw Karl follow Dave into the loos and then all hell let loose. Juliette's really upset.'

'Maybe we should call your Mum; get you both home?' Clarkey suggested.

'Don't you dare!' said Heidi, 'I want to see the other band. You'll be fine won't you Juliette?'

'I'd like to go and see if David's OK,' Juliette sobbed.

'Come on, I'll take you outside; see if we can find him. I'm sure he's OK,' Clarkey said, taking Juliette by the elbow, 'you coming outside too Tim?'

'Nah, think I'll get another beer.'

It was that sixth lager that did it.

Five minutes later, as the headline band ambled onto the stage, the room started to spin violently. My stomach lurched.

'Sorry,' I told Heidi, and without waiting for a reply, I made a dash for the nearest exit - the side door.

I only just made it; hurling cheese on toast and six pints of lager all over the pavement in Cheapside. Oh God, throwing up was becoming far too much of a habit.

The Manic Depressives were even louder than The Morbid Morsels, if mercifully a little more musically accomplished. Their thumping bass guitar throbbed in my head. I sat down on the concrete step, allowing the door to swing shut behind me. The street lights were doing a weird little dance; perfectly illuminating the spreading pool of vomit, a yard from my feet.

When I heard the door swing open behind me, I expected to see Heidi standing there, checking up on me. I turned my head; prepared to tell her to go back in and leave me alone. I was surprised to see it wasn't Heidi at all, but Jasmine, Frank Little's gorgeous girlfriend.

'Oh hi,' she said, taken by surprise.

I managed a little wave.

'It's so loud in there isn't it?' she said, wrapping her arms around herself as the cold wind blew up Cheapside.

'Yeah, very,' I muttered.

'It's Tim, isn't it? I'm Jasmine.'

Like I needed telling. She looked stunning, even with Frank's very unflattering duffel coat wrapped around her shoulders.

'Are you OK?' she said taking a step forward.

'One too many,' I smiled.

'Oh, so I see!' she said, cringeing, as she noticed my pavement-pizza.

'Can I get you some water?' she placed her hand on my back, as she spoke.

I shivered. 'No, thanks, I'll be fine in a minute.'

'Shall I get your girlfriend?'

'Uh? Oh, right, Heidi. She's not my girlfriend,' I said for the umpteenth time that evening.

'Oh, sorry, I just assumed...'

'An obvious mistake I suppose. Actually, my real girlfriend just dumped me. Great eh?' I said, letting out a very false sounding laugh. There was a strange prickling sensation at the corner of my eyes.

'Oh, right, sorry,' she said.

Jasmine was crouching next to me now, her arm loosely hanging on my back. She smelt lovely which is more than you could say for me. Her concern sounded genuine. I was touched; I felt really sick and miserable and here was this lovely girl feeling sorry for me. It was too much. I felt my eyes welling. Instinctively, I raised my hands to my face.

'Oh, Tim, come on love, chin up,' Jasmine said, now putting her arm around my shoulder. She rested her head against mine affectionately. Her breath smelt of cigarettes and alcohol.

I think she was slightly tipsy herself although clearly not completely "Brahms" like me.

A tear ran down my cheek. Great. I was crying like a baby in front of one of the sexiest girls I'd ever laid eyes on. Cool Tim. Really Cool.

'Hey, now then! Things aren't that bad surely? There are plenty of other girls out there you know? I bet loads of them are just dying to meet someone like you,' Jasmine said, placing her other hand in mine.

Thank God it wasn't the hand I'd used to cover my mouth when I was being sick. Hers was soft and cool. Just like her.

'Thanks,' I said, wondering what the hell she was on about. She didn't even know me. Mind you, right at that moment that didn't seem to matter in the least. I turned towards her, forcing a smile through my pathetic tears.

She returned my smile, squeezing my hand in hers. Oh God. Frank Little's girlfriend with her coffee coloured skin and big green eyes twinkling in the street light, was really quite stunning.

Then she did something that really surprised me; she leant across the cold concrete step and kissed me on the cheek.

'You'll be fine, just wait and see,' she said.

Well I was absolutely "Brahms" wasn't I? You couldn't really blame me, could you? Yes, you've guessed it. I went and did it. I went and made a really stupid, really clumsy pass at her.

As I moved in to kiss her cherry-red lips, she pulled away in shock, and I ended up kissing the very stale night air.

OK, it was a really dumb thing to do; but in my defence, Jasmine was drop dead sexy, and she was being really sweet to me.

In hindsight, it must have seemed like a bit of a lunge. In fact, I pretty much knocked her off the edge of the step as I leant over, grabbing her leg to stop myself from falling flat on my face as she moved her head away.

'Tim! What are you doing?' she screeched.

There was a gasp from behind us, which made me jump. I looked around. Heidi was stood there, holding the door. It was wide open but not as wide as Heidi's mouth.

'Tim? What's going on?' she asked.

'Er, nothing....'

She looked at me, then at Jasmine, and then, just to prove that things could indeed get even worse, she burst into tears.

Jasmine got up to comfort her.

'Heidi, you've got it all wrong,' Jasmine was saying, 'it was just a misunderstanding.'

'Oh right, you would say that!' Heidi shouted, growing hysterical, 'just because you don't want me to say anything to Frank.'

Oh shit.

'Now hang on Heidi…' I said, feeling suddenly very sober.

Then all hell broke loose.

'Heidi! Tim!' a voice shouted.

The three of us turned in the direction of the shouts; towards the Fine Fare supermarket on the opposite corner of London Road. It was Juliette. She was shouting as she ran around the corner towards us, waving frantically.

'Come quickly! It's Kevin!'

There were other cries coming from around the front of the shop. Suddenly, Clarkey appeared. He was trying to get away from someone who had him by the arm.

'Leave him alone!' Juliette was shouting.

Then Pete and Doddsy appeared around the corner too. Doddsy yanked Clarkey by his jacket sleeve. Clarkey slipped and fell back in a heap on the pavement outside the main entrance to the supermarket. I saw Doddsy stick out a boot and then Pete waded in too, aiming a kick at Clarkey, who had tightened himself up into a ball, like a small, startled, ginger hedgehog.

Juliette was screaming now.

Just as before, I was too drunk and too caught up in the moment, to think about what I was doing. Before I knew it, I was running across Cheapside and throwing myself at Pete. I knocked him off balance and we ended up on the ground in an untidy bundle of arms and legs.

Clarkey was lying feet away; Doddsy standing over him.

Pete tried to grab me but I had a momentary advantage; I was on top of him, my knee on one of his arms. With his spare hand, he aimed a punch at me. I felt a breeze as his fist missed my chin by a fraction of an inch and as I swung my head backwards to avoid contact, I felt arms grab me around the neck from behind. Doddsy jerked me backwards and I fell with a bump on my backside. Doddsy lost his grip on me. As I glanced up, I saw why; Clarkey had jumped on his back and the two of them teetered comically across the pavement, until Doddsy stepped off the kerb and they fell in a heap on the London Road. A passing taxi driver sounded a long, angry warning on his horn. I clambered to my feet and started towards them but Pete stuck out a leg. I tripped over it.

Juliette had flattened herself against the supermarket window, scared out of her wits. She was hysterical. Pete was on his feet now and as I tried to get up, he stuck his knee in my back and pressed me down face first on the cold, hard pavement.

'Get help!' I shouted at Juliette, although I had no idea where she was meant to get it from.

Juliette hesitated, as Pete grabbed a handful of my hair, forcing me to yelp in agony. This seemed to bring Juliette out of her trance. She started running back towards The Northern.

Just then, I heard more shouting; I assumed at first it was Clarkey and Doddsy; my head was twisted back and I couldn't see them. Then I heard the sound of running feet. Pete yanked me up and pushed me against the window; it vibrated nosily and for a moment I thought it might break. He was still holding my hair with one hand and before I knew what had hit me, he punched me hard in the stomach. He let go of my hair and I doubled up.

'Get off him!' a male voice shouted.

Then, I was aware of scuffling by the kerb but I was too badly winded to take it all in. All I could see was Pete's feet and the pavement. I was completely disorientated. My head was spinning. I felt uncomfortably warm and light-headed.

Punching me in the guts really hadn't been Pete's greatest move. Suddenly I heaved and threw up again; even more violently than the first time. Pete stepped back but he was too late. I emptied my sixth pint all over his legs, splattering his jeans and trainers.

'Fuckin' 'ell!' he shouted.

I heard laughing and looked up. Everything seemed out of focus. The shop window merged with the street lights, the twinkling stars and the herds of people standing over me. It was all just a blur.

'Oh, lovely job,' said a familiar voice.

Karl?

'Yeah, nice one mate!' said another voice I recognised.

My vision was all over the place. Dave Booth had three heads and at least two necks.

Eventually when my eyes focused I could see that he was holding Doddsy's arms behind his back. Doddsy struggled but Dave wasn't his only problem. Karl held him by the throat.

Next to me, Clarkey was dusting himself down, whilst laughing like a hyena at the sight of Pete, covered from the waist down in regurgitated Heineken.

Pete looked down at his legs and then up at me; his face a picture of fury. Oh shit.

'Pete, what's going on?' Humph said, as he walked up with Juliette. They were followed by a whole crowd of people from the pub, including Jacko, Fay, Wilf and Heidi. Doddsy continued to thrash around. It was taking the combined strength of both Dave and Karl just to hold him back.

'I'm just about to pummel your little mate's skull in, that's what's happening,' said Pete, grabbing me by the hair again and holding back his fist.

'Bloody hell Pete, they're only kids!' Humph said.

Kids? I'm two days older than you, I thought. Strange; the things that go through your mind when you're about to be "pummeled".

'He threw up all over me!' Pete said, tightening his grip on my fringe. I closed my eyes, braced myself. Nothing happened. Instead Pete's grip slackened.

'Let him go Mackay!'

I opened one eye, then the other.

Humph had wrapped his arm around Pete's neck. Pete looked stunned for a moment; he started wriggling, throwing his elbow back. Humph clearly anticipated this and easily dodged the blow, grabbing and twisting Pete's wrist in one Bruce Lee-like manoeuvre, pushing him to the ground.

'What the bloody hell are you doing?' Pete said, looking up at his mate.

'Something I should have done months ago,' said Humph.

My hero.

It was only then that the pub bouncers finally arrived on the scene. Better late than never I suppose.

Humph made me drink two pints of water.

We sat at the stage bar, neither of us saying much. Heidi hadn't spoken to me after the fracas with Pete and Doddsy. When her Mum came to pick her up at eleven (on the dot), she went home in the car with Juliette, both of them still upset by the evening's events. I wasn't offered a lift. Instead, Dave and Karl, now apparently firm friends again, climbed in the back seat with Clarkey and went with them. Jacko, Fay and Wilf had gone too - apparently off to some club or other on the seafront. I was touched by their concern.

'Great evening mate!' Jacko had said, as they were going, 'you lot were far more entertaining than the band!'

At least I'd made someone's evening.

Slowly, I was starting to sober up. Humph insisted on staying with me until the end of the Manic Depressive's set. The bar had an extension until midnight and most people had buggered off home by the time the band finished their encore. The Manic Depressive's weren't bad actually - although, as I might have anticipated given their chosen name, not exactly a bundle of laughs.

'Well, that was some evening!' Humph laughed as I sipped my second pint of water.

'Yeah, sorry about Pete and Doddsy,' I said, 'I expect work will be a bit tricky on Monday eh?'

'They'll be fine. Anyway, bugger them. They were well out of order.'

'Cheers anyway.'

My shoulder was throbbing and my scalp was sore from where Pete Mackay had yanked me by the hair, but otherwise, I was relatively unscathed. Somehow, I had survived. Cocking up at the football, being dumped by Roxanne, assaulted by Pete and Doddsy, making a clumsy, drunken pass at Jasmine and upsetting Heidi. Even by my sorry standards that had to rank as one of the worst days on record. Still, I suppose if it hadn't have been for Humph, things could have been even worse.

Humph offered to drop me off in his taxi, but he was heading in the wrong direction, so I declined. Besides, I was feeling sorry for myself and fancied some more fresh air. I'd missed the last bus from St. Peters church, so I sat on the bench and took out Roxanne's note.

You're a lovely lad Tim James. I'm sure you will find someone really special.

I folded the note and tore it into pieces, before letting it drift off in the wind up the Lewes Road and burying my aching head in my hands.

'Hello Tiger Tim,' a familiar voice said.

'Alison? What...?'

She placed her hand on my injured shoulder. It made me wince.

'Oops sorry,' she said, sitting down next to me on the bench.

350

'Not a good night then eh?' she said, putting her arm around my shoulder and pulling me into her.

A solitary tear slid down my cheek and on to Alison's shoulder.

'Where's Kong ...er Jez?' I said without looking up.

'Not sure. I think he went home in a taxi with Frank and Jasmine,' she said.

'Really?'

'Yeah, he's OK is Jez, but he's not stupid. We all know he's not the one for me, don't we?'

It was true. I was never exactly going to be a rocket scientist but even I knew that Jez had never stood a chance.

'I've called my Dad. He'll be here in a second. He'll give you a lift too I'm sure.'

'No, that's OK...'

'Shut up Timothy, I'm not leaving you out here to freeze to death.'

I didn't pursue the argument.

'Hey, I'm really sorry about what I said earlier - you know; about Roxanne,' she said, 'I didn't mean it. It was just vodka talk.'

'That's OK, plenty more fish in the sea eh?'

'Yep, just try to avoid the sharks next time though eh?' she laughed, hugging me. She kissed the top of my head. She was so lovely.

It was all I could do not to burst into a flood of tears.

You'd have thought I'd have learnt my lesson after Jasmine and Heidi, but no, I was still capable of doing, or saying, stupid things. It just sort of slipped out.

'I really love you, you know?'

How had I forgotten just how beautiful Alison Fisher was?

'I know you do, and I love you too,' she said, 'and now let's get you home to bed.'

Alison pulled me to my feet, as her Dad's car pulled up at the kerb.

'Heading back to the common room?' Alison asked.

Here we go, time for twenty questions.

'Tim, can you hang behind for a few minutes, so we can catch up on what you've missed?' Candice Morris called out, as I packed my untouched books into my bag.

'Sorry,' I shrugged at Alison, relieved to postpone the grilling I was sure to get from them.

'See you in the canteen for lunch?' Alison said.

'OK,' I agreed reluctantly.

'So, how have you been?' Alison asked, whilst munching on some very unappealing looking salad leaves.

'Not great.'

Blood awful actually. Like there's a hole where my heart used to be.

'What's been wrong?' Sara asked, a small smile playing across her lips.

'Nothing.'

Everything.

'Nothing? You've been off for four days!' Alison said.

'Just a bug.'

And losing the will to live.

'Nothing catching I hope?' Sara said, theatrically leaning away from me.

'No.'

Not unless you're a useless loser.

The girls exchanged glances; Alison picking at her lettuce; Sara devouring a jumbo sausage- roll.

'So..' Alison started, gazing into the middle distance.

Here we go.

'...heard anything from Roxanne?'

Just as I thought.

'What do you think?'

'And have you tried to contact her?' Sara said, her mouth full of half-chewed pastry, crumbs falling on the formica table top.

I shook my head, pushing my egg mayonnaise sandwich away. I couldn't face it.

'I think you should...' Alison started.

'Think I should what?' I snapped.

'Eat!' she pushed my sandwich back under my nose.

'Not hungry,' I mumbled.

We sat in silence for a few moments.

'So, you're not going to call her then?' Sara said.

I gave her a look.

'You really should you know,' Alison added.

'What's the point?'

'You should tell her how you feel.'

'So you said.'

'And?'

'Don't you think it might be a bit late?' I said sarcastically, 'you know what with her being ever-so-slightly engaged to be married?'

'Well it would be better to tell her now than waiting 'til she's actually married,' Sara shot straight back.

'Yeah, I'll just wait until the big day, creep into the back of the church and do my best impersonation of Dustin Hoffman in The Graduate shall I?'

'Eh?'

'It should have been me!' I pretended to shout down an imaginary aisle.

Sara smirked.

Alison just shook her head.

'All we're saying is that you should talk to her. You'll kick yourself if you don't.'

I certainly felt like kicking *someone*.

After lunch, I couldn't face English Lit. Instead, I slumped down on one of the old sofas in the common room and caught up with the latest pop and rock gossip. The "Record Mirror" being infinitely preferable to a discussion on Shylock and his pound of flesh. Shakespeare had lost the very little appeal he had ever had for me.

"Sting; The Present Day God" the article read.

Apparently, my hero was taking a break from touring to play the part of an angel in a TV play; he had apparently been chosen for the part because the director regarded him as a "present day God". He was currently filming in Denmark before heading back to work on the new Police album to be released later in the year.

I put the magazine aside, stretched and stood up, staring out at a seemingly never-ending grey sky. Someone opened a locker behind me and I caught sight of my face, reflected in the rain-spattered window. My zits were back with a vengeance and you could cook chips in my hair. My face looked like someone had been sleeping in it - which was ironic, as I hadn't been sleeping at all myself.

Present Day God. Why hadn't the TV director chap called me for the part, I wondered?

Probably for the same reason that the girl I was obsessed with had dumped me for a chinless wonder.

'Where were you?' Alison said as she breezed through the door at the end of the English Lit lesson. She slung her bag over the PVC covered sofa and jumped into the seat next to me, letting her long legs rest in my lap. In the past that might have presented me with an embarrassing little problem but I was so depressed I couldn't even muster an unwanted below-stairs salute.

'Des was asking after you.'

Des Manthorpe was our English teacher. He was OK was Des, in a slightly odd upper-class- twit sort of way. I did feel a little bit guilty - but not much.

'Don't worry I covered for you. Told him you'd hurried back to school too soon. So don't forget when he asks where you were - you had a relapse, OK?'

I mumbled a begrudging 'thanks'.

'Aren't you lucky to have a mate like me Mr. James?' she said, leaning over and punching me playfully on the arm.

'Am I?'

'Too bloody right you are! Not everyone would tell your teacher lies for you.'

'S'pose not.'

'So, you've been moping around in here all afternoon have you?' she said, standing with her hands on her hips.

'I am *not* moping.'

'Oh, what do you call it then? Feeling sorry for yourself; missing lessons just to stare out of windows? It seems pretty much like moping to me.'

I don't know what came over me but I wasn't standing, or sitting, for that.

'Well you should know about moping if anyone should. You've done it for months.'

Of course, I felt lousy as soon as I'd said it.

Alison's face dropped.

'Thanks. I suppose I asked for that?' She picked up her bag; started to walk away; turned back. She looked angry.

I wanted to say sorry but for some reason my mouth wouldn't move. Perhaps Mum had been right all along; I'd pulled a face once too many times, and it had finally stuck that way.

'OK, well, as I'm clearly such an expert, take some advice Tim. Moping doesn't help with anything. Either go and talk to her or ..,' she hesitated.

'Or what?' I said, finally forcing my sulky mouth to form actual words.

'Or find someone else to lie to Des for you.'

I hadn't consciously decided to head into Brighton.

It was only after the school bus had pulled away from my stop, and I found myself still on board, that I realised that's where I was heading. Even then, when it pulled in at Churchill Square, I hesitated. I seemed to have actually lost the power to make any sort of decision whatsoever. Then, just as the last kid traipsed off and the bus lurched to pull away, I sprang to my feet and made a mad dash for it before the driver could close the door.

Once the bus had pulled away behind me, I stood there on the busy pavement like a complete lemon, whilst crowds of people bustled by, going about their everyday business. I stared off into the middle distance, as if waiting for some divine intervention to urge my feet to carry me in one direction or the other. Eventually, they must have kicked into auto-pilot, because before I knew why or how, I found myself in my usual position, nose pressed up against the glass of the HMV shop front. I thought of that line from the Talking Heads song; *'Well, how did I get here?'*

And more to the point, what was I actually going to do now?

For once, the shop wasn't busy. The staff outnumbered the customers. There was no obvious sign of Roxanne on the shop floor. Of course, she could have been out back in the stockroom, or upstairs,

355

advising some idiot on what Country & Western cassette to send to his fictitious pen-pal. But, of course, it was easier to tell myself she wasn't there and walk away. So, that's exactly what I did.

Yet again, I noticed that even if my brain hadn't consciously decided where to go, my feet knew exactly where I was heading. So, there I was, twenty minutes later, trudging up St. James Street towards my inevitable destination; Upper Rock Gardens - Roxanne's street.

And before I knew it, there I stood; hands in pockets, gazing up the road, towards her flat.

Mentally, I counted off the houses in my head and from a distance, identified the familiar painted black railings. OK, now what?

I didn't need to provide an answer. As I stared at the gap in the railings where her steps led down to the basement flat, a man appeared, carrying a large cardboard box. I was maybe fifty feet away but I could see him quite clearly.

I realised in that moment that I'd never actually seen him before, yet somehow I knew instantly that this was Rob. Tall, well-built, long, lank Johnny Ramone hair, leather biker jacket and a Desperate Dan jaw, covered with Bob Geldof stubble. Not so chinless after all then?

Any doubt I may have had about the identity of this fit young man, who had now disappeared with his cardboard box, around the back of a white Transit van, was dispelled by the presence of the pretty, petite red-headed girl who emerged from the stairs behind him. She was wearing the very pixie boots I'd thrown up on in Churchill Square before Christmas. And she was carrying the same box of pots and pans I'd helped her move from her Mum's garage in Weybridge. She was laughing and joking with her fiance. She looked really happy.

For a split second, she started to turn towards me.

I felt sure she would see me.

Then the open door of the van caught in the wind and knocked the box from her hands. Pots and pans clanked on the pavement as she stooped in an attempt to catch them. Her boyfriend came dashing over to her, nearly tripping on the kerb. As he stumbled and stuck a leg out to steady himself, his booted foot stepped into the largest saucepan and wedged there. He clumsily lifted his foot with the saucepan still dangling from his leg. The two of them laughed and laughed as Rob hammed it up; hopping around the pavement in his new aluminium footwear, like a demented dancing robot.

I couldn't help but smile myself.

356

He looked like he didn't take himself too seriously, this Rob guy. The sort of bloke I could probably get on with.

For a few moments, I watched them, making fun of each other, as they bent down to retrieve the kitchenware that would no doubt take up pride of place in the new they were presumably about to set up together.

I suddenly felt self-conscious standing there.

So, I turned and headed back around the corner and down St. James Street, to the nearest bus stop.

Part Two
Six Months later

29 - Darkness

'Maybe you should try being a shirt-lifter?'

I screwed up my face; shuddered comically for effect, and took another sip from my pint.

'You might have more luck that way. There's a poofy lad on campus. Dafydd Thomas; "Flower" we call him. He looks a bit like you; big eyes, cute bum. He gets plenty of action. I think you would too, if your bread was buttered that way.'

'You're really not helping,' I said, although to be fair, my cousin Joanne had at least put a smile on my face - albeit a slightly uncomfortable one - which was something.

'Yeah, you'd make a good shirt-lifter,' she cackled in her lilting Welsh accent. She always sounded like she was going to break into song any minute. I reckon that's why my brain always does that irritating thing when I listen to my Welsh relations talking; turning what they said into a little jingle, which goes around and around in my head and refuses to budge. This time it was to the tune of "Hey Big Spender" by Shirley Bassey, which was appropriate I suppose.

"Hey shirt-lifter, lift a little shirt with me.."

'I mean, think of it this way. You'd be doing us sisters a favour too - sort of helping to balance the numbers out. After all, if there were only loads of us dykes and not an equal number of shirt-lifters, by my reckoning, there'd be a huge surplus of horny young hetero men, jerking themselves to death.'

'You've always had a way with words Jo.'

The stud in her nose caught the light as she laughed.

'Don't get me wrong though. Some of my best friends at Uni are pillow-munchers, so they are. They don't mind me having a laugh at their expense either. They've got a far better sense of humour than you uptight straights.'

'Perhaps they've more to laugh about,' I muttered into my beer.

'Exactly. Perhaps that's why you should give it a go. Don't knock it until you try it, that's my motto.'

I just shook my head; smiled.

'Fancy another?' I said, picking up my empty glass.

'Go easy Tiger, the night is young!'

'Well, I'm getting myself one anyway,' I said, rising from my seat.

Jo's hand clutched my arm, dragged me down.

'Seriously, pace yourself will you? You're drinking way too much, don't you think?'

'Who's counting?' I said, shrugging her off and heading towards the bar.

In truth, I wouldn't be drinking much more tonight - this was the last of my paper-round money - but I didn't like Jo, or my Mum and Dad, or anyone else for that matter, telling me I was drinking too much. It was my life. Or 'my funeral' as my Dad was fond of reminding me.

The Peds was its usual bustling self, for a Friday night. The clientele was almost into double figures. Fred had been doing a crossword as I strolled up, waving my empty glass.

'Same again Tim?' he said, throwing his paper on the bar, 'you're knocking them back a bit tonight aren't you?

Don't *you* start.

'Where are the others tonight? I haven't seen them for a while.'

'Girlfriends,' I said, like it was a dirty word.

'Ah!' Fred said knowingly, 'well, you look like you're doing alright for yourself on that score,' Fred continued to pull my pint whilst gesturing over to where Joanne was sitting.

'Very nice,' he winked.

'My cousin.'

'Ah well, no harm in keeping it in the family eh?' he laughed.

I looked over at Jo. She waved.

'A real looker though eh?' Fred said, 'I can certainly see the family resemblance.'

It was an odd thing to say. I often wondered about Fred.

The usual builders were sitting at the end of the bar. I could see them giving my cute cousin the eye. Best of luck there boys.

With her big brown eyes and her Siouxsie Sioux hair, and in her black PVC dress-cum-bin-liner, Jo was certainly striking - in an unconventional, punky sort of way.

'Fifty-five new pence,' Fred said.

'Bloody hell Fred, have you put the prices up?' I dug deep into my pockets.

He smirked. 'Maybe you should buy a round more often?'

'I'll get it Rothschild,' said Jo, appearing at my elbow, 'as long as it's the last one, OK? I'll have a Vodka and Lime please.'

'OK lovey, coming up,' Fred smiled.

'What are you, my mother or something?' I asked Jo.

'She's worried.'

'About what?'

'About you, stupid!'

'Why?'

'Well, for one thing, you're drinking half your body-weight in lager most weeks.'

'Huh, I wish! If only I could afford it.'

Fred plonked the drinks down in front of us.

Jo paid the man and we shuffled back to the privacy of our corner table.

'You could have done something radical like getting yourself a proper summer job, like every other sixth former in the country, instead of lying around in your room, feeling sorry for yourself and cultivating your zits.'

'I tried,' I said defensively, covering my spotty chin with my hand, 'there was nothing decent around. It was either shelf-filling at Fine Fare or collecting the trolleys in Sainsburys' car park.'

'Ah, the temporary brain surgeon positions were all taken were they?'

'What?'

'For Christ's sake Tim, just what were you expecting as a summer job? The Police's road manager? Warm-up man for Morecambe and Wise?'

'Toyah's personal dresser?' I suggested.

Jo was trying not to smile. She was trying to play the older, wiser cousin and I wasn't playing along.

'So, is that the reason for your sudden unannounced visit then? Did my mum drag you all the way down from Pembroke just to give me a pep talk? Does she think you're my guardian angel?'

'No, don't be silly.'

'After all, you'll be back down in six weeks for the wedding of the year.'

'I think Charlie and Di might have something to say about that description, don't you?' Jo smirked.

Prince Charles and Diana Spencer had married back in July. Even now, nearly two months later, the papers were still full of it.

'Well, true. I suppose St. Mary Magdalene's church is not exactly St. Paul's Cathedral is it?'

'No, and I don't suppose the royal couple held their reception at Denton Community hall either.'

'No, they tried, but it was already booked up. Denton Under 12's annual awards ceremony.'

'Ah well, never mind. Charlie and Di probably don't know enough people to fill it anyway, do they?'

Joanne sipped on her vodka, whilst checking on her black lipstick in a cracked vanity mirror.

'But you will be down for Princess Cheryl and Prince Lee won't you?' I asked.

'Of course.'

'So why come down now?'

'Well for one thing, it's the summer holidays. Everyone's left Cardiff for the summer and it was either holidaying with my favourite cousin in Brighton or hanging around my old haunts in Pembroke. It wasn't a tough choice. And anyway, for another thing....' her voice trailed off.

'And for another thing?'

'Well, if you must know, I needed some space from Cerys. Things have been a bit...claustrophobic.'

'Love's young dream wearing off is it?'

'Mind your own business.'

'Huh, that's rich coming from you, Marjorie Proops!'

Jo laughed.

'Seriously though, "Cerys" - couldn't you have found someone a bit more Welsh sounding?' I sniggered with sarcasm.

'You don't know the least of it - her surname's Jones-Evans.'

I spluttered on a mouthful of lager.

'Couldn't she find room for Williams in there somewhere too?'

'That's her step-dad's name. She did try.'

How we laughed.

'So, Cardiff's exciting is it?'

'By Welsh standards yeah, it's OK.'

'And what's this Cerys like?'

'Gay. But you're welcome to have stab at converting her. She'll be coming down for the wedding.'

'Really?'

'Yeah, she's got to meet the family sometime.'

'Phew. That's brave.'

'Yeah. I think I've got more reason for hitting the bottle than you, don't you?'

'Maybe, I suppose.'

Jo had finally come out to her Mum and Dad before she'd gone off to Uni the previous summer. Other than her immediate family, I was the only other person she'd confided in. No-one else knew - officially. By the sounds of it, my sister's wedding was going to put paid to that. She'd met Cerys Jones-Evans in fresher week. They'd been together ever since.

'So, what about you then? Do you fancy the Uni idea?'

'Huh, fat chance. The way my end of year exams went, I'm not sure I'll even be going back to the upper sixth.'

'Well, that's just plain stupid.'

'Is it? Humph and Jacko seem to be having a whale of a time working for a living.'

'They're only a couple of bankers.'

'Only Jacko works in a bank. Humph doesn't.'

'Who was talking about their jobs?'

'Oh, boom-boom.'

'Really though? You can't possibly envy them? Stuck behind a counter, shuffling paper or freezing your 'nads off on a building site. Have you thought it through? What are you going to do?'

'And what's the option? Another three or four years of studying and being skint?'

'You'll be working long enough. What's the hurry?'

'You sound like my Dad.'

'As long as I don't look like him.'

The conversation fell into another pause. It was so quiet in the bar, you could hear the clock ticking. Some Friday night - we were living the dream.

'So, talking of Humph. What's going on with him and the lovely Alison these days?'

'Seeing each other again.'

'Really?'

'Just friends apparently.'

'Yeah, right,' Jo raised her eyebrows; shook her head.

'And what about you?'

'What about me?'

'Still buying your records from Virgin are you?'

That made me smile.

'They're cheaper.' I said.

'Cheaper or safer?'

'Touche.'

'You'd better watch out or you'll be "shopping at Virgin" (she made speech mark signs with her fingers) for the rest of your life.'

'Very droll.'

'Well all I'm saying is that if you made a bit more effort, you know, rediscovered shampoo and your Mum's washing machine, used a bit of Clearasil now and then, you'd have no trouble finding someone else.'

'What makes you think I want someone else?'

'Emily's still got a crush on you.'

Emily was Jo's little sister. Last time I saw her, she was showing promise. She could do with losing a few more pounds and the braces on her teeth, but she was certainly turning into a bit of a looker.

'Is she, you know?'

'Is she another closet dyke do you mean? I don't think so somehow. Tony Hadley and Adam Ant all over her walls.'

'Single. I was going to say "is she single?"' Has she got a boyfriend?

'As far as I know, the last time I heard - no.'

I shrugged and went back to my beer.

'You could always take her to the wedding as your plus one.'

I groaned.

'I take it you are taking a guest?'

'Hadn't even thought about it.'

For once I wasn't being evasive. I really hadn't.

'Well, like I said, there's always Flower.'

'Uh?'

'Dafydd Thomas,' she winked, raising her glass, 'he'd be up for it.'

30 - Invisible Sun

'Sting's finally realised that the little girls have got Adam Ant now; they don't need him anymore.'

'What?' said Clarkey, sitting bolt upright on the end of the bed,'who *is* this prick?'

'Shh!' I told him again.

Clarkey's timing was lousy. I'd been waiting all week for this show and he'd gone and shown up unannounced, just as Kid Jensen finished introducing the song, and had instantly started babbling on about what he was going to wear to Cheryl's reception (Clarkey, not Kid - he hadn't been invited). As if I cared what Clarkey was going to bloody wear!

Kid Jensen's "Round Table" was required listening. Ever Friday tea-time I'd tune in to Radio 1 as Kid played the week's new releases. Then a panel of guests would debate whether they were any good. It was a sort of radio version of "Juke Box Jury". I loved it; it was one of the highlights of my week.

The previous week Kid had made a huge thing of the fact that this week he'd be playing the brand new Police song; the first single from their forthcoming album.

I'd been preparing ever since I'd got home from college; adjusting the recoding level on my tape deck, winding my brand new C90 tape to just the right place, pressing the "record" and "pause" buttons to capture the opening bars the moment Kid stopped talking.

'And here it is as promised, the very first national radio air-play for the brand new Police single; from their forthcoming album, "Ghost In The Machine", this is called "Invisible Sun"...'

And Clarkey chose that precise moment to ring our doorbell. I could have killed him - or Mum, for telling him to "go on up" - now, I wasn't sure if I'd pressed the record button at the right moment or if I'd missed the first few seconds. If I'd missed the start, I'd swing for bloody Clarkey.

The single wasn't being released in the shops for another week or so - I wanted to make sure I captured every second, so I could listen to it over and over again. Everyone at school would be talking about it on Monday.

The song had shut Clarkey right up. We'd both sat there gobsmacked. It wasn't anything like we were expecting; "Invisible Sun" certainly wasn't one of Sting's usual songs of heartbreak and angst, like "So Lonely" or "Message in A Bottle". There were none of the band's trademark reggae rhythms. Instead, the song was dark and moody, with Sting counting menacingly up to six, over an intro that built slowly to verses all about the troubles in Northern Ireland. The lyrics contained references to guns and killing. I was shocked but thrilled. When the song had finally reached it's brooding end, I'd left the tape running to capture the comments of Kid and his guests.

'And he's stopped singing in that silly high pitched voice and the cod-Jamaican accent,' the controversial guest continued.

'This geezer's an absolute toss-pot!' said Clarkey.

'It's Elvis Costello,' I said.

Clarkey's mouth fell open.

'Really?'

'Yes!' I said, putting my finger to my lips.

Elvis Costello was one of our heroes. It was weird to hear him bitching about a fellow performer.

'Must be jealousy,' Clarkey whispered, 'hasn't had a hit in a while, has he?'

'He's doing Country and Western now. He was saying earlier. They played his new single too.'

'Country and Western? He's lost the plot. No wonder he's jealous!'

'It was OK actually,' I said, turning the volume up on the radio, to drown out Clarkey's running commentary.

'That's actually a really good moody piece of music,' Costello continued.

'Well, that's something, I suppose,' Clarkey said.

I looked around the room for something to use as a gag. The look on my face seemed to do the trick though. Clarkey finally shut up, whilst Kid revealed that he'd seen a sneak preview of the video for "Invisible Sun". Apparently, it contained "stark black and white newsreel" of the troubles; he also added that there were rumours that it would be banned by the BBC.

'It'll still be number 1,' Clarkey observed.

'Hope so. Tainted Love seems to have been number one forever,' I pointed out.

'Well, it's much better than that new Adam & The Ants rubbish. Prince Charming? He's sold out big time. And Costello's never going to have a hit with ruddy Country and Western is he?'

I wasn't listening. I was busy re-winding the tape. It whirled to the start and I eagerly pressed "play". Fortunately for Clarkey, I'd caught the beginning. I'd leave off killing him for another occasion.

'So, I'm really looking forward to the reception tomorrow.'

'Really?' I said, still not really listening.

Sting was counting the song in again.

'Yeah, it'll be ace. Thanks again for inviting me.'

Clarkey seemed really chuffed that I'd invited him to Cheryl and Lee's reception as my "plus one". I didn't like to point out that he had been far from my first choice - although, judging by his line of questioning, he'd pretty much worked that out for himself.

'Shame about Jacko being away,' he said.

'Ah well, he'd probably have shown me up anyway,' I said.

Jacko had gone on holiday with Fay and her parents - to Gran Canaria - wherever that was.

'And you didn't want to invite Humph?'

We'd already had this conversation - at least twice.

'Hardly ever see him these days.'

It was true. Humph was either out with his work mates or seeing Alison. They seemed to be giving it another go. So, I could hardly invite one, without the other. And my invitation said "Plus guest" - not "guest loved-up couple".

'And you're sure there's no-one else you'd rather take along?'

'Of course not,' I said, trying to keep the growing irritation from my voice. Right at that moment, just about anyone would have been preferable. Did he ever shut up? I was trying to listen to the bloody song.

It had been a bit of a quandary who to invite but as it turned out, I'd sort of arrived at Kevin Clarke due to a process of elimination. Jacko was away, Humph off the scene and Alison strictly out of bounds again. Dave, as always, was doing something with Juliette. I didn't like to ask. Karl and his family were visiting his Mum's relatives in Germany. It wasn't like I'd been left with a lot of choice.

'No girls you could ask?' Clarkey continued.

'Given them up for lent.'

I tried turning up the volume again but he wasn't taking the hint.

'What about Heidi Bloom?' Clarkey checked his reflection in my wardrobe door mirror.

'What *about* Heidi Bloom*?'*

'You could ask her.'

I stood behind him, gave him a look in the mirror.

'What?' he said, 'After all, she's a fifth year now.'

'Yes, and I'm in the Upper Sixth. The age gap hasn't got any less over the last few months you know.'

I gave up on "Invisible Sun"; pressed pause. It could wait for later, when big mouth had gone home.

'Hey, I was listening to that,' he said.

'Chance would be a fine thing,' I muttered, pressing 'rewind'.

'She really likes you,' Clarkey ran his fingers through his hair, making it stand up like a cock's comb.

I smirked at his reflection.

'She does *not,'* I said, 'not after the Northern fiasco.'

'According to Karl she still *really* likes you. She's had other offers. She's turned them down. Still pining for the great Tim James apparently,' Clarkey twirled his finger around in a small circle, near his left temple, signifying that he thought Heidi was clearly bonkers.

He was full of it was Clarkey. Still, I couldn't help feeling a bit smug. If Heidi Bloom was a bit older...

'Are you trying to talk yourself out of an invite?' I asked him.

'No, not at all. I'm just saying, that's all.'

'Yeah, and you're like a broken record - turn it over, the B-side must be more interesting.'

Clarkey continued to ponce around with his barnet.

'I'm having it done tomorrow morning.'

'Bloody hell, it's my sister who's getting married, not you!'

'I think I'm going to take in the cover of "Scary Monsters"; ask them to copy Bowie's cut.'

'Scary Monster sounds about right.'

'Jealousy will get you nowhere,' he laughed.

He sat back on the bed, picked up my guitar, which was gathering dust in the corner.

'Did you hear about Karl's new band?' he asked.

'Yeah, I heard a rumour. He's gone all New Romantic hasn't he?'

'Yeah. But it's only him and a couple of the blokes from The Morbid Morsels. In fact, all they've done is ditched the hippy

369

drummer. They're calling themselves the Men Machine now, you know after the Kraftwerk album?'

'Can any of them play synths? They need to play synths to be proper New Romantics don't they?'

'They're advertising. Haven't you seen the poster up in the Common Room? "Keyboard player required. Must have own synthesizer"'

'That's just ridiculous. Where are they going to find someone with a synth at Denton?'

'Julie Wise is interested apparently. She can play the piano.'

'Julie Wise? The really big girl?'

'That's her. Dave says she looks like she's *swallowed* a piano,'

'Harsh,' I said, smirking, 'but she would look a bit out of place in Ultravox.'

Clarkey smiled; went back to plucking the guitar.

'So, how about you?'

'Me? Play the synth?'

'No,' he said, strumming the strings, 'I meant how are the lessons going?'

'They're not. My dad only paid for five for Christmas. I can't afford any more. I haven't had a lesson since April.'

'You're always skint. Don't you think you should get a Saturday job?'

'Don't *you* start. I've had enough of that from my family.'

'They're advertising in HMV.'

'You must be joking!'

'Why? You'd love that; all those cheap albums. You could play records all day to your heart's content and actually get paid for it.'

When he put it like that, it did sound quite appealing.

'Aren't you forgetting something?' I said.

Clarkey looked down at his feet.

'Hasn't Karl told you what Poppy said?' he asked.

'Told me what?'

He looked dead uncomfortable.

'What Clarkey? What hasn't Karl told me?'

'She's left. She's gone to Uni.'

The tape finished re-winding.

All of a sudden, I wasn't bothered about hearing it again.

'Yeah,' Clarkey continued, 'Leeds apparently, or so Poppy reckons.'

'So that's your type is it?' Joanne whispered in my ear, as I filled my paper plate from the wedding buffet, watching Clarkey fill his mouth with mini Scotch Eggs, at the far end of the long trestle table, ' he's not as butch as my friend Daffyd, but if that's what lights your candle.'

'Very funny Jo, you should be on the stage.'

'No fair play though love, at least you're out of that closet.'

'Excuse me whilst I repair my splitting sides.'

Jo munched on an egg sandwich.

'So, I understand you decided to do the sensible thing and get back to school then?' she said, as we stood, watching kids chasing each other around the edge of the dance floor.

'Like you said, I'll be working long enough. What's the hurry?'

And what I didn't say was, 'besides, I had no idea what else I wanted to do.'

Cheryl glided by; a huge smile on her face; the train of her satin wedding dress, trailing through discarded paper hats and streamers.

'What did you think of the service?' I asked Jo.

'It was a wedding. What can I say?'

Yep, that pretty much summed it up, I suppose. I'd pretty much yawned my way through the whole thing.

'Cheryl looks... happy,' Jo said, watching her newly married cousin as she chit-chatted to a long lost uncle, 'not so sure about the mechanic though.'

'Lee's OK. You just have to get to know him,' I said, glancing over to the dance floor where the groom and several of his mates were attempting to dance to a Michael Jackson song.

They all looked slightly pissed - mind you, I doubted whether any of them would have been up there if they hadn't had a drink or five. It was pretty embarrassing to watch. Michael might have been blaming it on the boogie - my bet was on the Stella Artois.

'He's not exactly a looker is he?' Jo observed.

'Cheryl says his face is lived-in,' I laughed.

'He should get an eviction order,' Jo said.

We watched my new brother-in-law dancing like a badly-wired Kenwood Chef.

'He does....you know, know that I'm....you know....*with* Cerys, doesn't he? Only he keeps trying to hit on her.'

'He'll probably work it out eventually - give him a year or two.'

'Poor Cheryl.'

We stood at the edge of the dance floor. My Dad had just dragged my Aunt Sylvia - Jo's mum - up to dance. They appeared to be jiving to Disco music. Jo and I exchanged glances. It was hard to say which of us was more mortified.

I spotted Jo's Welsh girlfriend across the dance-floor. One of Lee's mechanic mates was hovering around her now; trying to impress her by strutting his funky stuff. Silly sod.

'She's very....pretty,' I said.

And she was - in a slightly goofy, long-limbed way. She reminded me of Dee Hepburn, the "Gregory's Girl" actress.

'Thanks. Don't sound so surprised. We don't all look like Marty Feldman in drag you know.'

Clarkey wandered over, his plate piled to the ceiling.

'Love what you've done with your hair,' Jo told him.

'Thanks,' Clarkey said, preening himself with his spare hand. He'd put gel in his red hair and brushed it back. He looked even more of a cock than usual.

'Think's he's the Thin White Duke,' I muttered from the side of my mouth.

'Thin White Puke more like,' Jo muttered back.

I almost choked on my sausage roll.

'So,' said Clarkey turning to Jo, 'your sister...?' he gestured over to Emily, who was dancing with her Dad.

'No, she's not gay,' Jo said, 'don't worry, it doesn't run in the family.'

'No,' spluttered Clarkey, blushing, 'I just wondered if she's, you know, seeing anyone?'

'Blimey, you've got a rival,' Jo said, grinning at me.

'Oh, are you....interested in your *cousin* then?' Clarkey asked, a sarcastic emphasis on the word 'cousin'.

'No, don't be silly. Go for it. Ask her to dance.'

Clarkey gulped as he studied Emily across the dance-floor. She was one of Cheryl's bridesmaids. She used to be chubby when she was a kid, but she'd really blossomed. She looked very grown up today, in her shocking pink dress, with the huge puffed sleeves.

'But be careful,' laughed Jo, 'she might bite; you could get an electric shock!'

Right on cue, Emily looked over and smiled, flashing her braces at us. She did look nice in that dress though. If Clarkey didn't ask her to dance in a minute...huh, who was I kidding? I wasn't nearly pissed enough to dance. Yet.

An hour later, Clarkey and I were pogoing along to The Undertones and "Teenage Kicks".

I was as Brahms as the proverbial newt.

And I needed the loo.

It was as I was coming out of the gents, wondering if the splashes on my black shoes were visible to anyone else, that I quite literally bumped into the chief bridesmaid.

'Oh, sorry!' I said, as we collided in the doorway.

'Tim!'

'Stacey!'

There was an awkward silence. I had sudden, disturbing visions of hot soup and calamine lotion.

'So, how are you?' I finally managed to say.

'OK, thanks,' she smiled.

Her bottle-blonde hair was piled up in a bun on the back of her head; ringlets dropping down into her eyes. She would have looked gorgeous even if I was sober. Thanks to my mate Carlsberg, she was possibly the best looking bridesmaid in the world.

'Nice dress,' I smiled.

'Do you think so?' she said, looking down at the floor-length pink creation, 'not really me though is it?'

I laughed. 'No, but a micro-mini skirt might have been a little inappropriate today, don't you think?'

'Cheeky!' she grinned, 'probably true though.'

We both laughed, a little too self-consciously. There was another lull in the conversation. I looked over her shoulder, looking for an escape route. She didn't seem in a hurry to move on.

I couldn't think of anything to say. Then I remembered her boyfriend.

'How's Mehmet?'

'He's history,' she shrugged, trying to look as if she couldn't care less. Her bottom lip wobbled, betraying her true feelings on the matter.

'Oh, sorry. I had no idea. I did wonder why he wasn't around.'

'Sunning it up in the mediterranean somewhere, with some bimbo or other on his arm I should think.'

'Oh right, sorry.'

'He was a jerk anyway.'

'Sorry...'

'Stop saying "'sorry"!' she laughed, 'good riddance to bad rubbish, that's what I say. Fancy a dance with the chief bridesmaid?' she grabbed my arm.

Apparently, it had been a rhetorical question. All of a sudden, I didn't feel that drunk anymore. I started to protest, but there was no escaping her clutches. She led me back to the dance-floor, wrapping her arms around my waist. Then, to everyone else's amusement, Stacey Groves started to slow-dance me through "Hurry Up Harry" by Sham 69. The girl knew no shame.

I wouldn't have thought it possible for one person to put a tongue that far down another person's throat. It felt as if Stacey was trying to ensnare my internal organs and yank them out. I was gasping by the time she finally let me up for air. The taxi driver shot me a look in the rear view mirror. All I could see were raised eyebrows - I wasn't sure if he was shocked or amused; probably a bit of both. As I had begun to sober up, I'd started to wonder if I'd made the right decision by accepting her invitation. Not that she'd really given me that much choice.

We'd danced to the slowies at the end of the evening. One of them, the Fern Kinney song, had made me think of Roxanne. For a few moments, I felt miserable, but then I thought 'what the hell' and decided it was time I moved on.

Stacey Groves was awful. Somehow, whilst we were dancing, in the middle of a packed dance floor, she had managed to get her hand down the back of my suit trousers and given my bum a playful squeeze through my pants. Thankfully, no-one seemed to be paying Stacey's hands, or my bruised arse, too much attention.

Lee and Cheryl danced, entwined, in the centre of the floor. Lee looked knackered, but Cheryl was still full of beans - or Pernod more like. She looked raring to go. Poor Lee. Or lucky Lee, depending on your perspective.

To my left, Clarkey was dancing with Emily, a stupid grin on his face. The cat that had got the cream. Emily looked happy enough though. She was laughing at his jokes and didn't seem too bothered by the stray hand that had crept down to rest on the huge pink bow on the backside of her bridesmaid dress. Mum and Dad were up, so were my Aunts and Uncles; even my Grandparents were boogieing on-down.

During David Soul's "Don't Give Up On Us Baby", Stacey pressed her body as close to mine as it was humanly possible to get, without actually being a siamese twin. We weren't really dancing as such. We were sort of leaning on each other, like the couples in that film, *They Shoot Horses Don't They?*. We turned around and around in an ever decreasing circle, underneath one of the mirrored disco balls, which had been suspended from the dusty old beams of Denton Community Hall. I began to feel ever so slightly sick.

'Hey, guess what?' she shouted in my ear, as David Soul crooned on about there still being a little love left.

'What?' I said.

'I'm staying in Brighton tonight. At Eve's place.'

Eve was the salon manager at the shop where Cheryl and Stacey worked. I'd heard Cheryl moaning about her enough times to know that.

'Oh right, Eve. Which one is she?' I glanced around at the mass of smooching couples.

'She's not here. She's in Benidorm with her mate Chrystal. They're away for a fortnight. I'm house-sitting.'

'Oh great. Easier than getting back to Burgess Hill.'

'Yeah. Means I can get dead drunk and not worry.'

I'd never have noticed.

'The house is brilliant,' she went on, 'all mod cons - huge colour TV, video, microwave, the lot. And best of all....,' Stacey glanced around, then pressed her mouth right up to my face so that her breath tickled my ear, '...she's got a huge double bed.'

'Oh, great,' I said, slow on the uptake as usual. I hadn't yet grasped the full implications of what, or why, she was telling me.

'It's much too big for one.'

'Huh,' I gulped, 'like The Bed's Too Big Without You.'

'What?'

'You know, The Police song?'

'Never heard of it.'

375

Bloody hell. Why did really sexy girls like Stacey never have any taste in music?

'Fancy keeping me company?' she said.

'Eh?'

'It'd be much snugger with two,' she said, her eyes twinkling, the colour rising in her cheeks.

'Oh, yeah, right...brilliant.'

Sodding hell.

Lee hadn't even finished making his drunken "thank you" speech, at the end of the evening, when Stacey dragged me over to the cloakroom to retrieve our coats.

'I've phoned a taxi,' she'd explained.

'Cool,' I said.

Oh. My. God.

I blinked, rubbed my eyes. A searing pain shot across the back of my eyes. I lifted my head from the pillow. Bad mistake. Laid back down. Told myself not to move. The pain went away if I kept my eyelids closed and kept my eyeballs perfectly still.

A few moment passed; I lifted my head again. Winced. Put my head back. Nice soft pillow.

There were clues everywhere, but still, it took me a few moments to remember where I was.

It was too dark and the light from the gap in the curtains was coming from the wrong direction.

Why wasn't I wearing pyjamas?

The pillow didn't smell right. Perfume. Pernod. Cigarettes.

Oh.....OH!

Yeah.

Right.

The wedding reception.

The taxi.

Stacey Groves.

Eve's house.

And then flashes came back to me; like a film trailer montage; edited highlights; an action replay but without the slow motion. The taxi journey through Brighton; Stacey's eager tongue darting in and out of my mouth. Stacey fumbling for door keys, giggling. Walking

376

into a strange flat, butterflies in my stomach. Shifting nervously on a leather sofa, a kettle being boiled in the kitchen. Managing precisely two sips of coffee before that tongue was at it again. Frenzied necking, whoopee-cushion farts as flesh met leather. The warmth of her skin on my fingers. My shirt being unbuttoned, heart beating like a mad-thing, clothes being ripped off, being dragged to the bedroom - pink, girly bedroom; being pushed back onto the bed. The unfamiliar sensation of flesh on flesh; seeing Stacey - a real, live, warm-blooded woman - absolutely naked - blood rushing to my head and then heading south. Soft curves being pressed against me. Worrying if I would be up to the job; would I know what to do and when to do it? Stacey taking control, the older woman showing the innocent young boy the ropes. *Are you trying to seduce me Mrs. Robinson?* And all the time, humming the words to "Invisible Sun". Surely something else would have been more appropriate? Anything else! "Together We Are Beautiful" maybe, or even "Teenage Kicks"? "Invisible Sun" though? What was all that about? Would I ever be able to listen to that song again without thinking of her? Would it always make me get a stiffy on? I sincerely hoped not - what if they played it in Fine Fare, whilst I was shopping with Mum?

Stacey.

Oh God.

Oh well, I'd have to face her sometime.

Ignoring the blinding pain behind me eyes, I turned over.

The bed was empty.

The only sign of Stacey Groves was the waft of her perfume on the sheets. Her bag had gone, her clothes had gone; she had gone.

My body ached and shivered as I crawled out from under the duvet. My throat felt like I'd swallowed razor blades, my mouth was like a desert. I had to fight the urge to gag. I needed water. I needed the loo. Where was the bathroom?

Fumbling my way across the bedroom, I spotted my clothes. They had been folded into a neat little pile on a linen chest in one corner. Stacey must have picked them up and folded them, before she sneaked off. She'd folded all my clothes into a small neat pile. Crikey, she'd even folded my pants. Ruddy hell. I picked them up - inspected them. No skid-marks. Thank God.

377

After a wrong turn into an airing cupboard full of women's underwear, I found the bathroom, relieved my grumbling bladder and greedily and gratefully, splashed water into my mouth and onto my face. The reflection in the bathroom mirror stared back at me. One of Clarkey's Scary Monsters. Deathly pale skin, bloodshot eyes. A line from "Invisible Sun" came rushing back. *Looking like something that the cat brought in.*

Bloody Sting.

Writing my life story.

I stayed in that loo for what seemed an eternity, spending the next five minutes closely inspecting the salon manager's u-bend as a large percentage of my sister's wedding buffet made an unwelcome return appearance. I retched until there was nothing left to retch – and then I retched a little bit more. Was this what it felt like to die?

Finally, the convulsions came to an end. I stared at the floor until it came back into focus. The cool linoleum was inviting. Carefully, I pressed my hot face against it and closed my aching eyes. I must have curled up on the bathroom floor and fallen asleep. I lost all track of time.

Eventually I came around. To my relief the pain in my head had subsided a little – from excruciating down to merely agonizing. I summoned enough energy to pull myself to my feet, flushing away the evidence of the night before and wiping the seat with toilet paper.

The flat was empty. Tentatively, I called Stacey's name – there was no reply. A church bell sounded in the distance. An occasional car went by in the street outside. Birds tweeted, far too noisily for my liking. Otherwise, the only sound was a clock ticking. Bloody hell. Ten past twelve. I should get home - my absence would be noted by now. Mum would be panicking.

Back in the bedroom, I retrieved the eerily neat pile of clothes. It was only after I sat down on the bed to pull on my socks that it dawned on me.

Bloody hell.

I'd finally left the boys club.

Shouldn't I feel..............different? Where were the fireworks? Shouldn't there have been fireworks or something?

I suppose I didn't quite know what I'd been expecting, but it was probably more than this; more than a few blurry, drunken memories of being used as a human pogo stick and then being abandoned in a stranger's flat. It certainly wasn't like this in the movies.

As I picked up my shirt from the pile of clothes, something dropped onto the floor; a piece of paper. I recognised what it was immediately; after all I'd spent hours helping Cheryl's to put them all into envelopes. It was Stacey's invitation to my sister's wedding.

Pre-printed, it read *"Mr and Mrs. Shaun James request the pleasure of the company of..."*

<u>*Miss. Stacey Groves plus guest ...*</u>

Stacey's name was written in Cheryl's very best handwriting. It must have been one of the first she'd written out - towards the end of the evening, the names had become completely illegible.

___*'....at the wedding of their daughter Cheryl to Lee...'*

Then I spotted the message.

Scrawled underneath the date and the venue, in what looked like the bright pink shade of lipstick Stacey had been wearing at the reception, were three little words.

'DON'T TELL CHERYL!'

Charming.

And they said romance was dead.

31 - Every Little Thing She Does is Magic

'Relax mate, I told you. She doesn't work here anymore.'

Clarkey could sense my hesitation; even though he had told me that Roxanne was up in Leeds, at least eleven times before, and although I had no reason at all to suspect he was bullshitting me, I was still reluctant to go in.

It was months since I'd been anywhere near HMV; I'd avoided it like the plague. Just seeing the oh-so-familiar shopfront, with it's huge cardboard cut-out Jack Russell, brought it all back to me. My stomach churned; someone was playing the castanets under my rib-cage. It was as much as I could do to put one foot in front of the other.

'Maybe Virgin have got "Invisible Sun" on special offer?' I said.

Clarkey slowly shook his head.

'She's gone mate. You need to move on.'

I took a deep breath and swallowed. 'Come on then.'

Clarkey nudged me with his elbow, pointing to the sign on the window, next to the door. I'd already seen it but had deliberately kept my mouth shut. I'd hoped Clarkey wouldn't spot it; I hoped he'd forgotten. He hadn't.

Saturday staff required, apply within.

'Well?' Clarkey said.

I shrugged; smiled uncertainly.

'There'll be too many people applying,' I said.

'Well if you don't ask....'

We found the single easily enough in the "new releases" section. There were rows upon rows of seven inch "Invisible Suns". The record cover, like the song, was a bit of a surprise - no pictures of the famous blonde threesome, no familiar band logo emblazoned across one corner. Instead, the plain black cover had a simple, bright yellow, sun motif. It was cool. It fitted the drama of the song perfectly. Clarkey and I both picked up our copies.

Even though it was early on Saturday morning, there were already small queues forming at the only two tills that the shop had operating, and before we approached, I carefully scrutinised the faces of the staff serving at each of them. At the first till, there was a young Oriental looking girl, who I'd never seen before. At the second, a very familiar, very buxom blonde. Poppy Bloom. I started edging towards the Oriental girl.

'Come on, there's Poppy,' said Clarkey, joining the end of her queue.

At the sound of her name, Poppy glanced up. She saw us. Poppy and Clarkey exchanged waves. Poppy went back to serving her customer; an aging rocker with an Elvis quiff. Two minutes later, armed with his newly purchased Shakin' Stevens LP, he shot us a slightly embarrassed look and moved off.

'Good morning gentlemen! Long time, no see. And how are we this fine morning?' Poppy asked in an uncharacteristically chirpy voice. Blimey, what had happened to her? She usually had a face like Red Rum.

'Fine, thanks Poppy, you?' asked Clarkey.

'Good, thanks. Just been promoted,' Poppy pulled at the material of her snug-fitting black HMV T-shirt to give us a closer view of her name badge.

Poppy Bloom, Assistant Manager.

'Brilliant. Congratulations!' Clarkey enthused, just about managing to force his eyes back into their sockets.

'Thanks,' she said, beaming; turning her head towards me, 'so, how are you doing Tim?' her voice softened, like she was addressing a favourite puppy.

'I'm OK, thanks,' I said, smiling as widely as I could, determined to show that I wasn't bothered in the least by what she obviously assumed I would be bothered by.

'So, did Karl tell you...?' she said in a hushed, concerned voice, better suited to someone working in a funeral parlour.

'Sorry?' I said, knowing exactly what she was referring to, but refusing to acknowledge the fact.

'Ah well, never mind eh?' she said, giving me a condescending little smile.

Yep, I was clearly a lovely soft little puppy. I half expected her to scratch behind my ears and offer me a Good Boy choc-drop.

'Ah,' she said, relieving me of my "Invisible Sun" single, 'I should have guessed. Still a big fan then eh? Great isn't it? It's a real departure for them, don't you think?'

'Yeah, definitely,' I said, pleased she'd finally changed the subject and that she'd stopped talking like Barbara Woodhouse.

'Mind you, it wouldn't surprise me if you hadn't even heard it, knowing you.'

Poppy placed my single in a bag and tapped the till keys.

Clarkey snorted knowingly.

'Of course I've heard it,' I said, glaring at Clarkey.

'Yeah but be honest, you'd buy it even if it was three minutes of silence, wouldn't you?' he laughed.

Poppy's chest bounced up and down as she laughed, closely pursued by Clarkey's eyeballs.

'Very funny Kevin,' I said, 'remind me again, how many copies of "Ashes To Ashes" did you buy? Just the seven inch, the twelve inch and the cassette single wasn't it?'

That shut him up; for the briefest of moments at least.

'So, are you going to ask her then?' Clarkey said, nudging me in the ribs, as he handed Poppy a crisp new pound note.

'Eh?' I said, feigning ignorance.

'Tim wants to apply for a Saturday job,' Clarkey told Poppy.

'Hang on,' I started to protest.

'Really? That's excellent,' Poppy said, 'you'd be really good at it,' she said.

I smiled. I was a sucker for flattery. 'Do you think so?'

'Yeah,' she said, 'and just think, you'd get to work with me.'

'Mmm, just think.'

'And you'd get a free HMV T-shirt just like mine,;

'Amazing.'

And you'd get a staff discount on everything in the shop.'

'Really? A discount?' I said. Suddenly it didn't seem such a daft idea. The new Police LP was out in a few weeks.

'Well, we've had a load of applicants of course, but being Assistant Manager does have certain privileges,' Poppy winked, 'I'll get you a form shall I?'

'Best years of your life'

That's what my Dad's always telling me;

'School days; college days. It's all down hill from there."

If that's true, I thought to myself, I might as well top myself now and be done with it.

Only two weeks from my eighteenth birthday, my so called 'coming of age' - and there I was on a Saturday night, stacking shelves in a freezing cold stock room at the back of HMV. Outside, it was a cold, wet and miserable October evening. Leaves and discarded sweet wrappers scurried past the windows. Churchill Square was the epicentre of a ghost town, illuminated only by the lights of the shop windows; inside of which, I reckoned, must be hordes of other bored, spotty teenagers, just like me; stock-taking and refilling shop displays with goods they could never actually afford to buy.

Meanwhile, a few hundred yards away, older, richer people - the ones with proper jobs - were having fun, meeting members of the opposite sex, drinking themselves silly in the town centre pubs and clubs, stuffing their faces in the swanky restaurants in Preston Street, and gambling the night away in Sgt. York's casino; i.e. generally having a great time, whilst I was stuck there, emptying yet another box of Barry Manilow cassettes.

Best years of your life? God; Dad's life must have been shit.

I'd only been working at HMV three weeks, and I'd already reached a conclusion. Stock taking was boring. Shelf stacking even more so. The only saving grace of the Saturday evening shift I'd been assigned to - apart from the "generous" (5%) staff discount - was that after the shop had closed for business, the staff got to choose what music to play.

According to Elvis Costello, the roses were having a much better year than I was. Frank, the Saturday shift duty manager, was a big Elvis fan. "Good Year For The Roses" was OK, if you liked Country music, but by the time I'd listened to it for the umpteenth time that day, I was seriously tempted to invest in some weed killer. Frank's self-elected 'HMV Record Of The Week' was coming to an end (again) and this time, I was poised and ready.

Frank had first choice, but after that it was pretty much a free for all. Strictly speaking, as Assistant Manager, Poppy had second dibs, but she never seemed that bothered. I wasn't sure why Poppy worked in HMV really; she didn't even seem to like music that much.

You had to be on your metal, if you wanted to get your own choice played. Maria, one of the other Saturday shifters, always wanted to play dance stuff like Shalamar or Linx. I hated it. Disco music was utter crap.

Elvis's song was fading out.

Under starters' orders....

As soon as I heard the needle lifting, I dashed over to the deck, a copy of "Ghost In the Machine" in my hand.

Maria looked daggers from across the room, her crappy Shalamar album already poised in her fingerless glove. Too late love. You have to be quick in this game.

The already familiar opening bars of "Spirits In The Material World" received a mixed reception. One or two people cheered, gave me the thumbs up. There were groans from Frank and one or two of the older women.

'Not this crap again,' I heard Maria say, to no-one in particular but not so quietly that I wouldn't hear her.

'Better than shagging Shalamar, or bloody Linx,' I muttered, in a similarly loud whisper.

Maria gave me a look.

I stared her out.

'Intuition my arse,' I added.

Poppy wandered over, laughing and shaking her head, 'Charming,' she said.

'Uh?'

'I said "charming". That's a lovely attitude towards your colleagues. Are you always such a pleasure to be with?' Poppy teased.

I grunted.

'You really are a right little charmer, Tim, do you know that? No wonder you scare all the girls off,' she giggled.

That's right, kick a man when he's down.

I shrugged, like I wasn't bothered but I could feel the hackles standing up on the back of my neck.

Poppy wandered across the stockroom, a box of records balanced on one shoulder. As she passed by, she tousled my hair with her spare hand.

There was no doubting it. I was her puppy.

'Sorry, I suppose that was a bit uncalled for, wasn't it?' she said

What could I say? *"Yes actually it was totally out of order"?*

Poppy was my boss now. I didn't want to get on the wrong side of her. I bit my lip, let it go.

A bit later we carried our boxes out to the shop, in order to replenish the record racks. For the next fifteen minutes or so, we worked side by side, pretty much in silence, listening to The Police's new album. Occasionally Poppy would comment on the music.

'I love this one,' she said when "Every Little Thing She Does Is Magic" came on.

I nodded.

'More like the old Police sound, isn't it?'

She seemed desperate to strike up a conversation with me, but I wanted to listen to the album, and besides I was still smarting about the "scaring off all the girls" comment.

'I didn't mean it you know,' she said, as if reading my mind, 'I was only joking'.

'Can you pass me those scissors?' I said, deliberately ignoring her.

She stood with her hands on her hips, equally deliberately ignoring my request.

'You're not still upset about Roxy are you?' she suddenly asked.

'No, of course not,' I said, my voice suddenly an octave higher than usual.

'Did Karl tell you, her and Rob have split up again?'

Poppy handed me the scissors.

'No,' I said, cutting through the thick brown tape on a box of records. As hard as I tried, I couldn't stop a stupid smile from spreading across my face, 'that's awful,' I said, with absolutely no conviction.

'Apparently she's seeing a really sweet Scottish guy now. Fergus or Hamish or something. Met him at Uni.'

'Oh right.'

I felt the smile disappearing from my face as quickly as it had appeared.

'Or is it Angus? Anyway, I told her you were working here now. She said to say "hello".'

'Oh, great, thanks.'

'I'll send her your love shall I?'

'Like she wants it,' I muttered.

'Sorry, I'm being a bit insensitive again aren't I?'

A fraction?

'So, are you seeing that hairdresser again then?' she said, completely out of the blue.

'Who?' I said, puzzled.

'Your sister's mate - you know, from the wedding.'

What? How the hell did Poppy know about Stacey?

'It's just that...Karl.. mentioned, you know.'

Karl? How the hell did he find out?

'Mentioned what?'

'You know? That you two...' Poppy put her box down, giggled, did that really annoying thing with her fingers, making speech marks in the air, '"celebrated", after your sister's wedding.'

Clarkey.

I'd kill him. It could only be Clarkey. He was the only one who I'd been stupid enough to tell about Stacey. I'd made him promise he wouldn't say anything. So much for promises.

'Oh that,' I said, nonchalantly, the heat rising in my cheeks. I buried my face in the "T" racks - somewhere between Traffic and The Tubes.

'So, has she been in touch?'

'No, but I'm not bothered.'

'Oh right, that's OK then,' Poppy smiled an annoying smile, before returning to her task of sticking price labels on Bad Manners singles. "Walkin' In The Sunshine"?

Huh, good luck with that Buster.

It had been chucking it down for weeks - ever since the day of the wedding.

Oh God, the wedding.

Why should I be bothered about Stacey Groves? It was just one of those one night stand things wasn't it? I mean, people have them all the time don't they? It was no skin off my nose.

OK, so admittedly, I'd thought about calling her a couple of times - after Cheryl and Lee had gone off down to Ilfracombe on their honeymoon; down to Lee's folks' caravan, but I wasn't bothered at all really. I was only keen to make sure she'd got back home safely that Sunday morning. Then I realised; I didn't even know her home number. I did look but Cheryl had obviously taken her address book with her. And yeah, I did sort of half wonder whether Stacey might pop around to the house that first week, but I wasn't that surprised really when she didn't. And then, yeah, OK, I'd sort of thought about going down to the salon once, but I'd forgotten they closed early on Wednesdays. It didn't phase me at all when they were shut - I was sort of relieved really. Nah, I wasn't really bothered about Stacey one bit.

'So, you're not seeing anyone now then?' Poppy said, still busy with her label gun.

'No, not at the moment,' I said casually.

386

'Oh right.'

I should have left it there. I waited for her to go on, but when she didn't say anything, I felt the need to fill the uncomfortable silence.

'Why do you ask?'

'Oh no reason.'

She was weird sometimes was Poppy.

I went back to re-stocking the U's. I liked the U's - some of my favourite bands were U's. UB40, The Undertones, Ultravox - and that new band U2 that Jacko and Karl were always raving on about.

As it turned out, Poppy wasn't yet finished with her inquisition.

'Are you going to Karl's new bands' gig? You know, down the Richmond, next Saturday? We're all going down there after work.'

'Dunno. I hadn't thought about it.'

It was a lie but only a small white one. I had thought about it but after the last bloody gig of his I'd been to, I'd decided to give it a wide berth.

'Oh, OK, only if you change your mind, I know an attractive.., well..., not totally hideous, young lady, who wouldn't mind a chaperone.'

Of course.

I was such an idiot sometimes. I finally saw where Poppy's interrogation had been heading and buried my head in a box of LP's.

'If you do decide to go, I'm sure she'd love to hear from you.

The inside of the box was fascinating.

'Oh well, you know where to find her.'

Sting and the boys came to my rescue.

'Oh, that's the end of side one.' I said lifting my head out of the box, cradling an armful of vinyl, 'I'd best turn it over.'

As it turned out, the "hairdresser" Poppy had asked about, just happened to visit Cheryl later that very evening.

It was gone ten o'clock. I was knackered after my shift. I heard her as soon as I turned the key in the door. The voice, and the laugh, were pretty unmistakable.

'And you'll never guess,' she was squealing.

For a moment, I thought, 'Oh God, what is she talking about?'

Then I remembered the note. *"Don't Tell Cheryl"*

Maybe I didn't need to worry.

I tried to creep up the stairs but Lee spotted me through the open lounge door.

'Hey mate, you're missing a cracking Match of the Day.'

I hesitated; which was fatal.

'Tim! Come and say hello to Stacey!' Cheryl shouted.

Stacey looked sheepish as I walked through the door. Lee and Dad were watching the football. Mum and Cheryl were sitting with Stacey at the dining table; they were all enjoying a glass of wine.

'Hi Stacey,' I said.

'Hello Tim, are you ok?' she asked.

'Fine, you?'

Everyone seemed to be staring at Stacey.

'Well, aren't you going to show him then?' Mum said.

Stacey blushed.

'Stacey's got some news. It's dead exciting!' Cheryl gushed.

Stacey slowly held out her hand. I didn't know what I was meant to be looking at.

'It's so romantic,' Cheryl said, 'Mehmet's asked Stacey to marry him.'

Mehmet? Was this the same Mehmet that she'd called all the names under the sun, less than a month ago?

'She's engaged,' said Mum, 'look at the lovely ring.'

'Cool,' I managed to say.

'You're not jealous are you mate?' my Dad piped up.

'What?' I said, feeling the heat rise in my cheeks as I tried to form a smile.

'Well, the way you two were dancing at that reception, I thought there might be some romance blooming,' Dad said, winking at my Mum and then at Stacey.

Everyone laughed as if Dad had cracked the joke of the century.

Stacey looked dead embarrassed.

Stacey and me? Yeah, I suppose that was the joke of the century.

'Were you dancing with my kid brother, you old flirt?' laughed Cheryl.

'Yes, he was very gallant, weren't you?' Stacey said, squeezing my arm, 'he was the perfect gentleman!'

'The perfect gentleman eh?' Dad said, 'I can see I'm going to have to have that conversation with you boy, eh? What do you think Mum?'

'Oh, leave the boy alone, he's blushing,' Mum kindly pointed out.

388

'I'm just getting a drink and then I'm off up to bed,' I said, turning to leave the room as quickly as I could..

'Liverpool are on in a minute,' Lee said.

Sod Liverpool.

'I'm shattered,' I mumbled.

'Ah, poor lad,' my Mum said.

'Up the workers!' My dad shouted, as I walked towards the kitchen.

On my way back with my glass of squash, Stacey was in the hallway, making a play of putting something away in her handbag. Conveniently, she just happened to stand up, just as I was passing, heading for the stairs. The lounge door was open and she grabbed my wrist and pulled me to one side.

'You OK?' she asked.

'Of course,' I said, looking as puzzled I could, as if I hadn't a clue what she meant.

After all, why shouldn't I be OK?

'Good. It's our little secret yeah?'

'Oh, yeah, right, of course.'

'And you won't say anything to anyone?'

'Of course not.'

'Only Mehmet can get a bit...jealous, you know?'

'Yeah, right. No problem.'

'Thanks,' she stood on tip toe and kissed me on the cheek. Then she turned to go back into the lounge. She turned as she reached the door.

'Don't look so down,' she giggled, lowering her voice, 'you weren't *that* bad.'

Then Stacey disappeared back into Match of the Day and her celebratory drinks.

Not *that* bad eh?

Huh. Judging by the engagement ring, not *that* good either.

Sometimes, I have to admit, I can be pretty slow on the uptake. Looking back, I should have smelt an enormous rat, especially given the conversation I'd carefully avoided with Poppy Bloom just a few days before.

My relationship with Karl Bloom had improved a little of late. He finally seemed to have forgiven me for what he saw as my part in

Dave's betrayal with Juliette - frankly not before time - I mean get over yourself. It wasn't as if I was the one who'd snogged her face off all the way through a Police gig! And besides, he was as thick as thieves with Dave again these days; only the other day, I'd overheard them in the common room, fiercely debating which was the best single ever made. Karl reckoned it was "White Man in Hammersmith Palais". Dave said that the Clash song was "alright" but that it was nowhere as good as "Down In A Tube Station at Midnight". I'd have happily told them that "Message in a Bottle" and "Can't Stand Losing You" were better than anything by The Clash or The Jam, but I couldn't get a word in edgeways. They were arguing as if they'd never fallen out in the first place. So it was a bit rich for Karl to still be harbouring any ill feeling towards me.

He also had finally appeared to have forgiven me for ruining his chances of glory in the Thatcham match. Mind you, since I'd now resumed my usual place on the subs bench for the School First XI, I'd had little or no chance to deprive him of any further opportunities of becoming a hat-trick scoring hero in front of his adoring fan club (which admittedly now seemed to consist exclusively of Glenda); although from what I'd seen, he was pretty good at depriving himself anyway - he wasn't exactly Trevor Francis.

There was a kind of truce. We'd been seeing a bit more of each other, since the new term started, but if I'm honest, we still weren't exactly what you would have called bosom buddies. And if I'd have given it serious thought, I'd have realised that Karl wasn't exactly in the habit of inviting me round for tea after school every five minutes. So, like I say, I suppose I should have twigged, but I guess I was so keen to believe it was part of his bridge-building exercise, that I chose to ignore the bleeding-obvious; the ulterior motive, behind his sudden invitation.

'It's was my Mum's idea. She was asking after you the other day,' he explained.

'Really?'

'Yeah, she seems to have taken a bit of a shine to you.'

'Your Mum? Taken a shine to me? Why?'

'Who knows?' Karl shrugged, 'there's no accounting for taste.'

I gave him the finger and walked off down the corridor. Privately, I was pretty chuffed that Mrs. Bloom would even have remembered my name.

'So, what shall I tell her?' he called after me, 'will we have a guest on Friday for fish and chips, or not?'

Fish and chips? That swung it; I loved fish and chips.

I turned, shrugged.

'Why not? Yeah, OK, thanks, that'll be....nice.'

The last time I'd been to the Bloom's, had been the night of The Morbid Morsels gig, all those months ago. Given the way that had turned out, I felt pretty nervous as I strolled up the garden path. However, from what Karl had said, at least his mother didn't bear any hard feelings towards me.

Checking my reflection in the small frosted glass panel of the door, I braced myself and rang on the doorbell. Poppy answered. She had her coat on.

'Hi mate,' she said - I was always 'mate' now, since we'd started working together, 'come in, I'll give Karl a shout.'

Poppy shouted up the stairs.

Faint strains of music were coming from one of the bedrooms - it was pretty easy to identify the tune; it was one of the biggest hits of the year so far - I felt like I'd heard it about three million times - Soft Cell's "Tainted Love".

Eventually, Karl came jogging down the stairs, wearing the trench coat he usually reserved for gigs.

'Right,' he said to Poppy, 'shall we?'

'Are you two off somewhere?' I said, confused.

Marc Almond was still doing his stuff upstairs.

'Just off to pick up the grub. Ordered you a large cod. Hope that's OK?'

'Sure. Shall I come too?'

'No, that's OK, you wait here,' Poppy said, exchanging glances with her brother, 'we'll only be five minutes.'

Poppy opened the door, started heading out. Karl was putting a fiver in his coat pocket.

'Oh right, shall I say hello to your Mum and Dad then?' I said, gesturing towards their living room.

'Good luck with that, they're in Dorset for the weekend,' Karl said.

'Oh, really? What shall I do...?'

Karl closed the door behind him. I stood there looking at the front door, feeling like a lemon. This was weird.

391

Then it got weirder.

I heard a key being turned in the door. For a moment, I thought they'd forgotten something and were coming back in. Then it sounded like the latch was being slipped; like the door was being locked. Puzzled, I reached for the handle and turned it; it wouldn't budge.

'Karl?' I said.

Then I jumped back. Something was poking me in the nether regions; I glanced down; it was the letter box. Something was being pushed through. It was a slip of paper. I watched as it drifted onto the welcome mat.

'Karl?' I said again; this time louder.

There was no answer.   I knew they were still there; I could see the vague outlines of their bodies through the frosted glass. The slip of paper came to rest against my foot.

'Karl? Poppy? What's going on?'

Still no answer. I tried the handle again. It wouldn't move; the buggers had locked me in.

Bending down; I picked up the paper, turned it over. It contained a few of lines, in what looked like Poppy's writing.

Go upstairs, first bedroom on the left.

You're not leaving until you've asked her to the gig. And don't tell her we made you do it!

Good luck, luv Poppy and Karl.

There were two kisses underneath Poppy's name, plus a smiley face drawn under Karl's.

And a PS.

P.S. - No fish and chips for you, unless you do it.

Oh, Ruddy Hell.

Their silhouettes grew smaller as they moved away from the glass. I thought I heard them whispering and sniggering.

Grabbing the handle, I shook it. The door rattled but didn't budge. I put my ear to the door but the whispering had stopped. All I could see through the glass panel were the blurred shapes of parked cars on the road outside.

My stomach rumbled.

No fish and chips unless you do it.

Bugger.

Marc Almond was now crooning through "Where Did Our Love Go?". Heidi obviously had the twelve inch single, on which Tainted Love segued straight into Soft Cell's cover version of the old Supremes, Motown number - I'd heard it loads of times in the shop.

Marc had a yearning, burning feeling inside him. So did I; I was starving.

As I got nearer to her door, I could hear her singing along. Don't give up your day job, I thought. Not that she had one of course; she was only in the fifth year.

My stomach was churning. And it wasn't just hunger pains.

Bloody hell - I'd swing for Karl. Mind you, he was about six inches taller than me.

I'd swing for Poppy then. But she was my boss - maybe not.

I stood there staring at the door. Turned away, glanced back down the stairs - the front door was still closed. I wondered if Karl and Poppy had really gone up the chippy, or whether they were just waiting at the end of the front garden.

You're not leaving until you've asked her to the gig.

Bugger this. I knocked at the door.

Heidi stopped singing. There was a pause. Nothing happened. I knocked again. This time, I heard the needle being lifted from the record. Marc had been interrupted mid-surrender.

There was the unmistakable sound of small footsteps padding across the carpet, and then the door opened, very slightly. Heidi peered around the corner. She jumped back as if someone had clouted her around the face. Then she put one hand up to her mouth and the other across her chest. Her eyes were smiling now, as she opened the door a little wider.

'Bloody 'eck Tim, you made me jump out of my skin!' she said, pulling the door wide open now, her free hand still resting on her chest. She was wearing a long Smurfette T-shirt, which came down to her knees; the sort of thing girls wear to bed.

Her hair was tied back in a pony-tail - I noticed she'd gone blonde again. She looked older than I remembered. Even in a scruffy old T-shirt, she looked OK - her eyes were sparkly; I really liked her eyes. Dana's eyes. I'd forgotten.

'What are you doing here? Oh no, I must look a right mess,' she said, placing a protective arm across the Smurfette.

'Er, hello Heidi, ...er Karl invited me round for dinner.'

'Oh right, is it ready? I'll just get dressed and come down....,' she started to close the door.

I grabbed it. 'No, it's not...er...quite ready yet,'

'Oh, right. So, why are you up here?'

Good question.

Her legs were bare beneath the long T-shirt which reached just above her knees. Her legs were pale but shapely. Soft and smooth. Instinctively, she tugged at the hem of the t-shirt, pulling the thin material so that it clung to the contours of her body. The Smurfette came to life in stunning 3D. Fawn's antlers appearing through her blue forehead. The collar of my sweatshirt felt damp and there was a tingling sensation in my throat and round the back of my neck; what Peter Parker would refer to as his 'spider sense'. Maybe I was developing super powers? That could be useful. I could just climb out of her window and scale down the wall to freedom.

'I was just wondering,' I gulped, 'have you seen Karl's new band play?'

It was twenty minutes before Karl and Poppy came back with the grub. By then, Heidi and I were sitting at the kitchen table, drinking Mrs. Bloom's home-made lemonade. It was delicious - but more like bitter lemon than R Whites.

'Oh, still here then Tim?' said Poppy, smirking, as they came through the door. The aroma of fish and chips made my mouth water.

'Decided to stay for some grub have you?' said Karl meaningfully.

'What do you think, Heidi? Does he deserve any? Should we feed him?'

A huge beaming smile spread across Heidi Bloom's face.

'Yeah, let him stay - why not?' she giggled.

'So, are you coming to the gig then Tim?' Karl asked nonchalantly, as Poppy pulled plates from a cupboard.

'We're both going!' Heidi said, smiling 'Tim asked me to go with him.'

'Never!' said Karl.

'Get outta here!' said Poppy, 'what really?'

They were bloody awful actors.

It was amazing what gluttons for punishment most people were. The Men Machine gig attracted pretty much the exact same audience

394

as the Morbid Morsels. Friends, relatives, acquaintances, friends of friends. As hot tickets went, it was barely lukewarm.

Mrs. Bloom had offered to give us a lift to The Richmond, but I'd said it was fine, we'd get the bus. Heidi's mum had already gone through her pre-gig warm-up; telling me not to let Heidi drink too much; to get her home on time; I couldn't face the whole "keep your hands to yourself" speech all over again. We made a speedy exit.

As usual it was raining. Would it ever stop? Heidi had brought an umbrella with her. Girls always thought of things like that.

I was wearing my new black and red "Ghost In The Machine" T-shirt. It was soaked by the time we reached the pub. The Richmond, on the other side of St.Peter's Church from The Northern, wasn't as dark and dingy inside, but if anything it was smaller. It's size had a welcome side-effect from Karl's viewpoint though; it played the neat trick of making the gig look almost popular. Mercifully, Men Machine were better than The Morbid Morsels - or at least they were quieter, which in my book, amounted to pretty much the same thing. The improvement was mostly down to the new synth player; the rotund, but clearly talented Julie Wise.

'Julie has really slimmed down hasn't she?' Heidi pointed out.

Frankly, it was hard to tell. Julie appeared to be wearing a loose fitting tent. But she could certainly play the synthesiser. Some of the songs even seemed to have what you could vaguely call a tune.

'Great aren't they?' Heidi enthused.

Great was stretching it a bit.

'Someone tapped me on the shoulder and I heard a voice in my ear. 'Not bad are they?'

It was Alison. She was with Humph. They both looked happy enough. Maybe this time they'd stick together for good? And then again....Alison pecked me on the cheek and then, when Heidi stopped dancing long enough, Alison gave her a big hug, before resuming her position, behind my right shoulder.

'Good choice,' she whispered in my ear.

'Uh?' I said, half turning round.

I assumed she was referring to the tune. I think it was supposedly one of the band's own compositions - but OMD could easily have sued for infringement of copyright.

'And not before time,' Alison added, poking me in the ribs.

What was she on about? I shrugged in Humph's general direction as if to silently give voice to my question.

Humph just winked and returned my shrug. Was he tapping his feet? Bloody hell, move over Brotherhood of Man, Chris Humphreys might just have a new favourite band.

Glancing around the room, as Karl and The Men Machine brought their OMD-alike number to a close, I spotted other familiar faces. Jacko and Fay were huddled over in one corner, leaning on a huge amp. I had to suppress a giggle. Either Jacko had turned New Romantic or they'd got dressed in the dark and he'd put Fay's blouse on by mistake.

Dave and Juliette were there too. Not that they seemed to be that bothered by the gig. They were snogging each other's faces off as usual, over in another corner. At least twice, I noticed Karl casting looks that could kill in their general direction. Good to see he didn't harbour grudges then.

A few feet away from the young lovers, Wiffy Wilf stood in a small cloud of smoke, wearing tartan bondage trousers and puffing away on a cigarette, which I suspected wasn't Benson and Hedges. People around him moved away as the cloud became denser. Wilf had a serene grin on his face. I tried to attract his attention but he wasn't on the same planet.

Clarkey, meanwhile, was leaning on the side of the stage, like he was an honorary band member. He glanced over, we exchanged raised thumbs. I had to smile. Karl had pulled a master-stroke there. Clarkey had been "employed' as a would be roadie, which basically meant he got to hump all the band's equipment from the van to the stage and back out to the van again - pretty much on his own. When I'd first noticed him, I assumed he'd got caught in the downpour, but then I realised that his "Scary Monsters" T-shirt was actually plastered to his body, due to the exertions of his new roadie duties. His face was red and shining underneath the cheap strobe lighting, which Men Machine had set up as an essential part of their backdrop, along with some very wispy swirls of dried ice, which gave the impression that someone was enjoying a crafty fag underneath the stage. The effect was more Ultra-naff than Ultravox.

In return for Clarkey's hard work, Men Machine had introduced a passable cover of Bowie's "Heroes" into their set. Clarkey regarded that as payment. He was happy as Larry. Larry was a complete sucker.

396

So, the whole gang was there, with two notable exceptions - I scanned the "crowd" carefully - which frankly didn't exactly take long, and breathed a sigh of relief. There was no sign of Pete or Doddsy, for which I was eternally grateful.

Not surprisingly, Karl's band were not the headline act. There were two other bands on afterwards. We gave both a brief glance before deciding that neither of them would be troubling the charts any time soon. We all traipsed down to the saloon bar, huddled around a table and made fun of the headline bands, as they did their thing above us. Only Wilf and Karl stayed upstairs to the bitter end; and I was pretty confident that at least one of them would be struggling to remember much about the set-list by the following morning.

Having exhausted our supply of insults relating to the standard of musical entertainment on offer, Dave went off on his hobby horse and roped Jacko into the "best single ever" argument. To my surprise, Jacko, who had always been a massive fan of both The Clash and The Jam, didn't agree with either of the candidates put forward by Dave and Karl earlier in the day.

'Perfect Day?' Dave said, shaking his head and looking around the table at the rest of us for affirmation that Jacko had lost it.

'Lou Reed,' said Jacko, cuddling up to Fay in a cosy-corner of the leather sofa seat, 'pure genius.'

'Better than Tube Station by The Jam? You must have gone soft,' Dave scoffed.

'You're both wrong,' Alison piped up, 'the best single ever is "Your Song" by Elton John.'

There were hoots of laughter all around the table.

'You boys wouldn't understand,' Alison said dismissively, as she possessively placed her hand on Humph's leg, humming Elton's love song to herself.

The baton of the conversation was passed on and continued around the table. There were votes for "Heart of Glass" (Juliette) and "Love Will Tear Us Apart" (Fay).

'We don't need to ask you do we Tim?' Alison laughed.

'Ooh, yeah, let's guess shall we?' Dave said, a stupid grin on his face.

'Mmm, I wonder what on earth it might be?' said Jacko, rubbing his chin, as if deep in thought.

'Don't Stand So Close To Me?' suggested Alison

397

'Walking On The Moon?' Humph piped-up.

'Well, at least it's not Save All Your Kisses For Me!' I said.

Everyone laughed at Humph's expense.

He clipped me around the head.

'Roxanne?' said Juliette.

There were sharp intakes of breath, followed by smirks from around the table. Jacko almost spat his beer over Fay's lap.

'Oops, sorry, I didn't mean...' Juliette said, flushing scarlet, holding her hand to her mouth.

'Don't worry,' I said, 'it was never really my favourite one of theirs anyway,' I smiled.

'It would have to be something by The Police though, wouldn't it?' Fay said.

'Yeah, but it's tricky. They're all so good,' I said, emulating Jackos' chin rub, whilst giving the matter serious consideration.

Heidi interrupted my thought process.

'Well, I think, the best single ever is either "Message In A Bottle", or "Can't Stand Losing You",' she said, a determined smile on her face, like she wasn't going to be listening to any objections. 'There's nothing to choose between them really, so I'll vote for both.'

'That's cheating!' Juliette protested.

'No, credit where credit's due,' I said, 'this here, is a girl with brilliant taste,' I continued, placing my arm around Heidi's shoulder.

'Not from where we're sitting,' Jacko said.

Everyone laughed.

'I didn't mean...'

You could have lit a fire from my face.

Heidi didn't seem to mind; she leant into my arm, before I could pull it away.

'So? Come on Mr. James, which classic Police single is it to be?' said Alison.

'Every Little Thing She Does is Magic,' I said firmly.

I pulled Heidi closer to me.

The vital debate of the evening continued, as we made our way home.

'Do you really think "Every Little Thing She Does is Magic" is the best single ever made?' Heidi asked, as we strolled across the road, towards the bus stops by St. Peter's church.

398

We'd said our goodbyes to the others and headed off early; Mrs. Bloom's warning about getting Heidi home in time, still ringing in my ears.

'This month I do, yeah, but next month, The Police might issue a new one and I'll probably think that's the best one ever.'

'Can you ever foresee a time when your favourite single ever might be by another group?' she laughed.

'Doubt it - unless Sting ever goes solo; God forbid.'

Large drops of rain splashed onto the pavement in front of us. Here we go again, I thought. It must have been all of an hour since it last rained. Heidi put her brolly up, put her arm through mine and snuggled up to me as we walked along.

'It's weird the songs some people like isn't it?' she observed, squeezing my arm, 'I mean Elton John? That's really old hat isn't it? You'd think Alison was in her twenties or something.'

Ruddy hell; Heidi was so young.

'And "Perfect Day" by Loo Rolls?' she continued, 'what on earth is that? I've never even heard of it.'

'Lou *Reed*. It's very good actually,' I said, 'and it's funny you should say that. It reminds me, I've got something I've been meaning to give you,' I said, gently releasing her grip from my arm and fumbling in the inside pocket of my denim jacket.

I pulled out the little package and offered it to her.

'For me?' she said, beaming from ear to ear.

'Yeah, I made it for you especially,' I said. Well, it was only a *little white* lie.

Heidi studied the words on the end of the cassette tape and read aloud.

'Songs for Heidi, Volume 1. Wow, did you really do this just for me?'

'Yeah, it's nothing really,' I said, which was true, considering it used to be called songs for Tim volume 6 - but at least I'd swapped the old cover with Jacko's scrawl, for a new one, lovingly written out in my neatest handwriting. That had taken me all of ten minutes to do. And it's the thought that counts anyway isn't it?

Heidi's expression suggested I might have just given her a diamond ring. She looked dead chuffed. She leant over and kissed me on the lips. In doing so, she tilted the umbrella towards me and a small torrent of water splashed onto my face.

'Hey watch it!' I laughed, pulling my lips away from hers.

Heidi noticed the water running down my face and laughed out loud.

'Ruddy hell Heidi, do you mind? It's a big enough umbrella isn't it?' I said.

And it was; but I had a feeling it was always going to be me who ended up getting wet.

Acknowledgements

Firstly, a very big thanks to anyone and everyone who begged, purchased, borrowed, or even stole a copy of *Does Everyone Stare The Way I Do?* I'm really grateful for all the kind feedback, comments and words of encouragement I've received.

I must again thank my creative writing tutor Graham Jordan who was responsible for sowing the initial seed of an idea for the first book, which has now germinated and flourished into the two volumes. Also, thanks to my friends at the Portslade writing group; to Sara and Robin Bowers at The Steyning Bookshop, Gina Parsons at What the Dickens, and Ted Smith at Youwriteon.

Grateful thanks also go to all of my wonderful extended family (Muirs, Eartheys and the various offshoots of each), and to all my friends for their support and enthusiasm. Special mentions to my brother Eddie, for his tireless efforts in promoting the book to all and sundry, and to my sister-in-law Linda, for persuading her reading group to study and feedback on my humble offering. My brother Duncan (Sunshine Designs) has also been incredibly patient in helping me to 'master' photoshop and in co-designing the book cover with me.

So many people have offered encouragement that I'd need another chapter to list and thank you all individually, but you know who you are! Consider yourself thanked to within an inch of your lives.

However, a promise is a promise and therefore, to those people who offered specific ideas and contributions in response to my online plea for period anecdotes; a very big thanks to you especially; Simon Huggett, Chris Lelliott, Pete Hill, Glenn Simmonds, Paul Adams, Paul Weston, Rachel Roberts, Peter Merrick, Barbara Lambert-Smith, Ez Lane. And to anyone else I've inadvertently omitted to mention and have now mortally offended, I offer my sincere apologies and hope to remain on your Christmas card lists.

Finally, last but not least, I must thank Karen, for reading, re-reading and re-reading again; editing and improving on my stupid ideas. Your mouth; the home of comedy!